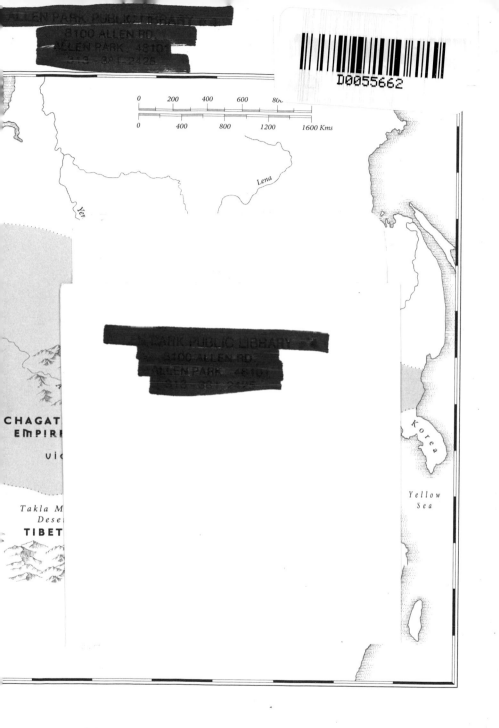

D0055662

Lena

Yen

CHAGAT
EMPIRE

vic

Takla M
Dese
TIBET

Korea

*Yellow
Sea*

GENGHIS
BONES OF THE HILLS

BY CONN IGGULDEN

Emperor: The Gates of Rome
Emperor: The Death of Kings
Emperor: The Field of Swords
Emperor: The Gods of War
Genghis: Birth of an Empire
Genghis: Lords of the Bow
Genghis: Bones of the Hills

BY CONN IGGULDEN
AND HAL IGGULDEN

The Dangerous Book for Boys

GENGHIS

BONES OF THE HILLS

Conn Iggulden

DELACORTE PRESS

GENGHIS: BONES OF THE HILLS
A Delacorte Press Book / April 2009

Published by Bantam Dell
A Division of Random House, Inc.
New York, New York

Book design by Glen M. Edelstein

Delacorte Press is a registered trademark of Random House, Inc., and the colophon is a trademark of Random House, Inc.

ISBN-13: 978-0-385-33953-7

Printed in the United States of America

To my son, Arthur

PROLOGUE

THE FIRE ROARED at the center of the circle. Shadows flickered around it as dark figures leapt and danced with swords. Their robes swirled as they howled over other voices raised in ululating song. Men sat with stringed instruments across their knees, plucking out tunes and rhythms while they stamped their feet.

At the edges of the fire, a line of Mongol warriors knelt bare-chested with their hands bound behind them. As one, they showed the cold face to their triumphant captors. Their officer, Kurkhask, had been beaten savagely in the battle. Blood caked his mouth and his right eye was swollen shut. He had known worse. Kurkhask was proud of the way the others refused to show fear. He watched the dark-skinned desert warriors shouting and chanting to the stars, waving curved blades marked with the blood of men he had known. They were a strange breed, Kurkhask thought, these men who bound their heads in many thicknesses of cloth and wore loose tunics over wide-legged trousers. Most were bearded, so that their mouths were just a red slash in black bristles. As a group, they were taller and more heavily muscled than the largest of the Mongol warriors. They reeked of strange spices and many of the men chewed at dark roots, spitting brown clots on the ground at their feet. Kurkhask hid his distaste for them as they jerked and yelped and danced, building themselves into a frenzy.

The Mongol officer shook his head wearily. He had been too confident, he knew that now. The twenty men Temuge had sent with him were all seasoned warriors, but they were not a raiding party. By trying to protect the carts of gifts and bribes, they had reacted too slowly and been caught. Kurkhask thought back to the months before and knew the peaceful mission had lulled him, made him drop his guard. He and his men had found themselves in a hard land of dizzying mountain passes. They had passed valleys set to straggling crops and traded simple gifts with farmers as poor as any they had ever seen. Yet game was plentiful and his men had roasted fat deer on their fires. Perhaps that had been a mistake. The farmers had pointed to the mountains in warning, but he had not understood. He had no quarrel with the hill tribes, but in the night, a host of warriors had overtaken them, coming out of the darkness with wild cries and curved swords slashing at the sleeping men. Kurkhask closed his eyes briefly. Only eight of his companions had survived the struggle, though he had not seen his oldest son since the first clash of arms. The boy had been scouting the path ahead, and Kurkhask hoped he survived to carry word back to the khan. That thought alone gave him pleasure to set against his vicious resentment.

The carts had been looted of their trinkets, the silver and jade stolen by the tribesmen. As Kurkhask watched from under lowered brows, he saw many of them now dressed in Mongol deels with dark splashes of blood on the cloth.

The chanting intensified until Kurkhask could see white spittle gather at the edges of the men's mouths. He held his back very straight as the leader of the tribe drew a curved blade and advanced on the line, screaming. Kurkhask exchanged glances with the others.

"After tonight, we will be with the spirits and see the hills of home," he called to them. "The khan will hear. He will sweep this land clean." His calm tone seemed to drive the Arab swordsman to an even higher pitch of fury. Shadows flickered across his face as he whirled the blade over a Mongol warrior. Kurkhask watched without expression. When death was inevitable, when he felt its breath on his neck, he had found all fear could be put aside and he could meet it calmly. That at least gave him some satisfaction. He hoped his wives would shed many tears when they heard.

"Be strong, brother," Kurkhask called. Before the warrior could reply, the sword swept down and took his head. Blood gouted and the Arabs hooted and beat their feet on the ground in appreciation. The swordsman grinned, his teeth very white against dark skin. Again the sword fell and another Mongol toppled sideways on the dusty ground. Kurkhask felt his throat constrict in anger until he could almost choke on it. This was a land of lakes and clear mountain rivers, two thousand miles west of Yenking. The villagers they had met were in awe of their strange faces, yet friendly. That very morning, Kurkhask had been sent on his way with blessings and sticky sweets that gummed his teeth together. He had ridden under a blue sky and never guessed the hill tribes were passing word of his presence. He still did not know why they had been attacked, unless it was simply to steal the gifts and trade goods they carried. He searched the hills for some glimpse of his son, hoping again that his death would be witnessed. He could not die badly if the boy watched. It was the last gift he could give him.

The swordsman needed three blows to take the third head. When it finally came free, he held it up by the hair to his companions, laughing and chanting in their strange language. Kurkhask had begun to learn a few words of the tongue, but the stream of sound was beyond him. He watched in grim silence as the killing continued, until at last he was the only man still alive.

Kurkhask raised his head to stare up without fear. Relief filled him as he caught a movement far beyond the firelight. Something white shifted in the gloom and Kurkhask smiled. His son was out there, signaling. Before the boy gave himself away, Kurkhask dipped his head. The distant flicker vanished, but Kurkhask relaxed, all the tension flowing out of him. The khan would be told.

He looked up at the Arab warrior as he drew back the bloody length of steel.

"My people will see you again," Kurkhask said.

The Afghan swordsman hesitated, unable to understand. "Dust be in thy mouth, infidel!" he shouted, the words a babble of sound to the Mongol officer.

Kurkhask shrugged wearily. "You have no *idea* what you have done," he said.

The sword swept down.

PART
ONE

CHAPTER ONE

THE WIND HAD FALLEN on the high ridge. Dark clouds drifted above, making bands of shadow march across the earth. The morning was quiet and the land seemed empty as the two men rode at the head of a narrow column, a *jagun* of a hundred young warriors. The Mongols could have been alone for a thousand miles, with just creaking leather and snorting ponies to break the stillness. When they halted to listen, it was as if silence rolled back in over the dusty ground.

Tsubodai was a general to the Great Khan, and it showed in the way he held himself. His armor of iron scales over leather was well worn, with holes and rust in many places. His helmet was marked where it had saved his life more than once. All his equipment was battered, but the man himself remained as hard and unforgiving as the winter earth. In three years of raiding the north, he had lost only one minor skirmish and returned the following day to destroy the tribe before word could spread. He had mastered his trade in a land that seemed to grow colder with each mile into the wastes. He had no maps for his journey, just rumors of distant cities built on rivers frozen so solid that oxen could be roasted on the ice.

At his right shoulder rode Jochi, the eldest son of the khan himself. Barely seventeen, he was yet a warrior who might inherit the nation and perhaps command even Tsubodai in war. Jochi wore a similar set of greased leather and iron, as well as the saddle packs and weapons all the warriors carried. Tsubodai knew without asking that Jochi would have his ration of dried blood and milk, needing only water to make a nourishing broth. The land did not forgive those who took survival lightly, and both men had learned the lessons of winter.

Jochi sensed the scrutiny and his dark eyes flickered up, always guarded. He had spent more time with the young general than he ever had with his father, but old habits were hard to break. It was difficult for him to trust, though his respect for Tsubodai knew no limit. The general of the Young Wolves had a feel for war, though he denied it. Tsubodai believed in scouts, training, tactics, and archery above all else, but the men who followed him saw only that he won, no matter what the odds. As others could fashion a sword or a saddle, Tsubodai fashioned armies, and Jochi knew he was privileged to learn at his side. He wondered if his brother Chagatai had fared as well in the east. It was easy to daydream as he rode the hills, imagining his brothers and father struck dumb at the sight of how Jochi had grown and become strong.

"What is the most important item in your packs?" Tsubodai said suddenly.

Jochi raised his eyes to the brooding sky for an instant. Tsubodai delighted in testing him.

"Meat, General. Without meat, I cannot fight."

"Not your bow?" Tsubodai said. "Without a bow, what are you?"

"Nothing, General, but without meat, I am too weak to use the bow."

Tsubodai grunted at hearing his own words repeated. "When the meat is all gone, how long can you live off blood and milk?"

"Sixteen days at most, with three remounts to share the wounds." Jochi did not have to think. He had been drilled in the answers ever since he and Tsubodai had ridden with ten thousand men from the shadow of the Chin emperor's city.

"How far could you travel in such a time?" Tsubodai said.

Jochi shrugged. "Sixteen hundred miles with fresh remounts. Half again as far if I slept and ate in the saddle."

Tsubodai saw that the young man was hardly concentrating, and his eyes glinted as he changed tack.

"What is wrong with the ridge ahead?" he snapped.

Jochi raised his head, startled. "I..."

"Quickly! Men are looking to you for a decision. Lives wait on your word."

Jochi swallowed, but in Tsubodai he had learned from a master.

"The sun is behind us, so we will be visible for miles as we reach the crest." Tsubodai began to nod, but Jochi went on. "The ground is dusty. If we cross the high point of the ridge at any speed, we will raise a cloud into the air."

"That is good, Jochi," Tsubodai said. As he spoke, he dug in his heels and rode hard at the crest ahead. As Jochi had predicted, the hundred riders released a mist of reddish grit that billowed above their heads. Someone would surely see and report their position.

Tsubodai did not pause as he reached the ridge. Digging in his heels, he sent his mare over, the rear legs skittering on loose stones. Jochi matched him and then took a sharp breath of dust that made him cough into his hand. Tsubodai had come to a halt fifty paces beyond the ridge, where the broken ground began to dip to the valley. Without orders, his men formed a wide double rank around him, like a bow drawn on the ground. They were long familiar with the firebrand of a general who had been placed over them.

Tsubodai stared into the distance, frowning. The surrounding hills enclosed a flat plain through which a river ran, swollen with spring rain. Along its banks, a slow-moving column trotted, bright with flags and banners. In other circumstances, it would have been a sight to take the breath, and even as his stomach clenched, Jochi felt a touch of admiration. Ten, perhaps eleven thousand Russian knights rode together, house colors in gold and red streaming back over their heads. Almost as many followed them in a baggage train of carts and remounts, women, boys, and servants. The sun chose that moment to break through the dark clouds in a great beam that lit the valley. The knights shone.

Their horses were massive, shaggy animals, almost twice the weight of the Mongol ponies. Even the men who rode them were a strange breed to Jochi's eyes. They sat like they were made of stone, solid and heavy in metal cloth from their cheeks to their knees. Only their blue eyes and hands were unprotected. The armored knights had come prepared for battle, carrying long spears like lances, but tipped in steel. They rode with the weapons upright, the butts held in leather cups close behind the stirrups. Jochi could see axes and swords hanging down from waist belts, and every man rode with a leaf-shaped shield hooked to his saddle. The pennants streamed back over their heads and they looked very fine in the bands of gold and shadow.

"They must see us," Jochi murmured, glancing at the plume of dust above his head.

The general heard him speak and turned in the saddle. "They are not men of the plains, Jochi. They are half blind over such a distance. Are you afraid? They are so large, these knights. I would be afraid."

For an instant, Jochi glowered. From his father, it would have been mockery. Yet Tsubodai spoke with a light in his eyes. The general was still in his twenties, young to command so many. Tsubodai was not afraid, though. Jochi knew the general cared nothing for the massive warhorses or the men who rode them. Instead, he placed his faith in the speed and arrows of his Young Wolves.

The jagun was made up of ten *arbans,* each commanded by an officer. By Tsubodai's order, only those ten men wore heavy armor. The rest had only leather tunics under padded deels. Jochi knew Genghis preferred the heavy charge to the light, but Tsubodai's men seemed to survive. They could hit and gallop faster than the ponderous Russian warriors, and there was no fear in their ranks. Like Tsubodai, they looked hungrily down the slope at the column and waited to be seen.

"You know your father sent a rider to bring me home?" Tsubodai said.

Jochi nodded. "All the men know."

"I had hoped to go further north than this, but I am your father's man. He speaks and I obey, do you understand?"

Jochi stared at the young general, forgetting for a moment the knights who rode in the valley below.

"Of course," he said, his face showing nothing.

Tsubodai glanced back at him, amused. "I hope you do, Jochi. He is a man to follow, your father. I wonder how he will respond when he sees how well you have grown."

For a moment, anger twisted Jochi's face before he smoothed his features and took a deep breath. Tsubodai had been more like a father than his own in many ways, but he did not forget the man's true loyalty. At an order from Genghis, Tsubodai would kill him. As he looked at the young general, he thought there would be some regret, but not enough to hold the blow.

"He will need loyal men, Tsubodai," Jochi said. "My father would not call us back to build or rest. He will have found some new land to tear to pieces. Like the wolf, he is always hungry, even to the point of bursting his own stomach."

Tsubodai frowned to hear the khan described in such a way. In three years, he had seen no affection when Jochi spoke of his father, though sometimes there was a wistfulness that showed less and less as the seasons passed. Genghis had sent away a boy, but a man would return to him, Tsubodai had made certain of that. For all his bitterness, Jochi was a cool head in battle and the men looked on him with pride. He would do.

"I have another question for you, Jochi," Tsubodai said.

Jochi smiled for an instant. "You always have, General," he replied.

"We have drawn these iron knights after us for hundreds of miles, exhausting their horses. We have captured their scouts and put them to the question, though I do not know of this 'Jerusalem' they seek, or who this 'white Christ' is." Tsubodai shrugged. "Perhaps I will meet him one day over the length of my sword, but the world is large and I am but one man."

As he spoke, he watched the armored knights and the trailing baggage lines behind them, waiting to be seen.

"My question, Jochi, is this. These knights are nothing to me. Your father has called me back and I could ride now, while the ponies are fat with summer grass. Why then are we here, waiting for the challenge?"

Jochi's eyes were cold as he replied.

"My father would say it is what we do, that there is no better way for a man to spend his years than at war with enemies. He might also say you enjoy it, General, and that is all the reason you need."

Tsubodai's gaze did not waver.

"Perhaps he *would* say that, but you hide behind his words. Why are we here, Jochi? We do not want their big horses, even for meat. Why will I risk the lives of warriors to smash the column you see?"

Jochi shrugged irritably. "If it is not that, I do not know."

"For *you,* Jochi," Tsubodai said seriously. "When you return to your father, you will have seen all forms of battle, in all seasons. You and I have captured towns and raided cities, ridden desert and forests so thick we could hardly cut our way through. Genghis will find no weakness in you." Tsubodai smiled briefly at Jochi's stony expression. "I will be proud when men say you learned your skill under Tsubodai the Valiant."

Jochi had to grin at hearing the nickname from Tsubodai himself. There were no secrets in the camps.

"There it is," Tsubodai muttered, pointing to a distant messenger racing to the head of the Russian column. "We have an enemy who leads from the front, a very brave man."

Jochi could imagine the sudden dismay among the knights as they looked into the bowl of hills and saw the Mongol warriors. Tsubodai grunted softly as an entire rank peeled off the column and began trotting up the slopes, the long spears ready. He showed his teeth as the gap began to narrow. They were charging uphill, in their arrogance. He longed to teach them their error.

"Do you have your *paitze,* Jochi? Show it to me."

Jochi reached behind him to where his bow holder was strapped to the saddle. He lifted a flap in the stiff leather and pulled out a plaque of solid gold, stamped with a wolf's head in profile. At twenty ounces, it was heavy, but small enough for him to grip in his hand.

Tsubodai ignored the men rising doggedly up the hill to face the eldest son of Genghis.

"You have that and the right to command a thousand by my hand, Jochi. Those who command a jagun have one of mere silver, like this." Tsubodai held up a larger block of the whitish metal. "The difference is that the silver paitze is given to a man elected by the officers of each arban below him."

"I know this," Jochi said.

Tsubodai glanced back at the knights laboring closer. "The officers of this jagun have asked to have you lead them, Jochi. I had no part in it." He held out the silver paitze and Jochi took it joyfully, passing back the plaque of gold.

Tsubodai was solemn and deliberately formal, but his eyes were bright. "When you return to your father, Jochi, you will have known all ranks and positions." The general gestured, cutting the air with his hand. "On the right, the left, and the center." He looked over the heads of the straining knights cantering up the hill, seeing a flicker of movement on a crag in the distance. Tsubodai nodded sharply.

"It is time. You know what you have to do, Jochi. Command is yours." Without another word, Tsubodai clapped the younger man on the shoulder and rode back over the ridge, leaving the jagun of riders in the care of one suddenly nervous leader.

Jochi could feel the combined stares of the hundred men on his back as he struggled to hide his pleasure. Each arban of ten elected one man to lead them, then those men elected one of their number to lead the hundred in war. To be so chosen was an honor. A voice in his mind whispered that they only honored his father, but he crushed it, refusing to doubt. He had earned the right and confidence swelled in him.

"Bow lines!" Jochi called. He gripped his reins tightly to hide his tension as the men formed a wider line so that every bow could bear. Jochi glanced over his shoulder, but Tsubodai had truly gone, leaving him alone. The men still watched and he forced the cold face, knowing they would remember his calm. As they raised their bows, he held up a clenched fist, waiting while his heart thumped painfully in his chest.

At four hundred paces, Jochi dropped his arm and the first flight of arrows whipped into the air. It was too far and those that reached the knights splintered on their shields, now held high and forward, so that almost the entire man was protected. The long shields showed their purpose as a second flight struck the ranks without a single rider going down.

The powerful horses were not fast, but still the gap closed and Jochi only watched. At two hundred paces, he raised his fist once more and another hundred arrows waited on creaking strings. At such a distance, he did not know if the knights' armor would save them. Nothing ever had.

"Shoot like you have never owned a bow," he shouted. The men around him grinned and the arrows snapped out. Jochi winced instinctively at shafts that went clear over the enemy heads, as if loosed by panicking fools. Only a few struck, and of those, still fewer brought a horse or man down. They could hear the thunder of the charge now and saw the front ranks begin to lower their spears in anticipation.

Facing them, Jochi smothered his fear in a sudden bloom of rage. He wanted nothing more than to draw his sword and kick his mount down the slope at the enemy. Shaking with frustration, he gave a different order.

"Retreat over the ridge," Jochi shouted. He wrenched at his reins and his horse jerked into a run. His jagun shouted incoherently, turning in chaos after their general. Behind him, he heard guttural voices yelling in triumph and acid rose in his throat, though whether it was from fear or anger, he did not know.

Ilya Majaev blinked sweat out of his eyes when he saw the Mongols turn like the filthy cowards they were. As he had a thousand times before, he took a loose grip on his reins and tapped himself on his chest, praying to Saint Sophia to bring enemies of the faith under his hooves. Beneath the chain mail and padded tunic lay a fragment of her finger-bone in a locket of gold, the most precious thing he possessed. The monks at Novgorod had assured him he would not be killed while he wore it, and he felt strong as his knights hammered over the ridge. His men had left the cathedral city two years before, carrying messages east for the prince before they finally turned south and began the long trek that would take them to Jerusalem. Ilya had pledged his life with the others to defend that holy place from the unbelievers who sought to destroy her monuments.

It should have been a journey of prayer and fasting before they brought their skill in arms against godless men. Instead, they had been stung over and over by the Mongol army raiding the area. Ilya ached to have them close enough to kill, and he leaned forward in the saddle as his mount lunged after the fleeing riders.

"Give them unto me, O Lord, and I will break their bones and trample on their false gods," he whispered to himself. The Mongols were racing wildly down the far slope, but the Russian horses were powerful and the gap closed steadily. Ilya sensed the mood of the men around him as they snarled and called to each other. They had lost companions to flights of arrows in the darkness. Scouts had vanished without a trace, or worse, been found with wounds to make a man vomit. In a year, Ilya had seen more towns burned than he could remember, the plumes of black smoke drawing him in desperate pursuit. The marauding Mongols were always gone by the time he arrived. He urged his mount to gallop, though the weary animal's sides were already heaving and clots of white saliva flicked up to strike his arms and chest.

"On, brothers!" Ilya shouted to the rest. He knew they would not tire with the tribesmen at last within reach. The Mongols were an affront to everything Ilya valued, from the peaceful streets of Novgorod to the quiet calm and dignity of the cathedral of his blessed saint.

Ahead, the Mongol warriors raced in disarray through a cloud of their own dust. Ilya snapped orders and his men closed into a solid column, fifty ranks of twenty abreast. They tied their reins to the saddle horns and leaned forward over the horses' necks with shield and spear, urging the animals on with just their knees. Surely there had never been such a force of men and iron in the history of the world! Ilya showed his teeth in anticipation of first blood.

The route of the fleeing Mongols took them past a hill shrouded in ancient beech and elm trees. As Ilya thundered past it, he saw something move in the green gloom. He barely had time to shout a warning before the air was filled with whining shafts. Even then he did not hesitate. He had seen the arrows break on his men's shields. He bawled an order to hold formation, knowing they could smash their way through.

A horse screamed and thumped into him from his left, crushing his leg and almost unseating him. Ilya cursed in pain, taking a sharp breath as he saw the rider hanging limp. Flight after flight of arrows came from the dark trees, and in horror, he saw his men falling from their saddles. Arrows passed through chain mail as if it were linen, punching out in a spray of blood. Ilya shouted wildly, kicking his exhausted mount on. Ahead, he saw the Mongols wheel in perfect unison, their commander staring straight at him. The Mongols did not stop to bend their bows. Their ponies lunged forward as one, the warriors loosing shafts as they rode.

Ilya felt an arrow pluck at his arm, then the two forces clashed together and he braced himself. His long spear took a warrior in the chest, wrenching it from his grasp so quickly he thought he had broken his fingers. He drew his sword with a hand almost too numb to grip. Red dust was everywhere, and in the midst, the Mongols rode like devils, calmly sending arrows into the packed ranks of his men.

Ilya raised his shield and was knocked backwards as an arrow struck it, the head showing clearly through the wood. His right foot came out of the stirrup and he swayed, all balance lost. Another shaft hit him in the thigh before he could recover, and he cried out in pain, raising his sword as he rode at the archer.

The Mongol watched him come, his face blank of any emotion. He was little than a beardless boy, Ilya saw. The Russian swung his blade, but the Mongol ducked under the blow and shoved him as he passed. The world spun in silence for a moment and then Ilya crashed to the ground, stunned.

The nosepiece of his helmet had been jammed in with the impact, breaking his front teeth. Ilya rose, blind with tears and spitting blood and fragments. His left leg buckled and he fell clumsily, desperate to find the sword that had fallen from his hand.

He heard hoofbeats behind just as he saw the weapon lying on the dusty ground. He reached for the relic at his chest and murmured a prayer as the Mongol blade came down on his neck, almost severing his head. He did not live to see the rest of his men slaughtered, too heavy and slow to defend against the warriors of Tsubodai, general to Genghis Khan.

Jochi dismounted to examine the dead, once he had ordered a dozen of his men to sweep the area and report the movement of the main column. The Russian chain mail had not saved them. Many of the sprawling bodies were struck through more than once. Only the helmets had held. Jochi could not find a single man brought down with a shaft to the head. He picked up a helmet and rubbed a finger over a bright slash of metal where an arrow had glanced away. It was a good design.

The ambush had gone just as Tsubodai had planned, Jochi thought wryly. The general seemed to read the minds of their enemies. Jochi breathed deeply, making an effort to control the trembling that beset him after each battle. It would not do for the men to see him shake. He did not know they watched him stride with clenched fists and saw only that he was still hungry, a man never satisfied no matter what he had achieved.

Three other jaguns had taken part in the ambush. Jochi saw the officers ride out of the trees where they had lain in wait all night. After years with Tsubodai, he knew each man like a brother, as Genghis had once told him to do. Mekhali and Altan were solid men, loyal but unimaginative. Jochi nodded to them both as they trotted their ponies to the field of the dead. The last of them, Qara, was a short, sinewy warrior with a scarred face from an old wound. Though he was faultlessly formal, Jochi sensed a dislike he could not understand. Perhaps the glowering man resented him for his father. Jochi had met many suspicious of his rise in the ranks. Tsubodai was not subtle in the way he included Jochi in every plan and stratagem, just as Genghis had once done with the young boy from the Uriankhai who had become his general. Tsubodai looked to the future, while men like Qara imagined they saw only a spoiled young prince, promoted beyond his skill.

As Qara rode up and grunted at the sight of the dead knights, Jochi realized he was no longer the man's superior. He had accepted the silver with a battle looming and still felt the honor of being trusted with a hundred lives. Yet it meant that for a time at least, Qara no longer had to watch himself around the khan's son. One glance told Jochi the wiry little warrior had already thought it through.

"Why are we waiting here?" Qara said suddenly. "Tsubodai will be attacking as we smell the grass and stand idle."

Jochi resented the words, but he spoke lightly as if Qara had merely greeted him. If the man had been a true leader, he would already have begun the ride back to Tsubodai. In a flash of insight, Jochi understood that Qara still looked to him to respond, despite his drop in rank. Glancing at Mekhali and Altan, he found they too were watching him.

Perhaps it was just their habit, but he felt an idea begin to form and knew he would not waste the moment.

"Do you see their armor, Qara?" he responded. "The first piece hangs from the helmet, covering their faces except for the eyes. The second cloth of iron rings reaches right to their knees."

"It did not stop our shafts," Qara said with a shrug. "When they are unhorsed, they move so slowly it is easy to bring them down. We do not need such poor protection, I think."

Jochi grinned up at the man, enjoying the confusion it brought.

"We do need it, Qara."

High in the hills above the valley, Tsubodai waited on foot, his pony snuffling among dead pine needles. Almost five thousand men rested around him, waiting for his decision. *He* waited on the scouts he had sent out. Two hundred had ridden in all directions, their reports allowing the general to form a picture of the area for many miles around.

He knew Jochi's ambush had been a success almost before it was over. One thousand fewer of the enemy left only ten, but it was still too many. The column of knights moved slowly through the river valley, waiting for the attack group to return victorious. They had not brought bowmen into the wilderness, a mistake that would cost them dearly. Yet they were large men and so strong that Tsubodai could not risk a simple frontal assault. He had seen knights stuck with arrows who had still fought through to kill two or even three of his. They were warriors of great courage, but he thought it would not be enough. Brave men come forward when they are attacked, and Tsubodai planned accordingly. Any army could be routed in the right conditions, he was certain of it. Not his own, of course, but that of any enemy.

Two of the scouts galloped in to mark the latest position of the Russian force. Tsubodai made them dismount and draw on the ground with sticks so he could be sure there was no misunderstanding.

"How many scouts do they have out?" he asked.

The warrior drawing with a stick replied without hesitation. "Ten in the rear, General, on a wide sweep. Twenty to the front and flanks."

Tsubodai nodded. He knew enough to move, at last.

"They must be killed, especially the ones behind the knights' column. Take them when the sun is highest and do not let even one escape. I will attack as soon as you signal by flag that the scouts are down. Repeat your orders."

The warrior spoke quickly, word perfect as he had been trained to be. Tsubodai allowed no confusion in the field. For all the use of flags to communicate over vast distances, he was still forced to rely on dawn, noon, and sunset as the only markers for time. He looked up through the trees at the thought, seeing that the sun was not far off midday. It would not be long and he felt the familiar flutter in his stomach that came before a battle. He had told Jochi it was to train him, and that was true, but not the whole truth. Tsubodai had held back that the knights traveled with portable forges in their baggage train. Blacksmiths were more valuable than any other artisan they could capture, and Tsubodai had been intrigued by reports of iron carts belching smoke as they rolled.

Tsubodai smiled to himself, enjoying the rising excitement. Like Genghis, he could find no love for the sacking of towns and cities. It was something that had to be done, of course, as a man would pour boiling water on a nest of ants. It was the battles Tsubodai wanted, each one proving or increasing his mastery. He had found no greater joy than out-thinking his enemies, confounding and destroying them. He had heard of the strange quest the knights were on, to a land so distant that no one knew its name. It did not matter. Genghis would not allow armed men to ride his lands—and all lands were his.

Tsubodai scuffed the drawings in the dirt with the toe of his boot. He turned to the second scout, who waited patiently, in awe of the general.

"Ride to Jochi and find what has delayed him," Tsubodai ordered. "He will sit at my right hand for this attack."

"Your will, lord," the scout said, bowing before he scrambled to his horse and went careering through the trees at breakneck speed. Tsubodai squinted through the branches at the sun. He would move very soon.

In the thump and thunder of ten thousand horses, Anatoly Majaev glanced over his shoulder at the ridge little Ilya had disappeared behind. Where had his brother gone? He still thought of him as little Ilya, despite the fact that his brother outweighed him in both muscle and faith. Anatoly shook his head wearily. He had promised their mother he would look after him. Ilya would catch up, he was certain. He had not dared halt the column now that the Mongols had shown they were in the area. Anatoly had sent scouts all around, but they too seemed to have vanished. He looked behind again, straining his eyes for the banners of a thousand men.

Ahead, the valley narrowed in a pass through hills that could have been part of the Garden of Eden. The slopes were green with grass so thick a man could not hack through the roots in half a day. Anatoly loved this land, but his eyes were always on the horizon, and one day he would see Jerusalem. He muttered a prayer to the Virgin under his breath, and at that moment, the pass darkened and he saw the Mongol army riding out against him.

The scouts were dead then, as he had feared. Anatoly cursed and could not help but look back for Ilya once more.

Shouts came from behind and Anatoly turned completely in the saddle, swearing at the sight of another dark mass of riders coming up fast. How had they gone around him without being spotted? It defied belief to have the enemy move like ghosts through the hills.

He knew his men could scatter the Mongols in a charge. Already they had unhooked their shields and raised them, looking to him for orders. As the eldest son of a baron, Anatoly was the most senior officer. Indeed, it had been his family who had financed the entire trip, using some of their vast fortune to earn the goodwill of the monasteries that had become so powerful in Russia.

Anatoly knew he could not charge with the entire baggage train and rear ranks exposed. Nothing unnerved fighting men more than being struck from before and behind at the same time. He began to shout an order for three of his officers to take their centuries and wheel around to charge the rear. As he turned, a movement on the hills caught his eye and he grinned in relief. In the distance, a line of Russian heavy horse came back over the ridge, banners flying lightly in the breeze. Anatoly judged the distances and made his decision. He called a scout over to him.

"Ride to my brother and tell him to hit the force at our rear. He must prevent them from joining the battle."

The young man raced away, unencumbered by armor or weapons. Anatoly turned to the front, his confidence swelling. With the rear secured, he outnumbered those who were galloping toward him. His orders had taken only moments and he knew he could punch through the Mongols like an armored fist.

Anatoly pointed his long spear over his horse's ears.

"Charge formation! For the white Christ, onward!"

* * *

Anatoly's scout raced along at full gallop across the dusty ground. Speed was everything with two armies converging on the column. He rode with his body pressed as low as he could go, the horse's head lunging up and down by his own. He was young and excited and rode almost to Ilya Majaev's men before pulling up in shock. Only four hundred had come back over the crest and they had been through hell. Brown slicks of blood showed on many men as they approached, and there was something odd about the way they rode.

The scout suddenly understood and wrenched at his reins in panic. He was too late. An arrow took him under a flailing arm and he tumbled over the horse's ears, making the animal bolt.

Jochi and the other Mongols did not look at the prone figure as they galloped past. It had taken a long time to pull the chain mail off the dead, but the ruse was working. No force rode out to cut them off, and though the Russians didn't know it, they were being attacked on three sides. As the slope lessened, Jochi dug in his heels and brought the heavy spear out of its leather socket. It was a cumbersome thing and he had to strain to hold it steady as he and his men thundered toward the Russian flank.

Anatoly was at full gallop, more than half a ton of flesh and iron focused on a spear point. He saw the front ranks shudder as the Mongol archers loosed their first shafts. The enemy were fast, but the column could not be held back, or even turned at that speed. The noise of shield impacts and hooves was deafening, but he heard screams behind him and wrenched himself back to clarity. He was in command, and as his mind cleared he shook his head in horror. He watched Ilya strike the main flank, cutting into the very men who had pledged themselves to the Majaev family on the pilgrimage.

As he gaped, Anatoly saw the men were smaller and wore bloody iron. Some had lost their helmets in the first clash to reveal yelling Mongol faces. He blanched then, knowing his brother was dead and the twin attack would crush the rear ranks. He could not turn, and though he bawled frantic orders, no one heard him.

Ahead, the Mongols let them come in, loosing shafts by the thousand into the Russian horsemen. The shields were battered and the column jerked like a wounded animal. Men fell by the hundred. It was as if a scythe had been drawn across the face of the column, cutting through living men.

Behind, the Mongols rolled up the baggage train, killing anyone on the carts who raised a weapon. Anatoly strained to think, to make out details, but he was in among the enemy. His spear ripped along a horse's neck, opening a great gash that spattered him in warm blood. A sword flashed and Anatoly took the blow on his helmet, almost losing consciousness. Something hit him in the chest and suddenly he could not breathe, even to call for help. He strained for just a cupful of air, just a sip, but it did not come and he collapsed, hitting the ground hard enough to numb his final agony.

At the fires that evening, Tsubodai rode through the camp of his ten thousand. The dead knights had been stripped of anything valuable, and the general had pleased the men by refusing his personal tithe. For those who received no pay for their battles, the collection of blood-stained lockets, rings, and gems was something to covet in the new society Genghis was creating. A man could become wealthy in the army of the tribes, though they thought always in terms of the horses they could buy with their riches. The knights' forges were of more interest to Tsubodai, as were the spoked cart wheels themselves, ringed in iron and easier to repair than the solid discs the Mongols used. Tsubodai had already instructed the captured armorers to demonstrate the skill to his carpenters.

Jochi was examining the forehoof of his favorite pony when Tsubodai trotted up to him. Before the younger man could bow, Tsubodai inclined his head, giving him honor. The jagun Jochi had commanded stood with pride.

Tsubodai lifted his hand to show Jochi the gold paitze he had taken from him before noon.

"You had me wondering how Russians could come back from the dead," Tsubodai said. "It was a bold stroke. Take this back, Jochi. You are worth more than silver, no matter what jagun wants you to lead them."

He tossed the gold plaque through the air and Jochi caught it, struggling to keep his composure. Only the praise of Genghis himself would have meant more at that moment.

"We will ride home tomorrow," Tsubodai said, as much for the men as Jochi. "Be ready at dawn."

CHAPTER TWO

CHAGATAI FELT AN ITCH in his left armpit, where sweat dribbled under his best armor. Though he was the second son of the khan, he sensed it would not be right to give the spot a good scratch while he waited for the king of Koryo.

He risked a quick glance at the man who had brought him to the distant, walled city of Songdo. The hall of kings was stifling in the midday heat, but Jelme showed no discomfort in his lacquered armor. Like the courtiers and the royal guards, the Mongol general could have been carved out of wood.

Chagatai could hear water running in the far distance, the gentle sound somehow magnified in the oppressive heat and silence. The itch became maddening and he struggled to think of something else. As his gaze rested on a high ceiling of white plaster and ancient pine beams, he reminded himself that he had no reason to feel intimidated. For all their dignity, the Wang dynasty had not been able to crush the Khara-Kitai when those people came into their land from Chin territory and built fortresses. If Jelme had not volunteered his army to burn them out, the Koryon king would still be a near prisoner in his own palace. At fifteen years old, Chagatai felt a vague smugness at the thought. He had all the pride and arrogance of a young warrior, yet in this case, he knew it was justified. Jelme and his warriors had come into the east to see what armies might stand against them and to view the ocean for the first time. They had found enemies in the Khara-Kitai and driven them out of Koryo like whipped dogs. Chagatai knew it was only just that the king pay a tribute, whether he had asked for help or not.

Sweating in the heavy air, Chagatai tortured himself with memory of the breeze off the sea in the south. The cool wind had been the only good thing about that blue vastness, in his opinion. Jelme had been fascinated by the Koryon ships, but the thought of wanting to travel on water baffled Chagatai. If it could not be ridden, he had no use for it. Even the memory of the royal barge swaying at anchor made his stomach clench.

A bell sounded out in the courtyard, the tone echoing through gardens where bees buzzed in hives around acacia blossoms. Chagatai pictured the Buddhist monks heaving on the log that struck the great bell, and he straightened, once more aware of how he stood. The king would be on his way and his torment would come to an end. He could stand an itch a little longer: just the thought of relief made it seem bearable.

The bell boomed again and servants slid back screens, opening the hall to the scent of pines from the surrounding hills. Despite himself, Chagatai let out a sigh as the intense heat began to lessen. The crowd moved subtly as they strained to see the king, and Chagatai used the distraction to dig two fingers into his armpit and scratch vigorously. He sensed Jelme's gaze flicker to him and resumed his impassive expression as the king of the Koryon people entered at last.

None of them were tall, Chagatai thought, as he saw the diminutive monarch waft through a carved doorway. He supposed the man's name was Wang, after his family, but who knew or cared how these wiry little people named each other? Chagatai looked instead at a pair of serving girls in the king's retinue. With their delicate golden skin, they were far more interesting than the man they served. The young warrior stared as the women fussed around their master, arranging his robes as he seated himself.

The king did not seem aware of the watching Mongols as he waited for his attendants to finish. His eyes were almost the same dark yellow as Genghis's, though they lacked his father's ability to inspire terror. Compared to the khan, the Koryon king was just a lamb.

The servants finished their tasks at last and the king's gaze finally focused on the arban of ten warriors Jelme had brought. Chagatai wondered how the man could bear such thick cloth on a summer's day.

When the king spoke, Chagatai could not understand a word. Like Jelme, he had to wait for the translation into the Chin language he had struggled to master. Even then he could hardly catch the meaning and listened in growing frustration. He disliked foreign languages. Once a man knew the word for a horse, why use another? Obviously Chagatai understood that men from far lands might not know the right way of speaking, but he felt they owed it to themselves to learn and not continue their gibberish, as if all tongues were of equal value.

"You have kept your promises," the translator said solemnly, interrupting Chagatai's thoughts. "The Khara-Kitai fortresses have burned for many days, and that foul people have gone from the high and beautiful land."

Silence fell again and Chagatai shifted uncomfortably. The court of the Koryo seemed to delight in slowness. He recalled his experience of the drink they called *nok cha*. Jelme had frowned at the way Chagatai emptied his cup in a gulp and held it out for another. Apparently, the pale green liquid was too valuable to be drunk like water. As if one warrior should care how another ate or drank! Chagatai ate when he was hungry and often forgot to attend the elaborate meals of the court. He could not understand Jelme's interest in pointless rituals, but he had not spoken his thoughts aloud. When he ruled the Mongol nation, he would not allow pretension, he vowed to himself. Food was not something to linger over, or prepare in a thousand flavors. It was no wonder that the Koryon people had come so close to being conquered. They would be required to speak one language and eat perhaps no more than two or three different dishes, prepared quickly and without fuss. It would leave more time for training with weapons and exercise to make the body strong.

Chagatai's wandering thoughts stilled as Jelme spoke at last, apparently having weighed every word.

"It is fortunate that the Khara-Kitai chose to attack my scouts. Our needs met in their destruction. I speak now for the Great Khan, whose warriors have saved your country from a terrible enemy. Where is the tribute promised by your ministers?"

As the translation droned, the king stiffened slightly in his seat. Chagatai wondered if the fool took some insult from the words. Perhaps he had forgotten the army camped outside the city. At a single command from Jelme, they would burn the polished beams around the king's head. It was still a mystery to Chagatai why they had not. Surely Genghis had sent them out to hone their skills? Chagatai appreciated distantly that there was an art in negotiating that he had yet to learn. Jelme had tried to explain the need to deal with foreign powers, but Chagatai could not see it. A man was either an enemy or a friend. If he was an enemy, everything he owned could be taken. Chagatai smiled as he completed the thought. A khan needed no friends, only servants.

Once more he daydreamed about ruling his people. The tribes would never accept his brother Jochi, if he was even the khan's son at all. Chagatai had done his part in spreading the rumor that Jochi was the result of a rape, many years before. Genghis had allowed the whispers to grow deep roots by his distant manner toward the boy. Chagatai smiled to himself at the memories, allowing his hand to drift past the hilt of his sword. His father had passed it into his hands over Jochi, a blade that had seen the birth of a nation. In his most private heart, Chagatai knew he would never take an oath to Jochi.

One of the king's ministers leaned close to the throne to exchange whispered words. It went on long enough for the ranks of courtiers to wilt visibly in their robes and jewels, but at last the minister retreated. Once more the king spoke, his words translated smoothly.

"Honored allies may accept *gifts* in token of a new friendship, as has been discussed," the king said. "One hundred thousand sheets of oiled paper have been prepared for you, the labor of many moons." The assembled crowd of Koryon nobles murmured at the words, though Chagatai could not imagine why paper would be seen as valuable. "Ten thousand silk vests have been sewn and the same weight added in jade and silver. Two hundred thousand kwan of iron and the same in bronze have come from the mines and the guild of metalworkers. From my own stores, sixty tiger skins have been wrapped in silk and made ready to travel with you. Finally, eight hundred cartloads of oak and beech are the gift of the Wang dynasty, in thanks for the victory you have brought to the Koryon people. Go now in peace and honor and count us always as allies."

Jelme nodded stiffly as the translator finished.

"I accept your tribute, Majesty." A slight flush had appeared on his neck. Chagatai wondered if the general would ignore the king's attempt to save face. Tribute was given to conquerors and Jelme stood in silence for a long time as he considered the king's words. When he spoke again, his voice was firm.

"I ask only that six hundred young men between the ages of twelve and sixteen be added to it. I will train them in the skills of my people, and they will know many battles and great honor."

Chagatai struggled not to show his approval. Let them choke on *that*, with their talk of gifts and honored allies. Jelme's demand had revealed the true balance of power in the room, and the courtiers were visibly distressed. The silence stretched in the hall and Chagatai watched with interest as the king's minister bowed close once more. He saw the king's knuckles whiten as his grip on the armrest tightened. Chagatai was tired of their posturing. Even the smooth-limbed women at the king's feet had lost their allure. He wanted to get out into the cool air and perhaps bathe in the river before the sun lost its heat.

Yet Jelme did not move a muscle and his glare seemed to make the men around the king nervous. Their darting glances were wasted on the silent warriors as they stood and waited for a certain outcome. The city of Songdo had less than sixty thousand inhabitants and an army of no more than three thousand. The king could assume whatever airs he wanted, but Chagatai knew the truth of the situation. When the answer came at last, it was no surprise.

"We are honored that you would accept so many young men into your service, General," the king said. His expression was sour, but Jelme responded to the interpreter, mouthing further expressions of goodwill that Chagatai drowned out. His father had called Jelme home after three years of scouting the east. It would be good to see the mountains again and Chagatai could barely restrain his impatience at the thought. Jelme seemed to think this paper would be important, though Chagatai doubted Genghis would value it. In that at least, his father was predictable. It was a good thing Jelme had demanded silk and hard woods as well. Those things were worth having.

Without an obvious signal, the bell sounded again in the courtyard outside, ending the audience. Chagatai watched the servant girls as they readied their master to stand and fell in behind him. He sighed as the room relaxed subtly around him, taking pleasure in scratching his armpit once more. Home. Jochi would be coming back as well, with Tsubodai. Chagatai wondered how his brother would have changed in three years. At seventeen, he would be fully grown, and no doubt Tsubodai had trained him well. Chagatai cracked his neck with his hands, relishing the challenges to come.

In the southern half of Chin lands, warriors of the third army of Genghis were drinking themselves senseless. At their backs, the citizens of Kaifeng waited behind high walls and gates, already despairing.

Some of the Chin had accompanied the emperor himself as he had come south from Yenking three years before. They had seen the smoke in the northern sky as that city burned. For a time, they thought the Mongols had passed them by, but then the army of Khasar came after them, drawing lines of destruction across the ground like a hot iron across flesh.

The streets of Kaifeng were almost empty and would have been eerily silent if not for the distant cheering of the Mongol host. Those who had armed guards could climb to the walls and look down on the besieging army. What they saw brought no comfort or hope. To the Chin, even the casual nature of Khasar's siege was an insult.

On this day, the Great Khan's brother was amusing himself with a wrestling competition amongst his men. Khasar's host of gers lacked a clear pattern, and his vast herds of animals wandered aimlessly over the land, only rarely disturbed by the long whips of herdsmen. The Mongols had not so much surrounded Kaifeng as made camp there. To the Chin who hated and feared them, it was galling to see the enemy enjoying games and sports while Kaifeng began to go hungry. Though the Chin were no strangers to cruelty, the Mongols were more callous than they could comprehend. Khasar's army cared nothing at all for the suffering inhabitants of Kaifeng and only resented them for delaying the fall of the city. They had been there for three months and they showed a terrible, limitless patience.

The emperor's city of Yenking had fallen to these primitive horsemen. Its great armies had not held them. With that example, no one in Kaifeng had real hope. The streets had become lawless and only the strong dared go out at all. Food was distributed from a central store, but some days they had nothing. No one could know if the food was running out, or if it had been stolen on the way.

In the camp, Khasar rose to his feet, roaring in excitement with Ho Sa as the wrestler known as Baabgai, the Bear, heaved his opponent up over his head. The vanquished man struggled at first, but Baabgai stood unmoving, beaming like a stupid child at his general. The bets dwindled to a trickle and then nothing. The man he held was so battered and exhausted that he only tugged feebly at Baabgai's square fingertips.

Khasar had found the wrestler among his Chin recruits, marking him apart immediately for his size and strength. He looked forward to having the massive idiot challenge one of the champions at home. If he judged the wagers well, he could beggar a few men in one match, his brother Temuge among them.

Baabgai waited impassively with his squirming burden, waiting for Khasar's order. Few others could have supported a grown warrior for so long, and Baabgai's face was pink and shiny with sweat.

Khasar stared through the big wrestler, his thoughts returning to the message from Genghis. The scout his brother had sent still stood where Khasar had placed him hours before. Flies were sucking at the salt on the scout's skin, but the young man dared not move.

Khasar's good mood vanished and he gestured irritably to his wrestling champion.

"Break him," he snapped. The crowd took a sharp breath as Baabgai dropped suddenly to one knee, bringing his opponent down on the outstretched thigh. The crack of a broken spine sounded across the clearing, and all the men roared and exchanged betting tokens. Baabgai beamed toothlessly at them. Khasar looked away as the crippled man's throat was cut. It was a kindness not to leave him alive for dogs and rats.

Sensing his thoughts turning darker, Khasar signaled for the next bout and a skin of black airag: anything to distract him from his gloom. If he'd known Genghis would be recalling the armies, he'd have made better time heading into Chin lands. With Ho Sa and Genghis's son Ogedai, he'd spent leisurely years burning cities and executing their populations, all the time moving closer to where the boy emperor had taken refuge. It had been a very happy time for him.

He was not a man given to thinking too hard about himself, but Khasar had come to enjoy being in command. For men like Genghis, it came naturally. Khasar could not imagine Genghis allowing anyone to lead him to a toilet pit, never mind a battle. For Khasar, it had come slowly, the need growing like moss. For three years, he had not spoken to any of his brothers, Genghis, Kachiun, or Temuge. His warriors had expected him to know where to ride and what to do once they arrived. Khasar had found it exhausting at first, just as a lead dog will last only so long at the head of a pack. He knew that well, but he discovered another truth, that leading was as exciting as it was exhausting. His mistakes were his own, but his triumphs were also his own. As the seasons passed, Khasar had changed subtly, and he did not want to go home. Waiting for Kaifeng to fall, he was father to ten thousand sons.

He looked around at the men he had brought so far from home. His second in command, Samuka, was sober as always, watching the wrestling with detached amusement. Ogedai was yelling and sweating with drink, looking small at the shoulder of warriors. Khasar let his gaze drift over the boy, wondering how he would take the news of their return. At Ogedai's age, everything was new and exciting, and Khasar thought he would be pleased. His mood soured further as he studied his men. Every one of them had proved his worth. They had taken women by the thousand, horses, coins, and weapons, too much to spend a lifetime cataloging. Khasar let out a long sigh. Yet Genghis was the Great Khan and Khasar could no more imagine rebelling against his older brother than he could sprout wings and fly across the walls of Kaifeng.

Ho Sa seemed to sense the general's mood and raised a skin of black airag to him, the noise of the wrestling bout swelling around them both. Khasar smiled tightly, without pleasure. With Samuka, Ho Sa had heard the scout's message. The day had been ruined and both men knew it.

The Xi Xia officer would once have shuddered at the thought of drinking with lice-ridden tribesmen. Before the Mongols had come, Ho Sa had lived a life of simple austerity, proud of his place in his king's army. He had woken each dawn for an hour of exercise before bathing, then begun the day with black tea and bread dipped in honey. Ho Sa's life had been almost perfect and he sometimes longed for it, while dreading its dullness at the same time.

On very dark nights, when all the pretenses of men are laid bare, Ho Sa knew he had found a place and a life he would never have enjoyed in the Xi Xia. He had risen to third in command of a Mongol army, and men like Khasar trusted him with their lives. The bites of fleas and lice were a small price to pay in return. Following Khasar's black gaze, Ho Sa too glowered drunkenly at Kaifeng. If all an emperor could do was cower behind high walls, he was no emperor as far as Ho Sa could see. He took another gulp of the clear airag and winced as it stung a cut on his gums.

Ho Sa did sometimes miss the peace and routines of his old life, but somewhere, he knew, they continued. That thought brought him comfort when he was tired or wounded. It also helped that he had a fortune in gold and silver. If he ever did return home, he would have wives, slaves, and wealth.

The second match finished with a broken arm and both men bowed to Khasar before he gave them leave to have their wounds treated. The day's events would cost him perhaps a dozen injured and a few killed, but it was worth it to inspire the others. They were not delicate young girls, after all.

Khasar glared at the scout. It had been Khasar himself who had taken the lonely forts the Mongols now used as way stations for their messengers. They stretched in an unbroken line all the way back to the charred remains of Yenking in the north. If Khasar had realized the new trade road would enable Genghis to send a recall order only *eighteen* days before, he might not have done it. Would his brother understand if he waited another year for the fortress city to fall? Khasar kicked at a stone, startling the scout as he stood there. He knew the answer. Genghis would expect him to drop everything and return, bringing the khan's son Ogedai with him. It was galling and Khasar stared at Kaifeng as if he could bring the walls down with anger alone. He hardly saw the third bout of wrestling, though the hard-drinking crowd appreciated it.

"Recite the orders again," Khasar said suddenly. Over the yelling warriors, he had to repeat himself twice to be heard. The scout bowed his head, at a loss to understand the mood his message had created.

"'Come home and drink black airag with our people, my brother. In the spring, we will drink milk and blood.'"

"That is all?" Khasar snapped. "Tell me how he looked when he sent you out."

The scout shifted uncomfortably. "The Great Khan was discussing plans, lord, with his senior men. They had maps weighted with stones of lead, but I did not hear what they said before I was summoned."

Ho Sa raised his head at that, his eyes glassy with drink. "'Milk and blood' will mean he plans a new war," he called. The noise of the crowd dropped suddenly at his words. Ogedai had frozen to listen. Even the wrestlers paused, unsure whether they should go on. Khasar blinked and then shrugged. He didn't care who heard.

"If my brother had his precious maps out, that must be it." He sighed to himself. If Genghis knew he stood before the walls of Kaifeng, surely he would wait. The boy emperor had escaped them at Yenking. The thought of the Imperial Chin court watching the Mongols leave was almost unbearable.

"Has my brother summoned Tsubodai and Jelme?" Khasar said.

The messenger swallowed nervously under the eyes of so many. "I did not carry the messages, lord."

"You know though. Scouts always know. Tell me, or I will have your tongue."

The young messenger swallowed his doubts and spoke quickly. "Two other men rode out to bring the generals back to the khan, lord. This I heard."

"And the armies at home? Are they drilling and making ready, or just waiting?"

"They are under orders to train the winter fat off them, lord."

Khasar saw Samuka grin and he cursed under his breath.

"Then it *is* war. Go back along the path I made and tell my brother 'I am coming.' It is enough."

"Shall I say you will be there before the end of summer, lord?" the scout asked.

"Yes," Khasar replied. He spat on the ground as the scout raced away. He had taken every city for a hundred miles around Kaifeng, surrounding the emperor with destruction and cutting his supplies. Yet he would leave, just when victory was assured. He saw Ogedai's eyes were wide with excitement and Khasar looked away.

It would be good to see his brothers again, he realized. He wondered idly if Jelme or Tsubodai could match the wealth he had taken from the Chin cities. Whole forests had been cut to provide carts enough to carry it all. He had even recruited from among the Chin, so that he returned with two thousand more men than he had taken with him. He sighed to himself. What he had wanted was to bring Genghis the bones of an emperor. He cared nothing for the other spoils of war.

CHAPTER THREE

GENGHIS LET HIS MARE have her head on the open plain, hitting full gallop so that the warm air rushed by him and sent his long black hair streaming in the wind. He wore only a light tunic that left his arms bare, revealing a dense web of white scars. The trousers that gripped the mare's flanks were old and dark with mutton fat, as were the soft boots in the stirrups. He carried no sword, though a leather bowcase rested behind his thigh and a small hunting quiver bounced on his shoulders, its leather strap running across his chest.

The air was black with birds overhead, the noise of their wings clattering as hawks tore through them, bringing prey back to their masters. In the distance, three thousand warriors had formed an unbroken ring that dawn, riding slowly and driving every living thing before them. It would not be long before the center was filled with marmots, deer, foxes, rats, wild dogs, and a thousand other small animals. Genghis could see the ground was dark with them, and he grinned in anticipation of the killing ahead. A deer ran bucking and snorting in panic through the circle, and Genghis took it easily, sending a shaft into its chest behind the foreleg. The buck collapsed, kicking, and he turned to see if his brother Kachiun had witnessed the shot.

There was little true sport in the circle hunt, though it helped to feed the tribes when meat was running low. Nevertheless, Genghis enjoyed it and awarded places at the center to men he wished to honor. As well as Kachiun, Arslan was there, the first man to take an oath to him. The old swordsman was sixty years of age and knife thin. He rode well, if stiffly, and Genghis saw him take a pigeon from the air as the bird flew overhead.

The wrestler Tolui galloped across his vision, leaning low on the saddle to drop a fat marmot as it streaked across the grass in panic. A wolf came from a patch of long grass and made Tolui's pony shy, almost unseating him. Genghis laughed as the massive warrior struggled upright. It was a good day and the circle was almost upon them. A hundred of his most valued officers raced here and there as the ground darkened into a solid stream of animals. They swarmed so thickly that more were crushed by hooves than spitted on killing shafts. The circle of riders closed until they stood shoulder to shoulder and the men in the middle emptied their quivers, enjoying themselves.

Genghis spotted a mountain cat in the press and kicked his heels in after it. He saw Kachiun on the same run and was pleased when his brother wheeled away to leave him the shot. Both men were in their late thirties, strong and supremely fit. With the armies returning, they would take the nation into new lands, and Genghis was glad of it.

He had come back from the Chin capital worn out and racked by illness. It had taken almost a year for him to regain his health, but the weakness was now only a memory. As the end of summer approached, he felt his old strength and with it the desire to crush those who had dared to kill his men. He wanted his enemies proud and strong, so that he could cast them further down in his vengeance.

Genghis reached for another arrow and his fingers closed on nothing, making him sigh. The boys and girls of the camps would now run in with hammers and knives to finish the slaughter and begin preparing the carcasses for a great feast.

The scouts for the khan had reported that the armies of Khasar and Tsubodai were only a few days' ride away. His generals would be honored with rice wine and black airag when they returned. Genghis wondered how his sons would have grown in the years apart. It was exciting to think of riding to war with Chagatai and Ogedai, taking new lands so that they too could be khans. He knew that Jochi was returning, but that was an old wound and he did not dwell on it. He was done with peaceful years with his wives and the young children. If the sky father had a purpose for him, it was not to spend his time quietly while the world slept.

Genghis rode to Kachiun as his brother clapped Arslan on the shoulders. Between them, the ground was red with blood and fur, and boys darted almost under the hooves as they yelled and called to each other in excitement.

"Did you see the great cat I brought down?" Genghis said to the two men. "It took two arrows just to slow it."

"It was a fine kill," Kachiun shouted, his face glowing with sweat. One scrawny boy came too close to Kachiun's stirrups as he spoke, and he reached down to cuff the lad, knocking him sprawling to the amusement of his companions.

Arslan smiled as the little boy picked himself up and glared at the khan's brother before racing off.

"They are so young, this new generation," he said. "I can hardly remember being so small."

Genghis nodded. The children of the tribes would never know the fear of being hunted as he and his brothers had. Listening to their laughter and high-pitched voices, he could only wonder at what he had achieved. Just a few herdsmen roamed the valleys and mountains of his homeland now. He had gathered the rest and made them a nation under one man and the sky father. Perhaps that was why he yearned to answer the challenge from the desert tribes. A man without enemies grew quickly soft and fat. A nation would fare badly without someone peering into their camps. He smiled at the thought. There was no shortage of enemies in the world, and he thanked the spirits that they teemed in their millions. He could not imagine a better way of spending a life, and he had good years ahead.

Arslan spoke again and the lightness had gone from his voice.

"I have thought for many months, lord, that it is time I gave up my position as general. I am getting too old to stand a campaign in winter and perhaps too cautious. The men need someone younger who can risk it all on a single throw of the bones."

"You have years in you yet," Kachiun replied as seriously.

Arslan shook his head, looking to see how Genghis reacted to his words. "It is time. I will wait for my son Jelme to return, but I do not wish to leave my homeland again. My oath is to you, Genghis, and I will not see it broken. If you say ride, I will ride until I fall." He spoke of death. No warrior could fall from a saddle while he still lived. Arslan paused to see the khan understood his loyalty before going on.

"No man can ride forever. My hips and shoulders ache and my hands are stiff at the first touch of cold. Perhaps it is all the years of beating metal, I do not know."

Genghis pursed his mouth, edging his mount closer so that he could grip his general's shoulder.

"You have been with me from the first days," he said softly. "No one has served with more honor. If you want to see your final years out in peace, I will release you from your oath."

Arslan bowed his head, visibly relieved. "Thank you, my lord khan." When he looked up, his face was flushed with emotion. "I knew you when you were alone and hunted. I saw greatness in you then when I pledged my life. I have known this day would come and prepared my second for command of my *tuman*. It is your decision, but I recommend Zurgadai to replace me."

"No one could replace you," Genghis said immediately. "But I will honor your choice and your wisdom this last time. I know this Zurgadai, the one they call 'Jebe,' the Arrow."

Arslan grimaced slightly. "As you say. You met him first when we rode against the Besud clan years ago. He killed your horse."

Genghis let out a surprised exclamation. "I thought I knew the name! By the spirits, he could shoot a bow. Was it three hundred paces? I remember I almost broke my head open."

"He has mellowed a little, lord, but not too much. He has been loyal to you ever since you spared him that day."

Genghis nodded. "Then pass your gold paitze to him and invite him to my council tent. We will make the feast a celebration of your life. The storytellers will sing your praises to the sky father, and all the young warriors will know a great man is gone from the ranks." He thought for a moment as Arslan colored in pride.

"You will have a thousand horses from my own herd and a dozen women as servants for your wife. I will send three young men to guard you in your old age. You will not be lonely in your retirement, General. You will have sheep and goats enough to make you fat for a hundred years."

Arslan dismounted and touched his head to Genghis's foot in the stirrup.

"You honor me, lord, but I need very little. With your permission, I will take my wife and just a small herd of breeding goats and horses. Together, we will find a quiet place by a stream and there remain. There are no thieves in the hills any longer, and if by chance there are, my bow and sword still speak for me." He smiled at the man he had seen grow from a boy to a conqueror of nations. "Perhaps I will build a small forge and make one last sword to be buried with me. I hear the sounds of the hammer in my mind even now and I am at peace."

Genghis found tears in his eyes as he viewed the man who had been like a second father to him. He too dismounted and embraced Arslan briefly, causing the shouting children around them to fall silent and staring.

"It is a good dream, old man, but first we wait on your son Jelme and feast a good life."

The lands around the Orkhon River were a deeper green than could be found anywhere else. The river itself was wide and clear. It had to be to support two hundred thousand men and women, with twice that number of horses when Khasar and Tsubodai arrived within a day of each other. Under the khan's ruling hand, the nation had grown and there were always children squalling somewhere. Since his return from the Chin capital, Genghis had made a near permanent camp at the river, rejecting the plain of Avraga. It was true that Avraga would always be sacred as the place he had forged a nation, but it was a dry, flat land. In comparison, a nearby waterfall beat the waters of the Orkhon into white spray, and the horses and sheep could drink their fill. Genghis had swum many times in its deep pools, regaining his strength.

Khasar had come in first and embraced his brothers: Genghis, Kachiun, even Temuge, who was no warrior, but ran the camps and settled disputes between families. Khasar brought Ogedai with him. The boy was barely thirteen years old, but stood muscular and long-limbed, with the promise of his father's height. In the sharp planes of Ogedai's face, the brothers could see an echo of the boy who had once kept them alive when they were banished and alone, just a few scraps of food away from starvation and death. Khasar gripped the back of Ogedai's neck as he sent him forward to see his father, showing his pride.

"He is a good hand with a bow and sword, brother," Khasar said, tilting a skin of black airag and directing a line of the spirit down his throat.

Genghis heard the delighted cry of his wife Borte from the family ger and knew his son would be surrounded by women in just a few moments.

"You have grown, Ogedai," he said awkwardly. "I will want to hear all about your travels tonight." He watched as Ogedai bowed formally, the boy's face hiding any emotion. Three years was a long time to be away, but Genghis was pleased with the stripling warrior who had returned to him. Ogedai had the same yellow eyes and Genghis approved his stillness and calm. He did not test it by embracing him, not with so many warriors watching who would perhaps follow Ogedai in a charge one day.

"Are you old enough to drink, boy?" Genghis asked, hefting a skin in his hands. When his son nodded, he tossed it over and Ogedai took it cleanly, overwhelmed with the sights and sounds of his people all around. As his mother came forward and embraced him, he remained stiff, trying to show his father that he was not a little boy to melt into her arms. Borte hardly seemed to notice and held his face in both hands, weeping at his safe return.

"Let him stand, Borte," Genghis muttered at her shoulder. "He is old enough to fight and ride with me." His wife ignored him and Genghis sighed to himself, his mood mellow.

Genghis felt his chest tighten as he saw Tsubodai trotting through the crowded plain toward him, Jochi at his side. Both men dismounted and Genghis saw Jochi walked with the springy step of a natural warrior. He had grown an inch taller than the khan, though his dark eyes still reminded Genghis that some other man may have fathered him. He had not known how he would react to Jochi, but on instinct, Genghis spoke directly to Tsubodai, ignoring him.

"Have you carried them all before you, General?" he said.

Tsubodai responded with a chuckle. "I have seen many strange things, my lord khan. I would have gone further if you had not called us back. Is it war then?"

A shadow crossed Genghis's face, but he shook his head.

"Later, Tsubodai, later. I'll have dogs for you to whip, but Arslan is stepping down as my general, and when Jelme comes in, we will feast his life."

Tsubodai showed sadness as he heard the news. "I owe him a great deal, lord. My poet is a fine man. May I offer his service?"

Genghis grinned. "For the swordsmith general, I have a dozen poets and storytellers fighting like cats for the honor, but your man may as well join them."

Genghis could feel Jochi's mother watching him as he spoke. Borte would be looking for some public acceptance of her firstborn son before she too welcomed him home. As silence fell, Genghis turned at last to Jochi. It was hard not to bristle under that flat, black stare. It had been a long time in the camps since any man dared to meet the eyes of the khan in such a way, and Genghis felt his heart thump faster, as if he faced an enemy.

"I am pleased to see you well and strong, Father," Jochi said, his voice deeper than Genghis had expected. "When I left, you were still weak from the assassin's poison."

Genghis saw Tsubodai's hand twitch, as if he wanted to raise it to Jochi in warning. The general had sharper wits than Jochi, it seemed. The young warrior stood proudly before him as if he were not a rape-born whelp, barely welcome in the gers of his family.

Genghis struggled with his temper, very aware of the silent presence of his wife.

"It seems I am a difficult man to kill," he said softly. "You are welcome in my camp, Jochi."

His son remained still, though for Genghis to grant him guest rights like any common warrior was a subtle barb. He had not said the words to Tsubodai or Khasar; they were not needed between friends.

"You honor me, my lord khan," Jochi said, bowing his head so that his father could not see his furious eyes. Genghis nodded, weighing the young man as Jochi took his mother's hands gently in his own and bowed, his face pale and strained.

Borte's eyes filled with tears of joy, but there was more restraint between mother and son than there had been with Ogedai. In such an atmosphere, she could not embrace the tall young warrior. Before Genghis could speak again, Jochi turned to his younger brother, and all the stiffness left him in a rush.

"I see you, little man," Jochi said. Ogedai grinned and came forward to punch Jochi on the shoulder, prompting a brief wrestling match that ended with his head jammed into Jochi's armpit. Genghis watched irritably, wanting to say something else that would prick Jochi's easy manner. Instead, Jochi walked Ogedai away over his muffled protests at having his head rubbed. The khan had not actually dismissed his son, and Genghis opened his mouth to have him brought back.

"Your son has learned well, lord," Tsubodai said before he could speak. "He has commanded a thousand in battles against the warriors of Russia, and the men respect him."

Genghis scowled, knowing the moment had somehow escaped him.

"You have not raised him too fast?" he said.

A weaker man might have agreed under those yellow eyes, but Tsubodai shook his head immediately, loyal to the young man he had fostered for three years. "He learned quickly what it means to command, lord, to have every man look to you alone for strength. My poet has many verses about Jochi and the men speak well of the khan's son. He can lead. I have no greater praise."

Genghis glanced over to where Jochi was laughing with Ogedai. Together, they looked younger, more like the boys who had grown in his ger. He nodded grudgingly, but when he spoke again, Tsubodai's hopes fell.

"Bad blood may come to the surface at any time, General. In a charge, or a battle, he could turn. Be careful not to risk your life on that one."

Tsubodai could not contradict the khan without giving insult, though he burned to speak against the unfairness. In the end, his struggle remained internal and he bowed his head.

"Jelme and Chagatai are only three days away," Genghis said, his expression lightening. "You will see a son of mine then, Tsubodai, and know why I am proud of him. We will light the land with lamps and eat and drink enough so that men will talk of it for years."

"As you say, lord," Tsubodai replied, hiding his distress. Over three years, he had seen Jochi grow into a fine man, one capable of leading armies. Tsubodai had seen no weaknesses in him and he knew he was a good judge of men. As he followed the khan's gaze to his oldest son, Tsubodai grieved for the hurt Jochi must feel. No man should ever be rejected by his father. If Jochi had every other general at his feet and the scorn of Genghis, he would feel only the scorn. As Genghis turned away with Khasar and Kachiun, Tsubodai shook his head slightly before he reasserted the cold face and joined the other men in preparing for the feast. Jelme and Chagatai were coming and Tsubodai did not look forward to seeing Genghis praise his second son over the first.

CHAPTER FOUR

SOMETHING WRENCHED JELME from a deep sleep. In complete darkness, he sat up, listening intently. The smoke hole in his ger was covered and his eyes could not adjust to the lack of light. At his side, a Chin woman stirred and he reached out to touch her face.

"Be quiet," he whispered. He knew the sounds of the camp: the whickering of ponies, the laughter or weeping in the night that eased him into sleep. He knew the sounds of his people and the slightest change in them. Like a wild dog, some part of him never fully slept. He was too much an old hand to dismiss the prickling sense of danger as a bad dream. In silence, he threw back his furs and stood bare-chested, wearing just an old pair of leggings.

It was low and distant, but the sound of a scout's horn was unmistakable. As the note died away, Jelme grabbed for a sword hanging from the central pole. He pulled on soft boots, threw a heavy coat over his shoulders, and ducked out into the night.

The camp was already waking around him, warriors mounting with murmurs and clicks to their animals. They were barely a day's ride from Genghis, and Jelme had no idea who could be mad enough to risk the legs of precious horses in the dark. One marmot hole in the wrong place and a foreleg could snap. Jelme could not imagine an enemy on the empty plains, not one who would dare to attack him. Still, he would make ready. He would not be surprised in his own camp.

Chagatai came running across the black grass, his stumbling gait showing the quantity of airag he had put away that evening. The young man winced as lamps were lit around Jelme's ger, but the general had no sympathy. A warrior should always be ready to ride, and he ignored the sallow features of Genghis's son.

"Take a hundred men, Chagatai," he snapped, his strain showing. "Scout around for an enemy, anything. Someone is out tonight."

The young prince moved away quickly, already whistling for his sub-officers. Jelme drew men in, organizing them without hesitation. The scouts had given him time and he did not waste it. Ranks coalesced in the blackness and the night was suddenly noisy as every man, woman, and child prepared weapons or stowed supplies and bound up carts. Heavily armed guards ran in pairs through the camp, looking for assassins or thieves.

Jelme sat at the center of the storm, sensing the swirl of movement all around him. There were no cries of alarm, not yet, though he heard the distant scout's horn sound once more. In the flickering, hissing light of mutton fat lamps, his servants brought his favorite gelding and he took the full quiver handed up to him.

By the time Jelme trotted out into the darkness, his army was alert and ready. The first five thousand warriors rode with him, a force of blooded men, well practiced in battle. No one liked to fight in the dark, and if they had to charge, men and horses would be killed. Jelme clenched his jaw against the cold, feeling it for the first time since he had woken.

Genghis galloped in the darkness, blind drunk and so light he felt the stirrups served a purpose in preventing him from floating away. As tradition demanded, he had begun each skin of airag by flicking a few drops for the spirits that guarded his people. He had spat more over the feast fires, so that the flash sent him reeling in sweet smoke. Despite all that, a fair amount had reached his throat and he had lost count of the skins he had thrown down.

The feast had begun two days before. Genghis had welcomed his returning sons and generals formally, honoring them all before the people. Even Jochi's constant glower had softened as great platters of meat from the hunt were served. Khasar and Ogedai too had fallen on the best cuts with a cry of pleasure. They had eaten many strange things in the years away, but no one in Koryo or Chin lands could have brought a platter of green earth mutton to the groaning tables. That meat had been buried the previous winter and brought out whole for the return of the generals. Khasar's eyes had filled with tears, though he claimed it was the bitterness of the rotted meat rather than nostalgia for the rare delicacy. No one believed him, but it did not matter.

The feast had built to a climax of noise and debauchery. The strongest warriors prowled through the gers, looking for women. Those of the people were safe, but Chin slaves or captured Russian women were fair game. Their cries were loud in the night, almost drowned by the drums and horns around the fires.

Poems had begun that would take a full day to finish. Some were sung in the ancient style of two tones from the same throat. Others were spoken aloud, competing in the chaos for any who would listen. The fires around Genghis grew more crowded as the first night wore into dawn.

Khasar had not slept even then, Genghis thought, looking for his brother's shadow in the dark. As the second day came to an end, Genghis had seen how the poets kept back their ballads for Arslan, waiting on the general's son. It had been then that Genghis refilled Arslan's cup with his own hand.

"Chagatai and Jelme are just a short ride from here, Arslan," he had said over the twang and screech of wind and string. "Will you come with me to meet our sons?"

Arslan had smiled drunkenly, nodding.

"I will take the poets to them to hear the tales of you, old man." Genghis told him, slurring his words. It was a grand idea, and with a warm feeling, he summoned his council of generals to him. Tsubodai and Jochi called for horses as Khasar and Ogedai came staggering up. Ogedai had looked a little green and Genghis had ignored the sour smell of vomit around his son.

It was Kachiun who had brought the khan's gray mare, a fine animal.

"This is madness, brother!" Kachiun called to him cheerfully. "Who rides fast at night? Someone will go down."

Genghis gestured at the darkness and then his companions. "We are not afraid!" he had declared, the drunken men around him cheering the sentiment. "I have my family and my generals. I have the swordsmith Arslan and Tsubodai the Valiant. Let the ground fear *us* if we fall. We will crack it open with our hard heads! Are you ready?"

"I will match you, brother," Kachiun had replied, catching the wild mood. Both men trotted to the head of their small column. It grew by the moment as others joined them. The shaman Kokchu was there, one of the few who seemed sober. Genghis had looked for his last brother, Temuge, and saw him on foot, shaking his round head in disapproval. It did not matter, Genghis thought. The useless bastard never could ride.

He had looked around him, at his family, checking to see they all had full skins of airag and rice wine. It would not do to run short. A dozen poets had joined them, their faces bright with excitement. One had already begun declaiming lines and Genghis was tempted to kick him off his pony and leave him behind.

There was a little starlight and he could see his sons, brothers, and generals. He chuckled for an instant at the idea of some poor thief stepping out in front of this group of cutthroats.

"I will give a white mare to any man who beats me into the camp of Jelme and my son Chagatai." He had paused a heartbeat to let this sink in and catch the wild grins of the men.

"Ride hard, if you have the heart!" He had roared then, thumping in his heels and jerking his mare into a gallop through the camp. The others were almost as quick, yelling as they raced in pursuit. Perhaps two thousand had followed the khan into the deep darkness, all those who had been within reach of their horses as the khan leapt up. Not one faltered, though the ground was hard and to fall was to throw a life and not know if it would come down.

Riding at full speed over rushing black ground helped to clear Genghis's head a little, though an ache had come to throb behind his left eye. There was a river somewhere near, he recalled. The thought of dipping his head into the freezing water was very tempting.

His light mood tore into shreds as he sensed a flanking movement in the darkness. For a single heartbeat, he wondered if he had risked his life, without banners, drums, or anything else that marked him out as khan. Then he kicked his mount forward and yelled madly. It had to be Jelme's men forming horns on either side of him. He rode like a maniac toward the center of the line, where he knew he would find his general.

Khasar and Kachiun were close behind and then Genghis saw

Jochi come past, riding flat on the saddle and yipping to his mount as he went, urging the animal on.

Together the spear point of the ragged column plunged toward Jelme's lines, taking their lead from the khan. Two fell as their horses struck unseen obstacles. More crashed into the sprawling men and ponies in the darkness, unable to stop. Another three broke legs and were thrown. Some of the men bounced to their feet laughing and unhurt, while others would not rise again. Genghis knew none of it, so intent was he on the menace of Jelme's men and catching his own errant son.

Jochi did not call out a warning to Jelme's lines, so Genghis could not. If his son chose to ride right down the throats of nervous men with drawn bows, Genghis could only swallow the sudden chill tugging at his drunkenness. He could only ride.

Jelme squinted into the blackness, his men ready. The warriors who rode like madmen in the dark were almost upon him. He had extended the wings around their column, so that they rode into a deepening cup. Though he could hardly see more than a black mass in the starlight, he could fill the air with shafts in a heartbeat.

He hesitated. It had to be Genghis, riding at the front. Who else could be so reckless? Yet no warning had been called. Jelme knew he would not let an enemy crash straight into his best men. He would send a storm of arrows first.

He squinted, turning his head left and right to make the moving shadows clear. Could it be the khan? He could have sworn he heard someone singing in the column that was charging right at him. In the dark, he alone stood in the light of a torch, to be seen. He raised his arm, and all along the lines, thousands of bows bent as one.

"On my order!" Jelme bellowed, as loud as he could. He could feel sweat chilling in the wind on his face, but he was not afraid. There was no one to ask, no one to tell him what to do. It was his decision alone. Jelme took one last look at the black riders coming and he smiled tightly, shaking his head like a nervous twitch. He could not *know*.

"Stand down!" he roared suddenly. "Let them come in! Wide formation!"

His officers repeated the orders down the line to those that could not hear him. Jelme could only wait to see whether the riders would stop, or hit his lines and begin the killing. He watched the blur of shadows come to a hundred paces, deep in the cup made by the wings. Fifty paces and still they followed the man who led them, into the mouth of their destruction.

Jelme saw some of them slow and men in the wings began calling out as they heard the voices of friends and family. Jelme relaxed, thanking the sky father that his instinct had been correct. He turned back to the front and his jaw dropped open as the tight-knit front rank punched into his own men with a crash loud enough to hurt the ears. Horses and warriors went down and suddenly every hand held a sword or a drawn bow once again.

"Torches! Bring torches there!" Jelme snapped. Slaves ran up through the ranks to light the scene of groaning men and kicking, sprawling horses.

Jelme recognized Genghis in the heart of it and he paled slightly, wondering if the khan would demand his head. Should he have fallen back or opened a path for them through the host? He let out a slow breath as Genghis opened his eyes and swore, sitting up with an effort. Jelme gestured for two warriors to help the khan to his feet, though he batted away their arms.

"Where are you, General?" Genghis called, shaking his head. Jelme stood forward, swallowing nervously as he saw Genghis touch his jaw and come away with a smear of blood.

"I am here, my lord khan," he said, standing painfully straight. He dared not look at the other men lying around and groaning, though he recognized Khasar's angry voice as he tried to get someone unconscious off him. Genghis turned to Jelme and his eyes focused at last.

"You will note, General, that no other man reached your lines before me?"

Jelme blinked. "I believe so, my lord khan," he said.

Genghis nodded blearily to those behind him, satisfied. "The night is barely begun and already I have a sore head." Genghis grinned and Jelme saw he had broken a tooth on the right side of his face in the impact. He watched as Genghis spat blood onto the grass, glaring at a nearby warrior who shrank back visibly.

"Light fires, Jelme. Your father is somewhere around, though he was not as quick as me, not even close. If Arslan is still alive, we will toast his life in rice wine and airag and whatever food you have."

"You are welcome in my camp, my lord khan," Jelme said formally. As he caught the riotous mood of the men who had ridden in, he began to grin. Even his father was chuckling in disbelief as he pulled himself upright and leaned on a stoic young warrior for support.

"You didn't stop, then?" Jelme murmured wryly to his father.

Arslan shrugged and shook his head, his eyes shining at the memory. "Who could stop? He pulls us all in."

Jelme's ten thousand continued the feast in the wilderness. Even the youngest children were woken and brought to see the Great Khan as he strode through the camp. Genghis made a point of laying his hand on the heads of young ones, but he was distracted and impatient. He had heard horns sound the recall to the flanking riders and knew Chagatai was coming in. He could not fault Jelme for his preparations, but he wanted to see his son.

Jelme's servants brought wine and cold food to the newcomers as huge fires of fine Koryon lumber were built and lit, casting pools of gold and darkness. The damp grass was covered in heavy sheets of felt and linen. When he took his place of honor, Genghis sat cross-legged with Arslan on his right hand. Kachiun, Khasar, and Tsubodai joined him in front of the roaring flames, passing a skin of rice wine from one to the other. As the places in the circle filled, Jochi secured a place on Khasar's right, so that Ogedai was further down the line. The senior men did not seem to notice the way the circle filled, though Jochi thought Kachiun saw everything. The shaman Kokchu gave thanks to the sky father for the conquests Jelme had made and the riches he had brought back. Jochi watched the shaman spin and shriek, throwing drops of airag to the winds and spirits. Jochi felt one droplet touch his face and trickle down his chin.

As Kokchu sank back to his place, musicians cracked out rhythms across the camp, as if released. The thump of sticks blurred and wailing notes mingled and turned around each other, calling back and forth across the flames. Men and women pounded out songs and poems in the firelight, dancing until sweat spattered off them. Those who had come in with Jelme were pleased to honor the Great Khan.

The fire's heat was strong on Jochi's face, licking out from a heart of orange embers and strange paths to the core. As he sat, Jochi stared at his father's generals and met Kachiun's eyes for an instant before sliding away. Even in that brief contact, there had been some communication. Jochi did not look back, knowing that Kachiun would be watching him with sharp interest. The eyes showed the soul and they were always hardest to mask.

When Chagatai rode in, it was to the yelling accompaniment of his jagun of warriors. Jelme was pleased to see the waxy look to Chagatai's skin had vanished with a bit of fast riding. Genghis's second son looked vital and strong as he jumped down over the horse's shoulder.

Genghis rose to greet him and the warriors shouted in appreciation as the father took his son's arm and pounded him on the back.

"You have grown tall, boy," Genghis said. His eyes were glassy from drink and his face was mottled and puffy. Chagatai bowed deeply to his father, the model of a perfect son.

Chagatai maintained a cool manner as he gripped hands and clapped shoulders with his father's men. To Jochi's slow-burning irritation, his brother walked well, his back straight and white teeth flashing as he laughed and smiled. At fifteen, his skin was barely scarred beyond the wrists and forearms and unmarked by disease. Genghis looked upon him with visible pride. When Jochi saw Chagatai welcomed to a seat close to Genghis, he was glad that the great fire hid his flush of anger. Chagatai had glanced at Jochi for an instant of cold recognition. He had not bothered to find words for his older brother, even after three years. Jochi's face remained calm, but it was astonishing how anger sprang in him from just that glance. For a few heartbeats, he wanted nothing more than to stride through the drunken fools and strike Chagatai to the ground. He could feel his own strength swell in his shoulders as he imagined the blow. Yet he had learned patience with Tsubodai. As Genghis filled Chagatai's cup, Jochi sat and dreamed of murder, smiling with all the rest.

CHAPTER FIVE

AS DAWN CAME, Tsubodai's poet was in the middle of telling the tale of the Badger's Mouth, where Arslan had fought the largest army ever seen by any of the people. With Genghis and the generals watching, the poet was more honest than usual as he told Arslan's exploits. They had all done well in that mountain pass before Yenking. Each man recalled those bloody days with pride and awe mingling with the wine in their blood. No one else would ever understand what it had meant to stand together there against the Chin empire—and see it humbled. The Badger's Mouth had been the womb that shoved them out into a new world, stronger and more dangerous. They had gone east and Yenking had burned.

The rising sun brought sight of thousands of riders streaming across the land from the camp by the Orkhon River, many with women and children on the saddles. Genghis was the khan and could ride where he wished, but they all wanted to hear the stories of Arslan. As the morning sun rose in the sky, poems and tales were declaimed from a hundred throats, over and over until the poets and shamans were hoarse.

Even Genghis had not realized so many would want to hear of the early days, but his people sat rapt for the performances, including those who were drinking heavily and stuffing their faces with greasy mutton and goat meat. He heard again how Arslan had rescued him from a pit, and he blinked in painful memory at names he had not recalled for years. Arslan had been the first man to take oath to him, to promise horses, gers, salt, and blood. That, when Genghis had nothing but his mother and sister, a few wild brothers, and starvation as his companions. It had been an immense act of trust, and Genghis found himself reminded and moved once more by the changes Arslan had wrought and witnessed. That was the purpose of the truth-telling of a man's life, that all those who heard would remember what he had meant to them and what he had accomplished as he flung the years.

The recitals broke off for the storytellers to rest their throats in preparation for the evening performances. By then it was clear that the entire Mongol nation would drift into that place.

It was not where Genghis had intended to honor his first general. The river was too far away, the grazing was sparse, and the ground itself was rocky and dry. Yet it was that lack of permanence that made him grunt in satisfaction as he peed into the earth. His people should not become used to comfort, he told himself blearily. Their hard lives kept them stronger than those who lived in cities.

As Genghis tucked himself away, his thoughts were interrupted by shouts and cheers nearby. Warriors seemed to be clustering around one spot like a swarm of bees. As Genghis blinked, he saw Chagatai climb a cart to address them. Genghis frowned as another sound stilled the crowd, a yowling, coughing roar that made the hairs on his neck bristle. Genghis dropped his hand to his sword hilt as he strode through his people, letting them fall back before him rather than touch the khan and lose a hand or a head.

His generals had gathered around an iron cage on the cart, but Genghis did not look at them, nor at Chagatai, who stood like a proud owner. The animal behind the bars was larger than any great cat he had ever seen. Genghis could only shake his head in amazement, closing one eye against the ache from his broken tooth and a throbbing headache. To numb the pain, he gestured for more airag and scored his throat with a line of it. Even then, his eyes did not leave the beast that prowled back and forth, showing its curved white teeth in a display of anger. He had heard of the orange-and-black-striped tiger, but to see its jaws and hear the thump of its tail as it padded back and forth in the cage set his own heart beating quickly. There was a challenge in its yellow eyes that raked the awed crowd.

"Is it not a gift for a khan?" Chagatai said. Genghis merely glanced at him, but Chagatai lost some of his cockiness in that warning. The crowd around them had fallen silent as they waited for the khan's reaction. Jelme was visibly uncomfortable and Genghis nodded to him in appreciation.

"I have never seen such an animal, General. How did you capture him?"

"The tiger is a gift to you, lord, from the king of Koryo. It was raised from a cub, but they cannot be tamed. I am told it will run down even a man on a horse and kill both the mount and the rider."

Genghis stood very close to the bars, staring into the tiger's eyes. As they met his, the animal moved without warning, its weight rocking the cage as it hit the bars. Genghis was too drunk to dodge and felt a tearing impact on his arm as a paw lunged at him. He looked in dim surprise at the blood on his torn sleeve. A single claw had caught him and gashed his flesh deeply.

"So fast...," he said in wonder. "I have seen slower snakes. And at such a size! I can believe the tale of it killing a man and his horse. Those jaws could break a skull." He swayed slightly as he spoke, but no one there mentioned the wound in case it shamed the khan.

"In Koryo, there are warriors who hunt the tigers," Chagatai said more humbly, "though they work in groups and use bows, spears, and nets." Chagatai's gaze fell on Jochi as he spoke, and his expression became thoughtful. His older brother was as fascinated by the beast as Genghis himself and stood too close to the bars.

"Be careful, Jochi," Chagatai warned him loudly. "He will strike you too."

Jochi glared. He wanted to contradict him, but he could not boast of his speed while his father stood and bled.

"Have you hunted one of these tigers, in Koryon land?" Jochi asked.

Chagatai shrugged. "They are not common around the king's palaces." Under Jochi's flat stare, he could not help going on. "I would have taken part, if one had been found."

"Perhaps," Jochi said, frowning. "Though I doubt Jelme would have risked the life of a young boy against such a monster."

Chagatai's whole face flushed as some of the men chuckled. Moments before, he had been the master of the crowd. Somehow, his father and Jochi had stolen his moment from him, so that he had to defend his pride. At fifteen years old, he had only spite, and he lashed out without a thought at the only one he dared challenge.

"You think you could face a tiger, Jochi? I would wager a fortune to see that."

Jelme opened his mouth, but Jochi's anger leapt and he spoke rashly.

"Name your terms, brother," he said. "I will consider teaching your cat a little respect. He has shed my father's blood, after all."

"This is drunken foolishness," Jelme snapped.

"No, let him try," Chagatai replied as fast. "I will wager a hundred cartloads of my share of the Koryon tribute. Ivory, metal, gold, and lumber." He waved a hand as if it mattered nothing. "If you kill the tiger, it will be yours."

"And you will kneel to me, in front of all the tribes," Jochi said. Anger consumed him, making him reckless. His eyes glittered as he stared up at Chagatai, but the younger man still sneered.

"For that, you will have to do more than kill a tiger, brother. For that you will have to be khan. Perhaps not even that will be enough."

Jochi's hand dropped to his sword hilt and he would have drawn if Jelme had not laid a hand on his wrist.

"Will you fight like children in front of the camp? On the night my father is honored? The tiger is a king's gift to the khan. No one else may decide what is to be done with him." His eyes were furious and Chagatai dipped his gaze, instantly meek. During his training, he had endured harsh punishments and scathing lectures from the general. The habit of obedience ran deep.

Genghis spoke at last, having watched the entire exchange.

"I accept the gift," he said. His yellow eyes seemed the same color as those of the big cat yowling at their backs. Jochi and Chagatai bowed their heads low rather than have the khan's temper erupt. When he was drunk, Genghis was likely to knock a man down for staring.

"We could pack a circle with armed warriors," Genghis said thoughtfully, "pointing swords and lances to the center. One man could face the beast then, if he wanted."

"These animals are more dangerous than anything else I have seen," Jelme said, his voice strained. "With women and children all around..." He was caught between the need to obey his khan and the madness of what Genghis seemed to be considering.

"Move the women and children back, General," Genghis replied with a shrug.

Jelme's training was too ingrained to argue and he bowed his head to the inevitable. Chagatai did not dare look at him.

"Very well, lord. I could have my men tie heavy planks together all the way around. We could use the catapults to form the structure."

Genghis nodded, not caring how the problems were solved. He turned to Jochi as the young man stood stunned at where his bickering and pride had led. Even Chagatai seemed awed, but Genghis was making all the decisions and they could only look on.

"Kill this beast and perhaps your brother will bend a knee to you," Genghis said softly. "The tribes will be watching, boy. Will they see a khan in you?"

"Or a corpse, or both," Jochi said without hesitation. He could not back down, not with his father and Chagatai waiting for it. He looked up at the tiger in its cage and knew it would kill him, but somehow he could not care. He had ridden with death before, in Tsubodai's charges. At seventeen, he could gamble with his life and think nothing of it. He took a deep breath and shrugged.

"I am ready," Jochi said.

"Then form the circle, and place the cage within it," Genghis said.

As Jelme began to send his men for wood and ropes, Jochi beckoned to Chagatai. Still stunned, the younger brother leapt lightly down, rocking the cart and bringing a snarl from the tiger that scraped along the nerves.

"I will need a good sword if I am to face that animal," Jochi said. "Yours."

Chagatai narrowed his eyes, fighting to hide his triumph. Jochi could not survive against a tiger. He knew the Koryons would not hunt one without at least eight men, and those well trained. He was staring into the eyes of a dead man, and he could not believe his luck. On a sudden impulse, he unstrapped the sword Genghis had given him three years before. He felt the loss as its weight left him, but still his heart was full.

"I will have it back when that beast has torn your head off," he murmured. No one else could hear.

"Perhaps," Jochi said. He could not resist a glance at the animal in the cage.

Chagatai saw the look and chuckled aloud. "It is only fitting, Jochi. I could never have accepted a rape-born bastard as khan." He walked away, leaving Jochi staring at his back in rage.

As the sun set, the circle took shape on the plains grass. Under Jelme's watchful eye, it was a solid construction of oak and beech brought from Koryo, bound with heavy ropes and buttressed at all points by catapult platforms. Forty paces across, there was no entrance and no escape from the ring. Jochi would have to climb over the barricades and open the cage himself.

As Jelme ordered torches lit all round the circle, the entire nation pressed as close as they could. At first it looked as if only those who could climb the walls would have a view, but Genghis wanted the people to see, so Jelme had used carts as platforms in an outer ring, raising men on pyramids of pine ladders, nailed roughly together. They swarmed over the towers like ants and more than one drunken fool fell onto the heads of those below, packed so tightly that the ground was hidden from sight.

Genghis and his generals had the best places on the ring, and the khan had led them in drinking themselves almost blind as the third day wore on. Arslan had been toasted and honored, but by then, the whole camp knew a khan's son would fight a foreign beast and they were excited at the closeness of death. Temuge had come with the last of the carts from the camp by the Orkhon River. He took most of the bets from the warriors, though only on the length of the fight to come. No one gambled on Jochi to win against the striped horror that lashed its tail and padded back and forth, staring out at them.

As night fell, the only light on the plains was that circle, a golden eye surrounded by the heaving mass of the Mongol nation. Without being asked, the drummer boys had begun to beat the rhythms of war. Jochi had retired to Jelme's own ger to rest that afternoon, and they waited on him, eyes turning constantly to catch the first glimpse of the khan's son coming out.

Jelme stood and looked down on the young man seated on a low bed, his father's sword across his knees. Jochi wore the heavy armor Tsubodai had given him, layered in finger-width scales of iron over thick cloth, from his neck to his knees. The smell of sour sweat was strong in the ger.

"They're calling for you," Jelme said.

"I hear," Jochi replied, his mouth tightening.

"I can't say you don't have to go. You do." Jelme began to reach out with his hand, intending to place it on the younger man's shoulder. Instead, he let it fall and sighed.

"I can say that this is a stupid thing to be doing. If I'd known how it would turn out, I'd have turned the cat loose in the Koryon forests."

"It's done," Jochi murmured. He looked up at his father's general with a bitter twist to his mouth. "I'll just have to kill that great cat now, won't I?"

Jelme smiled tightly. Outside, the noise of the crowd had grown in volume, and now he could hear Jochi's name being chanted. It would be a glorious moment, but Jelme knew the boy could not survive it. As the circle was being constructed and the cage lifted down from the cart, he had studied the animal and seen the smooth power of its muscles. Faster than a man and four times as heavy, it would be impossible to stop. He was silent with foreboding as Jochi came to his feet and flexed his shoulders. The khan's first son had inherited his father's blinding speed, but it would not be enough. The general saw sweat dripping down Jochi's face in a fat bead. Genghis had not allowed him room to interpret his orders, but he still struggled against ingrained obedience. Jelme had brought the tiger to the khan. He could not simply send a boy to his death. When he spoke at last, his voice was barely a murmur.

"I will be on the walls with a good bow. If you fall, try to hang on and I'll kill it." He saw a flicker of hope in the young man's eyes at that. Jelme recalled the only hunt he had seen in Koryo, when a tiger had taken a shaft in the heart and still disemboweled an experienced net man.

"You cannot show fear," Jelme said softly. "No matter what happens. If you are to die tonight, die well. For your father's honor."

In response, Jochi turned a furious gaze on the general.

"If he depends on me for his honor, he is weaker than I realized," Jochi snapped.

"Nevertheless, all men die," Jelme went on, ignoring the outburst. "It could be tonight, next year, or in forty years, when you are toothless and weak. All you can do is choose how you stand when it comes."

For an instant, Jochi's face cracked into a smile. "You are not building my confidence, General. I would value those forty years."

Jelme shrugged, touched at the way Jochi showed courage. "Then I should say this: kill it and your brother will kneel to you in front of the tribes. Your name will be known, and when you wear its skin, all men will look on you with awe. Is that better?"

"Yes, it is," Jochi replied. "If I am killed, be ready with your bow. I do not want to be eaten." With a deep breath, he showed his teeth for an instant, then ducked under the low doorway and out into the night. His people roared to see him, the sound filling the plains and drowning the growls of the waiting tiger.

*   *   *

The crowd parted to let him through and Jochi did not see their staring, cheering faces as he approached the walls of the ring. The light
from torches fluttered and spat as he climbed lithely to the top, then
leapt to the grass below. The tiger watched him with a terrifying focus,
and he did not want to open the cage. Jochi looked up at the faces of
his people. His mother was the only woman he could see, and he could
barely meet her eyes in case it unmanned him. As his gaze drifted over
her, he saw Borte's hands twitch on the wood, as if she wanted to reach
out to her firstborn son.

His father's face was set and unreadable, but his uncle Kachiun
nodded to him as their eyes met. Tsubodai wore the cold face and, in
doing so, hid the pain Jochi knew he would be feeling. The general
could do nothing to thwart the khan's will, but Jochi knew he at
least would not relish the fight. On instinct, Jochi bowed his head to
the general, and Tsubodai returned the gesture. The tiger roared and
opened his great mouth to gnaw at a bar in frustration, angered by the
ring of baying men. The animal was a young male, Jochi saw, unscarred
and inexperienced. He felt his hands shake and the familiar dry mouth
before battle. His bladder made itself felt and he took a strong grip on
the wolf's-head sword of his father. It was a fine blade and he had
wanted it for a long time. He had not known his grandfather Yesugei
and only hoped the old man's spirit would give him strength. He stood
tall and another deep breath brought calm.

Chagatai watched him with eyes that shone in the torchlight. Jochi
held his gaze for a time, showing the boy his contempt before he
turned to the cage. The noise of the warriors swelled as he approached
the bars and raised his hand to the iron pin that held the door shut. The
tiger seemed to sense his intention and stood waiting. Their eyes met
and Jochi murmured a greeting to the big cat.

"You are strong and fast," he said under his breath, "and so am I.
If I kill you, I will carry your skin in pride to the end of my days." He
yanked on the pin and threw back the cage door, moving quickly away.
The crowd fell silent, every warrior staring at the striped shape that
came sliding out like oil.

Jochi backed for six long strides and stood with his sword held forward and down, ready to lunge. His heart hammered in his chest and
he felt heavy-footed and clumsy in comparison with this beast he had
come to kill.

At first the tiger ignored him. It padded around the walls, looking for a way out. Its tail twitched in irritation and discomfort as the crowd resumed their roaring. Jochi looked on as the animal stretched to its full length against a wall, its clawed feet digging furrows in the hard wood. In the cage, its strength and grace had been less obvious. Moving, it was simply deadly, and Jochi swallowed nervously, waiting to be attacked.

It was aware of him. He saw its golden eyes pass over his and then fasten as it sank into a crouch, its head up. Its tail lashed on the grass and once more the crowd fell silent.

Jochi offered up his soul to the sky father. No man could stand against such a monster, he was certain. The shaking in his hands died away and he stood waiting.

The tiger attacked. When it came, it was with such an explosion of speed that Jochi was almost caught motionless. In three steps, it went from a statue to a blur and leapt straight at him.

Jochi did not try to use the sword. He threw himself to one side and was still too slow. The shoulder of the beast caught him and sent him rolling on the grass, desperate to regain his feet. He caught a glimpse of the animal landing and turning at impossible speed before it was on him once more. A jaw larger than his head clamped on his armored left arm, and he cried out in pain and shock as the pressure came on. He brought his right arm forward, thrusting the blade into the tawny chest as he went over backwards. They rolled together and the crowd went berserk, bellowing encouragement to the brave man fighting below.

Jochi felt pummeling blows as the cat's rear paws raked him. His armor protected his belly, though the iron scales went flying as they caught in claws as long as his fingers. He felt the bones in his arm grind and the lower limbs of the tiger kept up their strikes, thumping and battering him on the grass. The animal's breath was hot on his face as he shoved his sword in again and again, stronger in his terror than he had ever been. He could not rise with its weight on him, and when the tiger tried to release his arm to bite again, he jammed the armored sleeve deeper into its throat despite the pain.

The tiger coughed around the obstruction, wrenching its head from side to side to free its teeth. Jochi hung on as tendons tore, tears of agony filling his eyes. Had he hurt it? He did not know. The steel blade stabbed and stabbed, lost in the thick fur. He felt new pain in his legs as the beast clawed his armor to tatters. His sword was knocked from his hand and he drew a knife, plunging it into the matted neck as his left arm gave way.

Jochi screamed as stinking blood fountained over his face, blinding him. He could see nothing and the watching warriors were far away, their voices like the whispering of leaves. He felt death coming in a great wind, but he still worked the knife in deeper, sawing back and forth.

The tiger slumped suddenly, its weight pinning him. Jochi was lost in a world of pain and he did not see Tsubodai and Jelme leap down into the circle, bows drawn. He heard his father's voice, but he could not make out the words over the rasping breath of the tiger so close to his face. It still lived, but the blows to his belly and legs had stopped. Its panting filled the world and he worked his blade mindlessly even then.

As Jelme covered him with a bow, Tsubodai used his foot to shove the tiger off the broken warrior. The great head lolled as it fell on its side, but the chest still rose and fell and the eyes sparkled with rage and hatred. Blood gouted from its throat and the white chest was slick and foul with it. All those around the ring watched as the animal struggled to regain its feet, then collapsed, falling still at last.

Tsubodai reached down to Jochi, knocking away the hand that came blindly at him with a knife. The young man's left arm hung limp and his legs were gouged and dribbling blood from gashes right to his calves and feet. Not an inch of skin showed under the mask of blood that had almost drowned him. Tsubodai took away Jochi's knife and cleared his eyes with his thumbs, so that Jochi could see. Even then, the young man was dazed, unaware that he had survived.

"Can you stand? Can you hear me?" Tsubodai shouted to him. Jochi flailed, leaving a bloody print on the general's deel robe. Tsubodai took his wrist and lifted him to his feet. Jochi could not stand on his own and he was a dead weight on the general until Jelme dropped his bow and took him under an armpit. The two generals supported the khan's son between them and turned him to face his father.

"He lives, my lord khan!" Tsubodai declared in triumph. There was awe in the faces around the circle, as Jelme had predicted. Only Chagatai struggled to hide his fury. Jelme saw the bitterness in the young man he had trained for three years, and his mouth became hard. Jochi deserved much honor for his courage and Jelme conferred briefly with Tsubodai, letting him take the full weight as he stepped away. The general reached down to the bloody sword that lay on the grass, taking it in his hand.

"He has earned this blade, my lord, has he not?" he said, holding it up so that the wolf's-head hilt was visible to all. The warriors bellowed their approval, thumping the sides of the ring. Genghis showed them nothing, his face a mask.

Jelme stood waiting as the khan's son bled. The khan's thoughts swirled, pride and bloodlust mingling with irritation. He too had expected Jochi to die and he had not planned for this outcome. His headache returned as he stared down into the circle, and his mouth tasted sour. At last he nodded and Jelme bowed to his will.

Unheard by those around the ring, Jelme spoke to Jochi as he pressed the blade into unfeeling fingers.

"They will remember this, boy," he said into Jochi's ear. The young man gave no sign that he heard, and Jelme realized he was unconscious.

"His wounds may kill him yet," Tsubodai said to Jelme.

The general shrugged. "That is in the hands of the sky father. What matters is that he stood face to face with that beast. No one who saw it will forget."

As he spoke, Jelme looked up once more to Chagatai. The bitter face had vanished and he sighed. He was shifting his grip on Jochi's limp form when voices were raised outside the rim. Genghis had snapped an order into the darkness, and the crowd swirled around a point hidden from sight to those who stood in the ring. As Jelme looked to Genghis, the khan raised a hand, keeping him there with Tsubodai and his burden.

Chagatai appeared once more at his father's side, staggering as warriors pressed him forward. They had all heard his terms and it seemed Genghis would not let him vanish into the darkness. The khan didn't look at him, but a muttered order made Chagatai flush and climb over the wooden barrier. Jelme and Tsubodai watched in silence as Chagatai leapt down and approached them. An older man could have done it with a flourish, giving and receiving honor in a grand gesture. Chagatai lacked the skill to turn the situation to his advantage. He stood before his unconscious brother, shaking with anger and humiliation.

In silence Chagatai looked up once more at his father. There was no reprieve. He dropped quickly to one knee and the crowd roared and hooted. Chagatai rose more slowly, his face cold as he stalked to the wooden walls and accepted a hand to heave him back over.

Jelme nodded wearily to himself.

"I think you had the better son to train, my friend," he murmured to Tsubodai.

"I hope his father knows it," Tsubodai replied. The two men shared a glance of understanding before they called warriors down to begin skinning the tiger. The meat would feed as many as possible, half-burned scraps forced into the mouths of warriors. There were many who desired the speed and ferocity of such an animal. Jelme wondered if Chagatai would taste the meat, or just his own rage that night.

CHAPTER SIX

IT WAS ANOTHER THREE DAYS before Genghis came to see Jochi. After the riotous night that followed the fight with the tiger, almost all the camp had slept, and Genghis himself had risen only to vomit for an entire day and night after three spent solidly drinking. Another day had been spent in moving the great host back to the banks of the river Orkhon. Jelme's camp had been a fine place to feast Arslan's life, but the herds and horses needed water and sweet grass. With his customary vitality, Genghis had recovered during the ride, though his bowels remained watery as he stood before the ger of the shaman Kokchu. It depressed him to think he would once have thrown off the effects of so much drink in just a night's sleep.

Genghis opened the small door onto a peaceful scene that reminded him of the death of his father. He swallowed acid and ducked inside, his gaze hard as he looked over the bandaged figure in the shadows. Kokchu was washing Jochi and he twisted round in irritation before he saw who it was. The shaman came to his feet from kneeling and bowed low before the khan.

The shade was a relief after the hard sunlight, and Genghis relaxed slightly, pleased to be away from the bustling camp.

"Has he woken?" he asked.

Kokchu shook his head solemnly. "Only for moments, lord. His wounds have let a fever into his body, and he wakes and cries out before sleeping once more."

Genghis came closer, drawn by memories. At Jochi's side lay the sword he had won, a blade that Genghis himself had inherited. In its scabbard, it brought back many memories, and he could not help but sniff the air for the scent of rot. It was painful to recall the time he had come to his father as he died, the wasted body racked with poison. Genghis breathed deeply over the supine form of his son. Kokchu watched him closely and Genghis returned the stare rather than let it rest on him unchallenged.

"Will he live, shaman? I have lost count of the times I have been asked."

Kokchu looked back at the young warrior lying so still. The chest barely rose and fell and he could not say. He gestured at the bandages wrapping both legs and the splinted arm.

"You see his wounds, lord. The beast broke two bones in his lower arm as well as three ribs. He has dislocated a finger on his right hand, though that is minor enough. The gashes have swollen and weep pus." He shook his head. "I have seen men recover from worse."

"Have you sealed the cuts?" Genghis asked.

Kokchu hesitated, before speaking too quickly. In the fall of Yenking, he had taken books on medicine and magic that were worth more than all the gold and jade. He had not expected to have his treatment challenged and spoke without his usual confidence.

"I have Chin texts that are astonishing, lord, for what they know of the body. Their practice is to pour boiling wine into a gash before stitching. I have done that, as well as poultices to bring out the fever."

"Then you have not sealed them in the manner of our people," Genghis replied, his eyes cold. "Have an iron brazier brought to the ger and burn the cuts properly. I have seen it work."

Kokchu knew better than to argue further.

"Your will, lord." For the father, he would press red iron against each wound, though he now considered it a crude practice, beneath a man of his learning. He hid his distaste and Genghis seemed satisfied. Kokchu saw the khan intended to leave and spoke again, still trying to understand the man who led the tribes.

"The pain will be intense, lord. If it wakes him, shall I give him a message from you?"

Genghis turned his pale eyes on the shaman. He left without another word.

*   *   *

The generals gathered in the khan's ger, half again as high and twice as wide as any other in the camp. Khasar and Kachiun had come with Temuge, though he would only be responsible for the camp itself and would not ride with them. Tsubodai, Jelme, and Chagatai had been summoned and took their places on the ring of low beds that served as couches for the khan's council. The ger was as bare as that of the poorest herder, and they were all reminded that Genghis cared nothing for wealth or its trappings.

The last pair to enter before Genghis was Arslan and the young man he had chosen as his successor. Jebe, the Arrow, seemed unimpressed by the presence of so many leaders of his people in one place. As Arslan gestured for him to take a seat, he nodded to them as if he had every right to be there. The other men merely watched him, though they greeted Arslan openly, putting aside the cold face to show their appreciation of the old man. He also would not ride with them. All the men present knew that Arslan had tied packs to three mares and three stallions and that his wife and a small herd would travel with him into the wilderness.

Jelme's eyes were bright with pride for his father, and he made a point of vacating his seat for Arslan. The two men exchanged glances, and though they did not speak, Arlsan too seemed moved that the moment was finally upon him.

When Genghis entered the ger, the men within sat subtly straighter. He took his place on a pile of saddles and blankets facing the door and gestured to a servant for a cup of goat's milk to calm his stomach.

Arslan waited until the khan had finished the drink before speaking. "My lord, I commend this man to you, Jebe, whom you named."

Genghis looked across the ger at the new face, taking in his breadth of shoulder. Jebe wore an open robe over a bare chest, and his reddish skin shone with health and mutton fat. Even sitting, he seemed poised and alert, a warrior born. He made Genghis feel old.

"You are welcome in my ger, Jebe. With Arslan to speak for you, you will always be welcome. In the days to come, you will be tested. Be sure you honor his name in all that you do."

"I will, lord," Jebe replied. His confidence was obvious and Khasar grinned to himself as Genghis looked away.

Genghis took a deep breath and rested his hands on his knees. He knew as well as anyone that this meeting of generals would change the world, and he enjoyed the quiet moment while they waited for him to speak.

"When you left me to finish the siege of Yenking, I sent envoys to far lands. Some brought back trade goods and made alliances in my name. Others were attacked or have simply not returned." He paused, but no man spoke. They were hardly breathing as they listened to the man who would send them out like wolves on the hunt. The entire camp knew war was coming and it was a pleasure to be the first to hear the details.

"One group went into the west, more than two thousand miles. A single scout returned when the rest were slaughtered. At first I did not think too much of it. It was not so long ago that a raiding party in our own land would have been killed by whichever tribe came first upon them." Some of the older men nodded, though Tsubodai and Jebe could barely recall those times.

"I learned from the scout that the leader of that land is one who calls himself Shah Ala-ud-Din Mohammed." Genghis pronounced the name with difficulty, then gestured to Temuge. "On my brother's advice, I sent a group of four hundred warriors, well armed, but only as a threat. They traveled to the closest city, Otrar, and met the governor there. They took letters with my words on them for the Shah." Genghis grimaced at the memory. "I expected him to hand over the men involved, or at least to send word where they had their camp. I called him 'beloved son' and mentioned only trade and friendship." At that, he stared coldly at Temuge until his brother looked away. It had been his advice that had failed so spectacularly.

"The bazaar in Otrar is a public place. I sent three spies with the warriors to witness their treatment." He showed his teeth for an instant as anger swelled in him. "The governor commands a garrison of twenty thousand. They arrested my men and tore up my words in a gesture for the crowd." Once more he glared at Temuge.

"Even then, I did not react! This Shah is served by a fool, but I thought perhaps he could yet be made to walk a straight path. I learned of greater cities than Otrar in the east, and I sent three senior officers to the Shah himself, demanding that the governor be bound and handed over to me for punishment and my men freed. *In this too, I was scorned.*" His face had grown flushed and the men in the ger felt their own hearts beat faster in response.

"Shah Mohammed sent their heads back to me," Genghis went on. He clenched his right fist slowly. "I am not the author of this trouble, but I have prayed to the sky father to give me the strength to exact vengeance." In the distance, they heard a man's voice screaming, and more than one head jerked at hearing it. Genghis too listened and nodded, satisfied.

"It is Jochi. My shaman is tending his wounds." He looked at Chagatai as he spoke, and his son blurted out a question.

"Will he too ride with us?"

Genghis's eyes turned distant. "He killed the tiger, in front of the people. And our numbers have grown." His expression hardened at the memory of Chagatai kneeling. "As *you* have a place, so will he, if he lives. We will cross the Altai mountains to the west and show these desert men whom they have chosen to insult."

"And the Chin lands?" Khasar said. "There are cities more wealthy than any we have seen yet, and they lie untouched in the south."

Genghis was quiet at that. He still dreamed of bringing the southern Chin empire under his feet. Taking his nation into the west had its risks, and it was tempting to send at least one of the men in the ger to crush his ancestral enemy. He remembered the estimates of Chin numbers and grimaced again. Against millions, one tuman would not be enough. Reluctantly, he had decided the Chin must wait to see him on their horizon.

"They will still be there, my brother, when we come back for them. You will see Chin lands again, I promise you."

Khasar frowned at that and would have spoken again, but Genghis went on.

"Ask yourself this: for what purpose do we go to war and risk our lives? Is it for gold coins and to build the sort of palaces we tear down? I cannot care for those things. A man spends his life in struggle, from the pain of birth to the last breath." He looked round at them all then, his gaze falling finally on Jebe and Chagatai.

"There are some who will tell you they seek happiness, that there is nothing more to our lives than that simple aim. I tell you now that the sheep are happy on the plains and the hawks are happy in the air. For us, happiness is a small thing, one to be discounted in a man's life. We strive and we suffer because we know through those things that we are alive." He snorted. "You may want to see the Chin cities humbled, Khasar, but can I let this challenge go unanswered? How long will it be before every small king dares to spit on my shadow?" His voice grew harder as he spoke, so that it filled the ger. Outside, they could hear another scream from Jochi and it seemed a fitting counterpoint under those yellow eyes. "Can I let my people's deaths go unavenged? Never in this world."

He had them all. He knew it, as he had always known.

"When I am gone, I do not want men to say 'Look at his piles of wealth, his cities, his palaces and fine clothes.'" Genghis paused for a moment. "Instead I want them to say 'Make sure he is truly dead. He is a vicious old man and he conquered half the world.'" He chuckled at the idea and some of the tension went out of the group.

"We are not here to earn riches with a bow. The wolf does not think of fine things, only that his pack is strong and no other wolf dares to cross his path. That is enough."

His gaze swept them and he was satisfied. Genghis stood and his manner changed to one of respect as he gestured to Arslan.

"Your horses are ready, General," he said. "I will think of you resting your bones as we ride."

"Long life and victory, my lord," Arslan said. As they all stood, the ger became suddenly crowded. Having the highest rank, Genghis could have left first, but he stood back for Arslan to step out into the light. One by one, they followed until only Jebe remained to stare round at the khan's ger. The young warrior took it all in and nodded to himself, strangely satisfied at the lack of ornament. He felt the khan was a man to follow and everything Arslan had told him had been confirmed. Jebe grinned lightly with no one to see him. He had been born on a hillside and raised in winters so terrible that his father brought the sheep into the only ger to protect them. His eyes were bright at the memory. Now he would lead a tuman for the khan. If Genghis only knew it, he had loosed a wolf. Jebe nodded to himself, satisfied. He would show the khan what he could do. In time, every man and woman of the tribes would know his name.

Outside, Arslan checked his packs and mounts one more time, refusing to let the seriousness of the moment alter his routines. Genghis watched him test each knot and give instructions to three herd boys who would accompany him to his first camp. No one spoke until the old man was ready. When he was satisfied, Arslan embraced Jelme and they could all see the son's eyes were proud. Finally, Arslan stood before Genghis.

"I was there at the beginning, lord," Arslan said. "If I were younger, I would ride with you to the end."

"I know it, General," Genghis replied. He gestured to the vast camp on the banks of the river. "Without you, none of this would be here. I will honor your name always."

Arslan had never been a man who enjoyed physical contact, but he took Genghis's hand in the warrior's grip and then mounted. His young wife looked up at her husband, proud to see great men honor him with their presence.

"Goodbye, old friend," Genghis called as Arslan clicked his tongue and the ponies moved away. The herd boys used their sticks to move the animals with their master.

In the distance, they could hear the khan's son crying out, a mournful wail that seemed to go on and on.

Moving such a vast host of people and animals was no small task. As well as a hundred thousand warriors, a quarter of a million ponies had to be herded, with as many again of sheep, goats, yaks, camels, and oxen. The need for grazing land had grown to the point that the nation could remain in one place for only a month at a time.

On a frozen dawn, with the sun barely touching the east, Genghis rode through the busy camp, noting every detail of the cart lines with the huddled figures of women and young children on them. The column stretched for miles, always surrounded by the herds. He had lived with the sounds of animals all his life and hardly noticed the constant bleating of goats and sheep. His generals were ready; his sons were. It remained to be seen whether the Arab nations were ready to meet them in war. In their arrogance, they had invited annihilation.

Jochi had survived having his wounds burned. As Genghis had promoted Chagatai to lead a tuman of ten thousand warriors, he could hardly do less for an older son, especially one who had triumphed against a savage beast. The people talked of it still. Yet it would be months before Jochi was able to take his place at their head. Until then, he would travel with the women and children, tended by servants while he healed.

In the middle of the host, Genghis trotted past the ger of his second wife, Chakahai, who had once been a princess of the Xi Xia kingdom. Her father had remained a loyal vassal for almost a decade, and the tribute kept the Mongols in silk and valuable timber. Genghis cursed softly to himself as he realized he had not arranged a way for the tribute to follow him into the west. He could not trust the king to hold it for him. It was one more thing to tell Temuge before the tribes moved. Genghis passed the cart where Chakahai sat in furs with the three children she had borne. His oldest daughter bowed her head and smiled to see her father.

He did not leave the path to find the carts of Borte and his mother, Hoelun. The two women had become inseparable over the years and would be together somewhere. Genghis grimaced at the thought.

He passed two men boiling goat meat on a small fire while they waited. They had a stack of unleavened bread pouches ready to pack with meat for the trip. Seeing the khan himself, one of the men offered up a wooden platter with the head on it, touching the white eyes with a finger to make sure Genghis saw them. Genghis shook his head and the man bowed deeply. As the khan moved on, the warrior threw one of the eyes into the air for the sky father before popping the other in his mouth and chewing lustily. Genghis smiled at the sight. His people had not yet forgotten the old ways or been spoiled by looted riches. He thought of the new way stations that stretched in lines into the east and south, manned by crippled warriors and the elderly. A scout could change horses at a dozen of those places, covering land faster than Genghis would once have believed possible. They had come a long way from the hungry, quarreling tribes he had known as a boy, but they were still the same.

In a mass of carts and animals, Genghis dismounted at last, having ridden more than a mile from the head of the column. His sister Temulun was there, she who had been a babe in arms when his own tribe had abandoned him years before. She had grown into a fine young woman and married a warrior from the Olkhun'ut. Genghis had met the man only once, at the wedding, but he had seemed healthy and Temulun was pleased with the match.

As he adjusted the belly strap on his pony, she was ordering Chin servants to collect the last of her belongings. Her ger had been stored before dawn, leaving a black circle on the grass. As she saw Genghis, Temulun smiled and went to him, taking his reins.

"Don't worry, brother, we are ready, though I cannot find my best iron pot. No doubt it is at the bottom of the packs, under everything else." She spoke lightly, but her eyes were questioning. The khan had not visited her even once since she had been properly married. For him to come as they rode to war made her uneasy.

"It will not be long now," Genghis told her, losing some of his stiffness. He liked Temulun, though she would always be a child to him in some ways. She could not remember the first winters alone, when the brothers and their mother were hunted and starving.

"Is my husband well?" she asked. "I have not seen Palchuk in three days now."

"I don't know," Genghis admitted. "He is with Jebe. I have decided to have Palchuk command a thousand and carry the gold paitze."

Temulun clapped her hands with pleasure. "You are a good brother, Genghis. He will be pleased." A slight frown crossed her face as she considered giving her husband the good news. "Is it for him you have done this, or for me?"

Genghis blinked at her changing moods. "For you, sister. Should I not raise my own family? Can I have my only sister's husband in the ranks?" He saw her expression remained troubled. This sort of thing was beyond him, though he struggled to understand.

"He will not refuse, Temulun," Genghis said.

"I know *that*!" she replied. "But he will worry that the promotion comes from you."

"It does," Genghis replied.

Temulun raised her eyes at her brother's failings for an instant. "I mean it will matter to him that he did not earn the new rank."

"Let him prove he is worthy of it then," Genghis said with a shrug. "I can always take the paitze back."

Temulun glared at her brother. "You wouldn't dare. Better not to raise him at all, than lift and drop him as you please."

Genghis sighed to himself. "I will have Jebe tell him. He is still reordering Arslan's tuman. It will not be so strange, unless your precious husband is an idiot."

"You are a good man, Genghis," Temulun replied.

Genghis looked around to see who was close enough to hear.

"Keep it quiet, woman!" He chuckled to himself, remounting and taking back the reins.

"Leave the pot behind if you cannot find it, Temulun. It is time to go."

The restless urge that had made him tour the carts faded away as he rode back to the front. He nodded to his generals and saw that they too felt the same simple pleasure. Their people were on the move again and every day would bring a new horizon. There was nothing like the sense of freedom it brought, with all the world before them. As he reached his brothers and his generals, Genghis blew a long note on a scout horn and urged his pony to a trot. Slowly, the nation moved behind him.

CHAPTER SEVEN

IT WAS SNOWING in the high passes. The Altai mountains were further west than most of the families had ever traveled. Only the Turkic tribes, the Uighurs and the Uriankhai, knew them well and then as a place to avoid, a place of poor hunting and death in the winter.

Though the mounted warriors could have crossed the range in a single day, the heavily laden carts were ponderous, built for grassy plains and ill suited to deep snowdrifts and goat paths. Tsubodai's new spoked wheels did better than the solid discs that broke too easily, but only a few carts had been converted and progress was slow. Every day there seemed to be some new obstacle, and there were times when the slopes were so steep that the carts had to be lowered on ropes, held by teams of straining warriors. When the air was at its thinnest and men and animals grew exhausted, they were lucky to make five miles in a day. Every peak was followed by a twisting valley and another dogged climb to the best way through. The range seemed to go on endlessly and the families huddled miserably in their furs, exposed to the wind. When they halted, the rush to raise gers before sunset was hampered by frozen fingers. Almost all the people slept under the carts each night, covered in blankets and surrounded by the warm bodies of goats and sheep tethered to the wheels. Goats had to be killed to feed them, and the vast herds dwindled visibly as they traveled.

Thirty days out from the river Orkhon, Genghis called a halt early in the day. The clouds had come down so low that they touched the peaks around them. Snow had begun to fall as the tribes made a temporary camp in the lee of a vast cliff, soaring into whiteness above their heads. There was at least some protection from the biting wind in that place, and Genghis gave the order rather than take them over an exposed ridge that would see them still traveling as the light faded. He had riders out for a hundred miles and more ahead of them, a stream of young warriors who scouted the best path through and reported on anything they found. The mountains marked the end of the world Genghis knew, and as he watched his servants kill a young goat, he wondered how Arab cities would look. Would they resemble Chin fortresses of stone? Further than the scouts, he had sent spies to learn what they could of the markets and defenses. Anything could be useful in the campaign to come. The first ones out were beginning to return to him, exhausted and hungry. He had the beginnings of a picture in his head, but it was still in fragments.

His brothers sat with him in the khan's ger on its cart, above the heads of all the others. Looking out into the whiteness, Genghis could see gers like a host of pale shells, thin trails of smoke rising from them to the skies. It was a cold and hostile place, but he was not discouraged. His nation had no use for cities, and the life of the tribes went on all around him, from feuds and friendship to family celebrations and weddings. They did not have to stop to live: life went on regardless.

Genghis rubbed his hands together, blowing into them as he watched his Chin servants make a cut in the kid goat's chest before reaching in and squeezing the main vein around the heart. The goat stopped kicking and they began to skin it expertly. Every piece would be used and the skin would wrap one of his young children against the winter cold. Genghis watched as the servants emptied the stomach onto the ground, shoving out a mulch of half-digested grass. Roasting the flesh inside the flaccid white bag was faster than the slow boil the tribes preferred. The meat would be tough and hard on the teeth, but in such cold, it was important to eat quickly and take strength. At the thought, Genghis tested the stump he had broken in his drunken ride to Jelme and winced. It hurt constantly and he thought he might have to get Kokchu to pull the root out. His mood grew sour at the prospect.

"They'll have it on the fire in a little while," Genghis said to his brothers.

"Not soon enough for me," Khasar replied. "I haven't eaten since dawn." Around them in the pass, thousands of hot meals were being prepared. The animals themselves would get barely a handful of dry grass, but there was no help for it. Over the constant bleating, they could all hear the sounds and chatter of their people, and despite the cold, there was contentment in it. They rode to war and the mood was light in the camp.

In the distance, the generals heard a thin cheering, and they looked at Kachiun, who usually knew everything that went on in the gers. Under the stares of his brothers, he shrugged.

"Yao Shu is training the young warriors," he said. Temuge tutted under his breath, but Kachiun ignored him. It was no secret that Temuge disliked the Buddhist monk he and Khasar had brought back from Chin lands. Though Yao Shu was ever courteous, he had fallen out with the shaman, Kokchu, when Temuge had been Kokchu's most willing disciple. Perhaps because of those memories, Temuge regarded him with irritation, especially when he preached his weak Buddhist faith to fighting men. Genghis had ignored Temuge's protests, seeing only jealousy for a holy man who could fight better with his hands and feet than most men with swords.

They listened as another cheer went up, louder this time as if more men had gathered to watch. The women would be preparing food in the camp, but it was common enough for the men to wrestle or train when the gers were up. In the high passes, it was often the only way to stay warm.

Khasar stood and dipped his head to Genghis.

"If that goat won't be ready for a while, I'll go and watch, brother. Yao Shu makes our wrestlers look slow and clumsy."

Genghis nodded, seeing how Temuge grimaced. He looked outside at the bloated goat stomach and sniffed the air hungrily.

Kachiun saw Genghis wanted an excuse to watch the training and smiled to himself.

"It could be Chagatai, brother. He and Ogedai spend a great deal of time with Yao Shu."

It was enough.

"We'll all go," Genghis said, his face lighting up. Before Temuge could protest, the khan stepped out into the cold wind. The rest followed, though Temuge looked back at the roasting goat, his mouth watering.

* * *

Yao Shu was bare-chested, despite the altitude. He seemed not to feel the cold, and as Chagatai walked in a circle, making him turn, the falling snowflakes rested as they touched the monk's shoulders. Yao Shu was breathing lightly, though Chagatai was already flushed and bruised from the bout. He eyed the monk's stick, wary of a sudden strike. Though the little Buddhist disdained swords, he used the stick as if he had been born to it. Chagatai felt stabbing aches in his ribs and left leg where he had been struck. He had not yet landed a blow of his own, and his temper simmered close to the surface.

The crowd had grown, swelling with idle warriors. There was little else to do and they were always curious. The pass was too narrow for more than a few hundred of them to watch the practice, and they pushed and squabbled amongst themselves as they tried to give the fighters room. Chagatai sensed the movement in the crowd before he saw his father and uncles walking through, the ranks pressing back rather than jostle their generals. He clenched his jaw, resolving to get in at least one good blow while Genghis watched.

To think was to act and Chagatai darted in, bringing his stick around in a short, chopping blow. If Yao Shu had remained still, it would have cracked him in the head, but he ducked and tapped Chagatai sharply in the lower ribs before stepping away.

It was not a hard strike, but Chagatai colored with anger.

Yao Shu shook his head. "Remain calm," the monk murmured. It was the boy's chief failing in the practice bouts. There was nothing wrong with his balance or reflexes, but his temper undid him every time. Yao Shu had worked for weeks to get Chagatai to stay cold in battle, to put aside rage as much as fear. The two emotions seemed permanently linked in the young warrior, and Yao Shu was resigned to slow progress.

Chagatai circled, reversing his gait just as it looked like he might attack. Yao Shu swayed back to meet the stick as it came in low. He blocked it with ease, snapping out his left fist against Chagatai's cheek. He saw the boy's eyes flare and rage took over, as it had done many times before. Chagatai came in fast, his stick blurring. The crowd whooped at the cracking sounds as he was blocked again and again. Chagatai's arms were burning when he tried to step away, and at that moment, the monk trapped his foot under his own, sending Chagatai sprawling.

Their movements had taken them away from the open ground between two gers. Yao Shu would have spoken to Chagatai, but he sensed someone close behind him and turned, always alert.

It was Kachiun who stood there, his face showing nothing. Yao Shu bowed briefly to the general, still listening for the sound of Chagatai coming at him again.

Kachiun bent his head close, though the noisy crowd could hardly have overheard.

"Will you give him nothing, monk?" Kachiun murmured. "With his father watching and men the boy will command?"

Yao Shu looked up at the Mongol general blankly. He had trained to master his body. The thought of letting a blustering child like Chagatai strike him was a strange concept. If it had been a more modest warrior, one who would not crow about it for months, Yao Shu might have agreed. For the khan's spoiled second son, he only shook his head.

Kachiun would have spoken again, but both of them jerked as Chagatai attacked from behind, desperate for any advantage. Kachiun firmed his mouth in annoyance as he watched Yao Shu step clear with smooth strides, almost sliding across the ground. The monk was always in balance and Kachiun knew Chagatai would not touch him that day. He watched coldly as Yao Shu blocked two more blows, then attacked harder and faster than before, giving Kachiun his answer.

All the warriors heard Chagatai's "oof" as the stick thumped air from his lungs. Before he could recover, Yao Shu struck him on the right hand so that it sprang open and the stick fell. Without pausing, the monk passed his weapon through Chagatai's legs, so that the boy went tumbling on the frozen ground. The crowd did not cheer as Yao Shu bowed to the prostrate son of a khan. They expected Chagatai to return the gesture, but instead he rose with his cheeks flaming and stalked from the open space without looking back.

Yao Shu held the pose longer than necessary, showing his own anger at having been ignored. It was his habit to discuss the bouts with the young warriors, explaining where they had failed and done well. In five years with the tribes, he had trained many of the men Genghis commanded and kept a school of twenty of the most promising. Chagatai was not one of those, but Yao Shu had learned enough of the world to understand his permission to remain came at a price. Today, it had been too high for him. He passed Kachiun without even glancing at the general.

Though many in the crowd looked at Genghis to see how he reacted to his son's rudeness, the khan showed them the cold face. He turned to Temuge and Khasar after watching the monk pass Kachiun.

"That goat will be ready by now," he said.

Temuge smiled for an instant, though it was not at news of hot food. In his innocence, the monk had made enemies of violent men. Perhaps they would teach him humility. The day had turned out rather better than Temuge could have hoped.

Yao Shu was a small man, but he still had to duck low to pass into the ger of the khan's second wife. As he entered, he bowed to Chakahai, as befitted a princess of the Xi Xia. In truth, he cared nothing for the titles of men, but he admired the way the woman had made her place in Mongol society. It could not have been more alien to the court she had once known, but she had survived and Yao Shu liked her.

Ho Sa was already there, sipping the black tea her father sent to the camp. Yao Shu nodded to him, accepting a steaming cup from Chakahai's own hands before settling himself. The camp was a small place in some ways, despite the vast, sprawling size of it. Yao Shu suspected Kachiun would know exactly how many times the three of them met and perhaps even had listeners outside. The thought made the tea seem sour in his mouth, and Yao Shu grimaced lightly. This was not his world. He had come to the camps to spread the gentle teachings of the Buddha. He did not know yet if that had been the right choice. The Mongols were a strange people. They seemed to accept whatever he told them, especially if he phrased the lessons in stories. Yao Shu had passed on much of the wisdom he had learned as a boy, but when the war horns sounded, the Mongols shrugged off his teachings and rushed to kill. There was no understanding them, but he had accepted it as his path. As he sipped, he wondered if Chakahai was so accepting of her role.

Yao Shu hardly spoke for a long time, as Ho Sa and Chakahai discussed the welfare of Chin soldiers in the khan's tumans. Perhaps eight thousand men in the camp had once lived in Chin cities or been soldiers for the emperor himself. Yet as many had come from the Turkic tribes in the north. The Chin recruits should have had little influence, but Chakahai had seen to it that all senior men were served by her people. Through them, she knew as well as Kachiun himself what went on in the camps.

Yao Shu watched the delicate woman as she assured Ho Sa she would speak to her husband about the death rites for Chin soldiers. Yao Shu emptied his tea, taking pleasure in the bitter taste and the sound of his own language in his ears. That was something he missed, without a doubt. His drifting thoughts were dragged sharply back at his own name.

"... perhaps Yao Shu can tell us," Chakahai said. "He has been with my husband's sons as much as any other."

Yao Shu realized he had not heard the question and covered his embarrassment by holding out his bowl to be refilled.

"What do you want to know?" he asked.

Chakahai sighed. "You have not been listening, my friend. I asked when Jochi would be fit enough to take his place with his men."

"In another turn of the moon, perhaps," Yao Shu replied immediately. "His wounds have remained clear, though his legs and arm will always be scarred from the hot irons. He has to rebuild the muscles there. I can work with him. At least he listens, unlike his foolish brother."

Both Chakahai and Ho Sa stiffened slightly as he spoke. The servants had been sent away on an errand, but there were always ears to hear.

"I watched the practice, earlier," Ho Sa said. He hesitated, aware of delicate ground. "What did General Kachiun say to you?"

Yao Shu looked up, irritated at the way Ho Sa's voice had dropped to barely above a whisper.

"It is not important, Ho Sa, any more than it is important to guard my words in this ger. I speak truth as I find it." He sighed audibly. "And yet, I was once fifteen years old and stupid. Perhaps Chagatai could still grow into a strong man, I do not know. As it stands, he is too much of an angry boy."

For the monk, it was an astonishing outburst and Ho Sa blinked in surprise.

"That 'angry boy' may lead the tribes one day," Chakahai said softly.

Yao Shu snorted into his tea. "I think sometimes that I have been among the tribes for too long. I should care nothing for which man inherits the horse-tail standard of his father, or even if these new enemies see it trampled into the dirt."

"You have friends here, Yao Shu," Ho Sa said. "Why should you not care what happens to us?"

The monk frowned to himself. "I thought once that I could be a voice for reason in this camp, that I might have an influence on the khan and his brothers." He made a dismissive sound in his throat. "Such is the arrogance of young men. I thought then that I might bring peace to the fierce hearts of the sons." Yao Shu's cheeks flushed slightly under his skin. "Instead, perhaps I will watch as Chagatai comes to lead his father's people and takes them on to more destruction than any of us could imagine."

"As you said, he is yet a boy," Chakahai murmured, moved to see Yao Shu so distressed. "He will learn, or Jochi will lead the tribes."

The monk's face softened at her tone and he reached out to pat her on her shoulder.

"It has been a difficult day, Princess. Ignore what I have said. Tomorrow I will be a different man, with the past gone and the future unknown, as always. I am sorry to have brought my anger here." His mouth twisted wryly. "At times, I think I am a bad Buddhist, but I would not be anywhere else."

Chakahai smiled at him, nodding. Ho Sa refilled his own cup with the precious tea, deep in thought. When he spoke, his voice was very low and hard to hear.

"If Genghis falls in battle, it will be Kachiun who is khan. He has sons of his own and all of this would be like leaves in the wind."

Chakahai tilted her head to listen. She was beautiful in the lamplight, making Ho Sa think again that the khan was a lucky man to have such a woman waiting in his gers.

"If my husband named an heir from among his sons, I think Kachiun would honor it."

"If you push him to it, he will name Chagatai," Ho Sa said. "The whole camp knows he does not favor Jochi, while Ogedai and Tolui are still too young." He paused, suspecting that Genghis would not be pleased to have other men talking to his wife on such a subject. Still, he was curious. "Have you spoken to the khan about it?"

"Not yet," Chakahai replied. "But you are right. I do not want Kachiun's sons to inherit. Where would I be then? It is not so long since the tribes abandoned the families of dead khans."

"Genghis knows that better than anyone," Ho Sa said. "He would not want you to suffer as his mother suffered."

Chakahai nodded. It was such a pleasure to be able to speak openly in her own language, so far from the guttural breathiness of Mongol speech. She realized she would rather go back to her father than see Chagatai become khan as things stood, yet Ho Sa spoke the truth. Kachiun had his own wives and children. Would any of them treat her with kindness if her husband fell? Kachiun perhaps would give her honor, perhaps even send her back to the Xi Xia king. Yet there would always be some who looked to the old khan's wives and sons for a figurehead. Kachiun would be safest in having them all killed on the same day his brother fell in battle. She bit her lip as she thought it through, disturbed to have such dark thoughts come to her ger. Genghis would not accept Jochi, she was almost certain. He had been laid up to heal for more than a month, and a leader needed to be seen by his men if he were not to be forgotten. Even then, she did not know him, only that Chagatai would be a poor choice. Her children would not long survive his rise, she was certain. She wondered if she had the skill to bring Chagatai to her side.

"I will think about it," she told the two men. "We will find the right path through."

Outside the ger, they could hear the wind moaning through the carts and homes of the Mongol nation. Both men heard the sadness in Chakahai's voice as she dismissed them back to their posts to sleep.

As Yao Shu stepped out into the wind and snow, he shivered, pulling his deel close around his shoulders. It was not just the cold, which he hardly noticed after so many years wearing just a thin robe. At times, he felt he had taken a wrong turn in coming among the people of the horse. He liked them, for all their childlike arrogance and belief that they could order the world to suit them. The khan was a man to follow and Yao Shu had been impressed by him. Yet he had failed to find the right ears for the words of the Buddha. Only little Tolui seemed open to them and then only because he was so young. Chagatai laughed coarsely at any philosophy that did not involve grinding enemies under his heels, and Jochi seemed to listen with detached interest, letting the words and ideas flow over him without sinking in.

Yao Shu was lost in thought as he walked the snowy paths through the camp. Even then, he remained aware of his surroundings, and he knew the men were there as soon as they began to surround him. He sighed to himself. There was only one foolish boy who would have sent warriors to attack him that night. Yao Shu had not even brought his practice stick to the ger of Chakahai, believing himself safe.

Still, he was not a child to be ambushed by fools. He wondered if Chagatai had told them to kill him, or just break a few bones. It did not matter: his response would be the same. As the snow swirled, Yao Shu darted between two gers and attacked the first dark shape to loom up before him. The man was too slow and Yao Shu dropped him neatly with a strike to the chin while he blocked the back foot with his own. He did not intend to kill in that mountain pass, but he heard other voices answer the sound and knew there were many of them. Footsteps pattered lightly from all directions and Yao Shu controlled the growing anger in his chest. It was unlikely that he knew the men, or they him. There would be no malice in the assault, unless he killed one of them. He shrugged to himself, thinking again that time amongst the tribes had changed him subtly. The Buddha would have let them come in without raising a hand in anger. Yao Shu shrugged as he padded toward another shadow. At least he was no longer cold.

"Where is he?" a man hissed, only a pace away. Yao Shu stepped in behind him, pushing the man down before he could resist and slipping past. The warrior's surprised yell echoed back from the high hills, and Yao Shu heard other men closing fast.

The first to reach him was met with an explosive punch into the lower ribs. Yao Shu felt them break under his hand and drew back before he jammed the shards into vital organs. He ducked on instinct as something else moved, but in the whiteness, he had not seen two warriors and one of them tackled him around the waist, throwing him to the hard ground.

Yao Shu kicked out and his foot jarred against something solid, hurting him. He came to his feet as a ring of men closed, and looked around at the unsmiling faces. It distressed him to see three of them were from his own training group. They at least would not meet his eyes. The others were strangers carrying heavy sticks.

"We have you now, monk," one of them growled. Yao Shu readied himself, dropping slightly on bent legs so that he was in perfect balance. He could not defeat so many, but he was once again ready to teach.

Eight men fell into the center of the circle, and Yao Shu almost slipped between two and was away. By chance, one of them snagged his robe. Yao Shu felt fingers slip over the skin of his skull and he brought his head back sharply. The hard fingers vanished and the monk struck out with his right foot. Another man fell back with a cry, his knee shattered, but by then they had struck him many times and Yao Shu was dazed. He still hammered blows with hands, knees, and head wherever he could, but they knocked him down. The heavy sticks rose and fell with mindless anger. He did not cry out, even when one of them stamped on his right foot and broke the small bones.

Before he lost consciousness, Yao Shu thought he heard Kachiun's voice shouting and felt the hands on him falling away. The words of his own teachers spiraled in his mind then as he collapsed in the snow. They had told him that holding on to anger was like grasping a hot coal. Only he would be burned by it. Yet as the men scattered and he felt strong arms lift him up, Yao Shu held the hot coal closely and felt only warmth.

CHAPTER EIGHT

YAO SHU LOOKED UP as Kachiun came into the ger where the wounded were treated. By day, sick men and women traveled on the carts, well wrapped in furs. There were always some who needed a poisoned toe lanced or a wound bound. Yao Shu knew three of the men with him. They were the ones he had injured himself. He had not spoken to them and they seemed embarrassed by his silence and would not meet his eyes.

Kachiun brightened as he greeted Jochi, sitting on the edge of his bed and chatting lightly with him. He admired the striped tiger skin at Jochi's feet, running his hands over the stiff folds and flattened head as they talked. Yao Shu could see the two men were friends. Tsubodai too visited each dawn, and despite his seclusion, Jochi was well informed. Yao Shu watched the pair talk with some curiosity as he tested the splints on his foot and winced.

When conversation died away, Kachiun turned to the monk, visibly searching for words. He knew as well as anyone that it could only have been Chagatai who ordered the beating. He knew also that it would never be proven. Chagatai strutted around the camp and there were more than a few warriors who looked on him with approval. There was no shame for them in taking revenge, and Kachiun could guess what Genghis thought about it. The khan would not have relied

on others to make his point, but he would not have lost sleep about it
if he had. The camp was a hard world and Kachiun wondered how to
explain that to Yao Shu.

"Kokchu says you will be walking in just a few weeks," he said.

Yao Shu shrugged. "I heal, General. The body is just an animal, after all. Dogs and foxes heal and so do I."

"I have not heard anything else about the men who attacked you,"
Kachiun lied. Yao Shu's eyes drifted to the others in the small ger and
Kachiun flushed slightly. "There is always someone fighting in the
camp," he said, spreading his hands.

Yao Shu looked calmly at him, surprised that the general seemed to
be feeling guilt. He had played no part in it, after all, and was he responsible for Chagatai? He was not. In fact, the beating could have been much
worse if Kachiun had not come and scattered them. The warriors had
vanished back to their gers, bearing their wounded away. Yao Shu suspected Kachiun could have named each one if he wanted to, perhaps with
the names of their families as well. It did not matter. The Mongols loved
revenge, but Yao Shu felt no anger toward young fools following orders.
He had vowed to teach Chagatai another lesson in the fullness of time.

It troubled the monk that his faith came second to such a base desire, but he still relished the prospect. He could hardly speak of it with
Chagatai's own men in the ger, but they too were healing and it would
not be long before he was alone with Jochi. Though he might have
gained an enemy in Chagatai, Yao Shu had seen the fight with the tiger.
As he glanced at the great striped skin draped over Jochi's low bed, he
thought he had surely gained an ally as well. The Xi Xia princess would
be pleased, he thought wryly.

Kachiun stood automatically when he heard Genghis's voice outside. The khan entered and Yao Shu saw his whole face was swollen
and red, the left eye almost closed.

The khan registered the presence of the men in the ger and nodded
to Yao Shu before speaking to Kachiun. He ignored Jochi as if he were
not present.

"Where is Kokchu, brother? I have to get this broken tooth out of
my head."

The shaman came in as he spoke, bringing with him the strange
odor that made Yao Shu wrinkle his nose. He could not like the skinny
magic worker. He had found the shaman competent at splinting broken bones, but Kokchu treated the sick as if they were an annoyance,
then fawned on the generals and Genghis himself without shame.

"The tooth, Kokchu," Genghis growled. "It is time." Sweat beaded his brow and Yao Shu guessed he was in great pain, though the khan made a fetish of never showing it. Yao Shu sometimes wondered if they were insane, these Mongols. Pain was merely a part of life, to be embraced and understood, not crushed.

"Yes, lord khan," Kokchu replied. "I will take it out and give you herbs for the swelling. Lie back, lord, and open your mouth as far as you can."

With an ill grace, Genghis took the last bed in the ger and tilted his head far enough so that Yao Shu could see inflamed flesh. The Mongols had very good teeth, he thought. The brown stump looked out of place in the white ones. Yao Shu wondered if their diet of meat was responsible for their strength and violence. He shunned flesh himself, believing it to be responsible for bad humors in the blood. Still, the Mongols seemed to thrive on it, bad humors and all.

Kokchu unrolled a leather tube to reveal a small pair of blacksmith's pincers and a set of narrow knives. Yao Shu saw Genghis's eyes swivel to see the tools, then the khan met his gaze and a stillness came over him that was impressive to watch. The man had decided to treat the ordeal as a test, Yao Shu could see. The monk wondered if his self-discipline would hold.

Kokchu clacked the ends of the pincers together and took a deep breath to steady his hands. He looked into the khan's open mouth and pursed his lips.

"I will be as quick as I can, lord, but I have to take out the root."

"Do your work, shaman. Get it out," Genghis snapped, and again Yao Shu saw the pain must have been immense for him to speak in such a way. As Kokchu probed the broken tooth, the khan clenched his hands then let them fall loose, lying as if he slept.

Yao Shu watched with interest as Kokchu dug deep with the pincers, trying to get a purchase. The metal tool slipped twice as he brought pressure to bear. With a grimace, the shaman turned back to his roll and selected a knife.

"I have to cut the gum, lord," he said nervously. Yao Shu could see the shaman was shaking as if his own life were at stake. Perhaps it was. Genghis did not bother to reply, though once again the hands tensed and relaxed as he fought his body for control. The khan stiffened as Kokchu leaned on the knife, digging deeply. Genghis choked on a flood of pus and blood, waving Kokchu away so he could spit on the floor before settling back. His eyes were wild, Yao Shu saw, quietly awed at the man's strength of will.

Once more, Kokchu cut and jerked the blade, then reached in with the pincers, took a grip, and heaved. The shaman almost fell as a long shard of root came out and Genghis grunted, rising to spit once more.

"That is almost all of it, lord," the shaman said. Genghis glared at him, then lay back again. The second piece came out quickly and the khan sat up, holding his aching jaw and clearly relieved to have it end. The rim of his mouth was red and Yao Shu watched as Genghis swallowed bitterness.

Jochi too had observed the extraction, though he had tried to make it look as if he hadn't. As Genghis rose again, Jochi lay back on his bed and stared at the ribs of birch that made up the ceiling of the ger. Yao Shu thought the khan would leave without speaking to his son and was surprised when Genghis paused and tapped Jochi on the leg.

"You can walk, can't you?" Genghis said.

Jochi turned his head slowly. "Yes, I can walk."

"Then you can ride." Genghis noticed the wolf's-head sword that Jochi never let out of his sight, and his right hand twitched to hold it. It rested on the tiger skin and Genghis ran his fingers through the stiff fur.

"If you can walk, you can ride," Genghis told him again. He might have turned away then, but some impulse held him in place.

"I thought that cat would kill you," Genghis said.

"It nearly did," Jochi replied. To his surprise, Genghis grinned at him, showing red teeth.

"Still, you beat it. You have a tuman and we ride to conquer."

Yao Shu saw that the khan was trying to mend bridges between them. Jochi would command ten thousand men, a position of immense trust and not lightly given. To Yao Shu's private disappointment, Jochi sneered.

"What else could I possibly want from you, my lord?"

A stillness came into the ger then until Genghis shrugged.

"As you say, boy. I have given you more than enough."

The stream of carts and animals took days to spill out of the mountains to the plains. To the south and west lay the cities ruled by Shah Mohammed. Every man and woman of the people had heard of the challenge to their khan and the deaths of their envoys. They were impatient to bring vengeance.

Around the core of the people, scouts rode out in wide circles as they moved, leaving the cold mountains behind. The generals had gambled with knucklebones for the right to take a tuman raiding, and it had been Jebe who had thrown four horses and won. When Genghis heard, he had summoned Arslan's replacement to him for orders. Jebe had found the khan with his brothers, deep in conversation as they planned the war to come. When Genghis finally noticed the young man standing by the door, he had nodded to him, barely looking up from new maps being drawn with charcoal and ink.

"I need information more than piles of the dead, General," Genghis had said. "The Shah can call on cities as great as any in Chin lands. He will not be idle as we cross his lands. We must meet his armies, but when we do, it will be on my terms. Until that day, I need everything you can learn. If a town has less than two hundred warriors, let them surrender. Send their traders and merchants to me, men who know a little of the world around them."

"And if they will not surrender, lord?" Jebe had asked. Khasar had chuckled without looking up, but the khan's yellow gaze had lifted from the maps.

"Then clear the way," Genghis had replied. As Jebe turned to leave, Genghis had whistled softly. Jebe had turned to him questioningly.

"They are your warriors now, Jebe, not mine, nor any other man here. They will look to you first. Remember that. I have seen brave warriors who broke and ran, then stood against impossible odds just a few months later. The only difference was that their officers had changed. Never believe another man can do your job. You understand?"

"Yes, lord," Jebe had replied. He had struggled not to show his delight, though he felt light-headed with it. It was his first independent command. Ten thousand men would look to him alone, their lives and honor in his hands. Genghis had smiled wryly to himself, fully aware of the young man's sweating palms and thumping heart.

"Then go," the khan had said, returning to his maps.

On a spring morning, Jebe had ridden out with ten thousand veterans, eager to make his name. Within just a few days, Arab merchants rode into the camp as if the devil himself were behind them. They were willing to barter and sell information to this new force in the land, and

Genghis welcomed a stream of them to his ger, sending them away
with their pouches full of silver. Behind them, distant plumes of smoke
rose sluggishly into the heat.

Jochi joined his men two days after he had seen Genghis in the ger for
the sick. He was thin and pale from six weeks of seclusion, but he
mounted his favorite horse stiffly, setting his jaw against the pain. His
left arm was splinted and the wounds on his legs cracked and wept, but
he smiled as he trotted to the ranks. His men had been told he was
coming, and they formed up to greet their general and the khan's first
son. Jochi's expression remained stern, concentrating on his own
weakness. He raised a hand in greeting and they cheered his survival
and the tiger skin he had placed between the saddle and the horse's
skin. The dried head would always snarl at his pommel.

When he took his place in the front rank, he turned his pony and
looked back at the men his father had given him. Of the ten thousand,
more than four thousand were from the Chin cities. They were mounted
and armored in the Mongol style, but he knew they could not shoot arrows as fast or as well as his brethren. Two thousand more were from
the Turkic tribes to the north and west, dark-skinned men who knew
the Arab lands better than the Mongols themselves. He thought his
father had given them to Jochi as those of lesser blood, but they were
fierce and they knew the ground and the hunting. Jochi was pleased
with them. The last four thousand were of the people: the Naimans,
the Oirat, and the Jajirat. Jochi cast his gaze over their ranks and it was
there that he sensed a weakness in their grim faces. The Mongols knew
Jochi was not a favorite son of the khan, perhaps not even his son at
all. He read subtle doubt in the way they looked at each other and did
not cheer as lustily as the others.

Jochi felt his energy flag and summoned his will. He would have
liked longer for his arm to heal. Yet he had seen Tsubodai bind men together and he was eager to begin the work.

"I see men before me," he called to them. His voice was strong and
many grinned. "I see warriors, but I do not yet see an army." The grins
faltered and he gestured to the vast array of carts rolling out of the
mountains behind them.

"Our people have enough men to keep out the wolves," he said.
"Ride with me today and I will see what I can make of you."

He dug in his heels, though his legs had already begun to ache.

Behind him, ten thousand men began to trot out onto the plains. He would run them ragged, he told himself, until they were blind with exhaustion, or until his limbs hurt so much he could not stand it any longer. Jochi smiled at the thought. He would endure. He always had.

The city of Otrar was one of the many jewels of Khwarezm, made rich at the crossroads of ancient empires. It had guarded the west for a thousand years, taking a part of the wealth that flowed along the trade roads. Its walls protected thousands of brick houses, some of them three stories high and painted white against the hard sun. The streets were always busy and a man could buy anything in the world in Otrar if he had enough gold. Its governor, Inalchuk, gave offerings each day in the mosque and made public displays of his devotion to the teachings of the prophet. In private, he drank forbidden wine and kept a house of women chosen from the slaves of a dozen races, all picked for his pleasure.

As the sun dipped toward the hills, Otrar cooled slowly and the streets lost their mad energy as men and women returned home. Inalchuk wiped sweat from his eyes and lunged at his sword instructor. The man was quick and there were times when Inalchuk thought he allowed his master to take points. He did not mind as long as the instructor was clever. If he left too obvious an opening, Inalchuk struck with greater force, leaving a welt or a bruise. It was a game, as all things were games.

Out of the corner of his eye, Inalchuk saw his chief scribe halt on the edge of the courtyard. His instructor darted at him to punish the moment of inattention, and Inalchuk fell back before striking low so that the point of his blunt sword sank into the man's stomach. The instructor fell heavily and Inalchuk laughed.

"You will not tempt me to lift you up, Akram. Once is enough for each trick."

The instructor smiled and leapt to his feet, but the light was fading and Inalchuk bowed to him before handing over the blade.

As the sun set, Inalchuk heard the voices of the muezzins call the greatness of God across Otrar. It was time for evening prayers and the courtyard began to fill with the members of his household. They carried mats and lined up in rows, their heads bowed. Inalchuk led them in the responses, the thoughts and worries of the day vanishing as he took the first position.

As they chanted in unison, Inalchuk looked forward to breaking the day's fast. Ramadan was close to its end and even he did not dare to ignore its disciplines. Servants chattered like birds and he knew better than to provide them with evidence against him for the shari'a courts. As he prostrated himself, touching his forehead to the ground, he thought of the women he would choose to bathe him. Even in the holy month, all things were possible after sunset, and a man was king in his own home. He would have honey brought and dribble it onto the back of his current favorite as he enjoyed her.

"Allahu Akbar!" he said aloud. God is great. Honey was a wonderful thing, he thought, the gift of Allah to all men. Inalchuk could have eaten it every day if it were not for his expanding waist. There was a price for every pleasure, it seemed.

He prostrated himself once more, a model of piety in front of his household. The sun had set during the ritual and Inalchuk was starving. He rolled his prayer mat and walked swiftly through the yard, his scribe falling in behind him.

"Where is the army of the khan?" Inalchuk called over his shoulder. His scribe fussed with a sheaf of papers as he always did, though Inalchuk did not doubt he had the answer ready. Zayed bin Saleh had grown old in his service, but age had not dulled his intelligence.

"The Mongol army moves slowly, master," Zayed said. "Allah be thanked for that. They darken the earth all the way back to the mountains."

Inalchuk frowned, the image of honey-covered skin vanishing from his imagination.

"More than we thought before?"

"Perhaps a hundred thousand fighting men, master, though I cannot be sure with so many carts. They ride as a great snake on the land."

Inalchuk smiled at the image.

"Even such a snake has but one head, Zayed. If the khan is troublesome, I will have the assassins cut it off."

The scribe grimaced, showing teeth like yellow ivory.

"I would rather embrace a scorpion than deal with those Shia mystics, master. They are dangerous in more than just their daggers. Do they not reject the Caliphs? They are not true men of Islam, I think."

Inalchuk laughed, clapping Zayed on the shoulder.

"They frighten you, little Zayed, but they can be bought and there is no one as good. Did they not leave a poisoned cake on Saladin's own chest as he slept? *That* is what matters. They honor their contracts and all their dark madness is just for show."

Zayed shuddered delicately. The assassins ruled in their mountain fortresses and even the Shah himself could not command them to come out. They worshipped death and violence and Zayed felt Inalchuk should not be so casual in speaking of them, even in his own home. He hoped his silence would be taken as a subtle reproof, but Inalchuk went on as another thought struck him.

"You have not mentioned word from Shah Mohammed," he said. "Can it be that he has not yet answered?"

Zayed shook his head. "There are no reinforcements yet, master. I have men waiting for them to the south. I will know as soon as they appear."

They had reached the bathing complex in the governor's house. As a male slave, Zayed could not pass through the door, and Inalchuk paused with him, thinking through his orders.

"My cousin has more than a million men under arms, Zayed, more than enough to crush this army of carts and skinny goats. Send another message with my personal seal. Tell him...two hundred thousand Mongol warriors have come through the mountains. Perhaps he will understand my garrison can only retreat before so many."

"The Shah may not believe they will strike at Otrar, master. There are other cities without our walls."

Inalchuk made a tutting sound and ran a hand down the oiled curls of his beard.

"Where else would they come? It was here that I had the khan's men flogged in the marketplace. Here that we made a pile of hands as high as a man's waist. Did my cousin not guide me in that? I have followed his orders in the knowledge that his army would be ready to throw these Mongols back on their heels. Now I have called and still he delays."

Zayed did not respond. The walls of Otrar had never been broken, but Arab merchants were beginning to come in from Chin lands. They talked of the Mongols using machines that could smash cities. It was not beyond possibility that the Shah had decided to let the Otrar garrison test the mettle of the Mongol khan. Twenty thousand men rested within the walls, but Zayed did not feel confident.

"Remind my cousin that I once saved his life when we were boys together," Inalchuk said. "He has never repaid that debt to me."

Zayed bowed his head. "I will have word sent to him, master, by the fastest horses."

Inalchuk nodded curtly, disappearing inside the door. Zayed watched him go and frowned to himself. The master would rut like a dog in heat until dawn, leaving the campaign planning to his servants.

Zayed did not understand lust, any more than he understood men like the assassins who chose to eat the sticky brown lumps of hashish that banished fear and made them writhe with the desire to kill. When he was young, his body had tormented him, but one blessing of old age was relief from the demands of flesh. The only true pleasure he had ever known came from planning and scholarship.

Zayed realized dimly that he would need to eat to sustain himself in the long night ahead. He had more than a hundred spies in the path of the Mongol army, and their reports came in every hour. He heard his master's rhythmic grunting begin and shook his head as if at a wayward child. To act in such a way when the world was ready to topple mystified him. Zayed did not doubt Shah Mohammed had visions of becoming a new Saladin. Inalchuk had been just a child, but Zayed remembered the reign of the great king. He cherished memories of Saladin's warriors passing through Bukhara to Jerusalem more than thirty years before. It had been a golden time!

The Shah would not let Otrar fall, Zayed was almost certain. There were many leaders who had come to his banners, but they would be watching for weakness. It was the curse of all strong men, and the Shah could not give up a wealthy city. After all, the Chin had never been weaker. If Genghis could be stopped at Otrar, there was a world to win.

Zayed heard his master's grunting passion grow in volume and sighed. No doubt Inalchuk had his own eyes on the Shah's throne. If the Mongols could be broken quickly, perhaps it was even in his reach.

The corridor was cool after sunset and Zayed barely noticed the slaves lighting oil lamps along its length. He was not tired. That too was a blessing of old age, that he needed very little sleep. He shuffled away into the gloom, his mind on a thousand things he had to do before dawn.

CHAPTER NINE

JEBE HAD LOST COUNT of the miles he had ridden in a month away from the khan's army. At first he had headed south, coming across a vast lake in the shape of a crescent. Jebe had never seen such a body of fresh water, so wide that even the sharp-eyed scouts could not see the other side. For days he and his men had speared fat green fish they could not name, feasting on the flesh before moving on. Jebe had decided against trying to swim the horses across and took his tuman along the clay banks. The land teemed with animals they could eat, from gazelles and ibex to a brown bear that came bellowing out of a copse and almost reached a raiding group before arrows brought it down. Jebe had the bearskin draped over his horse's back, thick with rotting fat. He hoped to smoke-cure the skin before it was too far gone. Falcons and eagles soared the warm winds above their heads and the hills and green valleys reminded Jebe of home.

As Genghis had ordered, he left small villages alone, his men riding past in a dark mass as farmers ran or stared in dull fear. Such men reminded Jebe of cattle and he could only shudder at living such a life, trapped in one place for all time. He had destroyed four large towns and more than a dozen road forts, leaving the loot buried in marked spots in the hills. His men were coming to know him as leader, and they rode with their heads up, enjoying his style of striking fast and covering huge distances in just a few days. Arslan had been more cautious as a general, but he had taught Jebe well and the younger man drove them hard. He had a name to make among the generals, and he allowed no weakness or hesitation in those who followed him.

If a town surrendered quickly, Jebe sent its merchants north and east to where he thought Genghis might have reached with the slower carts. He promised them gold and tempted them with Chin coins as proof of the generosity they would receive. Many of them had been forced to watch their homes burned to the ground and had no love for the young Mongol general, but they accepted the gifts and rode away. They could not rebuild with Genghis coming south, and Jebe found them more pragmatic than his own people, more accepting of the fate that can raise one man and break another with no cause or reason. He did not admire the attitude, though it suited his own purposes well enough.

By the end of the new moon, which Jebe had learned was the Arab month of Ramadan, he reached a new range of mountains to the south of the crescent lake. Otrar was to the west and further on lay the golden cities of the Shah, with names Jebe could hardly pronounce. He learned of Samarkand and Bukhara and had Arab farmers draw their locations on rough maps that Genghis would value. Jebe did not travel to see those walled places. When he did, it would be with the Mongol host at his back.

As the moon vanished, Jebe rode on one last sweep into the hills of the south, mapping sources of water and keeping his men fit. He was almost ready to return and go to war. Though his tuman had stayed out for more than a moon's turn, he had no gers with him and made his camp in a sheltered valley, with scouts posted on all the peaks around him. It was one of those who rode back into camp, his pony lathered with sweat.

"I have seen riders, General, in the distance."

"Did they spot you?" Jebe asked.

The young warrior shook his head proudly. "Not in this life, General. It was in the last light before the sun set, and I came straight back." The man hesitated and Jebe waited for him to speak again.

"I thought...they could have been Mongols, General, from the way they rode. It was just a glimpse before the light went, but there were six men riding together and they could have been ours."

Jebe stood up, his meal of rabbit forgotten at his feet.

"Who else would have come so far south?" he muttered. With a low whistle, he had his men leaving their rations and mounting all around. It was too dark to ride fast, but he had seen a trail leading through the hills before sunset, and Jebe could not resist moving closer in the darkness. By dawn he would be in position. He passed on his orders to his officers and let them inform the men. In no time at all, they were clicking gently to their mounts, moving into a column.

Without a moon, the night was very dark, but they followed his orders and Jebe grinned to himself. If it was Khasar, or better still, Tsubodai, he would like nothing more than to surprise a Mongol force at dawn. As he walked his mount to the head of the line, he sent scouts out with whispered orders, knowing that the khan's generals would take pleasure in doing the same to him. Unlike the older men, he had a name to win for himself and he relished the challenge of a new land. Tsubodai's rise had shown Genghis valued talent over blood, every time.

Jochi woke from sleeping like a dead man in pine woods, halfway up a mountain slope. He lay still in pitch darkness, raising his left hand before his face and blinking wearily. The Arabs judged dawn as the time when a black thread could be distinguished from a white one, and it was not yet light enough for that. He yawned and knew he would not sleep again now that his battered body had dragged itself awake. His legs were stiff in the mornings and he began each day by rubbing oil into the raised scars from the hot irons and the tiger's claws. He worked the ridged skin with his thumbs, grunting in relief as the muscles relaxed. It was then that he heard hoofbeats in the darkness and one of his scouts calling.

"Over here," he said. The scout dismounted and came to kneel by him. It was one of the Chin recruits and Jochi handed him the pot of oil to continue as he listened. The scout talked quickly in his own language, but Jochi interrupted only once to ask for the meaning of a word.

"In three weeks, we've seen no sign of an armed force and now they come creeping at us in the dark," Jochi said, wincing as the Chin warrior's thumbs worked a tender spot.

"We could be miles away by dawn, General," the scout murmured.

Jochi shook his head. His men would allow him to run if he had some plan to draw an enemy into an ambush. To simply retreat would undermine him with all the groups of his tuman.

He cursed softly. In the moonless night, he could not know where the enemy were or how many came against him. His best trackers would be useless. His one advantage was that he knew the land. The isolated valley to the south had been his training ground for half a month, and he had used it to work his men to a new edge of toughness. Along with his scouts, he knew every back trail and piece of cover from one end to the other.

"Fetch my *minghaan* officers to me," he said to the scout. The ten senior officers could spread his orders quickly to the individual thousands of his tuman. Genghis had created the system and it worked well. Jochi had only added Tsubodai's idea of naming each thousand and each jagun of a hundred men. It led to less confusion in battle and he was pleased with them.

The Chin scout handed him the pot of oil and bowed his head before scurrying away. Jochi stood and was pleased to find his legs had stopped aching, at least for a while.

By the time his men were walking their mounts up to the ridge that led down into the valley beyond, two more scouts had come in. The sun was not yet up, but the gray light of the wolf dawn was over the hills, when men felt life stir in their limbs. Jochi saw the scouts were chuckling and gestured for them to come to his side. They too were of Chin stock, but the usually impassive warriors were visibly amused at something.

"What is it?" Jochi asked impatiently. The two men exchanged a glance.

"Those coming are Mongols, General."

Jochi blinked in confusion. It was true that he could make out the faces of the scouts in the dim light, but they had ridden through darkness to get back to him.

"How do you know?" he demanded.

To his surprise, one of them tapped his nose.

"The smell, General. The breeze is north to south and there is no mistaking it. Arab warriors do not use rancid mutton fat."

The scouts clearly expected Jochi to be relieved, but instead he narrowed his eyes, dismissing them with a sharp gesture. It could only be Arslan's tuman, led by the new man his father had promoted. He had not had the chance to know Jebe before Genghis sent him out. Jochi showed his teeth in the darkness. He would meet him on his own terms at least, on land Jebe could not know as well.

Jochi passed on new orders and they increased the pace, needing to be in the valley before dawn. They had all heard the news of another tuman in the area and, like their general, were eager to show what they could do. Destroying Shah Mohammed's armies could not bring them the satisfaction of confounding their own.

With the sun above the horizon, Jebe moved slowly forward. His warriors had crept through the last of the darkness, moving stealthily to surround a valley where they could hear warriors and horses. The whinnying calls carried far in the bowl of hills, and Jebe had left forty mares in season well back, where they would not call to stallions.

The first light made the young general smile to see the terrain ahead. Warriors moved in dark smudges on the land, surrounded on all sides by slopes and crags. The shamans told stories of great stones hurtling from the stars and gouging valleys. This looked like such a place. Jebe spotted a prominent ridge where he could direct the flanking groups and used the tree cover to move toward it, always out of sight from those on the valley floor. He did not intend to take lives, only to show the Mongol tuman that he could have destroyed them. They would not forget the sight of his armed lines coming thundering down the slopes.

Jebe's eyes were sharp over distance and he was pleased to see no sign of alarm in those he watched. They were clearly training and he could see a line of distant discs that could only be straw archery targets. Rank after rank galloped and shot their arrows at full speed before looping back for another try. Jebe chuckled as he heard the distant calls of Mongol horns.

With two senior men and two flag bearers, Jebe tied his reins to a pine tree and crouched, moving slowly to the ridge. For the last few paces, he approached on his stomach, worming forward until he could see the entire green valley. It was still too far to recognize the general, but Jebe nodded at the sharp formations as they wheeled and maneuvered. Whoever it was had trained his men well.

Half a mile away, Jebe saw a flash of red, gone as quickly as it had appeared on a high crag. His left flank had found themselves a slope they could ride, and they were ready. He waited for the right flank to do the same and his heart beat faster when a flag of blue flickered.

Something nagged at him then, spoiling his concentration. Where were the other scouts, the men who were meant to watch for exactly this sort of attack? The valley floor was vulnerable to any hostile force, and Jebe could not think of one of Genghis's generals who would leave himself blind. His men had orders to disarm the scouts before they could sound their horns, but that was down to luck. Perhaps the sky father was watching over his endeavors this day, and the scouts had been taken in silence. He shook his head warily.

"Where are the scouts?" he muttered. The closest man to him was Palchuk, who had married Genghis's sister, Temulun. Jebe had found him a solid choice, for all he suspected Genghis had broken his own rules to promote him.

"There is no large army close to this place," Palchuk said, shrugging. "Perhaps they have brought the scouts further in."

On the other side of the valley, Jebe saw a twinkle of light. The distance was too far for flags to be seen, but his man carried a piece of Chin glass and used it to reflect the sun. Jebe put aside his doubts and stood. A hundred paces behind the general lay two thousand men with their ponies beside them. The animals were well trained and hardly made a sound as the men removed their arms from the necks and allowed them to stand.

"Keep the bows in the saddle holders," Jebe called. "We are training men, not killing them."

Palchuk chuckled softly as he and Jebe mounted with the rest. They would charge on four fronts, converging in the center, where Jebe would meet the general. He reminded himself not to gloat when the man acknowledged him.

As Jebe raised his arm to give the order, he saw a red flash on the left, as if his flank were signaling again.

"What are they doing?" he said aloud. Before Palchuk could answer, men erupted from the ground on every side. Jebe's warriors shouted in confusion as warriors stood up from shallow pits, holding drawn bows. They had waited through the last of the darkness in complete silence, covered in a thick layer of leaf mulch and dead pine needles. In just moments, more and more of them were aiming sharp arrows at Jebe as he turned his mount in amazement.

He saw Jochi come striding out from between the trees and threw his head back to laugh. The khan's son did not reply until he had walked to Jebe's stirrup. Jochi dropped his hand to the wolf's-head sword.

"Your men are taken, General," he said. "No one is coming and you are mine." Only then did Jochi smile, and those closest surrounded Jebe, grinning evilly.

"I *knew* there should have been more scouts out," Jebe said. Accepting the mood, he handed over his own sword. Jochi bowed to him and handed it back, his face bright with success. As Jebe watched in amusement, Jochi blew a long note on a scout's horn that echoed across the valley. Far below, the warriors stopped their maneuvers and their cheering voices carried even to the heights.

"You are welcome in my camp, General," Jochi said. "Will you ride down to the valley with me?"

Jebe bowed to the inevitable. He waited until Jochi's men had put aside their weapons and horses had been brought up to the ridge.

"How did you know I would direct my men from here?" he asked Jochi.

The khan's son shrugged. "It's where I would have chosen."

"And you were trained by Tsubodai," Jebe replied wryly.

Jochi smiled, choosing not to mention the men he had hidden at four other places along the ridge. The hours of silent waiting had been damp and cold, but seeing Jebe's expression when they stood up had made the discomfort worthwhile.

The two generals rode together down the slope to the valley, comfortable in each other's presence.

"I have been giving thought to a name for my tuman," Jochi said.

Jebe looked at him, raising his eyebrows.

"Tsubodai has his Young Wolves and it has a better ring than 'Jochi's warriors' or 'Jebe's tuman,' don't you think?"

Jebe had witnessed this strange young man standing his ground when a tiger leapt at him. The striped skin lay under Jochi's saddle and Jebe was uncomfortably aware of the rotting bearskin he sat upon. Jochi did not seem to have noticed it.

"Are you thinking of tigers or something of that sort?" Jebe said warily.

"Oh no, it doesn't have to be an animal," Jochi said, and then he did glance at the bearskin.

Jebe felt his cheeks flush and chuckled again. He liked this khan's son, no matter what was said of him in the camps. Whether he was truly Genghis's son or not, Jebe relaxed. He sensed none of the blustering arrogance he had seen in Chagatai, and it pleased him.

They had ridden down to where Jochi's men waited in perfect squares. Jebe inclined his head to the officers, giving them honor in front of their men.

"They look dangerous enough," Jebe said. "What about the 'Iron Lance'?"

"Iron Lance," Jochi repeated, testing the sound. "I like 'Iron,' but I have too few lances to make the name work. It wouldn't seem right to make them retrain to fit the name."

"'Iron Horse' then," Jebe replied, caught up in the game. "They all have mounts, at least."

Jochi reined in. "I like that! Tsubodai has the Young Wolves. I have the Iron Horse. Yes, it is very stirring." He smiled as he spoke and suddenly both men were laughing, to the confusion of the officers around them.

"How did you know we were coming?" Jebe asked.

"I smelled that bearskin," Jochi replied, setting them both off again.

Jochi's men had hunted well and had meat enough for all Jebe's warriors. Taking the lead from the two generals who sat together like old friends, the tumans mingled easily and the mood was light. Only the scouts stayed high on the hills, and this time Jochi sent men out for miles as he had every day of the training. He could not be surprised in his valley.

Jebe allowed his men to train with Jochi and spent most of the day discussing tactics and the terrain they had covered. He accepted Jochi's offer to sleep in the makeshift camp, and it was not until the following dawn that he decided to leave. It had been a pleasant break from hard riding and trail rations. Jebe had eaten well and Jochi had provided the last of a stock of airag for the senior men. Jochi had not once referred to the way he had surprised the other general on the heights, and Jebe knew he was in his debt. The men would be talking about it for months.

"I will leave you with your Iron Horse, General," Jebe said as the sun rose. "Perhaps I will find a name for my own men in time."

"I will think on it," Jochi promised. For a moment, he lost his light manner.

"I have few friends, Jebe. Shall I call you one of them?"

Jebe did not reply at first. The khan's son walked a hard path and he felt a chill at the thought of being caught between Genghis and this tall young man. Perhaps it was the debt he owed, or simply because he

truly liked Jochi, but he had always been impulsive. With a quick gesture, he drew a knife and gashed his palm, holding it out.

Jochi stared, then nodded. He copied the gesture and the two men
clasped their right hands together. It was no small thing and the men
around them were silent as they looked on.

In the distance, two scouts were riding in, and the moment was
broken as they both turned. From the sheer speed, they knew in an instant that the scouts had news, and Jebe put aside his plans to leave until he had heard.

They were Jochi's men and Jebe could only stand and listen as they
reported.

"The enemy are in sight, General. Thirty miles south and coming
west."

"How many?" Jebe said, unable to stop himself.

The scout saw Jochi nod and answered.

"I cannot count such a force of men and horses, General. More
than all the khan's warriors, perhaps twice as many. They travel with
huge beasts I have not seen before, armored in gold."

"The Shah is in the field," Jochi said with satisfaction. "My Iron
Horse will ride to see them. Will your Bearskins come with us?"

"I do not like 'Bearskins' at *all*," Jebe replied.

"It is a fine name, but we will discuss it as we ride," Jochi replied,
whistling for his horse and bow.

CHAPTER TEN

THOUGH THEY MADE GOOD TIME on the hill trails that Jochi knew well, it took most of the day for the tumans to reach the point where the scout had seen the Shah's army. In mountainous lands, it was sometimes possible for two armies to pass only a valley apart and never know the other was there. Yet if the scout's estimates were right, such a host could not be hidden. In late afternoon, the generals were close enough to see a trail of reddish dust that hung in the air like a false horizon. Jebe and Jochi came together to discuss a plan for the first contact with the army of the Shah. With older men, deciding who would ride to the other might have been delicate. Jochi was the son of the khan, while Jebe was seven years more experienced. With the red lines still fresh on their palms, neither made an issue of it. They rode to a central point to discuss their plans and observe the enemy.

Jebe had lost the light mood of the morning. He nodded to Jochi as they trotted abreast, ahead of twenty thousand. As a man he liked the khan's son, but he did not know him as a general, and Jebe felt the first prickle of annoyance that he had to allow for another force on the field.

The Mongol armies rode through a high pass toward the dust trail. Ahead, the light was brighter as the land opened out, and both men aimed their mounts at a ridge that overlooked the plains beyond. Jochi at least had scouted it before. The dust hung like storm clouds in the distance, and he could only swallow dryly as he imagined an enemy force large enough to cause such a sight.

At last the generals halted, both men raising an arm to stop the warriors at their back. Their own dust trail moved in sluggish tails on the warm breeze. The enemy would know they were watched, but it was impossible to move such large forces without being seen in daylight.

Jochi and Jebe sat their mounts in grim silence as they watched a bannered host rumble west, just a mile away. It was an army to dwarf the khan's tumans, both in foot soldiers and a huge number of mounted men riding the wings. The foot of the valley was flat for miles, but still seemed too small to hold such a mass.

Jochi could see spears like the pines of a forest even at such a distance. In the brass light of the sun, iron armor glittered in the ranks. He looked across to Jebe to see how he was reacting and found the general leaning low in his saddle, staring in fascination.

"You see the bows?" Jebe asked, squinting.

Jochi had not, but he nodded, wishing Tsubodai was there to assess this force they would face in battle.

Jebe spoke as if he was already making his report. "Double-curved, like ours. They have good shields as well, larger than our own. So many camels! I have never seen so many in one place, nor seen them ridden to war. They will be faster over rough ground than our horses. We must be sure not to let them use that advantage."

There was something about Jebe that always lightened Jochi's mood.

"Do not forget those huge beasts," he said, "with horns, or teeth or whatever they are. They too will be new to our men."

"Elephants," Jebe replied. "Jelme talked of seeing one at the Koryon court. They are fearsome animals." He gestured at the black wings of the Shah's army, cutting the air with his hands.

"They use their cavalry on the edges, protecting the center. That is where we will find their generals." From the ridge, he could see the entire structure of the Shah's army, laid out before him. A smaller group of horsemen rode in the center, their ranks perfect. Jebe sucked his teeth while he considered. "You see the boxes on the backs of those elephants? Surrounded by riders? Those will be senior men." He paused and whistled to himself. "They are fine horsemen. See how they keep formation."

Jochi glanced sideways as he replied. "Frightening, aren't they?"

Jebe chuckled. "Do not be afraid, Jochi. I am here now."

Jochi snorted, though in fact he was afraid. His father's army could be swallowed up in so many, and he could not see a weakness in the dark lines.

Both men were aware that they had been spotted almost as soon as they showed themselves on the ridge. Riders were racing up and down the Shah's lines, and the Mongol generals watched with interest, learning everything they could. There was much they did not understand. Though Jebe had heard elephants described, the reality of seeing those huge animals looming over the riders was intimidating. The great heads looked armored in bone as well as glittering metal. If they could be made to charge, he could not see how to stop them.

As Jebe turned to point out a detail to Jochi, a vast host of Arab horsemen broke away from the main column and formed up in swirling dust. Horn calls brought the rest to a halt, and even in that, they could see the discipline of the Shah's men. Jebe and Jochi looked at each other in wild surmise.

"They are going to attack us!" Jebe said. "You should withdraw, Jochi, and take word to your father. Everything we have seen here will be useful in the days to come."

Jochi shook his head. His father would not look kindly on him if he simply left. The information could be carried by a single scout, and they had not come to the Shah's lands to retreat before his armies.

Jochi felt a pang of resentment that Jebe was with him. He had come a long way to lead his warriors, and it did not sit well with him to defer to a more senior man.

"We have the high ground at least," Jochi said. He remembered the Russian knights who had labored up a hill at him and knew the worth of such an advantage.

In the distance, the massive Arab formations kicked into a fast trot, and Jochi felt a sudden panic. He knew he could not lead the tuman straight at the enemy horsemen. There were easier ways to waste lives. He considered a running blow that would lead the Arabs out along the plain. His men were fit as only Mongols knew fitness, but he did not know if the Chin soldiers in his ranks would fall behind and be destroyed.

Jebe seemed blithely unaware of Jochi's whirling thoughts as he spoke.

"They will have to come straight up at us, with their Shah watching.

They will not know how many men we have behind this ridge. I should think they are as surprised as we are to meet in this place, so far from Otrar or the khan. Can you get around to the flank?"

Jochi looked into the distance before nodding. Jebe smiled as if they merely discussed a wrestling match or a wager.

"Then that will be the plan. I will wait until they have tired themselves riding up, then fall like a mountain on their heads. You will come from the flank and cut a wedge through to the center. Your lances will be useful there, I think."

Jochi looked down the steep slope. "It is only a shame that we do not have rocks to roll into them," he said.

Jebe nodded, surprised. "That is an excellent idea! I would give my second wife for pots of oil to roll down as well, but I will see what I can find." For an instant, both men sensed the strain in the other and exchanged a glance that had none of the lightness of their words.

"We cannot take so many if they are as good as their weapons and armor," Jochi said. "I will hit the flank, but then pull back and let them follow me far from the main force."

"Is that Tsubodai's voice I hear?" Jebe asked.

Jochi did not smile. "It is my voice, General. I will run them to exhaustion, well away from their reinforcements."

Jebe bowed his head to the khan's son. He did not mention that almost half of Jochi's tuman were of Chin stock. Though they rode hardy Mongol ponies, they would not have the endurance of men born to the saddle.

"Good luck, General," he called as he turned his mount. Jochi did not reply, already issuing orders to his men. Ten thousand of those behind the ridge gathered quickly and rode east to get around the steep slope. It would not be easy to charge over the loose shale, and Jebe honestly did not know which of them had the hardest task.

Khalifa Al-Nayhan was a worried man as he rode up the hill, his fine gelding already laboring in the heat and dust. He had grown up in those very mountains and knew the ridge he was assaulting. The Shah had given the order and he had formed his men without hesitation, but his stomach felt hollow. After the first shock of seeing Mongol scouts hundreds of miles from where they should have been, Shah Mohammed had settled into a fury Khalifa knew he could maintain for days or weeks. It was not a time to suggest that they wait for better terrain.

Khalifa urged his mount on over the broken ground, looking up at the ridge that seemed far above his head. Perhaps it was no more than a scout's camp at the top. By the time he arrived, they might well have galloped away, and then at least the Shah would be satisfied. No one knew how these savage Mongols had made a Chin emperor kneel, and the Shah needed quick victories to reassure his chieftains.

Khalifa shook the loose thoughts out of his head as he rode, feeling sweat sting his eyes. The summer had been mild so far, but climbing to the ridge was hard work. He trusted the men around him, many of them from his own tribe of desert warriors. The Shah had spared nothing in outfitting them for war, and though the new armor and shields were heavy, Khalifa felt the confidence they brought. They were picked men: the first into every battle, the breakers of walls and armies. He felt his bow slapping against his thigh, but they could not bring arrows to bear while riding up such a slope. Once more he thought of the Shah watching and shook his head against weak thoughts. They would win or they would be killed. It was all the same to Allah.

At the steepest point of the slope, Khalifa knew they were committed. The horses plunged on, but the ground was even softer than he remembered and progress was painfully slow. Khalifa felt exposed and made his peace with God as he drew the curved *shamsher* saber that had served him for many years. With his left hand, he raised his shield, and rode only with his feet in the stirrups. Like many of his men, he secretly despised the metal foot-holders that made it hard to dismount quickly. Yet they showed their use on such a slope, when he needed both hands for his weapons. A quick tap on his boot showed him his dagger was still there in the leather sheath, and he leaned forward into the warm breeze that came over the ridge.

In time of peace, civilization had no place for butchers like him, but still they were needed and would always be needed, when the jeweled cities and green parks were threatened. Khalifa had escaped two murder charges by joining the army and assuming a new name. It was what he did best. Sometimes he was paid and other times hunted, depending on how and when he practiced his skills. Riding with his men into the teeth of the enemy was what he loved. The Shah was watching, and if they bloodied their swords, there would be rewards of women and gold for the commanders.

"Hold the line straight, Ali, or I will see you whipped!" Khalifa roared across his men. He saw dust still rising from the ridge and knew the enemy had not run. He could hardly see in the clouds that his own men churned up, but there was only one objective and his horse was still strong.

Above him, Khalifa saw rocks grow in size as they were pushed to the edge. He called out a warning, but he could do nothing. He watched in fear as the boulders came bouncing down, ripping through men and horses in a series of sickening cracks. Khalifa cried out as one came close enough for him to feel the wind of its passage. As it passed, it seemed to leap like something alive, striking the man behind with a great crunch. He could see only six of the huge stones scything through his men, but each one took many lives and left the ground littered with pieces of armor and men. They were riding in close ranks and there was no room to dodge the stones.

As quickly as it had begun, the boulders stopped and a ragged cheer went up from those who still labored on the slope. The ridge was no more than four hundred paces away, and Khalifa kicked his mount on, hungry now to bring vengeance to those who killed his men. He saw a dark line of archers ahead and raised his shield instinctively, ducking his head beneath the rim. He was close enough to hear orders called in a strange language, and he clenched his teeth. The Shah had sent forty thousand men up that slope. No force in the world could do more than thin the ranks before they were among them and killing.

Firing downhill, the Mongol archers could send their shafts further than normal range. Khalifa could only keep his head down as arrows thumped against his shield. The one time he raised his head, it was immediately rocked back by a glancing blow that yanked the turban from his head and left it dangling. Rather than have it snag, he cut it free with part of his long hair and it bounded down the hill behind him.

At first the shields protected his men, but as they reached the last hundred paces, the air was thick with whistling shafts and men died in scores. Khalifa's shield was of wood, covered in the dried hide of a hippopotamus—the lightest and best of all the Shah's equipment. It held, though the muscles of his arm were bruised and battered until he could barely hold it. Without warning, he felt his horse shudder and begin to die.

Khalifa would have leapt clear, but his feet snagged in the stirrups and for a breathless moment of panic his right leg was trapped under the dying horse. Another mount crashed into his as it fell, and he jerked free, thanking Allah for his deliverance. He rose on sandy ground, spitting blood and wild with rage.

The entire front rank had been brought down by the archers, fouling those behind. Many of his men were yelling, tugging at shafts through their legs and arms while others lay sprawled and unmoving. Khalifa roared fresh orders and the men behind dismounted to lead their mounts through the broken dead. The gap closed further and Khalifa held his sword high, pointing it at the enemy above. One hundred paces and he was lost in his desire to kill. If anything, he was faster on foot, though every step on loose ground sapped his strength. He scrambled up with his sword ready for the first blow. The Shah was watching and Khalifa could almost feel the old man's eyes on his back.

The Mongols poured over the ridge, straight down the steep slope. Their ponies slid, with front legs straight and stiff while the back legs bunched to keep them upright. The desert warriors strained to take the first impact, but to Khalifa's shock, another wave of arrows punched them from their feet before the two forces met. He could not understand how the Mongols could draw and loose while guiding their mounts down such a slope, but the volley devastated his men. Hundreds died on foot or leading their mounts, and this time the shafts were followed by the Mongol front line crashing down on them. Khalifa heard their yelling swell until it seemed to echo back from the hills all around.

The Mongol horsemen came like a breaking wave, smashing anything in their path by sheer weight. Khalifa was standing behind the bodies of two horses and could only watch in astonishment as the charge roared past him, a wedge tipped with lances that struck deep and deeper into the climbing lines below.

He was left alive, but still they came. Khalifa could not climb further. The way was blocked by thousands of Mongol horsemen, guiding their mounts with just their knees while they loosed arrows at anything that moved. A long shaft ripped through his side, parting the steel links of his armor as if they had been made of paper. He fell, shouting incoherently, and it was then that he glimpsed another force cutting across the face of the slope.

Jochi's men hit the flank of the Arab riders below Jebe's charge. Their arrows tore a hole in the ranks, and they followed it with lances and swords, cutting men down while they were held in the press. Khalifa stood to see them, fear and bile rising in his throat. Arrows still whirred by his bare head, but he did not flinch. He saw the two forces meet in the center and the combined mass drove his men further down so that they almost reached the valley floor. Bodies covered the ground behind them and riderless horses ran wild, knocking fresh warriors from their saddles in their panic.

The Mongol charge from the ridge had passed him by, and Khalifa saw one horse with its reins trapped under a dead man. He ran to it, ignoring the pain in his side as he mounted, throwing his shield aside with a curse when the arrow shafts snagged. The air was thick with dust and the cries of dying brothers, but he had a horse and a sword and had never asked for more. Perhaps thirty thousand desert men still lived, struggling below to hold back the twin charge. Khalifa could see the Mongols had gambled their full force in the attack, and he shouted as he rode wildly down the hill toward the ranks. They could be held. They could be broken, he was sure of it.

As he reached his men, he bellowed commands to the closest officers. A solid square began to form, ringed with shields. The Mongols threw themselves at the edges and began to die as they met the swords of his tribe. Khalifa felt the battle like a live thing and knew he could still turn the losses to triumph. He had his men retreat in order back to the flat ground, harried all the way by the Mongol warriors. He drew them away from the slope they had used to such effect, and when the earth was hard under his mount, Khalifa ordered a charge into them, urging his men on with words of the Prophet.

"They shall be slain or crucified or have their hands and feet cut off on alternate sides, or be banished from the land. They shall be held up to shame in this world and sternly punished in the hereafter!"

His men were true Arabs of the blood. They heard and became fierce once more, taking the fight to the enemy. At the same time, the Shah moved at last, sending fresh soldiers racing in squares as the Mongols came within range. The lines met and a roar went up as the Mongols were knocked back, defending desperately as attacks came from more than one direction. Khalifa saw the Shah's ranks move wide to surround them, marching steadily in.

The Mongol warriors faltered, overwhelmed as Khalifa barged his horse through to the front rank. A young warrior came at him and Khalifa braced and took the man's head as he swept past. The Shah's riders advanced, their swords red. Discipline held them and Khalifa was proud. Once more he sensed uncertainty in the attacking horsemen, and suddenly they broke and ran, leaving the foot regiments in their wake as they galloped clear.

Khalifa ordered his lancers forward and was pleased with their formation as they took many of the fleeing men in the backs, hammering them from the saddles.

"For the prophet, brothers!" he roared. "Run these dogs down!"

The Mongol warriors were streaming across the plain on their ponies, riding flat out. Khalifa raised his hand and dropped it and the lines of Arabs dug in their heels to give chase. They would pass along the flank of the Shah's army, and Khalifa hoped the fierce old man would see and give thanks. As he rode, he glanced back to the slope leading up to the ridge. It was black with the dead and he felt new strength surge in him. These men had dared to enter his land, and they would find only fire and the sword.

CHAPTER ELEVEN

AFTER THE INITIAL RACE east along the valley, both the tumans and their pursuers settled into a slow gallop that ate the miles. Before the sun set, Khalifa's men tried to close the gap three times and were driven back with arrows fired by men turning in the saddle. Unlike the Mongols, the Arab horsemen were not accurate loosing arrows at full speed. Though their mounts were faster over short distances, they were forced to settle in for a long chase. By the time the sun touched the west behind them, they were more than a dozen miles from the Shah's army. The Mongol warriors rode in grim concentration, knowing that to fall behind was to die.

Jochi and Jebe had come together about halfway through the ranks of their men. They did not know how many of their number had been lost on the slopes under the ridge. The Arabs had fought well at the end, but both generals were pleased with what they had achieved. Genghis would be told of both strength and weaknesses in the enemy, and what they had learned would be vital to the khan in the days to come. Still, they had to survive the dogged pursuit. Both men knew it was easier to chase than to be hunted. As eagles and wolves had eyes to the front of their heads, so did man. Riding after an enemy kept the spirits strong, just as hearing the enemy always at their backs sapped the confidence of the tumans. Yet they did not falter.

"Will they follow us into the darkness, do you think?" Jochi asked.

Jebe looked back over his shoulder at the mass of riders. Perhaps thirty thousand men had come after them, and he could not know their quality. He and Jochi had left so many on the slopes that he thought anger would keep the Arabs on their trail for a long time. They had been thrown back in chaos in the battle, and they would not let them go without a chase. As he stared at the enemy, Jebe could admit that the Arabs were excellent horsemen. They had shown discipline and courage. Against that, the two tumans could only bring the stoic endurance they had learned on the brutal winter plains. They would not fall, if they had to run to the end of the world.

Jebe glanced back at the setting sun, now just a gold line that cast writhing shadows ahead of his men. He realized he had not answered the question and shrugged.

"They look determined enough and they have more speed in short bursts. If I were their commander, I would wait for true darkness and then close the gap when we cannot see to drive them back."

Jochi rode carefully, conserving his strength. His left arm ached and his legs were stiff, the old scars sending needles of discomfort along his thighs as they stretched. Even so, he struggled not to show his pride at the action on the ridge. His flanking charge had shattered the Arab soldiers, but Jebe had not mentioned it.

"When it is dark, then," Jochi said, "we should race for a mile and open a gap they cannot cross easily."

Jebe winced at the thought of pelting full speed across unknown ground. Their greatest fear was that the Arabs knew the valley would come to a sudden end, perhaps in a blocked canyon. The tumans could be riding right to their own destruction.

Jochi strained to see ahead, but the peaks on either side seemed to go on forever. A pang of hunger interrupted his thoughts and he reached into a pocket to pull out a lump of dried mutton. In the last light, he eyed the black twist dubiously, but tore off a piece and chewed before reaching out and offering it to Jebe. The general accepted the gift without speaking, pulling it apart with his fingers before passing the rest back. They had not eaten since the morning and both men were starving.

"When my father fought the Xi Xia kingdom," Jochi said, chewing, "the king used clusters of iron nails that could bring down a charging line."

"They would be useful now," Jebe replied, nodding. "If we had each man carry just a few, we could let these Arabs ride over a trail of them."

"Next time, my friend," Jochi said. "If there is one."

The sun set and a dim gray light crossed the valley, falling through shades to blackness. They had a little time before the new moon rose, its white crescent reversed. Jochi and Jebe gave orders that could barely be heard above the thunder of hooves, and the pace increased slowly. Both leaders depended on the sturdiness of the plains-bred ponies. The scouts were used to riding a hundred miles in a single day, and Jochi and Jebe counted on that to exhaust their enemy. Like the men who rode them, the ponies were as tough as old leather.

Behind them, both generals heard the rhythm of the Arab horses change to the fastest gallop, but they had already widened the gap. Jochi sent an order for the rear ranks to shoot three shafts each into the blackness. The decision was rewarded by crashes and yells that echoed from the hills. Once more the pursuers fell back and the generals settled to a fast canter, ready to gallop at any moment. The Mongol ponies had fought and charged already that day. Many of them were weary and already suffering without water, but there was no way to rest them.

"Did you see the flags of the Shah's army?" Jochi asked.

Jebe nodded, remembering the host of crescents all along the Arab ranks. The new moon was significant to their enemy, perhaps because it marked the beginning and end of their holy month. Jebe hoped it was not an omen of good fortune for those that rode behind him.

The crescent cast a silvery gloom on the armies that streamed through the valley. Some of the Mongol warriors used the dim light to loose arrows, until Jochi sent an order to conserve their stock. It was too hard to kill a man with a shield in the dark, and they would need every shaft.

Khalifa rode in furious silence at the head of his men. He had never experienced anything like this moonlight chase and could not escape the nagging feeling that he had deprived the Shah of his cavalry wing in territory that had already proved hostile. He had ridden down fleeing armies before, but that was a brief wild moment after an enemy broke, where a warrior could blood his sword joyfully on the necks of fleeing men, or shoot arrows until his quiver was empty. He remembered such times with great fondness, coming as they did after battles where he had ridden close to death.

This was something different and he could not understand the Mongol generals ahead. They rode in good order and every attempt to bring them down before sunset had been repulsed. Had their nerve gone? They did not ride in mindless panic. Instead, they seemed to be guarding the strength of their mounts, keeping only just enough ahead that he could not bring bows to bear against them.

Khalifa gritted his teeth in irritation, his wounded side throbbing. The Shah had chosen this valley as the fastest route west to support Otrar. The crease between mountains was more than a hundred miles long and opened out into a great plain close by the village where Khalifa had been born. Every mile took him further from the main army and made him wonder if the Mongols were not deliberately drawing him away. Yet he could not rein in and let them go. His blood cried out for vengeance for those they had slaughtered.

The moon rose, which brought some respite as he spent hours calculating angles from the red planet Merreikh to the moon and the eastern horizon. He could not decide if the results promised good fortune or not, and the mental game did not satisfy him. Could the Mongols have planned an ambush so far from the main battle site? Surely it was impossible. As the moon crept higher, he strained his eyes in the gloom for some sign that the Mongols were signaling to another force lying in wait.

He could see nothing but their backs, riding as if they were not pursued by a vast army of furious men intent on their deaths. In the dark valley, it was easy to imagine enemies in every shadow. Khalifa's anger sustained him as the cold became biting. He took a single gulp from his waterskin and shook it irritably. It had not been full at the beginning, and there was only a little left. He felt his men looking to him for orders, but he had no words for them. He would not return to the Shah only to tell him the enemy had escaped. He could not.

Jebe and Jochi had spent much of the night in conversation, developing a mutual respect that deepened with the hours in the saddle. Some of the men dozed in turns around them, always with a friend to take the reins in case their mounts began to drift back through the ranks. It was common practice for those who had been herdsmen to ride asleep, though usually at just a walking pace. No one fell, despite their drooping heads. The tumans had slowed as the moon began to descend, and the force at their heels had instantly kicked on to a gallop, closing the gap once more. Four times they had been forced to match the frantic pace before slowing, but as dawn approached, both armies were trotting, their mounts biting froth at their mouths as they panted and rode on.

Jochi saw the first wolf dawn and reached across to nudge Jebe. The moon was just a faint sliver on the hills, and a new day was beginning. Another attack was likely and the men around them rubbed tiredness from their eyes. The night they had spent seemed to have lasted forever and at the same time had vanished in an instant. Despite the enemy at their backs, it had been oddly peaceful as the men shared the last of their dried meat and passed skins of warm, sour water between them until they were empty.

Jebe was sore and dry-mouthed, feeling as if there was dust in every joint. His lower back ached and he could only wonder at the enemy who were still there when he looked back. As the light increased, he saw the Arab horses were exhausted from the ride. Their pursuers were lolling in their saddles, but they had not fallen, or allowed the tumans to get too far ahead.

Jochi was proud of the Chin who rode with his people. They had suffered more than anyone and so many had drifted back that they formed the rear of the tumans. Still, they went on. Less than half a mile separated the two armies, and that had not changed since the darkest hours.

As the sun rose in glory, Khalifa passed orders down to his senior men. He had suffered through the night, with cold and exhaustion. The end of the valley was in sight and he knew they had covered more than a hundred miles in one ride. When he had been young, he might have laughed at such a challenge, but at forty, his knees and ankles had begun to hurt with every stride of his mount. His men too were weary, though they had the grim endurance of desert Arabs. They lifted their heads as the order came to close the gap once more. Surely he could bring the Mongols to battle this last time!

There was no sudden surge of speed to alert the enemy ahead. Instead, Khalifa urged his panting mount on slowly, closing the gap to just four hundred paces before the Mongols reacted. Khalifa raised his hand then, roaring through the dust in his throat for a charge.

His men dug in their heels and the exhausted horses responded, hitting a ragged gallop. Khalifa heard a horse scream and go down, spilling a man to the ground. He could not see what had happened as he closed to two hundred paces and drew a long, black arrow from the quiver on his back.

The Mongols had seen the threat and answered it with a volley of shafts loosed behind them. Even then, the accuracy was terrifying and Khalifa saw men and horses plucked away to be trampled on every side. He snarled in frustration as his arrow feathers touched his cheek. His mount was foundering and still they managed to widen the gap. He let go, crying out in triumph as his shaft took an enemy high in the back, sending him crashing down. Dozens more were struck, though armor saved some. Those who fell went under the Arab hooves as they writhed in the dust, struck many times until their bones were shattered pulp.

Khalifa shouted raucously to his men, but they were finished. He could see from the way they swayed in the saddle that they had reached the end of their strength. Many of the horses had gone lame in the night. They drifted to the rear as their riders flailed uselessly with whips and sword scabbards.

He considered ordering a halt, but the effort was too much. Always, he thought he could hang on a little longer, just until the Mongols killed their horses and began to die themselves. His eyes were sore and red from the gritty dust he had ridden through all night, and he could only watch as the enemy drew ahead once more, to half a mile and further. There they stayed as the sun rose higher, and neither side could widen or close the gap. Khalifa put his bow back in the leather sleeve behind his right leg and patted his horse's neck.

"Just a little further, great heart," he murmured to the plunging animal. He knew that many of the horses would be ruined after such a ride. They had been pushed beyond anything they had known before, and the wind of many would be permanently broken. He heard another thump and cry as a horse fell somewhere behind him, staggering into those around it and collapsing. Others would follow, he knew, but still the rear ranks of the Mongols beckoned him on and he narrowed his eyes against the choking dust.

As the tumans came out of the shadowy valley onto a plain, their spirits lifted. They could see the morning smoke of villages in the distance, and they followed a road of packed earth into the east. Somewhere ahead lay the cities of the Shah and potential reinforcements for those who still followed. Jebe and Jochi had no idea how many men the Shah could bring to the field. His cities could have been stripped for the war, or left well manned and bristling for just such a raid into their territory.

The road was wide, perhaps because of the huge army that had trampled the earth in passing, just a few days before. The Mongol column narrowed to use the hard ground, riding in ranks of fifty across as they came out of the mountains in a whirl of dust. The sun passed noon and the heat brought horses and men crashing down on both sides, vanishing behind in a welter of hooves. The Mongols sweated and there was no water or salt to keep up their strength. Jebe and Jochi began to glance back more and more often in desperation.

The Arab horses were better than anything they had faced before in war, certainly better than Chin or Russian mounts. Yet as the heat sapped their strength, the pursuers began to fall further behind until Jebe ordered a slower pace. He did not want to lose them or allow them time to halt and regroup. He thought perhaps that they had led the Shah's riders for more than a hundred and fifty miles, approaching the limits of even the toughest Mongol scouts. The ponies were lathered in strings of soapy spit, their skin dark with sweat and fresh sores where the saddle had rubbed away patches of old callus.

Long into the sweltering afternoon, they passed a road fort with openmouthed soldiers on the walls, shouting challenges to them as they passed. The Mongols did not respond. Each man was lost in his own world, resisting the weakness of flesh.

Jochi spent the hot hours in pain as a raw spot appeared on his thigh, rubbed bloody in the ride. It went numb as the evening came once again, which was a blessed relief. His scars had eased, but his left arm felt weak and the ache there had become a hot iron in his flesh as he gripped the reins. There was no talking in the Mongol ranks by then. Their mouths were closed as they had been taught, conserving moisture in their bodies as they approached the end of endurance. Jochi looked to Jebe occasionally, waiting for the other man to judge the best time to break off the ride. Jebe rode stiffly, his eyes hardly leaving the horizon ahead. To look at him, Jochi thought the young general might well ride to the horizon.

"It is time, Jebe," Jochi called to him at last.

The general stirred sluggishly from his daze, mumbling something incoherent and spitting feebly, so that the wad of phlegm struck his own chest.

"My Chin warriors are drifting further back," Jochi went on. "We could lose them. Those who follow are letting the gap widen."

Jebe turned in the saddle, wincing as his muscles protested. The Arabs were almost a full mile behind. The lead animals were stumbling and lame and Jebe nodded, a tired smile crossing his face as he came fully alert.

"At this pace, a mile is only four hundred heartbeats apart," he said. Jochi nodded. They had spent part of the dawn judging speed with markers as they passed them and then took note of the Arab ranks drawing abreast at that point. Both Jochi and Jebe found the calculations easy and had amused each other estimating distance and speed to pass the time.

"Increase the pace then," Jochi replied. He forced his mount to a canter as he spoke, and the tumans matched them doggedly. The enemy dwindled with painful slowness as the generals called out the mark. When the first Arab riders passed a pinkish stone six hundred heartbeats after the last Mongol, the generals looked at each other and nodded grimly. They had come as far as any scout had ever ridden and further. All the men were weary and sore, but it was time. Jochi and Jebe passed orders down the line so that the warriors were ready. Though they had pushed themselves to the limit, Jochi and Jebe both saw something in the red-rimmed eyes of those around them that made them proud.

Jochi had sent orders to the minghaan officers of his Chin recruits at the back, and it was one of those men who rode up through the ranks to speak to him.

The Chin soldier was covered in dust as thick as paint, so that cracks appeared around his eyes and mouth. Even then, Jochi could see his anger.

"General, I must have misunderstood the order you sent," he said, his voice a dry croak. "If we turn to face this enemy, my men will be in the front rank. Surely you cannot mean to have us fall back?"

Jochi glanced at Jebe, but the Mongol general had fixed his gaze on the horizon.

"Your men are exhausted, Sen Tu," Jochi said.

The Chin officer could not deny it, but he shook his head. "We have come this far. My men will be shamed if they are taken from the line of battle at the end."

Jochi saw fierce pride in his officer and realized he should not have given the order. Many of the Chin would die, but they too were his men to command and he should not have tried to spare them.

"Very well. You have the first rank when I call the halt. I will send those with lances to you. Show me you are worthy of this honor."

The Chin officer bowed in his saddle before returning to the rear.

Jochi did not look again at Jebe, though the latter nodded in appreciation.

It took time for the orders to spread through the Mongol riders. For tired men, it seemed to act like a gulp of airag, so that warriors sat straighter in their saddles and readied their bows, lances, and swords. While they still rode, Jebe sent his lancemen to support the rear and waited until they were in position.

"We have come a long way, Jochi," Jebe said.

The khan's son nodded. He felt as if he had known Jebe all his life after the night ride. "Are you ready, old man?" Jochi said, grinning despite his tiredness.

"I feel like one, but I am ready," Jebe replied. Both men raised their left hands high into the air and circled their fists. The Mongol tumans ground to a halt and the gasping horses were turned to face the enemy riding toward them.

Jebe drew his sword and pointed it at the dusty Arab riders.

"Those are *tired* men," he roared. "Show them we are *stronger*." His mount snorted as if in anger and broke into a gallop, its sides heaving like bellows as they charged the pursuing enemy.

Khalifa rode in a daze, drifting in and out of alertness. At times, he thought of the vineyard near Bukhara, where he had first seen his wife tending the crop. Surely he was there and this ride was just a fever dream of dust and pain.

His men began to shout with dry throats all around him, and Khalifa raised his head slowly, blinking. He saw the Mongols had stopped and for a moment he took a searing breath in triumph. He saw the rear ranks raise lances and suddenly the gap between the armies was closing. Khalifa hardly had strength to speak. When he tried to shout, his voice was a feeble whisper. When had he emptied his water flask? That morning? He could not remember. He saw the approaching line and somehow Chin faces were grinning at him. Even then he could barely raise his shield.

The approaching lancers carried small shields in their left hands, some part of him noted. Archers needed both hands for the bows and were vulnerable just as they began to draw. Khalifa nodded to himself at the thought. The Shah would value such information.

The two armies came together with a numbing crash. The heavy birch lances broke shields and pierced men right through. On the narrow road, the column ripped into the Arab riders, deeper and still deeper, tearing them apart.

Arrows screamed past his ears and Khalifa felt something burn his stomach. As he looked down, he saw an arrow there and he plucked at it. His horse had stopped moving at last, falling to its knees as its heart burst in its chest. Khalifa fell with it, the cursed stirrups entangling his right leg, so that his knee tore and his body twisted as he fell. He gasped as the arrow drove further through him. Above his head, he could see Mongols riding like kings.

Khalifa could hear nothing but wind rushing in his ears. The Mongols had ridden them down and he feared for the armies of the Shah. He must be told, Khalifa thought to himself, but then he was gone.

"Kill them all!" Jochi shouted above the roaring hooves and men. The Arabs tried to rally, but many could barely lift their swords more than once and they fell like wheat. The generals smashed through them with their column, seeming to take new strength from every man they killed.

It took hours to turn the dusty road red. As it grew dark, the slaughter continued until they could not see to strike and those who tried to run were brought down by shafts or chased like lost goats. Jebe sent scouts to look for water and at last they made camp on the banks of a small lake just three miles further down the road. The warriors had to be watchful then, as their mounts would have drunk to bursting. More than one had to strike his pony hard on the nose to stop it taking too much water. Only when the animals had drunk did the men throw themselves into the lake, turning the dark waters pink with blood and dust as they gasped and drank and vomited it back up, cheering the generals who had brought them such a victory. Jochi took the time to commend Sen Tu for the way he had led the Chin recruits. They had hacked through the enemy with unmatched ferocity, and they sat at fires with tribesmen of both tumans, proud of the part they had played.

Jochi and Jebe sent aching men back along the road to quarter dead horses and bring them to the fires. The men needed meat as much as water if they were to make it back to Genghis. Both men knew they had done something extraordinary, but they fell into the routines of the camp with just a shared glance of triumph. They had deprived the Shah of his cavalry wings and given Genghis a fighting chance.

CHAPTER TWELVE

THE GATES OF THE CITY OF OTRAR were barred against Genghis. He stood on a hill overlooking the city, watching dark smoke lift sluggishly over the burning suburbs. He had spent three days scouting the land, but even for those who had taken dozens of Chin cities, there was no obvious flaw in the design. The walls had been built in layers of light gray limestone on a granite base, each slab weighing many tons. In the walls of the inner city, two iron gates led out to a sprawling maze of abandoned markets and streets. It had been strange to ride through those echoing passageways in sight of the great walls. The governor had known they were coming for months, and apart from a few stray dogs and broken pots, everything of value had been taken. Genghis's scouts had found a number of subtle traps set for them as they searched. One boy of only thirteen had kicked open a door and fallen back with a crossbow bolt in his chest. After two more deaths, Genghis had given Temuge the task of firing the outer city and Otrar still choked on black smoke. In the cinders and rubble below the hill, Tsubodai's Young Wolves used pikes to pull down the walls and give the khan a clear route to the inner city.

There was no shortage of information. In exchange for gold, Arab merchants even gave the location of wells within the walls. Genghis had ridden round the entire city with his engineers, noting the thickness of the stone.

The clearest weakness was the hill on the city's northern side, overlooking the walls. His scouts had found abandoned pleasure gardens there, rich with flowers and an ornamental lake and wooden pavilion. Two days before, Genghis had sent warriors to clear the crest, leaving the rest covered in ancient pine trees. If he sited his wall-breaking weapons where the pavilion had stood, they would have the height to send stones right down the throat of the governor.

Genghis looked down on the city, enjoying the sense of having it almost in his grasp. If he had been governor of such a place, he would have had the hill leveled rather than give an enemy any advantage. Yet he could not enjoy it. Thirty miles to the east, his own camp was protected by his brother Khasar, with just two tumans. The rest of them had sallied into the field against Otrar. Before the far scouts had ridden in, he had been confident that the walls could be broken.

That morning, his scouts had reported a huge army coming from the south. More than two men for every one of his eighty thousand were marching toward that position, and Genghis knew he must not be caught between Otrar and the Shah's army. Around him on the crest, twelve men drew maps and made written notes on the city. Led by Lian, a master mason from a Chin city, still more worked on assembling catapults and piling clay pots of fire oil. Lian too had been confident before the Shah's army had been sighted. Now the decisions would be military and the mason simply spread his hands when any of his workers asked what the future held.

"I'd let the governor of Otrar rot in his city if he didn't have twenty thousand to hit our rear the moment we move," Genghis said.

His brother Kachiun nodded thoughtfully as he turned his horse in place. "We can't bar the gates from the outside, brother," he replied. "They would let men down on ropes and pull the beams away. I can stay here while you take the army to meet our enemy. If you need reserves, send a scout and I'll come."

Genghis grimaced. The warriors of Jebe and Jochi had vanished into the valleys and hills, with no sign or contact. He could not leave the families in his camp without protection, and he could not let Otrar go free with so many men. Yet if the scouts were right, he would face a hundred and sixty thousand with only six of his ten tumans. No one had more faith in the fighting ability of his warriors than Genghis himself, but his spies and reports said that this was only one of the Shah's armies. Genghis not only had to crush it, but come through without serious losses, or the next army would end it all. For the first time since coming west, he wondered if he had made a mistake. With such a vast force available to him, it was no wonder the governor of Otrar had been so arrogant.

"Have you sent men out looking for Jochi and Jebe?" Genghis demanded suddenly.

Kachiun bowed his head, though the khan had asked the question twice already that morning.

"There is still no sign. I have scouts riding a hundred miles in all directions. Someone will bring them in."

"I would expect Jochi to be absent when I need him, but Jebe!" Genghis snapped. "If I ever needed Arslan's veterans, it is now! Against so many, it will be like throwing pebbles into a river. And elephants! Who knows how we can stand against those beasts?"

"Leave the camp undefended," Kachiun said.

Genghis glared at him, but he only shrugged.

"If we fail, two tumans would not be enough to get them home. The Shah would fall on them with everything he has left. The stakes are already that high, just by being here."

Genghis did not reply as he watched the spars of a catapult being lifted into position. If he had a free month, two at most, he could smash his way into the city, but the Shah would never give him such a respite. He scowled in irritation at the choices. A khan could not throw bones with his entire people, he told himself. The risk of being crushed between hammer and anvil was too great.

Genghis shook his head without speaking. A khan could do as he pleased with the lives of those who followed him. If he gambled and lost, it would be a better life and death than raising goats on the plains of home. He still remembered how it had been to live in fear of the sight of men on the horizon.

"When we were at the walls of Yenking, brother, I sent you out to bleed a Chin column. We know where the Shah is heading and I will not wait in patient squares and columns for him to come to us. I want his men under attack all the way to Otrar."

Kachiun raised his head when he saw the glitter come back to his brother's eyes. He took a scout map from a servant's arms and unrolled it on the ground. Genghis and his brother crouched over it, looking for terrain they could use.

"With so many men and animals, he will have to split his force *here* and *here*, or bring them through this wide pass in one group," Kachiun said. The land to the south of Otrar was a rough plain of farms and crops, but to reach it, the Shah had to cross a range of hills that would funnel the Arabs into a long column.

"How long before they reach the passes?" Genghis asked.

"Two days, maybe more, if they are slow," Kachiun replied. "After that, they are on open farmland. Nothing we have will stop them."

"You cannot guard three passes, Kachiun. Who do you want?"

Kachiun did not hesitate. "Tsubodai and Jelme."

The khan looked at his younger brother, seeing his enthusiasm kindle. "My orders are to thin them, Kachiun, not fight to the death. Hit and retreat, then hit them again, but do not let them trap you."

Kachiun bowed his head, still staring at the map, but Genghis tapped him on the arm.

"Repeat the order, brother," he said softly.

Kachiun grinned and did so. "Are you worried I will not leave enough for you?" he said.

Genghis did not answer and Kachiun looked away, flushing. The khan stood and Kachiun rose with him. On impulse, his brother bowed and Genghis accepted the gesture with a dip of his head. Over the years, he had learned respect came at the cost of personal warmth, even with his brothers. They looked to him for answers to all the problems of war, and though it made him a remote figure, it was a part of him and no longer a mask.

"Send for Tsubodai and Jelme," Genghis said. "If you delay the Shah long enough, perhaps Jochi and Jebe will support you. They too are yours to command. You have half my army, brother. I will be waiting here," Genghis said. He and Kachiun had come a long way from the young raiders they had once been, he thought. Ten generals would stand to face the Shah's army, and Genghis did not know whether they would live or die.

Chakahai came out of her ger to see what the sudden shouts meant. She stood in the hot sun with her Chin servants shading her skin, and she bit her lip when she saw the warriors coming out of their homes with supplies and weapons.

Chakahai had lived among the Mongols for long enough to know it was not just a scouting group that was forming. All the men but Khasar and his second, Samuka, were away at the city to the west and she bit her lip in frustration. Ho Sa would be with Khasar, of course, but surely Yao Shu would know what was happening. With a curt order, she started her servants moving with her, seeking out the Buddhist monk as the camp grew noisier all around. She could hear women screeching in anger and she passed one who was weeping on the shoulder of a young man. Chakahai frowned to herself, her suspicions hardening.

She passed the ger of Borte and Hoelun before she caught a glimpse of the monk. Chakahai hesitated outside, but the decision was made when Borte came out, flushed and angry. The two wives of Genghis saw each other at the same time, and both stood stiffly, not quite able to put aside the strain they felt.

"Do you have news?" Chakahai spoke first, deliberately giving the older woman honor. It was a small thing, but Borte's shoulders became less rigid and she nodded. Chakahai saw how weary she was as she spoke.

"Genghis is taking the tumans," Borte said. "Khasar and Samuka have orders to leave at noon."

One of Chakahai's servants made a terrified sound, and Chakahai reached out instantly, slapping the girl's face. She turned back to Borte, who was already staring across the camp at the men gathering in ranks.

"What if we are attacked?" Chakahai asked.

Borte winced and shook her head. "How many times have I been asked that since the orders came?" she said. She saw the genuine fear in the Xi Xia princess's eyes and softened her tone. The woman had been given to Genghis as a gift by her defeated father. She had seen chaos in her time and knew the terror that came with it.

"Do you think we will be defenseless, sister?" Borte said.

Chakahai too had looked away, but the term of friendship brought her gaze snapping back. "Are we not?" she demanded. "What can women and children do against soldiers, if they come?"

Borte sighed. "You were not raised in the tribes, Chakahai. If we are attacked, the women will take up knives and fight. Crippled warriors will mount as best they can and attack. Boys will use their bows. We have horses and weapons enough to hurt anyone who troubles us."

Chakahai stared in silence, her heart pounding. How could her husband have left her undefended? She knew why Borte spoke in such a way. Panic would destroy the camp before they even sighted an enemy. Families would be torn between the safety of numbers and the fact that the camp itself would draw danger to it. Left alone to protect their children, many wives and mothers would be considering leaving in the night to find a safe place in the hills. To a mother of young children, the idea was tempting, but Chakahai resisted. Like Borte, she was the khan's wife. The others would look to them for leadership. Of all the women left behind, they could not run.

Borte seemed to be waiting for a response and Chakahai thought carefully before replying. The children would be frightened as they saw the last warriors leave. They would need to see confidence, though it was all false.

"Is it too late for me to learn the bow, sister?" Chakahai said.

Borte smiled. "With those bony, narrow shoulders? It is. But find yourself a good knife."

Chakahai nodded, though uncertainty swept through her. "I have never killed a man before, Borte."

"Perhaps you will not have the chance. The knife is to cut and shape straw warriors to put on the saddles of spare horses. In poor light, an enemy will not see our men have gone."

Borte raised her eyes from her worries and the two women shared a glance before each one turned away, satisfied. There could be no true friendship between them, but neither had found a weakness in the other and both took comfort from that.

As the sun reached its highest point, Khasar looked back at the camp he had been told to abandon. It was as busy as an ants' nest as women and children scurried between the gers. Even without the tumans, it was a vast assembly, more than a hundred thousand people and gers by a small river. Around them, herds grazed, oblivious. Everything they had looted from the Chin was there, from jade to gold and ancient weapons. Temuge and Kokchu had their collection of manuscripts and books. Khasar bit his lip at the thought of the Shah's soldiers finding such a prize undefended. Perhaps a thousand elderly or crippled warriors would remain, but he did not hold out hope that those who had lost arms and legs would stop a determined enemy. If they came, the gers would burn, but his brother had called him and he would not disobey. He had three wives and eleven young children somewhere in the maze of gers, and he regretted not taking the time to speak to them before gathering his men.

It was done. The sun was high and he had been called. Khasar

looked at his second in command, Samuka. The man was caught between pride at his promotion to lead a tuman and shame at abandoning
the camp. Khasar clicked his tongue to catch the other man's attention,
then raised his arm and let it fall. His men kicked in their heels and rode
with him, leaving everything they valued behind.

Jochi and Jebe rode together at the head of the tumans. Jochi's mood
was light as they wound their way through valleys back into the west.
He had lost almost a thousand men. Some had fallen in the wild charge
across the face of the ridge, while more had been cut down or fallen
from sheer exhaustion in the long ride that none of them would ever
forget. Most of those had been from his Chin soldiers, but those who
survived rode with their heads high, knowing they had earned the right
to follow their general. Jebe had lost as many, but they were men he
had known for years under Arslan. They had died well, but would still
be denied the sky funerals, where bodies were taken to the highest
peaks to feed hawks and birds of prey. Both generals knew there was
no time to honor the dead. Genghis's brother-in-law Palchuk had been
among the bodies, found with a great gash across his face from an
Arab sword. Jebe did not know how Genghis would respond to the
news, and spent two days resting by the lake in grim silence.
    Jebe and Jochi were painfully aware of the threat to the khan, but
the horses were spent. They had been forced to let the animals recover
their strength before remounting. Even then, it was too early. Many
of the animals were still lame and it hurt the senior men to order the
ruined ones killed and the meat distributed. Dozens of warriors carried
a rack of ribs or a leg across their saddles, while others rode Arab
horses in little better condition. For men who saw horses as the only
true spoils of war, the battle in the pass had been a triumph worth
telling round the fires for a generation. With each warrior, two or three
of the Arab mounts ran alongside. Many were lame and broken-
winded, but their strength could be used and the Mongols could not
bear to leave them behind.
    Eighteen thousand men rode with the generals as they turned away
from the main valley and took a more tortuous route. As tempting as it
was to ride in their own steps, the Shah could well have left an ambush-
ing force somewhere ahead. The men needed time to recover before
facing an enemy once more.
    Water at least was plentiful. Many of the men had drunk until their

bellies were swollen. When they were being chased, they had emptied their bladders as the need came, letting the warm water cut through the coating of dust on their mounts. On the way back, they had food in them. The speed had been slowed by dozens at a time dismounting quickly and squatting on the ground before wiping themselves with rags and leaping back on. They were stinking, filthy, and thin, but hardened by the land they had ridden for so long.

It was Jochi who saw the scouts riding back from a ridge ahead. In Jebe, he had found a man who understood the need to know terrain as well as Tsubodai, and they were always surrounded by a ring of riders many miles out. Jochi whistled to catch Jebe's attention, but the other general had also seen and merely raised his eyebrows in surmise.

"Did I not send *two* men that way?" Jochi called. Three were returning and even from a distance, they could see the other rider was a scout like their own, without armor or anything but a sword to slow him down. Some even rode without that weapon, depending on speed alone.

Without a signal, the young generals kicked their mounts forward of the line, hungry for information.

The scout was not from their tumans, though he looked almost as weary and dusty as their own men. Jochi and Jebe looked on as the young man dismounted and bowed, holding his reins in his hands. Jebe raised a hand and the warriors came to a halt. At first the scout hesitated in the presence of two generals, unsure whom to address first. Jochi's impatience broke the silence.

"You have found us," he said. "Report."

The scout bowed again, overwhelmed to be speaking to a son of the khan.

"I was about to turn back when I saw the dust of your horses, General. Tsubodai sent me out. The Shah is in the field with a great army."

If the scout had expected any excitement at this news, he was disappointed.

"And?" Jebe asked.

The scout began to dip his head and hesitated again, his composure deserting him. "I was sent to bring you in at all speed, General. My lord Genghis will attack, but I do not know any more. I have been out for two days alone, looking for you."

"We could hit the rear if we get back into that valley," Jochi said to Jebe, ignoring the scout. Jebe looked back at his men, knowing they were still close to complete exhaustion. A warrior of the tribes could ride all day and still fight, but the horses had clearer limits to their strength. The value of staging an attack on the Shah's rear ranks would be lost if a fresh enemy turned and cut them to pieces. Jebe nodded grimly to Jochi. Genghis would expect them to push on.

"The Shah's army will have moved from where we left them," Jebe said. "It could be a hundred miles yet and then a battle to win."

Jochi turned his pony in place, preparing to ride. "Then we will have to make good time, General," he said. The scout watched the conversation warily, unsure whether he should say more. He eyed the herds of horses enviously, pony and Arab mount standing together.

"If you have a fresh horse for me, I will ride ahead and tell the khan you are coming," he said. For some reason, both generals shared a grin at his words.

"Do you see any fresh horses?" Jebe asked. "If you do, you should take one."

The scout looked again at the milling animals, seeing the way they stood to favor sore legs. He glanced at the ranks of dusty, grim warriors with them. Some had their arms and legs bound in strips of torn cloth, showing bloody patches under the grime. For their part, the warriors stared back indifferently, ready for orders. Their generals had shown them their own strength in that long ride through the valley. Those who had survived had come out with a confidence they had not known before. If they could ride thirty thousand Arabs to death, what could they not do?

Disappointed, the scout bowed to the generals once more, before mounting. He was barely more than a boy and Jochi chuckled to see his nervousness. With fresh eyes, the general looked over the mass of riders. They had been tested and they would not fail him. For an instant, he saw the pleasure his father took in leading men in war. There was nothing like it.

Jochi clicked with his tongue and the scout looked at him.

"Tell my father we are coming. If he has fresh orders, send scouts along the long valley just to the north. You will find us there."

The scout nodded earnestly and raced away, filled with the importance of his task.

CHAPTER THIRTEEN

SHAH ALA-UD-DIN MOHAMMED seethed as the elephant under him rocked like a ship at sea. The last he had seen of his cavalry had been watching it disappear into the east days before. After each dawn prayer, he could not resist turning to the sun to see if they were returning, but his hopes sank lower each time. The desert tribes could not be trusted and he was certain Khalifa was resting at some distant town, caring nothing for the betrayal. Ala-ud-Din swore there would be a reckoning, when the Mongols had been thrown back over their mountains, or destroyed.

All around the Shah, his army marched stolidly on, heading for the hills that would lead them to Otrar and the Mongol khan. The sight of the shining ranks never failed to lift his aging heart. In truth, the invasion had come at the right time for him. He had spent almost twelve years bringing kings and chieftains to heel, and when they were at their most rebellious, an enemy had swept in from the north, forcing them to choose loyalty over bickering and petty rivalry.

It was hard not to think of Saladin as the army strode on over rocky ground. The great king had captured Jerusalem and sent crusaders reeling. Saladin had faced enemies as fearsome as the Mongol khan and more so. Each night, when the army made its camp, Ala-ud-Din read lines by lamplight from Saladin's own record of his battles, learning what he could before tucking it under a thin pillow and finding sleep. Next to his copy of the Koran, it was his most prized possession.

The curtained howdah was still cool after the night, though the sun would be fierce as it rose. Ala-ud-Din broke his fast with a plate of dates and dried apricots, washing them down with a draught of cool yoghurt. His men carried dried mutton and flat bread that had long gone stale, but it did not matter. Otrar was not more than a few days away, and his idiot cousin, Inalchuk, would entertain him with the best of meats and fruit when they saved his city for him.

Ala-ud-Din jerked as his servant cleared his throat softly outside the curtains.

"What is it?" he demanded.

The curtain flicked back to reveal the man standing on a step set in the elephant's belly strap. "The last of the coffee, master."

Ala-ud-Din nodded and held out his hand for the cup. They had been on the move for almost an hour, and he was surprised to find the black liquid still steaming. He tipped it carefully so as not to dribble the precious drink onto his beard.

"How have you kept it hot?" he asked.

His manservant smiled to see his master pleased. "I put the pot in a leather bag, master, filed with ashes from the morning fires."

Ala-ud-Din grunted, sipping. It was bitter and delicious.

"You have done well, Abbas. This is very fine."

The curtain dropped as his servant stepped down. Ala-ud-Din heard him trotting at the side of the great beast for a while. No doubt he was already thinking of what he could scavenge for his master's next meal after the midday prayers.

If his men would have allowed it, Ala-ud-Din had considered granting a dispensation not to pray as they marched. They lost more than three hours a day to do so, and the delays chafed on him. It would be taken as weakness in the faith by those who looked to challenge him, and he brushed off the thought once more. It was their belief that kept them strong, after all. The words of the prophet formed the call to prayer, and even a Shah could not resist.

He had turned his army from the great valley at last, heading north to Otrar. Ahead was a range of brown hills, and beyond that, his men would fall on the Mongol host with all the ferocity of men bred to the harsh southern deserts. Ala-ud-Din closed his eyes in the rocking howdah and considered those he had brought to war. With the loss of Khalifa's riders, he had only five hundred horsemen, his own guard of noble sons. Already he had been forced to use them as messengers and scouts. For the sons of ancient families, it was an insult to their blood, but he had no choice.

Further back in the column, six thousand camels plodded, the supplies of the entire army on their backs. Half as fast as the best horses, they could carry immense weight. The rest of the army marched, while the Shah and the most senior men rode in comfort. He doted on his elephants for sheer power and strength, eighty bulls in their prime.

Looking out from the howdah, Ala-ud-Din took pride in the force he had assembled. Saladin himself would have been proud of them. The Shah could see his oldest son, Jelaudin, mounted on a superb black stallion, still uncut though the animal was vicious. The Shah's heart soared at the sight of the handsome young man who would one day succeed him. The men adored the prince and it was not hard to dream of his line ruling all the Arab peoples for centuries to come.

Ala-ud-Din thought again of Khalifa's horsemen and struggled to prevent anger from spoiling the morning. He would have them hunted down when the battle was over and leave not one of them alive. He swore it silently as his army marched on and the hills grew slowly closer.

Tsubodai's scouts came racing in as he crouched on one knee, overlooking the plains below the hills and the Shah's army. The view stretched for many miles and he did not need the young men to tell him the enemy was coming through the wide pass, the one he had chosen to defend.

As the scouts dismounted, Tsubodai waved a hand in their direction.

"I know," he said. "Go and tell the other generals. We will hit them here."

In the distance, he saw the Shah's outriders cutting dusty lines through scrub crops as they rode north. Tsubodai tried to put himself in the Shah's position, but it was hard. He would never have brought such an army through a single pass. Instead, he would have gone round the mountains entirely and let Otrar fall. The distances would have delayed the Shah for another month in the field, but the Mongol tumans would have been forced to meet him on open ground, with all advantages stolen away.

Instead, the Shah took the easiest route, revealing that he valued

Otrar. Tsubodai was learning everything he could, noting every decision that would help to destroy his enemy. He knew as well as anyone that Genghis was overextended in this realm. It was no longer a matter of bringing vengeance to one city, but simple survival for their people. They had stuck their hands into a wasps' nest every bit as furious as the Chin empire, and once again the stakes were at their highest.

Tsubodai smiled at the thought. Some of the men fought for new land, for exotic women, even for gold. From his private conversations with the khan, Tsubodai knew he and Genghis cared for none of those things. The sky father gave a man his life and nothing else. The khan's people were alone on the plains and it was a savage loneliness. Yet they could ride and conquer, take cities and empires one by one. Perhaps in time, those who followed them would be as weak and soft as the city dwellers they faced, but that did not matter to Tsubodai. He was not responsible for the choices of his sons and grandsons, only for the way he lived his own life. As he knelt on hard gray stone and watched the clouds of dust come closer below, he thought again that he had only one rule, which guided everything he did.

"Fight for every breath and step," he muttered aloud, the words a talisman to him. It was possible that the Shah's great army could not be stopped, that it would roll over the tumans of Genghis, right to the plains of home. Only the sky father knew. Like the khan, Tsubodai would still seek out anyone who might ever be a threat and hit them first and harder than they would believe. With that, when he came to the end of his life, he would be able to look back with pride and not shame.

Tsubodai broke off his thoughts as riders from Kachiun and Jelme cantered up to his position. After days in that place, he knew them all by name and greeted them. They dismounted and bowed deeply, honored by a general who remembered such details.

"The tumans are coming, General," one of them said.

"Do you have orders for me?" Tsubodai replied.

The scout shook his head and Tsubodai frowned. He did not enjoy being set under Kachiun's command, though he had found him a solid leader.

"Tell your officers that we cannot wait here. The Shah could still send men around us. We need to sting him, to force him along the route we have chosen."

Tsubodai looked up with the others as Kachiun and Jelme came riding in, leaping down from their horses and striding to the high crag. Tsubodai rose and dipped his head to Kachiun.

"I wanted to see for myself," Kachiun said, staring out onto the farmland below. The Shah's army was only a few miles away, and they could all see the front ranks through the dust. It came on as a solid block and the sheer size of it was enough to alarm any man.

"I have waited for your orders before moving, Kachiun," Tsubodai said.

Kachiun glanced sharply at him. He had known the young general when he was just another warrior, but Genghis had seen something valuable in him. He reminded himself that Tsubodai had repaid his brother's trust many times.

"Tell me what you have in mind," Kachiun said.

Tsubodai nodded. "This is a huge army, ruled by one man. The fact that he has chosen to come through this pass shows that he does not have our structure of officers. Why did he not trust two good men to take columns through the other passes? Know the enemy and you will know how to kill him. It is all useful to us."

Kachiun and Jelme looked at each other. As experienced as they were, Tsubodai had a reputation for keeping his warriors alive that was unmatched in the tribes. He spoke without haste and all the time the Shah's army was drawing closer.

Tsubodai saw Jelme glance over his shoulder and smiled.

"We hit them with that weakness," he continued. "We have thirty minghaans between us, each commanded by a man who can think and act on his own. Our strength is in that and in our speed." He thought again of wasps as he went on. "We send all but four out against them. Like a swarm. Let the Shah try and crush them with his clumsy hands. We are too fast for them."

"And the four thousand men who stay behind?" Kachiun asked.

"The best archers," Tsubodai replied. "The very best we have. They will line the pass, high in the rocks. You showed the power of our bows at the Badger's Mouth pass, did you not? I cannot find a better example."

Kachiun twisted his mouth at the praise. Against Chin cavalry, he had once stood with nine thousand men and hammered shafts at them until they had broken.

"If I keep the men low enough on the rocks to be accurate," he replied, "the Shah's archers will pluck them down with their own shafts. We don't even know how those elephants will act in war."

Tsubodai nodded, unconcerned. "No plan is perfect, General. You must use your judgment to place your men, of course, though they will have more range shooting down than up, no? I have said how I would tackle this Shah and his host. Even so, I will follow your orders."

Kachiun thought only for a moment. "Pray you are right, Tsubodai. I will send the men out."

Tsubodai chuckled, surprising both Jelme and Kachiun. "I do not pray to anyone, General. I think if I did, the sky father would say 'Tsubodai, you have been given the best fighting men in the world, generals who listen to your plans, and a foolish, slow-moving enemy, yet you are still looking for an edge?'" He chuckled again at the idea. "No, I will use what we have. We will take them apart."

Kachiun and Jelme looked once more at the immense enemy marching toward the pass. A hundred and sixty thousand men were coming with their blood up, but somehow they seemed less terrible after Tsubodai's words.

Shah Ala-ud-Din Mohammed jerked as his army let out a great shout all around him. He had been playing chess with himself to pass the hours, and the set slipped from the small table in the howdah, scattering pieces. He swore under his breath as he yanked back the curtains at the front, squinting into the distance. His eyes were not strong and he could only make out bodies of horsemen coming at his army. Alarm horns sounded across the host and Ala-ud-Din felt a spasm of fear as he turned to look for his servant. Abbas was already running alongside and leapt nimbly to the wooden mounting step. Both men stared across two miles to where the Mongols rode.

"Will you say nothing, Abbas?"

The servant swallowed nervously. "It is . . . strange, master. As soon as they are out of the pass, they sheer off and take different directions. There is no order to it."

"How many?" the Shah demanded, losing his patience.

Abbas counted quickly, his mouth moving with the strain. "Perhaps twenty thousand, master, but they move constantly. I cannot be certain."

Ala-ud-Din relaxed. The Mongol khan must have been desperate to send so few against him. He could see them better now as they galloped toward his marching army. They rode in strange patterns, weaving and overlapping the groups so that he could not see where they would strike first. No orders had yet been given and his men marched stoically on toward the pass, readying their shields and swords. He wished Khalifa's riders were there, but that was merely revisiting empty anger.

Ala-ud-Din beckoned to three sons of chieftains, riding behind his elephant. He saw his son Jelaudin riding close, his young face stern with righteous anger. Ala-ud-Din raised a proud hand in greeting as the scouts came up.

"Take my orders to the front," he told them. "Have the flanks move out to a wider line. Wherever the enemy strikes, we will surround them."

"Master," Abbas said, "they are already attacking."

"What?" Ala-ud-Din snapped. He narrowed his eyes, blinking in surprise at how close the Mongols had come. He could hear distant shouts as his front ranks met the first volleys of arrows with raised shields.

Columns of galloping Mongol horsemen were swinging in, passing the front and riding along the vulnerable flanks of his army. Ala-ud-Din gaped. Khalifa could have held them, but the man had betrayed his master. He could feel his son's eyes burning into him, but he would not send the guard out yet. They were his shield and they rode the only horses he had left.

"Tell the generals that we do not stop for these. March on and use the shields. If they come too close, make the sky black with arrows."

The noble sons raced to the front and the Shah fretted as the elephant strode on, oblivious to its master's concerns.

Tsubodai rode at full gallop along the flank of the Shah's army. He stood in the stirrups with his bow bent, balancing against the pony's rhythms. He could feel the strike of each hoof and then there would be a moment of flying stillness as all four legs were in the air. It lasted for less than a heartbeat, but he loosed an arrow in that instant and watched it strike a yelling enemy soldier, knocking him off his feet.

He could hear the Shah's officers bark commands, strange syllables on the wind. The man himself was well protected in the heart of the army. Tsubodai shook his head in amazement at the core of riders trapped in the center. What good did they do there, where they could not maneuver? The elephants too were deep in the ranks, too far to hit with his shafts. Tsubodai wondered if the Shah valued them more than his own men. It was one more thing to know. As he thought and rode, thousands of marching men raised their double-curved bows and loosed. Arrows whined at him and Tsubodai ducked instinctively. The Shah's bows had more range than anything he had faced in Chin lands. Tsubodai had lost men on his first pass down the flank, but he could not stay out of reach and still make his own shafts count. Instead, he brought his column swinging in, pounding the Arabs with arrows, then galloping away as the reply came snapping back at him. It was a risky maneuver, but he had begun to get a feel for how long he could delay to aim. The Arabs had to hit a fast-moving column, while his men could aim anywhere in the mass.

Around him, his minghaans adopted the tactic, each column of a thousand biting holes in the Arab lines before racing clear. The Shah's army marched on, and though the shields saved many, a trail of broken dead marked their path toward the pass in the hills.

Tsubodai pulled his men in a wider curve than the last three strikes, straining his eyes to see the pass. Once the Shah's front ranks reached it, there would be no chance to slip back in and join Kachiun. The Shah's army advanced like a plug being forced into a bottle and there was not much time left before the pass was blocked. Tsubodai hesitated, his thoughts spinning. If the Shah continued at that speed, he would leave the flying columns behind and punch his way through to Otrar. Kachiun's four thousand would surely not stop such a mass. It was true that Tsubodai could continue the attacks on the rear as they advanced, and he knew that was a sound decision. He and his men could snatch thousands from the helpless ranks, and the Shah would be unable to stop them. Even then, there were two other passes to go round the army. Tsubodai could lead the minghaans through and still support Genghis at Otrar.

It was not enough. Though the Mongol riders had killed thousands, the Shah's army barely shuddered as they closed ranks over the dead and moved on. When they reached the plain before Otrar, Genghis would be left with the same problem Tsubodai had been sent to solve. The Shah would hit the khan from the front, while the Otrar garrison waited at his back.

Tsubodai led his men in once more, loosing arrows a thousand at a time. Without warning, another minghaan crossed his path and he was forced to pull up or crash into the young fool who led them. Arrows soared out of the Shah's ranks as soon as they saw him slow, and this time dozens of warriors fell, their horses screaming and bloody. Tsubodai swore at the officer who had ridden across his line and caught a glimpse of the man's appalled expression as the two forces separated and swung away. It was not truly his fault, Tsubodai acknowledged. He had trained his own tuman for just such an attack, but it was hard to weave trails around the Shah without some confusion. It would not save the man from public disgrace when Tsubodai caught up with him later on.

The Shah's army reached the pass and Tsubodai's chance to dart in ahead of them had gone. He looked for Jelme, knowing the older general was riding his own weaving path, but he could not see him. Tsubodai watched the tail of the great host begin to shrink as the Shah passed to what he thought was safety. If anything, the stinging attacks on the flanks intensified as the minghaans had less ground to cover. As the tail shrank, they struck again and again and Tsubodai saw some of the wilder men lead attacks with swords, cutting right into the marching lines. The Arabs screamed and fought, holding them off as best they could, but with every pace, the numbers fell in Tsubodai's favor. There would be a moment when the flying columns outnumbered those left in the tail, and he decided then to cut it off completely.

He sent his freshest men off to pass on the order, but it was hardly necessary. The Mongols had gathered round the last of the Shah's army, harrying them so closely that they had almost stopped. The ground was red around the mouth of the pass, and Tsubodai saw limbs and bodies lying everywhere as the carnage grew.

Forty thousand Arabs were still in the column before the pass when a shudder rippled through them. Tsubodai cocked his head and thought he could hear screams in the distance, echoing back from the hills. Kachiun's attack had begun. Tsubodai's quiver was empty on his back and he drew his sword, determined to see the Shah's tail wither in the sun.

Warning shouts broke his concentration as Tsubodai led his men in again, this time directly across the face of the column. He had chosen a spot close to the pass itself, and his heart was hammering as he kicked his mount into a gallop. At first he did not hear the shouts, but his instincts were good and he looked up for the source, raising his sword to halt his men before the attack.

For an instant, Tsubodai swore under his breath. He could see riders and an awful suspicion followed that the Shah had kept a rear guard to surprise their attackers at just such a moment. The fear passed as quickly as it had come. He saw his own people riding and his heart lifted. Jochi still lived and Jebe rode with him.

Tsubodai looked around sharply with fresh eyes. Perhaps thirty thousand Arabs still struggled to reach the pass, hammered and struck on all sides. The minghaans really did swarm around them like wasps, Tsubodai thought, but even a bear could be brought down in the end. He was not needed there, though he could not leave without telling Jelme.

It seemed to take an age before he found his fellow general, bloody and battered, but jubilant as he too readied his men to ride in once more.

"Like sheep to a slaughter!" Jelme shouted as Tsubodai rode up. Concentrating on the battle, he had not yet seen the riders, and Tsubodai only nodded in their direction.

Jelme frowned and let his fingers drop to a long shaft that had struck him in the shoulder. It had passed through armor to cut his flesh just below the skin. Jelme worked furiously at it, trying to pull it free. Tsubodai came close and took the shaft, snapping it quickly and throwing the pieces down.

"Thank you," Jelme said. "Is it our missing generals?"

"Who else has two tumans in this place?" Tsubodai replied. "We could have used them before, but I shall send them around the passes to attack the Shah as he comes out."

"No," Jelme replied. "You and I can do that well enough. Let these latecomers take our leavings and follow the Shah into the pass. I am still fresh, General. I will fight again today."

Tsubodai grinned and clapped Jelme on the shoulder. He sent two scouts back to carry orders to Jebe and Jochi before peeling off and calling his men after him. The closest pass was little more than a mile away.

In just moments, the attack on the rear had ceased and the last of the Shah's bloody soldiers passed between the hills. As shadow crossed their faces at last, they looked fearfully back at the wild horsemen who rode so swiftly toward somewhere else. No one cheered to have survived it. They were filled with dark foreboding and as they looked behind at the swathe of dead they had left, another army rode closer and closer, ready to begin the killing again.

Tsubodai forced his mount over broken ground, heading up into the hills. The second pass was a narrow trail and the Shah might well have discounted it for so many men. Still, it served a rank of ten across, and as he climbed, Tsubodai looked at the farmlands below, seeing a wavering red slash marking the path of the battle, quickly drying to brown. Over it came the tumans of Jochi and Jebe, and even from that distance, Tsubodai could see they were riding slowly. He saw the tiny figures of his scouts reach them and the pace picked up.

Tsubodai's view was blocked after that and he did not see them follow the Shah into the pass. Kachiun would be out of arrows and still the army was too large for the forces of Genghis at Otrar. Yet Tsubodai was pleased with the killing. He had shown the strength of the columns on their own and the best way to act against a slow enemy. He looked ahead to where Jelme rode, urging on his men. Tsubodai smiled at the older man's enthusiasm and energy, still undimmed. Every warrior there knew that they might have another chance to attack if they could get through the hills before the Shah reached open ground. There would be no place for stinging wasps then, Tsubodai realized. With the right timing, they would hit the Shah's right flank with the best part of twenty thousand men. Most of their arrows had gone. Shields and swords would have to finish what they had begun.

CHAPTER FOURTEEN

IN THE MORNING SUN, Genghis turned quickly enough to make Khasar jump. When he saw it was his younger brother, the khan's face grew a fraction less terrible, but the visible strain remained. Genghis had lived on anger and frustration for two days, while his men fought and died beyond the southern hills. If the walls of Otrar had been a little less thick, he would have had the catapults working all that time. Instead, it would have been a pointless gesture and he had waited. The city was not as important as surviving the Shah's army, but inaction had worn his temper to bare bones.

"Give me good news," Genghis snapped.

Khasar hesitated and Genghis scowled as he saw it.

"Then give me whatever you have," he said.

"The scouts report a battle before the pass. The generals have thinned the Shah's men as you ordered, but the army is still mostly intact. Kachiun is ready with archers on the high slopes. They will kill many, but unless the army breaks and runs, the Shah will come through. You knew it would be so, brother."

He watched as Genghis clenched his left fist hard enough to make the arm shake.

"Tell me how to stop twenty thousand warriors falling on us from behind and I will stand in the Shah's path as he comes out," Genghis said.

Khasar looked away at the city that mocked their preparations. With the camp stripped of warriors, five full tumans waited for orders, and Genghis chafed at every wasted moment. He did not underestimate the risk he had taken. As well as his wives, his sons Ogedai and Tolui had been left without protection as he tried to wring every advantage from the forces available to him. As the sun had risen on a second day, only Khasar had dared speak to his brother, and he could offer no solution.

Khasar knew as well as his brother that if the Shah made it through the hills with his army, the garrison at Otrar would attack as soon as they saw his banners. The tumans would be crushed. Khasar knew he did not have the brilliance of Tsubodai or even the wits of Kachiun, but he could see only one order to give. They could not hold Otrar. All they could do was retreat, drawing all the generals with them. Still, he waited for Genghis.

The black smoke of the burning suburbs had dwindled to nothing over the previous days. The air was clean and hot as Genghis looked over his army. The city was silent as they waited for deliverance.

"There will be other years, brother," Kachiun said at last. "Other battles."

"You would have me retreat, Khasar?" Genghis turned to his brother once more.

Khasar shrugged. "Better than being killed. If you take the tumans ten miles north, this Shah will join the garrison at Otrar and then at least we will face one army, with no one to attack the rear."

Genghis snorted in disdain for the idea. "Miles of plains and mountains that they know better than we do. They would batter us all the way home, and even my generals cannot stop so many. Yet if I can reach this pass, the Shah will not be able to maneuver. Even now, it would be hard to reach him before the sun sets, brother. Time is killing us."

Genghis fell silent suddenly, as a thought struck him. "The man who was your second, Samuka. Is he loyal?"

Khasar narrowed his eyes, wondering what Genghis was thinking. "Of course," he replied.

Genghis nodded sharply, making a decision. "Give him five thousand men and have him hold this place until I return. He does not have to win the battle, just prevent them from entering the field. Tell him I need time and that he must win it for me."

Khasar did not reply at first. Chagatai's tuman was closer to the city than Samuka's men, but Khasar knew Genghis would not send his son to certain death, as he seemed willing to do with Samuka.

"Very well, brother. I will tell him," he said. Genghis was already mounting his horse and turning it to take his place at the head of the army. Khasar rode back to the ranks, cutting across at a gallop to reach Samuka.

He found his old second in command standing with Ho Sa, discussing the riding order. Their faces lit up as they saw Khasar, and his heart sank at what he must say. With a gesture, Khasar drew them apart from the other officers and spoke in a low voice.

"My lord Genghis orders you to stay behind, Samuka. Take five thousand of the best archers and hold the city until we return."

Ho Sa stiffened as if he had been struck. Samuka's dark eyes searched Khasar's for a moment. All three men knew it was a death sentence. The garrison would cut them to pieces in their desperation to get out of the city.

"They will do their best to break through," Khasar went on. "It will be bloody work."

Samuka nodded, already resigned. Five thousand men would not be enough to hold two gates. As a thought struck him, he glanced to Ho Sa.

"I do not need this one, General. Let him go with you." Samuka smiled tiredly. "He is useless anyway and I will not need him here."

Ho Sa suffered through a moment of utter weakness. He did not want to die in a land he barely knew. Samuka had given him a chance to live. Khasar looked away rather than watch the turmoil on Ho Sa's face.

"I will stay," Ho Sa said.

Samuka looked to the skies and blew air out of puffed cheeks. "You are a fool then," Samuka said. He turned to Khasar and took a deep breath, his manner suddenly brisk. "How long must I hold?"

Khasar gave no sign that he had noticed Ho Sa's struggle. "Perhaps a day. I will relieve you myself."

Both Ho Sa and Samuka bowed their heads, accepting the task before them. On impulse, Khasar reached out and gripped Ho Sa's shoulder. He had known the Xi Xia officer for many years, ever since the first raids into Chin territory.

"Stay alive, brother," Khasar said. "I will come if I can."

"I will be watching for you," Ho Sa said, his voice rough. His face showed none of the fear that churned in his stomach.

Genghis was already at the head of his army, staring coldly across at the three men. He waited until Samuka shouted orders to five minghaan officers and they rode clear of the main army. Khasar delayed a while to collect four arrows from each warrior of Chagatai's tuman, passing them on in bundles. Samuka and Ho Sa would need every one. If they could hold the Otrar garrison even until dark, perhaps Genghis would have justified the waste of men.

As the order to remain spread among the five thousand, many heads turned to Khasar. They knew what the orders meant. He sat like a stone and was pleased to see no shouted arguments. They had learned discipline, his people, even unto death.

Genghis dug in his heels and his pony leapt forward. Chagatai and Khasar went with him toward the brown hills where the Shah battled the generals. Behind them, the people of Otrar cheered on the walls, and only the small, grim force with Samuka and Ho Sa rode back, dwarfed by the city.

The front ranks of the Shah's army marched out of the pass into bright sunlight, roaring at having survived. Arrows had fallen on them in tens of thousands as they forced their way through. Their shields bristled with spent shafts and many of the men used knives to cut them to stubs as they strode on toward Otrar.

Behind them, there was still screaming in the valley as the Mongols tore at the rear of his army, perhaps hoping the Arabs would panic and break. Shah Ala-ud-Din Mohammed smiled grimly at the thought. There was no shame in dying well and his men were strong in their faith. Not one of them had run from the bloody swords of the enemy. The Mongol bows had been silent at the back, and that was Allah's mercy, at least. The Shah wondered if they had used up their arrows on Khalifa's riders, and in his embattled state of mind, he hoped so. It was a better end for the desert thief than betrayal.

It had taken a long time to march through the storm of shafts from Mongols perched like hawks on the cliffs. The sun was long past noon and the Shah did not know if the devils would continue their assaults into darkness. Otrar was no more than twenty miles north, and he would push his men on until the city was in sight. He would make his camp where the people of the city would know he had come to save them.

He heard fresh death cries behind and snarled to himself. The Mongols were everywhere, and though his men had locked shields, it was hard to have an enemy killing where you could not see him. Many in the ranks looked back fearfully, but they were the best of those he could summon to war. Every one of them had fought in battles and raids. Only death would stop them reaching the city.

From his high position on the elephant's back, Ala-ud-Din was among the first to see Tsubodai and Jelme coming out of the mountains on his right side. He cursed under his breath, calling for his noble messengers once more. He cast a quick glance over his army, noting the strengths and regiments to hand, then nodded to the first man to ride close.

"Tell my son Jelaudin to destroy the flanking force. He may have twelve elephants and ten thousand men under General Faisal. Tell him I will be watching."

The rider pressed fingers to his lips and heart before racing away to pass on the order. Ala-ud-Din turned his gaze away from the right flank, knowing his son would ride them down.

The Shah smiled grimly as his army left the mountain pass behind. Nothing could stop him reaching Otrar. Somewhere ahead Genghis rode, but he had left it too late. Even if he was on his way, Inalchuk's garrison would hamstring him. The Mongols were fast and more mobile than Shah Mohammed could believe, but he outnumbered them still and his men would not run while he lived.

It would be a fine battle and Ala-ud-Din was surprised to discover he was looking forward to seeing the khan crushed. It was almost with regret that he must kill such a daring enemy. The last year had been more exciting and rewarding than any of the three before it. He sighed to himself, remembering a childhood tale of a Shah who feared black depression almost as much as the giddy heights of overconfidence. When he asked his advisers to find him a solution, they had forged a simple ring with the words "This too shall pass" cut into the gold. There was truth in such simplicity and the Shah was content as his battered army strode on to Otrar.

Tsubodai's columns formed into a wide charging line as they came out of the hills. The head of the Shah's army was already in sight, but

Tsubodai halted his men and made them pass arrows to the front ranks. There were very few. He had enough for three quick shots from five hundred men before it was down to swords.

Jelme came to ride at his side as the ponies surged forward.

"Jochi and Jebe are on the tail of this snake," Jelme said. "Can we cut off the head?"

"All things are possible," Tsubodai shouted over his shoulder. "I can hardly believe this enemy has weathered so many attacks without losing formation. It is one thing more to know, General: they have extraordinary discipline, almost as good as our own. Even with a fool for a leader, they will be hard to break."

They had just over a mile to ride before they hit the right wing. Tsubodai calculated the time in his head. At that speed, they could reach the lines in two hundred heartbeats.

As they bore down on the army spilling out of the pass, Tsubodai saw a great piece of it break off and face them. He frowned at a line of elephants coming to the fore, jabbed and whipped by their handlers. He felt rather than saw his men hesitate and shouted encouragement to them.

"The heads are armored. Aim for the legs," he called. "Anything that lives can be killed by us." Those who heard grinned as the orders flew across the lines. The archers bent their bows in readiness, testing their strength.

The elephants began to lumber forward, picking up speed quickly. Tsubodai saw foot soldiers running alongside them. The elephants were terrifying as they grew and grew before his eyes. Tsubodai readied his sword, swinging it lightly along his horse's flank, so that it swished the air. He could see the tumans under Genghis coming from the north and wondered idly how the khan had left Otrar at his back.

"Kill the elephants first!" he roared to his archers. They were ready and he felt his heartbeat pounding in his chest and throat. The sun was dipping toward the horizon and it was a good day to be alive.

Samuka had arranged his five thousand in two groups at either end of the city, each facing the high gates set into the walls. Ho Sa commanded the second and Samuka approved of the cold face the Xi Xia officer had learned in his time with the tribes. Once both men were in position, Samuka became calm. His men had assembled rough barriers braced against rocks that would protect them from arrows while they held the gate. Samuka sighed to himself. Genghis had left him only one advantage and he would use it to the best of his ability. He ran a silk banner through his fingers, enjoying the feel of it. He could see dark faces watching him from the high towers of Otrar, and he did not think he would have long to wait.

Genghis was not more than a few miles to the south when Samuka heard the garrison's orders echoing inside the walls. He nodded to himself and checked his officers were ready one more time. They were as grim as their general and no one was foolish enough to think they would survive the battle to come.

The iron door in the eastern wall opened slowly. At the same time, ranks of dark bowmen appeared on the walls, thousands of them. Samuka stared up indifferently, judging the numbers. In the days previously, the Mongols had cleared a path to the gate, using pikes to pull down the rubble of charred houses. It had been a good plan at the time, but they had made it easier for the inhabitants to come storming out. Samuka snapped an order and his men readied their bows, placing arrows carefully at their feet where they could be snatched up at speed. One of the makeshift wooden barriers collapsed and Samuka heard an officer swear as he sent men to brace it. Samuka smiled tightly. Genghis had placed him there and he would not be moved easily.

He did not know if the garrison would come at just this one place or try to force Ho Sa's gate as well, hidden from his sight. Either way, his path was set as he sat his pony just out of range and watched the iron gates pushed back. In the sunlit city beyond, ranks of well-armored men sat good Arab horses. Samuka squinted at them. They were the ones he had to destroy. Infantry could not reach Genghis in time.

For a man who loved horseflesh, it was a bitter order, but Samuka raised his head.

"Kill the horses," he shouted, his voice carrying far. Like an echo, it was repeated, though for such a small force, there could not have been many who did not hear him. The Mongol ponies were little use in a crescent formation that could not move, but it was comforting to sit his saddle and Samuka would not have wanted to stand on the ground with an enemy coming at him.

Voices roared in the city and the enemy lunged out. The gateway compressed their ranks, so that only five at a time could hit the gallop. Samuka raised his left hand, looking for the moment. A hundred men bent their bows at the gaps in the barricades. He knew he had to stagger the volleys to conserve the stock of arrows, but he wanted the first one to be terrifying.

The garrison had planned well enough, Samuka saw. They widened their rank as they came through the gate, getting as many men out as possible in the shortest time. Samuka watched impassively as they crossed the marker he had left at a hundred paces.

"Horses first!" he shouted again, and dropped his hand.

The crack that followed made his heart race. A hundred long shafts soared out, hardly slowing before they hit the emerging horsemen. The first rank collapsed like a burst waterskin, horses and men falling on the dusty ground. Samuka raised his hand again and dropped it almost immediately, knowing the next hundred would be ready. Nothing could resist such hammering blows. Though the Arabs wore armor and carried shields, they fell hard with their horses, then more arrows impaled those who staggered to their feet.

The air above the gates filled with whirring shafts as the archers on the walls bent and loosed. Samuka ducked instinctively, though the barriers protected him. Those that shot high dropped on the shields of his men. They were experienced and took the blows with a light hand, soaking up the impacts.

Still the riders came out. Samuka sent volley after volley at the lines until there were hills of dead men and horses before Otrar. Some of his men died as arrows from the walls beat past their guard, but it was only a few.

Lulls came as the garrison used their own wooden barricades to clear the bodies. It took time and the Mongols were pleased to wait before beginning the slaughter once more. Even then, Samuka despaired as he estimated the arrows remaining. If every shot took a life, it would still come to swords in the end.

The brutal exchange went on. If the garrison were willing to ride straight out, Samuka could at least hold them until dark, he was almost sure. His confidence was on the rise when he saw fresh movement on the walls. He glanced up quickly, assuming it was a change of men, or arrows being brought up to them. He grimaced at the sight of ropes spilling over the crest and soldiers clambering down, burning their hands in the need to reach the ground quickly.

Samuka swore, though he had expected it. Already, hundreds were forming up out of his range, and all the time, his men sent shafts into the gateway, killing screaming riders as they struggled to break out. Samuka summoned a scout and sent him to Ho Sa on the other side of the city. If the warriors there were still untouched, he could bring a few hundred around and sweep the new threat away. As Samuka watched, more and more ropes became black with climbing men and the ranks on the ground grew thicker and more confident. His heart sank as he saw them begin to run toward his position, swords and shields bright in the afternoon sun. Once more he dropped his hand to send arrows at riders urging their mounts over their own dead. He could not maneuver until the arrows were gone.

If the Otrar officers had decided to take a wide route around him, Samuka would have been forced to cut them off. It was too early to allow them to ride in support of the Shah. Samuka watched them carefully, but in his rage and excitement, the governor had clearly ordered them to sweep the Mongols away. They came at the run and Samuka had his mobile five hundred meet them with arrows as they closed, the shafts tearing through their ranks. More and more climbed out of the city, and Samuka clenched his jaw in anger and frustration as the first garrison soldiers met his.

While his men fought savagely, four hundred Mongol riders came racing round the city and charged straight at the infantry of Otrar. At first they cut through them, loosing one vicious wave of shafts before they drew their swords and fell to the killing. The garrison buckled under the onslaught, but every Mongol warrior was met by three or four Arab soldiers. Samuka saw their numbers dwindle as the charge came to a shuddering halt. Assailed on all sides, they fought well and no one broke, but the Arabs cut them down until just a few dozen remained in the press, hacking desperately at anything they could reach. They too fell at last and Samuka groaned aloud as almost ten thousand of the garrison re-formed. He had one last bone to throw and it would not be enough.

Inside the iron gate, he could see lines of fresh cavalry, shouting and holding up their shields. They knew they had the victory.

Wearily, Samuka pulled the silk banner from where he had stuffed it under a saddle cloth. The breeze made it flutter as he raised it over his head. He looked up at the hill behind the city and felt a shadow pass over his face before he heard the crack of the catapults.

Pottery balls shattered against the gate into Otrar, each as large as a man could carry. Samuka held out an arrow with the head bound in oil-soaked cloth and let a warrior light it from a shuttered lamp. He saw two more clay pots break in the gate, sending a horseman tumbling. Samuka sighted carefully and let the arrow go.

He was rewarded by a rush of flame that enveloped the gate and incinerated all those trying to come through it. The Chin fire oil was terrible to see, the heat so intense that many of the Mongol ponies danced back from it until they were brought under control. The catapults on the hill sent more clay pots over the heads of his men, adding to the inferno until the gate itself began to glow dull red. Samuka knew he could ignore the gate for a time. No one could cross those flames and live. He had intended to join Ho Sa on the other side while the first one roared in flames, but the plan was ruined by the mass of soldiers who had climbed down.

As his men turned their bows on the Arab infantry and crumpled them, Samuka shook his head to clear it. Foot soldiers could not trouble Genghis, he reminded himself. One sharp blast on a scout horn had his men turning their horses to him.

Samuka used his sword to point and kicked his mount forward, passing close enough to the fiery gate to feel its warmth on his cheek. Even as he did so, the city vomited fresh soldiers down the ropes to replace the dead, but no enemy remained to face them.

It was strange to leave a battle behind. Otrar was not a small city and Samuka saw blurred figures on the walls as he and his men raced along in their shadow, alone with the rhythm of hooves and the smell of smoke. He did not know how long the supply of Chin fire oil would last, and he suffered at the thought that a better thinker would have found a way to hold both gates.

He heard Ho Sa's men before he saw them, and Samuka drew his bow from its holder, an extension of his strong right arm. The walls rushed by and the sound grew until he came upon a scene of bloody chaos.

Ho Sa had struggled to hold the second gate, Samuka saw at a glance. Without the catapults, he and his men had been driven back by waves of soldiers. They roared at the Mongols, berserk to the point of pulling arrows from their own flesh as they marched and leaving bloody footsteps on the ground.

Samuka's last thousand men hit them from behind, cutting into the Arab regiments in an impact so colossal that they smashed almost through to Ho Sa's core of warriors in one sweep. Samuka felt them slowing around him as horses were killed, or hemmed in too close by dying enemies. He reached for an arrow, but found nothing and threw down the bow as he drew his sword once more.

He could see Ho Sa fighting for every step as the warriors were pushed back. Samuka grunted and hacked with all his strength to reach him, but more and more men came rushing round the city after him and he felt as if he were being swallowed in a dark and roaring sea.

The sun was dipping toward the west. Samuka realized he had been fighting for hours, but it was not long enough. The second gate was a hundred paces away and no flames burned there. He could see horsemen coming out and they did not join the others. Samuka cried out in rage and despair as they streamed away in a ragged column. Even a small number of cavalry hitting the khan's rear could mean the difference between life and death.

Samuka blinked blood out of his eyes as he kicked a man away from his right stirrup. Of the men Khasar had left him, just a few hundred still lived. They had killed many more than their own number, but this was the end. Somehow, Samuka had thought he would survive it, despite the odds. The image of his body cooling on the ground was beyond his imagination.

Samuka shouted Ho Sa's name across the swarming heads and hands of men clutching at him. He could feel their fingers tugging at his legs, and he kicked wildly and slashed with his sword as Ho Sa saw him. Perhaps for a moment, the Xi Xia officer thought he was calling for aid, but Samuka gestured with his sword after the fleeing cavalry. As Ho Sa turned to follow the gesture, Samuka saw him gashed across the neck, blood gushing as he collapsed.

Samuka howled in fury as he brought his blade down on fingers digging into his thighs. Bearded faces clustered so thickly around him that his horse came to a halt, and Samuka felt a sudden calm, mingling with surprise. Khasar had not come back. He was lost and alone and all his men were dying.

Hands gained purchase on some part of his armor, and to his horror, Samuka felt himself begin to slip. He killed another man with a wild swing, but then his arm was trapped and the sword torn from his hand. His horse lurched with unseen wounds and the men around him were so close that he could see their red throats as they yelled. Samuka slid into the mass, still flailing. The setting sun vanished as he fell at the feet of stamping, stabbing men. The pain was worse than he had feared. He told himself that he had done all he could, but it was still a hard death and the garrison of Otrar was out.

CHAPTER FIFTEEN

EVEN OVER THE NOISE OF GALLOPING HOOVES, Tsubodai could hear the crackle of feathers at his ear as he drew his bow. He rose from the saddle and sighted on the front legs of an elephant that was coming at him like a landslide. On every side, his men copied the action, and when he released, a black blur of arrows snapped out. None of the warriors had to think about their actions. They had trained for it ever since they had been tied to a sheep and taught to ride at two or three years old. Before the first arrows hit, they had a second on the string. Powerful cords of muscle swelled in their right shoulders as they pulled back again.

The elephants bellowed and reared in pain, swinging their heads from side to side. Tsubodai saw shafts sink into the massive gray legs, catching them in full stride and breaking the rhythm of the charge. Half of the enormous animals stumbled as a leg buckled. Others raised their trunks and showed yellow tusks in enraged challenge. If anything the speed increased, but the second wave of arrows cracked out and the elephants shuddered with the impacts. Arrows snagged between their legs, wrenching at wounds.

Tsubodai reached automatically for another arrow, but his fingers closed on an empty quiver. He was almost at the Shah's cavalry by then, and he dropped his bow back into the stiff leather fold on his saddle and raised his sword over his right shoulder, ready to chop down.

The men around him loosed one last shaft at the approaching lines, and Tsubodai stood in his stirrups as he saw the closest elephants rear on their hind legs, wild with pain. Their handlers screamed, beating wildly as they were spun around. His heart seemed to slow as he saw one of them plucked off a broad back and thrown to the ground with appalling force. The elephants turned in agony from the line of galloping warriors, knocking down horses and men.

Tsubodai shouted in triumph as the massive animals retreated blindly into the Shah's ranks. They cut lines through the advancing soldiers as if they waded through thick grass, using their tusks to toss aside fully grown men. Nothing could stop them in their madness. In just moments, Tsubodai faced broken front ranks, dazed and bloodied by the passing beasts. Some of the Arabs recovered quickly enough to send their own arrows whirring from double-curved bows. Mongol warriors and horses were cut down, but the others showed their teeth and rode. In the last instants before the forces met, Tsubodai picked his man and guided his pony with knees alone.

The Mongol warriors went over the first line into chaos. Tsubodai took the head of one soldier, then almost lost his seat as another aimed a blow at him and he ducked under it. As Tsubodai rose, he held out his blade and his shoulder wrenched at the impact against armor. His low stance and weight kept him in the saddle as an Arab fell and Tsubodai found himself in one of the bloody tracks the elephants had left. He could still see them charging away, tormented and blind to the destruction in their wake. Tsubodai silently thanked the monstrous animals as he looked around for another enemy.

The Shah's ranks had been shocked into immobility by the rampaging elephants. Arab archers scattered, dying as they bawled orders in fear while the Mongols came in hard, taking wounds without a sound while they hacked and chopped. Good blades were ruined on Arab armor, but their arms rose and fell without respite, and if a shield stopped one strike, they whipped another in above or below, cutting legs and throats. They were faster than those who faced them. Tsubodai clashed with a huge, bearded Arab, fighting in a mindless frenzy. Tsubodai could smell the man's sweat as he used his pony's shoulder to knock him off balance. In the instant before he was past, Tsubodai saw the curved sword had no guard and let his blade slide, cutting three fingers cleanly so that the weapon spun away. The Shah's men were large and Tsubodai wondered if they had been picked for their strength more than skill. Their blows hammered at his warriors, but again and again, Mongols ducked or swayed away, cutting back where they could and moving on. Many of the Shah's soldiers took three or four wounds before blood loss felled them.

Tsubodai saw hundreds of foot soldiers gather around a horseman riding a black stallion. Even at a distance, he could see the animal was very fine. Its rider was yelling orders and men formed up with him, making a wedge. Tsubodai braced for a counterattack, but instead they raised shields and began a fighting retreat back to the main lines.

The Mongol general did not have to give new orders. His minghaan officers were on their own and four of them sensed the withdrawal and raced to attack. Arrows would have slaughtered the retreating soldiers, but there were none left and the Arab ranks stayed together in good order, leaving hills of the dead behind them.

In the distance, Tsubodai heard scout horns moaning across the land. He looked up and saw the tumans of Genghis riding in. The khan had entered the field at last and Tsubodai wiped his eyes of sweat, filled with a terrible pleasure.

His men had shattered those sent against them, but Tsubodai still chafed. The orderly withdrawal had done its work, preventing him from collapsing the lines in on themselves and cutting the head from the Shah's main army. He and his men milled around on the edge of the battle, some still engaged in fighting the last few knots of weary infantry. Tsubodai wondered who the young officer had been who had prevented a complete rout. The man had held his soldiers together in the fire of battle, and Tsubodai added the knowledge to what he knew of the enemy. The Shah had at least one competent officer under his command, it seemed.

The minghaans re-formed in a landscape of broken men, littered armor and weapons. Some of them dismounted to yank precious arrows out of flesh, but only a few were good enough to be used again. Tsubodai felt his heartbeat settle and took in the battlefield, judging where he was needed. The Shah's army was out of the passes and he could see the tumans of Jebe and Jochi cutting them bloody in the rear. The sun was deep in the west and he thought Genghis would hardly have time to attack before the light faded.

Tsubodai nodded to himself. He could see the last of the Shah's infantry were back on the flank, staring out balefully at the Mongol warriors milling amongst the bodies. Most of the elephants had vanished, though some lay kicking where they had been hit with more arrows from the Shah's own ranks, rather than letting them smash through. Tsubodai was tired and he ached in a dozen places, but the battle was far from over.

"Form on me!" he shouted, and those who heard responded. As the Shah's ranks marched past, fresh foot soldiers came under Tsubodai's cold gaze. He could hardly believe it, but the Shah's soldiers were so determined to reach Otrar that they pressed on regardless of the attacking forces.

Tsubodai shook his head. The generals had shown the strength of mobile forces, with the officers acting on their own. Yet the Shah's army lumbered on, holding to a single command no matter what faced them. Tsubodai thought the Shah as ruthless as Genghis himself in the way he spent his men.

As Jelme's men formed with his into columns, Tsubodai saw frightened faces turn toward him in the Shah's army. They knew what was coming, even as he made the decision. He watched them bend their bows and make ready.

Tsubodai reached for the scout's horn at his neck, only to find it in two pieces, cut by a blow he could not remember. He swore to himself, blind to the grins his words produced in those close by.

"With me!" he bellowed. To his left, Jelme's men dug in their heels and rode.

Genghis had pushed hard for twenty miles to be in that place, changing to fresh mounts when the battle was in sight. He saw the Shah had come clear of the hills, but there was no help for that. He looked along the lines to where his son Chagatai galloped and further to Khasar. Fully fifty thousand men rode at his back, with a great tail of spare horses riding behind them. Yet they faced an army that stretched further than he could see. Tsubodai's flags were barely visible on his left, attacking the flanks. Behind the Arab host, dust clouds roiled and raged. Genghis thought Samuka and Ho Sa would be dead by then, but Otrar was far away and its garrison could not reach the battle that day. He had done all he could, but this was the final fling of the bones. It came to this and he had no other plan except to hit the Shah's column and envelop it in horns.

Genghis snapped an order to a bannerman and heard the fluttering as a gold flag went up. All along the line, thousands of bows creaked.

The Shah's army tried to brace for the impact, though their officers urged them on. No one wanted to face these grim warriors again, but there was nowhere to go. They screamed defiance as the gold flag dipped and the air blackened.

The Mongol lines struck at full speed, roaring, the sheer pace as dangerous as the weapons they carried. The wide Mongol horns spilled around the head of the Shah's army, racing along the flanks and cutting in. The light was already gray as the armies met, the sun sinking over the west. The evening was clear and perfect as the Mongols flung themselves at the host of their enemy.

Shah Ala-ud-Din Mohammed cried out in shock as a line of Mongols cut right through to him. His mounted guard slaughtered them to a man, but he was surrounded on all sides and half his army could not bring their weapons to bear. The Shah was close to panic as he looked in every direction. It would be dark very soon and yet the Mongols still fought like madmen. They did not make a sound, even when life was ripped from them. The Shah could only shake his head at such a display. Did they not feel pain? His son Jelaudin believed they were more like dumb animals than men, and he could have been right.

Still, the Shah's army moved, staggering as they fought the desire to run from this enemy. Ala-ud-Din saw bright columns of his men being smashed to pieces on the flanks, and always the rumble of the Mongols in the rear drove them on.

More and more of the khan's warriors died as they tried to fight their way to the center. The Shah's soldiers held formation and cut them to pieces as they came galloping through. They could not match the Mongol speed, but their shields stopped many of the arrows and those who came in were hacked and slashed as they went, sent reeling back time and again. As the light faded, Ala-ud-Din exulted in the enemy dead as his elephant passed over them.

Darkness came and for a time it was a vision of hell. Men cried out as they struggled in a heaving mass of shadows and knives. The Shah's army seemed to be surrounded by a growling djinn, the thunder of hooves in their ears. Marching soldiers jerked around as they struggled on, terrified that the noise of riders was coming straight at them. Above their heads, the stars were clear and bright as the crescent moon rose slowly.

The Shah thought that the Mongol khan might continue right to dawn, and he prayed constantly as he gave his orders, hoping that he would survive the dark hours. Once again his guards had to fight off a stray column of raiding warriors, killing eighty or so men and sending the rest galloping away to be cut down by others. The sons of the ancient houses were enjoying themselves, Ala-ud-Din could see. Their teeth flashed as they mimed good cuts to their friends. The army around them was being battered to pieces, but such noble sons would not count those losses. Allah gave and took away as he pleased, after all.

Ala-ud-Din thought dawn would reveal a bloody tatter of the host he had commanded. Only the thought of his enemy suffering as much kept him resolute.

He did not notice the sound dwindle at first. It felt like he had lived with the thump of hooves in all directions forever. When it began to fade, he was still calling for his sons, for fresh reports. The army marched on and Otrar would surely be somewhere close before dawn.

At last one of the Shah's senior men shouted that the khan had withdrawn. Ala-ud-Din gave thanks for his deliverance. He had known horsemen could not attack at night. With hardly any light from the moon, they could not coordinate their blows without crashing into one another. He listened to news as his scouts came in, estimating their distance from Otrar and passing on every detail they had seen of the khan's position.

Ala-ud-Din prepared to make camp. Dawn would bring an end to it and the cursed Mongols would have left their arrows behind in the bodies of his men. With Otrar in sight, he would widen his lines and bring more swords to bear on their stinging attacks. In the last hour, they had lost as many men as he had, he was certain. Before that, they had gutted his host. He looked around at the marching lines, wondering how many had survived the fight through the mountains. He had once seen a hunting party follow a wounded lion as it dragged itself away from their spears. The animal had left a trail of blood as wide as itself as it crawled on its torn belly. He could not escape the vision of his own army in just such a state, the red smear bright behind them. He gave the order to halt at last, and he could hear the massed sigh of thousands of men allowed to rest. The Shah began to dismount, but as he did so, he saw lights begin to spring up to the east. He knew the pinpoints of an army's fires well, and he stayed on the back of the elephant as more and more sprang into existence until they looked like distant stars. There was his enemy, resting and waiting for the dawn.

Around Ala-ud-Din, his own men began to make fires with wood and dried dung from the camel backs. The morning would see an end to it. The Shah heard voices calling the faithful to prayer and nodded fiercely to himself. Allah was with them still and the Mongol khan was bleeding too.

As the moon crossed the black sky, Genghis gathered his generals around a fire. The mood was not jubilant as they waited for him to speak. Their tumans had slaughtered many of the Shah's men, but their own losses were appalling. In the last hour before darkness, four thousand veteran warriors had been killed. They had cut their way almost to the Shah himself, but then the Arab swords had gathered against them and dug them out.

Jebe and Jochi had come into the camp together, greeted by Kachiun and Khasar while Genghis merely stared. Tsubodai and Jelme rose to congratulate the two young men, having heard the story of the long ride as it spread through the camp.

Chagatai too had heard the news and his expression was surly as he watched Jelme clap his older brother on the back. He could not understand why they seemed so pleased. He too had fought, following his father's orders rather than disappearing for days at a time. He, at least, had been where Genghis needed him. Chagatai had hoped to see Jebe and Jochi humiliated for their absence, but even their late arrival at the Shah's rear ranks was being treated as a stroke of genius. He sucked his front teeth, looking to his father.

Genghis sat cross-legged, with a skin of airag on his hip and a bowl of sour cheese curds on his lap. The back of his left hand was caked in blood, and his right shin was bound tightly but still seeped. As Chagatai turned his face from the foolish praise of his brother, Genghis cleaned the bowl with a finger and chewed the last of it. Silence fell as he put the bowl aside and sat perfectly still.

"Samuka and Ho Sa must be dead by now," Genghis said at last. "The garrison at Otrar cannot be far away, and I do not know how many survived the fire and arrows."

"They won't stop for darkness," Kachiun said. "Perhaps they will walk their horses, but they'll still reach the Shah before dawn." As he spoke, Kachiun stared out into the night, to where they could expect the garrison to arrive. Further still, he could see the fires of the Shah's camp, and even after so much death, there were still hundreds of the pinpoints of light, just a few miles away. No doubt Arab scouts were already riding back to join with the Otrar garrison and lead them in. The darkness would hide them well enough.

"I have scouts out in a ring around us," Genghis said. "If they attack tonight, there will be no surprises."

"Who attacks at night?" Khasar said. His thoughts were with Samuka and Ho Sa and he barely looked up from the dry goat meat he forced between his lips.

In the light of the flames, Genghis turned a cold gaze on his brother.

"We do," he said.

Khasar swallowed the meat faster than he had intended, but Genghis went on before he could reply.

"What choice do we have? We know where they are and the arrows are all gone anyway. If we strike from all sides, we will not foul each other's lines."

Khasar cleared his throat and spoke thickly. "The moon is weak tonight, brother. How could we see flags or know how the battle is going?"

Genghis raised his head. "You will know when they break, or when you are killed. It is the only choice left to us. Would you have me wait until a garrison of twenty thousand men joins them at dawn—fresh men who have not fought as we have?" In the firelight, he looked around at his generals. Many of them moved stiffly and Jelme's right arm was wrapped in bloody cloth, still wet.

"If I know Samuka, there won't be half that number," Khasar muttered, but Genghis did not reply.

Tsubodai cleared his throat and Genghis's eyes slid over to the young general.

"My lord khan, the flying columns worked well when we had arrows. In the night, each attack would be met by men with shields in solid ranks. We could lose them all."

Genghis snorted, but Tsubodai went on, his quiet voice calming the others.

"One column could cut its way in, but we saw that today. They do not run from us, these Arabs, not easily. Every step brings more and more men onto the flank of the charge until it is overwhelmed."

"You have an alternative?" Genghis snapped. Though his voice was hard, he was listening. He knew Tsubodai's sharp mind and respected it.

"We need to confuse them, lord. We can do that with a false second attack, circling around. They will send men to hold and we will roll them up from our side."

Genghis shook his head, considering. Tsubodai pressed on.

"What if we had a small number of men drive horses at the Shah's left wing, lord? Have them take all the spare mounts and make as much noise as they can. When the Shah commits his soldiers there, we attack the right with everything we have. It might make a difference."

He waited as Genghis thought it through, unaware that he was holding his breath.

"It is a good plan," he began. All the men at the fire stiffened as they heard a scout's horn sound in the night. Almost in response, a roar sounded in the distance, coming toward them. While they talked and ate, the Shah had attacked their fires.

As one, the generals surged to their feet, keen to get back to their men.

"This is simpler, though, Tsubodai," Khasar said as he passed.

Tsubodai grinned at the insolent tone. He had already planned for such an attack, and the warriors were ready.

CHAPTER SIXTEEN

AS HE TROTTED THROUGH THE DARKNESS, Jelaudin stared at the fires ahead of him. The men running at his stirrups were exhausted, but he had pressed his father for one more massed charge, knowing that their best chance lay in catching the Mongols asleep. He seethed at the thought of his father's precious guard still barely blooded. The Shah had refused his demands to have them accompany him, just when they would have justified their existence. Jelaudin cursed his father and Khalifa too, for losing the cavalry, then pressed away his anger to concentrate. Just one sweep through the enemy camp could be enough to break them at last. The moon was hidden by clouds and Jelaudin rode slowly over broken ground, waiting for the uproar that would follow.

It came sooner than he expected, as enemy scouts blew warning notes before they were cut down. Jelaudin drew his sword and risked his neck with a faster pace. The running men fell behind as he aimed his mount at the Mongol fires.

The khan had made only a rough camp after days of fighting. Jelaudin saw the left flank was a mass of lights, revealing the presence of many men. The nights were cold and they would be clustered close to the flames. On the right, the night fires were more widely spaced, dwindling to just a few points of light on the furthest edge. It was there that he led his men, racing to take revenge for the battering they had suffered.

He heard the Mongols rise against the attack, howling in their mindless anger. Jelaudin shouted a challenge into the night, echoed by his men. The fires came closer and suddenly there were men on all sides and the forces met. Jelaudin had time to shout in surprise before his stallion was cut from under him and he went flying.

Tsubodai waited with Jochi, Jebe, and Chagatai. It had been his idea to arrange the fires to draw in a careless enemy. Where the lights were thick, he had just a few men tending them. On the dark right flank, veteran tumans clustered with their ponies, far from warmth. They did not heed the night cold. For those who had been born on the frozen plains of home, it was nothing to them. With a great shout, they charged the Arab ranks coming in.

As the two forces came together, the Arabs were sent reeling, smashed from their feet by men who had fought and trained from the earliest years. Their right arms hardly tired as they punched through the enemy and rocked them back. Tsubodai bellowed orders to advance and they trotted forward, shoulder to shoulder, their mounts stepping delicately over dying men.

The moon rose above them, but the attack was broken quickly and the Arab force sent streaming back to their main camp. As they ran, they looked over their shoulders, terrified that the Mongols would ride them down. Not half of their number made it clear, though Jelaudin was one of them, humiliated and on foot. He staggered back to his father, still dazed from the chaos and fear. In the distance, the Mongols finished off the wounded and waited patiently for the dawn.

Shah Ala-ud-Din paced his tent, glaring at his eldest son as he turned. Jelaudin stood nervously, wary of his father's anger.

"How did they know you would attack?" the Shah snapped suddenly. "There are no spies in the ranks, not here. It is impossible."

Still smarting from his failure, Jelaudin did not dare to reply. Privately, he thought the Mongols had merely prepared for the possibility of an attack, not known of one, but he could not seem to praise them while his father raged.

"You see now why I did not give you my personal guard?" the Shah demanded.

Jelaudin swallowed. If he had ridden in with five hundred horsemen, he did not think the rout would have been so easy or so complete. With an effort, he strangled a retort.

"You are wise, Father," he said. "Tomorrow they will take the fight to the enemy." He fell back a step as his father rounded on him and stood close enough for the bristles of his beard to touch his son's face.

"Tomorrow you and I are dead," the Shah snarled. "When the khan sees how many men I have left, he will fall on us and make an end to it."

Jelaudin was relieved when he heard a throat cleared at the entrance to the tent. His father's body servant, Abbas, stood in the lamplight, his eyes flickering from father to son and judging the mood within. Jelaudin made an impatient gesture for the man to leave, but Abbas ignored him, coming in and bowing to the Shah. Jelaudin saw he carried a sheaf of calfskin vellum and a pot of ink and he hesitated before ordering the man out.

Abbas touched his forehead, lips, and heart in respect to the Shah before placing the writing materials on a small table to one side. Jelaudin's father nodded, his fury still evident in his clenched jaw and flushed skin.

"What is this?" Jelaudin said at last.

"This is vengeance for the dead, Jelaudin. When I have put my name to it, this is an order for the assassins to rid my land of this khan."

His son felt a weight lift from his shoulders at the thought, though he repressed a shudder. The sect of Shia fanatics had a dark reputation, but his father was wise to bring them in.

"How much will you send them?" he said softly. His father bent over the thick parchment and did not reply at first as he read the words Abbas had prepared.

"I do not have time to negotiate. I have offered a note for a hundred thousand gold coins, to be redeemed from my own treasury. They will not refuse such a sum, even for a khan's head."

Jelaudin felt his hands grow clammy at the thought of so much gold. It was enough to build a great palace or begin a city. Yet he did not speak. His chance to break the Mongols had been wasted in the night.

Once the Shah had signed the note for gold, Abbas rolled the thick sheets together and bound them with a strip of leather, tying the knot expertly. He bowed very low to the Shah before he left the two men alone.

"Can he be trusted?" Jelaudin said as soon as he was gone.

"More than my own sons, it seems," the Shah replied irritably. "Abbas knows the family of one of the assassins. He will see it safe to them and then nothing will save this dog of a khan who has shed so much of my people's blood."

"If the khan dies tomorrow, will the gold be returned?" Jelaudin asked, still thinking of the vast wealth his father had given away in just a moment. He sensed the Shah walk to him and turned his head from looking at the tent's entrance.

"Unless Allah strikes him down for his impudence, he will not die tomorrow, Jelaudin. Do you not understand even now? Did you not see as you came back to my tent?" He spoke with a flat intensity that Jelaudin could not understand, and the younger man stammered as he tried to reply.

"See...what? I..."

"My army is finished," the Shah snapped. "With the men you lost tonight, we have hardly enough left to hold *one* of his damned generals in the morning. They have reduced us to less than thirty thousand men, and even if the Otrar garrison appears at this moment, we have lost. Do you understand now?"

Jelaudin hadn't and his stomach tightened in fear at his father's words. They had fought for days and the slaughter had been terrible, but the field of battle was vast and he had not known how bad the losses had been.

"So many dead?" he said at last. "How is it possible?"

His father raised a hand and for a moment Jelaudin thought he would strike him. Instead, the Shah whirled to pick up another sheaf of reports.

"Do you want to count them again?" he demanded. "We have left a trail of corpses for a hundred miles and the Mongols are still strong."

Jelaudin firmed his mouth, making a decision.

"Then give command to me, for tomorrow. Take your noble guard and travel back to Bukhara and Samarkand. Return in the spring with a fresh army and avenge me."

For an instant, the Shah's furious expression faded. His eyes softened as he stared at his eldest son.

"I have never doubted your courage, Jelaudin." He reached out and gripped his son's neck, pulling him into a brief embrace. As they parted, Ala-ud-Din sighed.

"But I will not throw away your life. You will come with me and next year we will bring four times as many warriors to root out these godless invaders. I will arm every man who can hold a sword, and we will bring fire and bloody vengeance on their heads. The assassins will have killed their khan by then. For so much gold, they will move quickly."

Jelaudin bowed his head. In the darkness outside the tent, he could hear the noises of the camp and the moaning of wounded men.

"We leave tonight then?"

If the Shah felt the sting of dishonor, it did not show.

"Gather your brothers. Hand command to the most senior man left alive. Tell him…" He trailed off, his eyes growing distant. "Tell him that the lives of our men must be sold dearly if they are to enter paradise. They will be frightened when they find I have gone, but they must hold."

"The Mongols will track us, Father," Jelaudin replied, already thinking of the supplies he must take. He would have to gather his father's mounted guard as quietly as possible, so as not to alarm those they left behind.

The Shah waved a hand irritably. "We will go west, away from them, then cut north and east when we are clear of Otrar. The land is vast, my son. They will not even know we are gone until tomorrow. Gather what we need and come back here when you are ready."

"And Otrar?" Jelaudin said.

"Otrar is lost!" the Shah spat. "My cousin Inalchuk has brought this disaster on us, and if I could kill the fool myself, I would."

Jelaudin touched his forehead, lips, and heart with his head bowed. His dream of riding at the head of a victorious army had been crushed, but he was his father's son and there would be other armies and other days. Despite the humiliation and horror of the battles against the Mongols, he thought nothing of the lives given for his father. They were the Shah's men and any one of them would die to protect him. As they should, Jelaudin thought.

He worked quickly as the moon passed overhead. Dawn was not far away and he needed to be well clear of the battle and the Mongol scouts by the time it came.

*   *   *

Genghis waited in the moonlight, dark ranks of men at his back. Khasar was with him, but neither brother spoke as they stood ready. The scouts had warned them of the Otrar garrison coming in. Even then it had been barely in time to beat back the night attack on their camp. Behind him, Genghis had given command to Tsubodai, the most able of his generals. He did not expect to get any sleep before the morning, but that was common enough to the warriors around him, and with meat, cheese, and fiery black airag, they were still strong.

Genghis cocked his head at a sound from the gloom. He clicked with his tongue to alert the closest men, but they too had heard. He felt a pang of regret at the deaths of Samuka and Ho Sa, but it passed quickly. Without their sacrifice, he would have lost it all the day before. He turned his head left and right, searching for more sounds.

There. Genghis drew his sword, and all along the line, the front rank readied lances. They had no arrows with them. Tsubodai had spent much of the night collecting the final shafts into full quivers, but they would need them when dawn came. Genghis could hear walking horses ahead and he rubbed tiredness from his eyes with a free hand. At times, it seemed as if he had been fighting all his life against these dark-skinned madmen.

With Jelme, he had chosen a spot to wait just under a low rise. Even in the moonlight, he would not be seen, but his scouts kept moving, leaving their horses and running in the dark to keep him informed. One of them appeared at his stirrup and Genghis dipped his head to hear the soft words, grunting in surprise and pleasure.

When the scout had gone, Genghis nudged his horse close to Khasar.

"We outnumber them, brother! Samuka and Ho Sa must have fought like tigers."

Khasar nodded grimly. "It's about time. I am tired of riding against their vast armies. Are you ready?"

Genghis snorted. "I have been waiting forever for his garrison, brother. Of course I am ready."

The two men parted in the darkness, then the Mongol line surged forward over the rise. Against them, the remnants of the garrison of Otrar were making their way south to join the Shah. They came to a shocked halt as the Mongol lines appeared, but there was no one to save them as the lances came down.

*   *   *

Shah Ala-ud-Din reined in as he heard the sounds of battle echo back from the hills. In the moonlight, he could see distant smudges of fighting men, but he could not guess what was happening. Perhaps the cursed Mongols had attacked again.

With only four hundred surviving riders, he and his sons had abandoned the army and ridden hard. The Shah glanced at the east and saw dawn was coming. He tried to fill his mind with plans for the future, numbing it to regrets. It was difficult. He had come to smash an invader and instead seen his best men bleeding out their strength. The Mongols were tireless killers and he had underestimated them. Only the thought of Abbas riding to the assassins' stronghold in the mountains gave him satisfaction. The men of shadows never failed and he only wished he could see the face of the khan as he felt their soot-blackened knives plunging into his chest.

Kokchu could smell fear in the camp, thick in the warm night air. It showed in the lamps that hung from posts at every intersection in the maze of gers. The women and children were afraid of the dark, with imagined enemies all around them. For Kokchu, the simmering terror was intoxicating. With the maimed warriors, Genghis's brother Temuge, and Yao Shu, he was one of very few men left among thousands of frightened women. It was hard to hide his arousal at their flushed faces. He saw them prepare as best they could for an attack, stuffing clothes and armor with dried grasses before tying them to spare mounts. Many of them came to him each day, offering whatever they had so that he would pray for their husbands to come back safe. He guarded himself rigidly at those times, forcing himself to remember that the warriors would return and ask their wives about the time alone. As young women knelt and chanted before him in his ger, their pathetic offerings lying in the dust, he sometimes placed his hand on their hair and grew flushed as he led them in their entreaties.

The worst of them was Genghis's sister, Temulun. She was lithe and long-legged, an echo of her brother's strength in her frame. She had come three times to ask for his protection over Palchuk, her husband. On the third time, the smell of sweat was strong on her. While small voices screamed warnings in his head, he had insisted on placing a charm on her skin, one that would extend to all those she loved. He felt himself grow hard at the memory, despite his misgivings. How she had looked to him with hope in her eyes. How she had believed! Having her in his control had made him reckless. He had told her of a most potent charm, one that would be like iron against enemy swords. He had been subtle in his doubts and in the end she had begged him for its protection. It had been hard to hide his excitement then as he bowed to her need.

She had removed her clothes at his order, standing naked before him as he began the chant. He recalled the way his fingers had shook as she closed her eyes and let him daub her body in a web of sheep blood.

Kokchu stopped his meandering path and swore to himself. He was a fool. At first she had stood proud and still, her eyes closed as he drew lines with a finger pressing into her flesh. He had marked her in wavering red until her stomach and legs were crisscrossed with patterns. His lust had been overwhelming and perhaps he had begun to breathe too hard, or she had seen his flushed face. He winced at the thought of her feeling him press against her thigh as he leaned close. Her eyes had snapped open from the trance, looking through incense smoke and suddenly doubting him. He shuddered as he recalled her expression. His hand was lingering over her breasts, marking them in shining blood, the scent of which filled his nostrils.

She had left in a rush then, gathering her clothes even as he protested the charm was unfinished. He had watched her go almost at a run, and his stomach had clenched at what he had dared to do. He did not fear her husband, Palchuk. There were few men who would even dare to speak to the shaman, and Kokchu did not doubt he could send the man away. Was he not the khan's own spirit-talker, the one who had brought Genghis victory after victory?

Kokchu bit his lip at the thought. If Temulun told Genghis her suspicions, of a hand too intimately on her thighs and breasts, no protection in the world would save him. He tried to tell himself she would not. In the cold light of day, she would admit she knew nothing of the spirits, or the manner of calling them. Perhaps he should consider daubing one of the maimed men in the same way, so that the news of the ritual would get back to her. He considered it seriously for a moment, then cursed his lust again, knowing that it had put everything in danger.

Kokchu stood at a crossroads, watching two young women lead ponies by the reins. They bowed their heads as they passed, and he acknowledged them graciously. His authority was absolute, he told himself, his secrets safe. Many of the women in the camp would not have men coming home to them. He would have his pick of them then, as he consoled them in their grief.

CHAPTER SEVENTEEN

BEFORE DAWN LIT THE PLAIN, the remains of ten tumans left the ashes of their fires and assembled. Not one was intact and the worst were reduced to just a few thousand men.

Those warriors too injured to fight remained at the makeshift camp, bloodied and bandaged, or simply left to die with their companions. The shamans who might stitch and heal them were all far away. Many of them asked for a clean death and were given it with a single blow from a sword, in all honor.

In the gloom, Genghis listened to a tally of the dead as a fresh breeze across the plain made him shiver. There were too many names to hear them all, but he bowed his head as each officer was recalled, especially senior men like Samuka and Ho Sa.

Twenty-three thousand had been killed, maimed, or lost in the battles against the Shah. It was the worst tally he had ever known and a terrible blow for the nation. Genghis felt a slow rage building whenever he looked for faces and found them missing in the ranks. His sister's husband, Palchuk, was among the dead, and he knew there would be rivers of grief when he returned at last to the camp.

Genghis looked up and down the lines as they formed. As well as his own tuman of ten thousand, he noted the banners of Khasar and

Kachiun, Jebe and Tsubodai, Chagatai, Jelme, and Jochi. He had given orders for broken tumans to fill the places of the dead, and eight tumans had formed out of the ashes. From the youngest boys of fourteen, they were veterans. He knew they would not fail him.

Genghis reached down to touch his lower leg and grimaced at the sick feeling and wetness he found. He had taken the wound the day before, but he could not remember how it had happened. He could not stand on it, but he had tied the foot into the stirrup so that he could still ride. Some of his warriors had lost part of their armor to arrows or sword blows, suffering gashes that they bound with strips of dirty cloth. Others had taken a fever through the wounds and poured with sweat in a dawn breeze that could not cool them. They sat their horses in grim anger, waiting for dawn and first sight of the enemy. No one had slept the night before and they were all bone tired, but there was no give in them, no weakness. They had all lost friends or relatives. The days of battle had burned away everything but a cold desire to avenge the fallen dead.

When there was enough light to see, Genghis stared out at the Shah's army. He heard distant horns blow an alarm as the Shah's scouts caught sight of the host waiting for them, but the Arabs were sluggish in their movements. The sight of the Mongol army unnerved them, and Genghis could see them mill aimlessly, all order gone.

He gave the command to trot and his tumans moved with him. His entire front rank of two thousand men weighed lances in their hands, feeling the strain on tired, torn muscles. The rest readied swords and the distance closed.

Genghis saw two men running out ahead of the forming lines, holding banners of white cloth. He wondered if they meant to surrender, but it did not matter. The time for mercy was long gone. Many of those who had died had been known to him, and he had only one answer to give, only one they would approve if their spirits still saw the world below. The men with white banners were killed as the Mongol line swept past them, and a low moan came from the rest as they saw and tried to brace for the charge.

Forty elephants were brought to the front, but Tsubodai ordered his archers to shoot for the legs and sent them rampaging back into the Arab army, causing more destruction than they ever could have against mounted men.

The great line of lances hit almost as one, and Genghis shouted the order for horns. His son Chagatai swept forward on the right, while

Jochi matched him on the left. The Mongol warriors began the slaughter as the sun rose over the east. They could not be held. They could not be thrown back.

Chagatai's tuman pinched in against the right flank, their speed and ferocity carrying them to the very center of the Arabs. In the chaos and noise, there was no calling him back. Jochi's wing spilled along the left flank, carving dead men out of living lines. Across the battlefield, he saw Chagatai had plunged too far into the mass of terrified men. He could see him only a few hundred paces away before the Arab ranks seemed to swallow him. Jochi cried out. He dug in his heels and led his men like a spear thrust into the jerking body of the Arab army.

The front ranks were hit so hard by Jebe and Tsubodai that they bowed right back in a bloody cup. No one had taken command and in the chaos, the tumans of Chagatai and Jochi sliced through them until the brothers were separated by just a few struggling, panting men.

The Arabs broke, terrified by the khan's warriors. Thousands threw down their weapons and tried to run, but none of the generals hesitated. Those who turned their backs were cut down without mercy, and by noon the army of the Shah was a morass of desperate, flailing groups. The slaughter continued without pause. Some of the Shah's men knelt and prayed aloud in shrieking voices until their heads were taken by galloping men. It was butcher's work, but the Mongols were willing. Many of them broke their swords in huge swings and had to pick up one of the curved sabers that littered the ground. Lances were snapped in Arabs too dazed to step out of the way.

In the end, just a few hundred remained. They had no weapons and held their arms high to show empty palms. Genghis grunted a final order and a line of lancers accelerated. The Arabs cried out in terror, then were silent as the riders rolled over them and returned, dismounting to hack the dead men into small pieces, until their fury and spite were spent.

The Mongol tumans did not cheer the victory. From the first light, there had been no fight in the Arab army, and though they had taken a savage pleasure in the killing, there was no more glory in it than a circle hunt.

The ground was soft with blood as individual warriors looted the dead, cutting fingers for rings and stripping the bodies of good boots and warm clothing. Flies gathered in great swarms, so that the Mongols had to bat them away from where they landed on lips and eyes. The buzzing insects crawled intimately over the dead, already beginning to corrupt in the heat.

Genghis summoned his generals and they came to him, bruised and battered, but with satisfaction in their eyes.

"Where is the Shah?" he demanded of each one. They had found camels laden with tents of silk, and Jebe's men had discovered a cache of jewels and already gambled or exchanged half of them.

When Genghis asked Tsubodai, the general shook his head thoughtfully.

"His horsemen are gone, Lord Khan," he replied. "I did not see even one."

Genghis swore, his weariness vanishing. "Get the scouts out looking for tracks. I want him hunted down."

Those scouts who heard jumped back into their saddles and raced away, while Genghis simmered.

"If he left last night, he has had almost a day to get away. He must not escape! The Arab merchants talk of armies five times the size of this one, more. Have your men join the scouts. Nothing is more important than this, *nothing.*"

Riders went in all directions and it was not long before two men of Jochi's tuman came racing back. Genghis listened to the report and paled.

"Tsubodai! Horses traveling west," he said.

Tsubodai stiffened. "His cities are in the east," he said. "He will turn north or south. May I ride to protect the camp, lord?"

Genghis swore under his breath. "No. Take your tuman and get after the Shah. If he reaches a city and finds fresh reinforcements, we are all dead."

Jebe was at the khan's side when he gave the order. He had seen the Shah's army when it was bright and strong. The thought of facing as many again was sickening. He turned to Tsubodai and raised his head.

"With my lord khan's permission, I will come with you," he said.

Genghis waved a hand and Tsubodai nodded as he dug in his heels. Tsubodai shouted an order to the closest officer, but did not pause as the man raced to gather Tsubodai's Young Wolves.

As the news spread, Jochi came riding up to his father. He bowed low in the saddle as he reined in.

"Is the camp in danger?" he asked. Genghis turned his pale gaze on the young general, noting the tiger skin draped across his pony. All of them had family there, but he bristled anyway. It had been his order to leave the camp undefended. There had been no other choice.

"I have sent Jebe and Tsubodai to hunt the Shah," Genghis replied at last.

"They are good men, the best you have," Jochi replied. His father's face was cold, but he went on carelessly, thinking of his mother.

"May I take my tuman and bring the families back here?"

Genghis considered grudgingly. He did not like the thought of Jochi announcing the victory to the women and children. No doubt the young man was already thinking of a hero's welcome. Genghis felt his stomach twist at the thought.

"I need you at Otrar," he said. "Give Chagatai the order."

For an instant, Genghis saw anger flash in Jochi's eyes. The khan leaned forward in his saddle, his hand dropping to his sword hilt. Even in that, he felt swelling bitterness, as Jochi carried the wolf's-head sword on his hip. The lapse was quickly masked and Jochi bowed his head and trotted away to speak to his younger brother.

Chagatai was at the center of a riotous group of young warriors. He did not see Jochi approach at first and was in the middle of laughing at some comment when he stiffened. The men with Chagatai took their lead from him, and Jochi walked his pony through their hostile stares.

Neither brother spoke a greeting. Jochi let his hand drop to the tiger skin at his pommel, his fingers toying with the stiff fur. Chagatai waited for him to speak, raising one eyebrow, so that his companions chuckled.

"You are to take your tuman back to the camp and bring them to the land around Otrar," Jochi said when he tired of the game.

Chagatai frowned. He did not want to nursemaid women and children while Otrar trembled for the first sight of them.

"Whose order is this?" he replied. "Whose authority?"

Jochi controlled his temper at the insolent tone. "Genghis bids you go," he said, turning his mount to ride away.

"So you say, but who listens when a rape-born bastard speaks?" Chagatai spoke knowing he was surrounded by his own men, all waiting for such a barb that they could repeat with relish at the campfires.

Jochi stiffened in the saddle. He should have left the grinning fools, but nothing in the world brought him to anger as easily as his younger brother's blustering arrogance.

"Perhaps he feels you are a fitting companion for the women after the way you knelt to me, brother," he replied. "I cannot know his mind."

With a tight smile, Jochi held his mount to a walk. Even with armed men at his back, he would not give them the satisfaction of seeing him urge his pony to a trot.

He heard the sudden rush of hooves and his hand fell automatically to the wolf's-head hilt before he snatched it away. He could not draw a blade on Chagatai in front of so many witnesses. It would be the end of him.

Jochi glanced back as unconcernedly as he could. Chagatai was closing the gap between them, with his tail of followers trotting behind. His brother was red faced with rage and Jochi had barely opened his mouth to speak again when the young man launched himself from the saddle, taking Jochi down hard.

As they hit and rolled, Jochi lost his temper and struck out, his blows thumping uselessly. They came apart and both of them leapt up with murder in their eyes. Even then, old habits were strong and they did not reach for their swords. Chagatai came at Jochi with his fists high, and Jochi kicked him as hard as he could between the legs.

Chagatai collapsed in agony, but his fury was so all-consuming that to Jochi's amazement, he struggled to rise and staggered into him again. By then his companions had dismounted and they pulled the two generals apart. Jochi wiped a smear of blood from his nose and spat contemptuously on the ground at Chagatai's feet. He watched as his brother recovered some semblance of calm, and only then did he glance over to Genghis.

The khan was pale with rage, and as his eyes met Jochi's, he dug in his heels and trotted closer. Not one of the warriors dared look up as they froze in his presence. His temper was legendary in the families and the youngest men were suddenly aware that their own lives might hang on a word or a gesture.

Only Chagatai seemed unaffected. As his father approached, he stepped forward and tried to backhand Jochi across the face. His brother ducked instinctively and was off balance when Genghis kicked Jochi hard between the shoulder blades, sending him sprawling.

Even Chagatai became still at seeing that, though his sneer remained. Genghis dismounted slowly, his fists tight on the reins until he forced them open.

When he turned to his sons, his anger was clear enough to make Chagatai step back. It was not enough. Genghis placed his hand on Chagatai's chest and pushed him flat to join Jochi on the ground.

"Are you children *still*?" Genghis said. He shook visibly at the young fools who dared to brawl while their men looked on. He wanted to take a stick and beat sense into them, but the last thread of his control held him back. If he thrashed them, they would never again command the respect of his warriors. Sly whispers would follow them the rest of their lives.

Neither Jochi nor Chagatai responded. Finally aware of the danger they were in, they chose to say nothing.

"How can you command...?" Genghis stopped before he destroyed them both, his mouth working soundlessly. Kachiun had galloped across the makeshift camp as soon as he heard, and his approach allowed the khan to break off his glare.

"What would you do with young fools like these?" Genghis demanded of Kachiun. "With all the enemies we still face, with our own camp in peril, they fight like boys."

His eyes pleaded silently with Kachiun to find a punishment that would not be the end for them both. If it had been Jochi alone, he would have ordered his death, but it had been Chagatai he had seen leaping off his horse to roll his brother in the dust.

Kachiun's face was stern, but he understood the khan's dilemma.

"It is almost twenty miles to Otrar, Lord Khan. I would have them make the journey on foot, before dark." He looked at the sun, judging the time. "If they cannot, perhaps they are not fit to lead their men."

Genghis breathed out slowly in relief he could not show. It would do. The sun was merciless and such a run could kill a man, but they were young and strong and it would serve as a punishment.

"I will be there to watch you come in," he said to the dumbfounded pair. Chagatai glared at Kachiun for the suggestion, but as he opened his mouth to object, Genghis reached down and picked him up in one smooth motion. His father's fist rested just under his chin as he spoke again.

"Remove your armor and go," he said. "If I see you fighting again, I will make Ogedai my heir. Do you understand?"

Both brothers nodded and Genghis stared at Jochi, incensed that he had thought the words were also for him. His temper flared again, but Kachiun deliberately chose that moment to call the men into ranks for the ride to Otrar, and Genghis let Chagatai go.

For the benefit of all those who could hear and repeat the words a thousand times, Kachiun forced a smile as Jochi and Chagatai began to run in the vicious heat.

"You won such a race when we were boys, I remember."

Genghis shook his head irritably. "What does that matter? It was long ago. Have Khasar bring the families back to Otrar. I have debts to settle there."

Shah Ala-ud-Din Mohammed reined in as he saw the thin trails of cooking smoke rising from the Mongol camp. He had ridden slowly west before taking a wide route north around Otrar, covering many miles since the first gray light of predawn. As the sun rose to burn off the morning mist, he stared at the filthy gers of the Mongol families. For an instant, the urge to ride among the women and children with his sword was overwhelming. If he had known the khan had left them so vulnerable, he would have sent twenty thousand to kill them all. He clenched his fists in frustration as the light grew. Warriors clustered on the edges, the heads of their ponies peacefully snuffling the dusty ground for grass. For once, there were no warning horns blown from the cursed Mongol scouts.

With a snarl, the Shah began to turn his mount away from the camp. They bred like lice, these Mongols, and he had only his precious four hundred to see him safe in the east. The sun was rising and his guards would soon be seen.

One of his men shouted something and Ala-ud-Din turned his head. The sun's light revealed what the shadows had hidden, and he grinned suddenly, his mood lifting. The warriors were no more than straw dummies tied to the horses. The Shah strained his eyes as the light grew, but he could not see a single armed man. Around him, the news spread and the noble sons laughed and pointed, already loosening their swords in the scabbards. They had all taken part in punishment raids on villages, when the taxes had been late. The sport was good in such places and the desire for revenge was strong.

Jelaudin did not share the men's laughter as he rode to his father.

"Would you have the men waste half a day here with our enemies so close?"

In response, his father drew a curved sword. The Shah glanced at the sun.

"This khan must be taught the price of his arrogance, Jelaudin. Kill the children and burn what you can."

CHAPTER EIGHTEEN

SLOWLY, almost ritually, Chakahai wrapped her hand in a length of silk, tying it to the hilt of a long dagger. Borte had told her to beware of the shock of impact, that a woman's hand could be jarred loose or sweat enough to slip. The process of winding the silk around her fingers and biting one end to hold a knot was somehow calming as she looked out through the gers at the Shah's riders. The knot of terror in her stomach was not under her control.

She, Borte, and Hoelun had done what they could to prepare the camp. They had been given little warning and the more elaborate traps were still unset. Still, they had weapons and Chakahai murmured a Buddhist death prayer as she readied herself. The morning was cold, though the air seemed heavy and promised another day of heat. She had hidden her children as best she could in the ger. They lay in perfect silence under piles of blankets. With a vast effort, Chakahai put her fear for them aside, leaving it in a separate place so that her mind was clear. Some things were fate, what the Indian Buddhists called *karma*. Perhaps all the women and children would be killed that day, she could not know. All she desired was the chance to kill a man for the first time, to fulfill her duty to her husband and her children.

Her bound right hand was shaking as she raised the blade, but she enjoyed the feeling of holding the weapon and took strength from it.

Genghis would avenge her, she knew. Unless he too had been killed. That was the thought she tried most to crush as it reared in her mind. How else could Arabs have come to the camp if not over a dead nation and the body of her husband? If Genghis still lived, he would surely have moved mountains to protect the camp. For a Mongol, the families were everything. Yet there was no sign of the khan on the horizon, and Chakahai struggled against despair, seeking a calm that came and went in flashes.

At the last, she took a deep breath and felt her heart settle to a slow, heavy thump, her limbs strangely cold as if her blood had chilled in her veins. The riders were trotting toward the city of gers. Life was just a restless fever dream, a short breath between longer sleep. She would reawaken and be reborn without the agony of memory. That, at least, was a blessing.

The herds of Mongol ponies stirred nervously as the Shah rode in with his men. He could see ripples running through the animals, and in the strange silence, he felt a sense of foreboding. He looked to the others to see if they too had a premonition of danger, but they were blindly eager for the hunt and leaned forward in their saddles.

Ahead, threads of cooking smoke lifted lazily into air. It was already growing warm and the Shah felt sweat trickle down his back as he reached the first gers. His guards spread themselves into a wide line as they rode into the maze, and the Shah felt his nerves tighten. The Mongol homes were high enough to conceal anything behind them. Even a mounted man could not see what lay beyond the next, and that made him uneasy.

The camp seemed deserted. If not for the cooking fires, Ala-ud-Din might have thought the place empty of life. He had intended to ride through in one great sweep, killing anyone who ran across his path. Instead, the lanes and paths were silent and the Arab horses drove deeper and deeper without seeing a living soul. Far above his head, an eagle circled, its head twitching back and forth as it searched for prey.

He had not appreciated the sheer size of the Mongol encampment. Perhaps twenty thousand gers were in that place, or even more, a true city sprung from nothing in the wilderness. They had claimed the land on the banks of a nearby river, and Ala-ud-Din could see drying fish tied to racks of wood as he passed. Even the flies were quiet. He shrugged to himself, trying to throw off the dark mood. Already some of his men were dismounting to enter the gers. He had heard the older men talk of threatening the children to make the women more pliable. The Shah sighed in irritation. Perhaps Jelaudin had been right. Once they were in the gers, the morning would be lost. The Mongols could not be far behind and he did not intend to be caught in that desolate place. For the first time, he wished he had simply ridden past the camp.

Ala-ud-Din watched as one of his son's friends ducked low to push open the door to a ger. The entrance was almost too small for his massive shoulders. The Arab soldier stuck his bearded face through the opening, squinting into the gloom. Ala-ud-Din blinked as the man suddenly shuddered, his legs quivering as if he had begun a fit. To his astonishment, the soldier dropped to his knees, then fell flat into the ger, his body still twitching.

As he took a breath to give orders, Ala-ud-Din caught a movement out of the corner of his eye and brought his sword round in a sweeping blow. A woman had been creeping up on him and the tip caught her across the face, gashing her jaw and breaking teeth. She fell back with blood pouring from her mouth, then to his horror, leapt at him and sank a dagger into his thigh. His second blow took her head off cleanly, then the silence shattered into chaos all around him.

The gers erupted and his warriors were instantly fighting for their lives. Ignoring the pain from his wound, the Shah spun his horse in place and used its bulk to shoulder down a woman and young boy who raced toward him, screaming and brandishing heavy knives. His men were veteran cavalry, used to defending their mounts from men on foot. Yet the Mongol women seemed to have no fear of death. They ran in close and cut either the horse or a man's leg before vanishing behind the nearest ger. Ala-ud-Din saw more than one hacked down, then stagger in before death took them, using their last breath to plunge a blade into flesh.

In heartbeats, every man of his four hundred was fending off more than one, sometimes four or five different women. Horses bolted wildly as their haunches were cut, and men cried out in fear as they were pulled from their mounts and stabbed.

The Arab guards held their nerve. More than half of them rode without care to surround the Shah, and the rest drew into close formation, each man watching for attacks on the others. The women darted at them from the side of every ger, appearing and disappearing like ghosts. The Shah felt hemmed in, but he could not ride free and let the khan tell the world he had run from women and children. One ger had collapsed as a horse crashed into it, and he saw an iron stove broken open. He snapped an order to his manservant, Abbas, watching eagerly as the man tore a great strip of felt and lit it from the scattered fire.

The attacks became more desperate, but his men had the rhythm by then. The Shah could see some wild fools had dismounted to rape a young woman on the ground, and he rode furiously to them, using his horse to knock them aside.

"Have you lost your minds?" he roared. "Get up! Up! Fire the gers!" In the face of his fury, they drew a knife across the throat of the struggling woman and stood, abashed. Abbas already had one ger aflame. The closest guards took up pieces of the burning material in their hands, riding away with them to spread the terror as far as they could. Ala-ud-Din coughed as he breathed in thick gray smoke, but he exulted at the thought of the khan coming back to a field of ashes and the cold dead.

Jelaudin was the first to spot the running boys. They darted through the gers near the river, weaving between paths, but always coming closer. Jelaudin could see hundreds of the devils, running bare-chested with their hair flying. He swallowed nervously when he saw they carried bows, like their fathers. Jelaudin had time to shout a warning to his men, and they raised their shields and charged down the paths at this new threat.

The Mongol boys held their ground as the Arabs thundered toward them. Jelaudin's men heard a high voice shout an order, then the bows bent and arrows were flying in the breeze.

Jelaudin yelled a curse as he saw men knocked down, but it was just a few. The boys were as accurate as the adults, but they did not have the power to batter shafts through armor. The only deaths came from an arrow in the throat, and those were good odds. As Jelaudin drew close, the boys scattered before his men, vanishing into the labyrinth. He cursed an arrangement that meant they had to turn only one corner to be lost to view. Perhaps that was how the Mongols had intended it when they laid out their camps.

Jelaudin cantered around a ger and found three of the boys in a huddle. Two loosed a shot as soon as they saw him, the arrows passing wide. The other took a heartbeat longer and released his shaft just as Jelaudin's horse crashed into him, shattering the boy's ribs and tossing him away. Jelaudin roared in pain, looking down in disbelief at the arrow that had ripped along his thigh under the skin. It was not a bad wound, but he raged as he drew his sword and killed the dumbfounded pair before they could react. Another arrow whirred past his head from behind, though when he spun his mount round, he could see no one.

In the distance, smoke rose in thick billows as his father's men set fires. Already the sparks would be landing on other gers, burying themselves deeply in the dry felt. Jelaudin was completely alone, yet he sensed movement all round him. When he had been a very young boy, he had once been lost in a field of golden wheat, the crop taller than he was. All around him, he had heard the scuttling, whispering movement of rats. The old terror surfaced. He could not bear to be alone in such a place, with creeping danger on all sides. Yet he was not a boy. He roared a challenge to the empty air and hammered along the closest path, heading for his father and where the smoke was thickest.

The Shah's men had killed hundreds of the Mongol women, yet they still came and died. Fewer and fewer of them managed to draw blood from the guards, now that they were prepared. Ala-ud-Din was astonished at their ferocity, as fierce as the men who had ravaged his armies. His sword was bloody and he burned with the need to punish them. He breathed heavy smoke and choked for a moment, delighting in the destruction as the fire spread from ger to ger. The center of the camp was aflame and his men had developed a new tactic. As they saw a Mongol home burn, they waited outside the door for the inhabitants to come rushing out. Sometimes the Mongol women and children cut their way through the felt walls, but more and more were slaughtered as they rushed armed and mounted men. Some were already on fire and chose to die on swords rather than burn.

Chakahai ran on bare feet toward a warrior with his back to her. The Arab horse seemed huge as she approached, the man on its back so far above her that she could not see how to hurt him. The crackle of flames hid the sound of her steps as she raced across the grass. Still he did not turn, and as he shouted to another man, she saw he wore a leather tunic decorated in plates of some dark metal. The world slowed as she reached the hindquarters of his mount and he sensed her. He began to turn, moving as if in a dream. Chakahai saw a glimpse of flesh at his waist, between his belt and the leather armor. She darted in without hesitation, ramming the blade upwards as Borte had told her to do. The shock of it thrilled along her arm and the man gasped, his head snapping back so that he stared at the sky. Chakahai yanked the blade and found it had wedged in him, trapped in flesh. She pulled at it in a frenzy and did not dare look at the Arab as he brought his sword arm up to kill her.

The blade came loose and she fell backwards, her arm covered in his blood. The Arab slumped and fell almost beside her, so that for an instant, their eyes met. She struck out again in panic, but he was already dead.

She stood then, her chest heaving as she was filled with a dark pleasure. Let them all die in such a way, with their bowels opening and their bladders darkening the ground! She heard galloping hooves and looked up dazedly as another Arab stallion came to smash her from her feet. She could not move in time and the exhilaration of the kill left her to be replaced by a vast weariness.

Facing the Arab soldier, she saw Yao Shu before he did. The Buddhist monk shot across the face of the horse, aiming a heavy stick at a foreleg. She heard a crack and the animal went down hard. As she watched in a daze, it turned right over in front of her, crushing the man on its back. Chakahai could only stare at the kicking legs, seeing that one of them hung at a vicious angle. She felt Yao Shu's hands pulling her between gers and then the world came back in a rush and she began to retch weakly.

The little monk moved as jerkily as a bird, looking for the next threat. He caught her staring at him and only nodded, raising the stick he had used in salute.

"Thank you," she said, bowing her head. She would reward him, if they survived it, she promised herself. Genghis would honor him before them all.

"Come with me," he said, letting his hand rest briefly on her shoulder before he led the way through the gers away from the fire. Chakahai looked at the blood staining the wrap on her right hand and felt only satisfaction at the memory. Genghis would be proud of her, if he still lived.

Ala-ud-Din turned his head as he heard a series of short, hard sounds. He did not understand the words, only that men were coming. His stomach twisted in panic that the khan had tracked him down already. He bawled new orders for his men to leave the gers and face the enemy. Many of them were lost to him in an orgy of destruction, their faces wild with fanatic madness. Yet Jelaudin heard as he raced in, and two more of his sons repeated the orders, shouting until they were hoarse.

The smoke was thick and at first Ala-ud-Din could see nothing, hear nothing but approaching hooves. The sound echoed through the encampment and his mouth went dry. Surely there were thousands coming for his head?

Out of the smoke, horses came at full gallop, the whites of their eyes showing clearly as they ran. They had no men on their backs, but in that confined place, they could not stop for the Shah's men. With Jelaudin, Ala-ud-Din was fast enough to dodge behind a ger, but others reacted too slowly. The horses ran like a river bursting its banks through the camp, and many of his guards were knocked down and trampled.

Behind the Mongol mounts came the maimed men. Ala-ud-Din heard their battle cries as they raced by in the host of horses. They were both young and old, many without limbs. One of them turned to kill the Shah, and Ala-ud-Din saw the man carried only a heavy stick in his left hand. His right was missing. The Mongol warrior died swiftly under Jelaudin's sword, but some of them held bows and the Shah shuddered at the song of arrows in the air once more. He had heard it too often over the previous month.

The smell of blood and fire was in the air, too thick to breathe as more and more gers took flame. Ala-ud-Din looked for his officers, but they were all defending themselves. He felt surrounded, helpless in the confining maze of gers.

"With me! To your Shah! With me!" he roared, digging in his heels. He had barely been able to hold his horse in place. Released, the animal moved like it had been shot from a bow, careering across the camp and leaving the smoke and terror behind.

Jelaudin repeated his order and the survivors followed, as relieved as their master to be away from the fighting. The Shah rode blindly, standing high on his stirrups for some sign that he was heading the right way. Where was the river? He would have given a second son for an elephant's height to let him see his way out. Even as his men fought free of the stampeding horses and the maimed men, he saw lines of children, boys and girls alike, rushing along the gers on either side. Arrows flew at his men and knives were thrown, but none fell and he did not stop until the river was in sight.

There was no time to look for a fording place. The Shah plunged into the freezing water, the shock of it numbing him as spray spattered on all sides. Allah be thanked it is not too deep! he thought as his horse surged across to the far bank. He almost fell from the saddle as the animal struggled up through mud worn smooth by the river. At last he had firm ground under him and he rested, panting and looking back at the burning camp.

Kokchu cowered in the shadow of a ger as Arab warriors raced past, unaware of him. The maimed warriors pursued them with guttural yells, and they were fearsome to behold. Kokchu had tended many of their wounds and cut limbs from screaming men as helpless as babies, but those who had lived had nothing left to lose. Men who could not walk could yet ride, and many of them gave their lives willingly, knowing that they would never again have a chance to fight for the khan. Kokchu saw one who was missing his right leg to the knee. His balance was all wrong, but when the Arabs slowed on the narrow paths, the warrior caught a straggler and threw himself at him, sending them both to the ground. The warrior held on tightly, desperate to kill before his enemy regained his feet. They had fallen next to Kokchu and the shaman saw the warrior's gaze fall on him, desperate for help.

Kokchu stood back, though he fingered his knife nervously. The felled Arab plunged a knife into the warrior's side and ripped it back and forth with savage strength. Still the man fought on, his arms iron strong from years supporting his weight. One of them was around the Arab's throat and it tightened convulsively, the fingers crushing. The Arab choked and stabbed in a frenzy as he grew purple.

Kokchu darted forward and used his knife to slit the Arab's throat, gashing the warrior's fingers as he did so. Blood poured as both men died together, but Kokchu stepped in, his fear vanishing in rage at a helpless enemy. As the Arab fell back, Kokchu jammed in the knife again and again, keening mindlessly to himself until he was chopping at dead meat.

He rose panting, his hands on his knees as he sucked great lungfuls of warm air. In the gloom of a nearby ger, he saw Genghis's sister Temulun staring at him and wondered what she thought she had seen. She smiled then and he relaxed. He could not have saved the maimed warrior, he was almost sure.

The flames around Kokchu seemed to heat his blood, perhaps also the wildness that came from feeling death pulse under his hands. He felt strong as he took three strides to the ger and pushed his way in with her, yanking the door closed behind them. The thought of her golden skin taut with lines of dried blood filled his mind, maddening him. She was not strong enough to resist as he pulled her deel from her shoulders, exposing her to the waist. The lines he had drawn were still there, pathetic proof of her faith. He began to devour them, licking off the bitter taste. He felt her hands striking at him, but they were distant and brought no pain. He told himself she felt the same passion as he pushed her back on the low bed, ignoring the desperate cries that no one else would hear. Part of him screamed that it was madness, but he was lost for a time as he moved in her, his eyes like black glass.

Tsubodai and Jebe had seen the smoke from afar and arrived at the camp in the early evening, their horses lathered and exhausted. Almost ten thousand gers had been burned and the stink of it was sour on the breeze. Even then, there were hundreds of women and children roaming the camp with leather buckets, pouring river water on anything that still smoldered.

Dozens of the Shah's guard lay dead on the ground to be kicked and abused by children as they passed by. Tsubodai came across the bodies of five girls lying sprawled between a ger. He dismounted and knelt with them for a time, saying quiet words of apology that they could not hear.

When he rose, Jebe was there and both men shared a complete understanding. The Shah would not escape them, no matter where he ran.

CHAPTER NINETEEN

THE NATION HAD GATHERED AROUND OTRAR, holding it in a fist. In normal times, the idea of the khan's sons running a race would have been an event for the warriors. They would have wagered fortunes on which brother would be first to touch the walls of the city. In the end, when Jochi staggered in with Chagatai some way behind, their arrival went almost unnoticed. The nation waited for news that the camp was safe, and every man there had parents, wives, or children. Jochi's tuman had not met his eyes when he caught sight of the tiger skin draped across his horse. The beast's dried head had been roughly hacked from it, the sole sign that Genghis had not forgotten his sons fighting in front of the ranks. Jochi had fingered the torn skin in silence for a time, then turned away.

When the first riders came a day later, the tumans reeled at the news, everything they had feared. For a time, they were left with hope that their families might have been spared, but Khasar arrived with the survivors and the dead. Warriors ran to each cart as it came in, searching for their wives and children. Others waited in silent agony as the weary women passed them, desperate for a face they knew. Some were rewarded by a sharp cry and an embrace. Most were left standing, alone.

*   *   *

It took more than a month to collect every fallen warrior on the path back through the hills in the south. The Arabs were left to rot, but those who had fought for Genghis were brought in and treated with honor. Their bodies were stripped of armor and wrapped in soft white felt before being taken on carts to the highest peaks they could see and laid out for the hawks and eagles of that realm. The women who had died were tended by their sisters and mothers, with Chakahai, Borte, and Hoelun overseeing the grim work.

Genghis had come to view the dead face of his sister when she was brought in. She had been found naked, with her throat cut in one great slash. His grief had been terrible to see. It was one more crime to bring to the feet of the Shah. His mother had aged overnight at the news, so that Hoelun seemed constantly dazed and had to be taken by the arm wherever she went. She had lost a son many years before, and ancient wounds bled again, leaving her ruined with tears. When Genghis turned his gaze on Otrar, those who saw knew the city would be reduced to dust in a hot wind.

The catapults had been destroyed on their hill, deliberately set on fire as the Otrar garrison broke out and raced away to their own destruction. Twelve good men had been found around the charred timbers, cut down as they held their posts to the last. Genghis had merely grunted when that news reached him and set his Chin artisans to making more with Koryon lumber. The end of summer was quiet as they rested and recovered, with simmering rage always close to the surface. The city waited for them and no one came to the high walls anymore, still marked with soot from the burning oil Samuka had sent against them.

Ho Sa and Samuka had been found among the heaped dead and been honored for the enemies they had taken with them. The story-tellers wove their tale into ballads for the evenings, while the empty flesh was taken with the rest, with no more ceremony than the lowest warrior of the tribes. In the distance, the peaks were covered with the dead, and birds of prey hung like a dark cloud above them, feasting.

Winter in that place was a weak thing compared to the bitter cold they knew in the north. Genghis could not know the mind of the governor of Otrar, but the onset of colder months seemed to bring agitation to the city while the Mongols waited for the catapults to be rebuilt. There was no sense of urgency in the tribes. They did not need to move to live, and one place was as good as any other. The city would

fall, and if the inhabitants suffered as they waited, that too was well deserved.

As the days grew shorter, Genghis could sometimes see distant figures on the walls, pointing and talking. Perhaps they could see the
frames growing on the hill outside the city. He did not know or care. At
times, he was almost listless, and even after the catapults were finished,
he did not give the order, preferring to stay in his ger and drink through
a black depression. He did not want to see accusation in the eyes of
those who had lost their families. It had been his decision and he tortured himself with grief and fury, sleeping only when the drink made
him pass out.

The gates of Otrar opened without warning on a day of gray clouds
and threatening rain. The Mongol army sent up a storm of sound, beating spears and bows on shields, showing their anger in the discordant
clashing. Before Genghis or his remaining generals could respond, a
small group of men came walking out and the gates closed swiftly behind them.

Genghis was talking to Khasar when he heard the howl of the warriors. He walked slowly to his horse and climbed stiffly into the saddle,
staring at Otrar.

Just twelve men had left the protection of the walls. As Genghis
watched, he saw his warriors riding hard at them, their swords bared.
He might have stopped them, but he kept his mouth firmly shut.

The twelve Arabs bore one of their number trussed between them,
his feet dragging on the dusty ground. They cowered back from the
warriors swirling around them and held up their free hands to show
they were unarmed. To the Mongols, that too was a provocation. Any
man fool enough to venture among them without a blade or bow just
excited their lust to kill.

Genghis watched impassively as the warriors galloped across the
face of the men's progress. Closer and closer they rode until one of
them clipped an Arab with his horse's shoulder, sending him spinning.

The small group paused in sudden terror and Genghis could see
them calling to their fallen companion as he tried to struggle up. More
warriors forced them on, yipping and urging as they might a lost sheep
or goat. The man was left behind and warriors dismounted to finish
him.

The sound of his screams echoed from the walls of Otrar. The group
of Arabs moved on, glancing back in horror. Another was knocked

down with a blow from a sword hilt, so that a flap of his scalp was torn and blood covered his face. He too was left behind in a welter of kicking, stabbing men. Genghis sat his horse in silence as he observed their progress.

Two Mongol women approached one of the Arabs and pulled him away from the others. He yelled something in his strange language and held both hands out and open, but they laughed at him and held him back from his companions. When they had passed, the man began to scream and this time he did not die quickly. The sounds grew in intensity, going on and on.

When there were just six left of the group, Genghis held up his hand, sitting straight backed in the morning sun. Those who had watched for his signal pulled away from the bloodied Arabs and allowed a path to the khan. The group staggered on, pale with what they had seen. When they reached Genghis, they fell to the ground, abasing themselves before him. Their prisoner writhed in the dust, the whites of his eyes showing.

Genghis watched coldly as one of the Arabs lifted his head and spoke in the Chin language, his words slow.

"My lord, we have come to discuss peace!" he said. Genghis did not reply and only looked back at Otrar to where the walls were once again black with small figures, watching. The man swallowed the dust in his throat and tried again.

"The city council has voted to hand over our governor to you, lord. We were led into war against our will and we are innocent. We beg you to spare us and take only Governor Inalchuk, who is the author of our troubles."

The man settled back to the dust now that the words were spoken. He could not understand why he and his companions had been attacked. He was not even sure if the khan had understood his words. Genghis gave no sign of it and the silence lengthened.

The governor had been gagged as well as tied. Genghis heard the moan of muffled words and gestured to Khasar to cut the gag. His brother was not gentle and the blade sliced across Inalchuk's lips as the cloth parted, making him cry out and spit blood.

"These men have no power over me!" Inalchuk said through his pain. "Let me negotiate for my life, Lord Khan."

Genghis had learned only a few words of Arabic and could not understand. He waited patiently while an Arab merchant was brought, one of those who spoke many tongues. The merchant arrived looking as nervous as the others lying in the dust. Genghis gestured for the governor to speak again and listened patiently to the translation into the Chin language. It occurred to him that he had better set Temuge to training more men in the task if he intended to stay long in Arab lands. It was hard to make himself care.

When he understood Inalchuk, Genghis chuckled cruelly, waving away a fly that buzzed around his face.

"They have tied you like a sheep for slaughter and delivered you to your enemy, yet you say they have no power over you?" he said. "What other power is there?"

As the interpreter stumbled through the reply, Inalchuk struggled into a sitting position and touched his bound hands to his bleeding face, wincing.

"There *is* no council in Otrar, lord. These are mere traders of my city. They do not speak for one appointed by the Shah himself."

One of the Arabs began to spit an answer, but Khasar lunged at him, kicking him onto his back.

"Be silent!" Khasar snapped. He drew his sword and the battered Arabs followed the movement with nervous eyes. No interpretation was needed and the man did not try to speak again.

"Spare my life and I will have six thousand *oka* of silver delivered to you," Inalchuk declared. The interpreter hesitated over the sum and Genghis looked over to him. Under that yellow gaze, the shaking Arab merchant lowered himself to the ground with the others.

"Lord, I do not know the word in the Chin tongue. It is a term of weight used by gold- and silversmiths."

"No doubt he offers a great deal," Genghis replied. "He has set the value of his own life, after all."

The interpreter nodded where he lay. "The weight in silver of many men, lord. Perhaps a hundred, or even more."

Genghis considered, glancing up at the walls of Otrar that still loomed over his army. After a time, he cut the air with his hand.

"These others will be given to the women, to use as they see fit. The governor will live for now," he said. He caught Khasar's surprise out of the corner of his eye, but did not respond to it.

"Fetch Temuge to me," Genghis went on. "They are watching us on the walls of Otrar. I will give them something to see."

His brother Temuge came quickly at the summons, barely glancing at the bloody dust, or the governor who still sat with his eyes darting from man to man.

"How much silver do we have in the camp, Temuge?" Genghis asked.

"Perhaps a hundred carts of it, my lord khan," Temuge replied. "I have accounted for every coin, but I would have to bring my records if—"

"Bring me the weight of a man in that metal," Genghis said. He sensed Inalchuk staring at him and smiled slowly.

"And one of the moving forges Tsubodai brought back. I want the silver to run like water before sunset. Do you understand?"

"Of course, Lord Khan," Temuge replied, though he did not understand at all. He hurried away to do his brother's bidding.

The population of Otrar crowded onto the walls of the city to see what would become of the governor they had sent out to the Mongol army. They had suffered through the battle between the garrison and Samuka's men. When the garrison had broken out at last, their mood had been jubilant. The Shah was coming to relieve the city and they would be saved. Instead, the Mongol army had come back unchallenged from the south to surround them. They did not know if the Shah still lived, but how could the khan sit outside their walls if he did? It had taken months for the merchants to form a council and days of secret talks before they had surprised Inalchuk in his bed and trussed him to be handed over. The Mongols had no grudge against the citizens of Otrar, only the man who had provoked them. Families stood together on the walls and prayed that they would be saved.

Before the sun set, Genghis had Inalchuk brought to within arrow shot of the walls. It was a dangerous thing to do, but he guessed rightly that the people within would not dare risk a shot at the one man who could choose to spare them. Just a hundred yards from the iron gates, he had Inalchuk kneel with his hands freshly tied in front.

The sight of the smoking forge had not been lost on the governor of Otrar. It too had been wheeled close to the walls of his city, and he could smell the tang of hot metal on the breeze. He doubled his offer and then doubled it again, until Genghis told the interpreter to hold his tongue or lose it.

They made a strange group, standing alone before the city. Three burly men worked the forge bellows under Temuge's direction. Genghis stood by the prisoner with Khasar, but the rest of the Mongol army stood back in silent ranks, watching.

At last the forge workers nodded that the silver coins were molten, held in a cauldron of black iron. One of them dipped a stick into the liquid within. It charred on contact, while drops of silver hissed and spat. Two of the men ran long wooden poles through the cauldron handles and lifted it clear of the iron box and the white heat of charcoal and bellows.

Inalchuk moaned in terror as he saw them bring it out, heating the air to a haze above the simmering contents.

"One hundred thousand oka of silver, lord," he said, sweating. The interpreter glanced up but did not speak, and Inalchuk began to pray aloud.

As the carriers came forward, Genghis stared into the bowl of liquid silver and nodded to himself.

"Say these words to him in his own tongue," he said to the interpreter. "I have no use for silver or gold."

Inalchuk looked up in desperate hope as the interpreter spoke.

"What is he doing, my friend? In the name of Allah, tell me if I am to die!"

The interpreter held his breath for a moment, staring in sick fascination at the silver as it slopped against the sides of the iron and coated them.

"I think that you are," he admitted. "It will at least be quick, so prepare your soul for God."

Oblivious to the exchange, Genghis went on. "Accept this gift from me, Governor of Otrar," he said. "You may keep what you can hold."

Genghis turned to Khasar, his face cold.

"Have him hold out his hands, but be careful you are not burned."

Khasar knocked Inalchuk down with a blow to his head that left him dazed. He mimed holding out his hands and the governor began to yell, refusing. Even a sword held to his throat would not make him raise his hands. In growing anger, Khasar took him by the elbow and shoulder and snapped a bone with his knee, as if breaking a stick. Inalchuk screamed, still struggling. Genghis nodded and Khasar walked round to break the other arm.

"Do as they want, brother!" the interpreter snapped. "You may live!"

Inalchuk heard through his madness and, sobbing, held out the bound hands, one supporting the other as it hung limp. Genghis nodded to the forge men and they tipped the cauldron, slopping silver toward the edge.

A flood of bubbling metal covered the governor's hands so that for a moment it looked as if he held shining rain. He opened his mouth to scream, but no sound came out. His fingers were welded together in the heat, the flesh dissolving.

He fell backwards, jerking away and landing on his face, drool spilling from his mouth as his lips made a paste of dust. His eyes were blank as Genghis came to stand over him, looking with interest at hands that seemed twice their usual size.

"You brought me to this dry land," Genghis told the shuddering figure. "I offered you peace and trade and you sent me the heads of my men. Now I have given you your precious silver to hold."

Inalchuk said nothing, though his lips worked soundlessly.

"Do you have no words to thank me?" Genghis went on. "Is your throat too dry? Accept this drink from me to slake your thirst. Then you will know a small echo of the pain you have caused."

The interpreter was silent in horror, but Inalchuk was past hearing. The khan did not bother to watch as the forge men brought up their pot and poured the rest of the metal over the governor's face. His oiled beard ignited and the open mouth filled, but Genghis only stared at the people on the walls. Many of them turned away, understanding at last that death would come for them.

"The catapults are finished, Khasar," Genghis said, still staring up at the city. "You will begin breaking the walls tomorrow at dawn. I want each stone removed from every other. Otrar will not be rebuilt when we have gone. This city will be swept from the face of the world, with every living thing in it."

Khasar shared the depths of his brother's hatred. He bowed his head.

"Your will, my lord khan."

The Old Man listened at a tiny grill set high in the wall of the cell. He could see only bare outlines in the gloom, but he heard the sounds of a young body stirring as it rose from drugged sleep. He was patient as he waited. How many times had he guided a boy through the ritual of awakening? He had shown the garden to his new recruit, with its glory enhanced by the drug in wine sweetened almost to syrup. He had shown him paradise and now, in the darkness, he would see hell.

The Old Man smiled to himself as he heard a voice cry out below in horror. He could imagine the shock and confusion, recalling how he had felt himself so many years before. The smell of dead flesh was strong in that little cell, the bodies greasy with loose flesh as they lay over the young warrior. The Old Man heard him whisper and sob as he struggled with the limp limbs covering him. It would seem as if only moments had passed since he sat in a place so beautiful that it was almost painful. The Old Man had perfected the garden and chosen the women well, down to the last detail. They were exquisite creatures and the drug had inflamed the young man so that every light touch on his skin had driven him almost to madness. Then he had closed his eyes for an instant and woken with the stinking dead.

The Old Man strained his eyes to see into the gloom. He could see flailing movement as the boy cast around him. He would feel soft matter under his hands in the darkness, perhaps feel the movement of maggots in the meat. The boy moaned and the Old Man heard him vomit. The stench was appalling and the Old Man pressed a pouch of rose petals to his nose as he waited. The moment was always delicate, but he was a master of his art.

The boy was naked in that place of the slippery dead. The Old Man saw him plucking at shreds of glistening skin where they had clung to his own. His mind would be fragile, his heart racing to the point of death. The Old Man thought only the very young could survive such an experience, but even they were haunted by it ever after.

The boy yelled suddenly, his attention caught by a shifting mass of rotting flesh. The Old Man smiled at his terrified imaginings and readied the shuttered lamp at his feet, where no stray glow could spoil the lesson. Below him, the boy prayed to Allah to deliver him from his stinking pit of hell.

The Old Man threw open the door to the cell, his lamp shattering the gloom, so that the boy was blinded and fell back with hands over his eyes. To the Old Man's pleasure, he heard the spatter of hot urine as the boy's bladder gave way. He had judged the moment well. Tears streamed below the clasped hands.

"I have shown you paradise," the Old Man said. "And I have shown you hell. Shall I leave you here for a thousand lifetimes; or shall I take you back to the world? Which one awaits you depends on how well you follow me. On your soul, speak truly. Will you dedicate your life to me to spend as I see fit?"

The boy was fifteen years old. As he knelt and wept, the last traces of sticky hashish faded from his young body, leaving him shaking and weak.

"Please! Anything you ask! I am yours," he said, sobbing. Still, he did not dare open his eyes, in case he found the vision gone and was left alone once more.

The Old Man pressed a cup to his lips and let him smell the resin that was said to give courage. The boy gulped at it, the purple wine running down his bare chest and arms. The Old Man grunted in satisfaction as the boy slumped back, his senses spinning away.

When the boy awoke, he lay on clean sheets in a bare stone room, somewhere in the fastness that was the Old Man's sanctuary from the world. Alone, he wept at what he had seen, unaware that he was still observed. As he swung his legs over and tried to rise, he was filled with determination never to see the demons of the dead room again. He shuddered to remember the way the bodies had moved and stared at him, each memory more vivid and terrifying than the last. He thought he would have gone insane if the garden had not remained also in his mind. Its peace had protected him, even in hell.

The wooden door to the room opened and the boy took a deep breath as he stood before the man of power who had brought him out of that place. The Old Man was short and burly, his eyes fierce in a face as dark as mahogany. His beard was oiled and perfect, but his clothes were simple as always, suited to one who refused all the tawdry trappings of wealth. The boy threw himself full length on the cool stone, prostrating himself for his deliverance.

"You understand at last," the Old Man said softly. "I have taken you by the hand and shown you both glory and failure. Which will you choose when the time comes?"

"I will choose glory, master," he said, shaking.

"Your life is just a bird's flight through a lit room. You pass from infinite darkness into endless night, with only a short time in between. The room does not matter. Your life does not matter, only how you prepare for the next."

"I understand," the boy said. He could feel the oily touch of dead limbs on his skin even then and he shuddered.

"Pity those who do not know what comes after death. You can stand strong among them, for you have seen both heaven and hell and you will not falter." The leader of the assassins raised the boy to his feet with a gentle hand.

"Now you may join your brothers. Men like you, who have been allowed to press their eye to a crack in the walls of reality. You will not fail them, or me, when you bring a perfect death to the feet of Allah."

"I will not, master," the boy replied, more certain than he had ever been in his young life. "Tell me whom I must kill. I will not fail."

The Old Man smiled, always touched by the earnest faith of the young warriors he sent out into the world. He had been one of them once, and when the nights were dark and cold, he still sometimes ached for the garden he had been shown. When death took him at last, he could only hope the real thing was as wonderful as the one he had created. Let there be hashish resin in paradise, he thought. Let him be as young and lithe as the boy before him.

"You will travel with your brothers to the camp of the Mongol khan, he who calls himself Genghis."

"Amongst the infidel, master?" the boy stammered, already feeling unclean.

"Even so. Your faith will keep you strong. For this and only this you have trained with us for five years. You have been chosen for your skill with languages. You may serve Allah well with his gift." The Old Man rested a hand on the boy's shoulder, his palm seeming to radiate heat. "Get close to the khan, and when the moment is right, tear his life from him with a single thrust to the heart. Do you understand the price of failure?"

The boy swallowed painfully, the pit fresh in his mind.

"I will not fail, master. I swear it."

PART
TWO

CHAPTER TWENTY

THERE WAS NO BREEZE IN THE SUMMER HEAT. The air was still and the sun emptied the streets for hours around midday. The city of Almashan was not much more than a walled fortress, ancient and dusty, though a shining river ran along its flank. There were no women and children out on the riverbanks that day. Almashan was shut tight, packed with people and animals from the farms all around. The market-places smelled of fear and cesspools that oozed their filth through to the surface and could not be emptied.

In the distance, the city merchants could hear a whispering thunder, growing all the time. Those on the ground could only look up to the guard posts on the walls and pray for deliverance. Even the beggars had ceased their calls for alms.

"Be ready!" Ibrahim called to the men at the gate below. He stared out over the wall, his heart thumping in his chest. Almashan was surrounded by thin soil, too poor to farm well. Yet they had never depended on crops for their wealth.

In the heat haze, a black line of riders approached at frightening speed. They were the reason Ibrahim's beloved city was packed with strangers. Merchants and trading caravans had raced inside the walls for safety. Ibrahim had levied a tax on all of them, fully half of the goods they sought to protect. None of them had dared complain. If they survived the Mongol attack, Ibrahim knew he would be an extremely wealthy man, but he was not confident.

His little city had stood for seven hundred years on the banks of that river. Its merchants had traveled as far as Chin lands and Spain, bringing back treasures and priceless knowledge, yet never so obviously that they excited the interest of kings and Shahs. The elders of Almashan paid their taxes on time while they made fortunes on the backs of infidel slaves. The little city had built its walls and granaries on those profits, becoming a hub for the sale of flesh. Farmland would not have brought Ibrahim the wealth he already enjoyed, or even a small piece of it.

He strained his eyes against the brutal glare, his splayed hands gripping dark stones that had been part of a fort more ancient than anyone could know. Before even that, the city had once been just a place for slave traders to rest by the river before heading south or east to the great markets. Almashan had risen from the ground and claimed them for its own.

Ibrahim sighed to himself. From what he had heard, the Mongols did not understand trade. They would see only an enemy city. His turban soaked up sweat, but he still wiped his hand across his face, leaving a dark patch on the cool white cloth of his robe.

Ahead of the Mongol riders, a lone Bedouin raced, looking back over his shoulder as he galloped. Ibrahim could see he rode a fine black horse, the animal's size and speed barely keeping him ahead of his pursuers. Ibrahim drummed his fingers on the rough stone as he considered whether to open the small door set into the gate. Clearly the desert warrior thought he was running to safety, but if the gates remained closed, perhaps the Mongols would not attack. If the man was allowed to enter, how long would Almashan withstand the assault that would surely follow?

Indecision racked Ibrahim as he turned and looked down. The souks and bazaars still chattered with news of the Shah's defeat, and he was desperate for fresh news, but not at the cost of his city. No. Ibrahim decided to keep the gate closed and let the man die. His mind filled with anger at the thought of the infidels snatching a Moslem right before the city, but Ibrahim had many families looking to him for their safety. Perhaps the Mongols would pass by once they had shed blood. Ibrahim would pray for the man's soul.

The Mongol line had come close enough for Ibrahim to see individual mounts. He shuddered at the sight of the fierce warriors who had undone Shah Ala-ud-Din Mohammed and broken his great host in sight of Otrar. Yet he saw no catapults or carts, no sign of the great raiding nation that had spilled out of mountains to the east. Perhaps three thousand men rode toward his city, but mounted men alone could not trouble Almashan. The stone under his hands reflected the wealth of centuries of slaving. The walls kept that wealth safe, as well those who lived there.

Ibrahim's heart was bitter as he watched the Arab rider rein in before the city gate. The man gestured desperately, spinning his horse in place as he yelled to those who watched.

"Let me in!" he yelled. "See those behind me!"

Ibrahim felt the gaze of other men rest on him. He stood very straight as he shook his head. The Mongols were just half a mile away and he could hear the rumble of their hooves. Almashan was independent and always had been. He could not risk the anger of this foreign khan.

The Arab below gaped, darting a glance back at the warriors running him down.

"For the love of Allah!" he roared. "Would you leave me to be killed? I have news you must hear!"

Ibrahim clenched his fist, shaking. He saw the man's horse was laden with saddlebags. Was he a messenger? What news could be so important? The Mongols, the infidels, were just heartbeats away. Ibrahim could hear the snorting mounts and the guttural calls of their men as they bent their bows. He cursed to himself under his breath as he looked away. What was one life in comparison to a city? Almashan would survive.

Below his feet, Ibrahim heard raised voices and he stepped back from the parapet to peer below at the source. To his horror, he saw his brother smash a guard across the face with his hand. The man fell and though Ibrahim cried out in anger, his brother lifted the locking bar and a beam of solid sunlight lit the gloom below. Before Ibrahim could shout again, the door closed and the panting Bedouin was safe inside. Red with rage, Ibrahim raced down the stone steps to the street below.

"You fools!" he roared. "What have you *done*?" The guards would not meet his eyes, but his brother only shrugged. The door in the gate shook suddenly, making them all jump. The bar rattled under an impact, and above, someone fell back from the wall with an arrow in his shoulder. Ibrahim winced as, outside, Mongol riders howled their frustration.

"You have killed us all," Ibrahim said in fury. He felt the cool gaze of the man who had entered Almashan and ignored it. "Send him back out to them and they may yet spare us."

His brother shrugged. "Inshallah," he murmured. Their fate was in God's hands. He had acted and the man was inside their city. The noise from outside increased in volume, making them all sweat.

The messenger was panting at his narrow deliverance. He stood for a moment with his hands on his knees, and Ibrahim saw that he had brought the saddlebags with him.

"My name is Yusuf Alghani," he said as he recovered. He had not missed the exchange between the two brothers, and his eyes were very cold as he addressed Ibrahim. "Do not fear for your city. The Mongol animals have no siege weapons. Your walls are safe from them. Be thankful that you did not earn Allah's displeasure with your cowardice."

Ibrahim crushed his rage and frustration to reply. "For you alone, my brother has put us all in danger. We are a trading city and only our walls keep us safe. What news is so important that you risked your life to come to Almashan?"

Yusuf smiled, showing very white teeth in his sun-darkened face. "I have news of a great victory, but not for your ears. Take me to the Shah and I will raise his heart."

Ibrahim blinked in confusion, looking to his brother and back to this confident young man.

"Shah Mohammed is not in Almashan, brother. Is that what you thought?"

Yusuf grinned, unabashed. "Do not play games, my friend. He will want to hear what I know. Take me to him and I will not mention how you nearly let me die before your walls."

Ibrahim spluttered in confusion. "Truly, he is not in Almashan. Is he coming here? Let me have drinks and food brought for you. Tell me what you know and I will pass it on when the Shah arrives."

The messenger's smile faded slowly as he understood, replaced by a great weariness.

"I had hoped he would be here," he muttered to himself. Ibrahim watched as the young man tapped the fingers of one hand on the leather saddlebags, as if the contents had grown too hot to hold comfortably.

"I must leave," Yusuf said suddenly. He bowed to Ibrahim, though the gesture was formal and stiff. "My words are for the Shah alone, and if he is not in this place, I must travel to the next city. Perhaps they will not make me wait until the very last moment to let me in."

Ibrahim would have replied, but the noise at the gate ceased as suddenly as it had begun. With a nervous glance at his idiot brother, he raced back up the stone steps to the walls. The other men followed him and together they gazed out.

The Mongols were riding away. Ibrahim breathed in relief and thanked Allah for his city. How many times had the council complained of the cost when he had reinforced and repaired the crumbling walls? He had been right and a thousand times right. The Mongols could not assault his home without their stone-throwers, perhaps not even then. Almashan scorned their swords and bows. Ibrahim watched in delight as the enemy warriors rode clear without looking back.

"They are clever," Yusuf said at his shoulder. "It could be that they seek to lull us. I have seen it before. Do not trust them, master."

Ibrahim's confidence had grown and he was expansive as he replied.

"They cannot break our walls, Yusuf. Now will you take cool drinks in my house? I am curious to know the messages you carry."

To his frustration, the young man shook his head, his attention still on the Mongol riders.

"I will not stay here. Not when the Shah is close by. He must be told. Greater cities than this one depend on me reaching him." Before Ibrahim could reply, the man leaned over the parapet, looking down.

"Did they kill my horse?" he asked.

Ibrahim's brother cleared his throat. "They took it," he said. Yusuf swore as he went on. "I have a good mount, a mare. You could have her."

"I will buy her from you," Yusuf replied.

Ibrahim's brother bowed his head, though he was relieved at the offer. "She is very strong. For the Shah's man, I will give you an excellent price," he said.

Ibrahim could only stand with his fists clenched as his brother sent a man to bring his second-best mare to the gate. The young messenger strode back down the stone steps, and Ibrahim was forced to follow with the others. He could not help glancing at the bulging saddlebags once more, silently considering whether the contents would be worth cutting a man's throat. As the thought formed, Yusuf seemed to sense it and smiled again.

"There is nothing of value in my bags, master," he said. He reached up and tapped his head. "My messages are all in here."

Ibrahim colored, flustered that the young man had guessed his thoughts. When the mare came, the messenger inspected the animal with the eye of one who knew horses. At last he was satisfied and paid Ibrahim's brother more than he had asked, honoring him. Sourly, Ibrahim watched the young man check the belly strap and reins. Above their heads, the guards called that the way was clear.

"I would pay well to hear those messages," Ibrahim said suddenly. To his surprise, the messenger hesitated. "In gold," Ibrahim went on, sensing the first weakness.

"Very well, master," Yusuf replied. "I need funds to continue my search for the Shah. But it must be quick." As Ibrahim fought to hide his pleasure, the messenger passed the reins to a guard and followed him to the nearest house.

The family within made no protest when Ibrahim told them to leave. In just moments, he was alone with the messenger, almost quivering to hear the news.

"The gold you promised?" Yusuf said softly.

In his excitement, Ibrahim did not hesitate. He took a full pouch from under his robe, still warm and damp from his skin. The younger man hefted it, glancing at the contents with a wry smile before making it disappear.

"This is for you alone, master," Yusuf said, his voice almost a whisper. "My poverty forces me to speak, but it is not for all ears."

"Tell me," Ibrahim urged. "It will go no further."

"Bukhara has fallen, but the garrison at Samarkand achieved a great victory. The khan's army was shattered in the field. For this year alone, they are weak. If the Shah returns to lead his loyal cities, he will have all their heads. *If* he comes, master. That is why I must find him quickly."

"Allah be praised," Ibrahim whispered. "I see now why you cannot delay."

The messenger pressed his hands to his forehead, lips, and heart in the ancient gesture.

"I am the Shah's servant in this, master. The blessing of Allah on you and your honorable house. Now I must ride."

Ibrahim moved quickly then, striding with more confidence back to the gate. He felt the eyes of all his men on him, and even his foolish brother stared as if he might discern what the messages had been.

Once more the small door in the gate opened to let in sunlight and air to that stifling place under the walls. The messenger bowed to Ibrahim and then led his mount through the gap. The door was shut and barred behind him, and he dug in his heels, riding hard across the dusty ground.

It was sunset before Yusuf caught up with the tuman of Tsubodai and Jebe. He rode into the makeshift camp they had made, acknowledging the calls of warriors. He was nineteen years old and more than pleased with himself. Even Tsubodai smiled at the young Arab's confidence as he dismounted with a flourish and bowed before the two generals.

"Is the Shah there?" Tsubodai asked.

Yusuf shook his head. "They would have told me, General."

Tsubodai pursed his lips in annoyance. The Shah and his sons were like wraiths. The Mongols had chased the man and his guards right through to the end of summer and still he evaded them. Tsubodai had placed his hopes on him going to ground in the city on the river, its walls too high for an assault.

"He is a slippery fish, that old man," Jebe said. "But we will catch him in the end. He cannot get past our lines without someone seeing him, even with the men he has left."

Tsubodai grunted. "I wish I could be so certain. He had the wit to send his men on a false trail. We almost lost him then and it is much harder to track just a few." He rubbed his arm where one of the Shah's guards had surprised him. It had been a well-laid ambush, but the guards had been vastly outnumbered. Though it took time, Tsubodai and Jebe had slaughtered them to the last man. They had checked the face of every dead Arab, but they had all been young and strong. Tsubodai bit his lip at the memory. "He could hide himself in a single cave and scrub out his tracks. We could have ridden past him already."

"They know nothing in the city, General," Yusuf said. "The Shah did not stop for supplies anywhere near here. The slavers would have heard and told me." He had expected to be congratulated on the success of his subterfuge, though it had been Tsubodai's idea. Instead the two generals were back to their discussions as if it had been nothing. He did not mention the pouch of gold he had won with a few lies. They had noticed the new mare he had brought back and would consider that enough of a reward for his work. The Mongol generals did not need to know everything.

"The scouts report a dozen villages and towns further west of here," Jebe replied after glancing at Yusuf. "If he has passed through, someone will remember an armed group and an old man. He cannot run forever."

"He has managed *this* far," Tsubodai snapped. He turned to Yusuf, who still stood there, shifting his weight from foot to foot. "You did well, Yusuf. Now leave us."

The young man bowed deeply. It was a good thing they paid well, these Mongols. If the Shah could evade them until winter came again, Yusuf would be a rich man. As he walked back through the camp, he nodded and smiled to some of the warriors he knew. They were quiet as the evening came, as wolves were quiet when there was no prey in range. He saw them sharpening their swords and repairing arrows, slow and steady in their work. Yusuf shuddered delicately. He had heard of the attack on their women and children. He would not like to see what happened when they finally caught the Shah and his sons.

Jelaudin rubbed his eyes, furious at his own weakness. He could not let his three brothers see his air of confidence fade, not when they looked to him every day with fear and hope.

He winced in the darkness at his father's laboring breath, in and out in a slow wheeze that seemed to go on forever. Every time it ceased, Jelaudin listened in despair, not knowing what he would do if the silence stretched and stretched around him.

The Mongols had brought the old man down, just as if they had struck him with one of their shafts. The pursuit across plains and mountains had never allowed the Shah to rest and recover. Damp ground and torrential rain had meant they all suffered colds and aching joints. At more than sixty years of age, the old man was like a bull, but the damp had seeped into his lungs and torn the strength right out of him. Jelaudin could feel tears spring fresh to his eyes, and he rubbed them too hard, digging the heels of his hands into the sockets so that the pain would ease his anger.

He had never been hunted before. In the first month, it was like a game to him. He and his brothers had laughed at the Mongols on their trail, coming up with ridiculous plans to lose them. As the rains had come, they had laid false trails, split their force, then split it again. They had ordered men to their deaths in ambushes that barely seemed to slow the implacable enemy who streamed after them.

Jelaudin listened as his father's breath crackled in the dark. His lungs were full of thick muck and he would wake soon, choking on it. Jelaudin would pound him on the back as he had so many times before until the old man's skin lost its waxy look and he could rise for one more day on the run.

"Curse them all to hell," Jelaudin whispered. The Mongols must have had men who could follow the path of a bird in flight. Four times Jelaudin had risked turning his father back to the east. On each occasion, they had seen a distant line of scouts, spread wide and watching for just such an attempt. On the last, they had been forced to run to exhaustion, losing themselves at last in a city market. Jelaudin had barely escaped with his life and his father's coughing had started two nights later, after sleeping on wet ground.

It had hurt the brothers to send the last guards away. It was just too easy to track large groups of men, or even the last few dozen who had stayed doggedly with the Shah they had pledged to serve. Now only Jelaudin remained with his three younger brothers to tend their father. They had changed their clothes and horses too many times to recall. They had only a little gold left for food and supplies, and when that was gone, Jelaudin truly did not know what would happen. He touched a small pouch of gems, hidden under his robe, taking comfort from the glassy click as he rolled them against each other. Away from the moneylenders in the great cities, he was not sure how he could sell even one safely. It was infuriating. He and his brothers could not live off the land the way the Mongols could. He had been born to silk, with servants to answer his slightest whim.

His father choked in the gloom and Jelaudin reached to him, helping him sit up. He could not remember the name of the small town where they had stopped. Perhaps the Mongols were riding into the outskirts even as the Shah heaved for breath.

Jelaudin shook his head, despairing. One more night on the ground would have killed his father, he was sure of it. If it was Allah's will that they be taken that night, at least it would be in dry clothes, with a meal inside their shrunken bellies. Better that than to have the wolves fall on them as they slept in fields like lambs.

"My son?" his father called, his voice querulous. Jelaudin pressed a cool hand to his father's forehead, almost recoiling from the heat there. A fever was raging through him and he was not certain the old man even knew him.

"Shh, Father. You will wake the stableboys here. We are safe for the night."

His father tried to say something else, but a coughing fit broke the words into meaningless bursts of sound. The Shah leaned over the edge of the bed to hawk and spit weakly into the bucket. Jelaudin grimaced at the sound. Dawn was close and he had not slept; could not sleep with his father needing him.

The Caspian Sea was more than a hundred miles west of that shabby little town in the middle of moonlit fields. Jelaudin had never traveled beyond it. He could hardly imagine the lands or the people there, but he would be hiding among them if the Mongol line continued to sweep them further and further from home. He and his brothers were desperate to break through those who herded them, but how could it be done? He had even left three men hidden under wet leaves, so that the Mongols would pass them by. If they had survived, they would have brought help as winter came, surely? Every noise in the night was terrifying to the Shah and his sons, and there were no smiles anymore at the enemy who would not stop, would not ever stop until they ran them into the ground.

Shah Ala-ud-Din Mohammed sank back exhausted onto the straw pallet Jelaudin had found for him. His sons would sleep in the filthy stable and still it was better than anything they had known for months. Jelaudin listened to his father's breathing become quieter and silently cursed the old man for his illness. They seemed to travel a shorter distance each day, and Jelaudin doubted the Mongols moved as slowly.

As his father slept, Jelaudin considered going to ground, as he had all through the hot months. He had needed the horses while there was a chance of breaking through, but if they sold or killed the animals and entered a city as a group of travelers, how could the Mongols ever find them? They were only men, for all the fiendish skill of their trackers. He had urged the Shah to stop at the ancient slave city of Almashan, but the old man would not hear of hiding like beggars. The very idea seemed to wound him. It had been hard enough to stop his father announcing their presence to the city elders and defying the Mongols from the walls.

To stop was to die, Jelaudin was certain of it. The army chasing his father brought terror with them, and few cities would sacrifice their own families for the Shah and his sons. The moment the Mongols surrounded a city, Jelaudin knew he would be handed over or murdered in his sleep. He had few choices left. Jelaudin stared through the darkness at the man who had given orders all his life. It was a hard thing to accept that the Shah was too frail to know best how to avoid the animals on their trail. Though Jelaudin was the oldest son, he did not feel ready to scorn his father's will.

"We will stop, Father," he whispered suddenly. "We will hide the horses and ourselves in a town. We have enough money to live simply while you recover your strength. They will pass us by. Let them be blind, Allah. If it is your will, let them pass us by."

His father could not hear through his delirium, the fever working its way into his lungs and leaving less and less each day to draw breath.

CHAPTER TWENTY-ONE

ON THE OUTSKIRTS OF THE TOWN OF NUR, Genghis strolled with his wives and brothers behind a cart drawn by camels. Though the days were short in winter, the breeze barely carried a chill. For those who had known ice and snow every year of their childhood, it was almost a spring day. His mind was clear and calm for the first time in months, and he looked with pride as little Tolui managed the animals with a slap of the reins. His youngest son was barely fourteen, but the wedding ceremony had come at the demand of the girl's father. Two years older than Tolui, she already nursed a baby boy in her ger and was pregnant with another child. It had taken a word from Borte to Genghis to make the marriage happen before one of the girl's relatives was reluctantly forced to declare blood feud on the khan's son.

The girl was already showing her second pregnancy, though her family had tried their best to conceal it with voluminous robes. No doubt her mother was looking after the firstborn boy, Genghis mused as he walked. Tolui and the girl, Sorhatani, seemed besotted with each other, if careless with the laws of the tribes. It was not uncommon for young girls to get themselves pregnant, though Sorhatani showed unusual spirit in binding Tolui to her without her father's consent. She had even come to Borte to ask that Genghis name the first son. The khan had always admired that sort of brazen courage and he was pleased with Tolui's choice. He had called the boy Mongke, meaning "eternal," a fitting name for one who would carry his blood. As Genghis walked, he considered declaring all children legitimate, whether they were born after marriage or not. It would save trouble in the future, he was certain.

"When I was a boy," Genghis said a little wistfully, "a young man might have traveled for days to reach his bride's tribe."

Khasar snorted at the idea. "I have four wives, brother. If I had to do that each time I wanted a new one, I'd never get anything done."

"I am amazed any of them put up with you," Borte said, smiling sweetly. She made a gesture with her little finger to Chakahai, causing her to giggle.

Genghis grinned at his first wife. It lifted his spirits to see her smile, standing tall and strong, her bare arms tanned from the sun. Even Chakahai's pale skin had taken a golden hue in the hot months, and both women glowed with health. He was pleased to catch Borte's wink as she noticed him looking her over. She and Chakahai seemed to have reached an understanding after the Shah's attack on the families. At least he did not have to watch them too closely when they were together, in case they erupted like cats in a bag. It was peace of a sort.

"The nation does need children, Borte," he replied. Khasar chuckled lasciviously in response, making Borte and Chakahai roll their eyes at each other. Khasar had fathered seventeen children that he knew of and was justly proud of having fourteen of them live. With the exception of Temuge, Genghis's brothers had done their part in swelling the nation with squalling brats to run wild among the gers. Temuge too had married, but the union had produced no children as yet. Instead, his youngest brother filled his days with the administration of tribal disputes. Genghis glanced at him, but Temuge was ignoring Khasar and watching Tolui step down from the cart. For once, Genghis felt mellow toward his youngest brother. Temuge had created his own little empire within the nation, with a staff of eighty men and women working for him. Genghis had heard he even taught them reading and writing. It seemed to work and Genghis was pleased his brother did not come to him with the problems he faced each day. In contrast to the long strides of his warrior brothers, Temuge walked in short, fussy steps and wore his long hair tied in a Chin style. He washed far too often and Genghis could detect a scent of perfumed oil about him as the breeze blew. There had been a time when Genghis had been ashamed for him, but Temuge seemed content and the tribes had slowly accepted his authority.

The bride's family had made their small camp to the west of Nur, setting out their gers in the traditional style. Genghis saw Tolui hesitate as armed men came racing out to intercept him. The blue robe and gold tunic his son wore were unmistakable even at a distance.

Genghis smiled as the men of the family put on their show. They seemed unaware of the thousands who had come to witness the union and waved their swords as if genuinely affronted. Tolui bowed deeply to Sorhatani's father. Genghis could not help but wince. Tolui was the son of the Great Khan, after all. With Sorhatani already a mother, her father would hardly have sent Tolui away for showing less respect.

Genghis sighed to Borte, knowing she understood. Tolui was a good son, though he seemed to lack the fire of his father and uncles. Perhaps it was growing up in the shadow of Jochi and Chagatai. Genghis slid a glance to his right, where those two young men walked with Ogedai. His two oldest sons had not put aside their differences, but that was a problem for another day.

The bride's father relented at last, letting Tolui into his gers to greet his wife-to-be. Genghis and his wives walked closer to the family gathering as Kokchu blessed the land and threw drops of black airag into the air for the watching spirits.

"He is a fine son," Kachiun said, clapping both his brother and Borte on the back. "You must be proud of him."

"I am," Genghis replied. "Though I doubt he could lead. He is too soft to hold men's lives in his hands."

"He is young yet," Borte said immediately, shaking her head in reproof. "And he has not had your life."

"Perhaps he should have. If I had left the boys to survive in the winters of home instead of bringing them here, perhaps they would all be khans." He could sense both Jochi and Chagatai listening, though they pretended not to.

"They will be yet, brother," Khasar said. "You'll see. The lands we have taken need men to rule them. Give him a few years and set him up as Shah of one of these desert kingdoms. Leave a tuman to support him and he'll make you proud, I do not doubt it."

Genghis nodded, pleased at the compliment to his boy. He saw Temuge turn with sudden interest at Khasar's words.

"That is a good thought," Temuge said. "In the Chin lands, we often had to take the same city more than once. Some resisted even after a second raid and had to be destroyed. We cannot just ride over them and expect them to remain defeated."

Genghis grimaced slightly at that "we." He did not recall Temuge riding against cities, but on such a day, he let it pass. His youngest brother went on blithely.

"Give me the word and I will have good men left behind in every city we take from this absent Shah, to rule in your name. In ten years or twenty, you will have an empire to match the Chin and Sung combined."

Genghis recalled an old conversation with a tong leader in the Chin city of Baotou. The man had suggested something similar then, all those years ago. It was a difficult concept for him. Why would a man want to rule a city when the plains were open and empty? Yet the idea intrigued him and he did not scorn his brother's words.

The bride's family could not possibly have fed so many, but Temuge had ordered every stove in the camps lit for the wedding feast. Vast mats of felt were unrolled on the dusty ground and Genghis sat with his brothers, accepting a skin of airag and a steaming bowl with a dip of his head. Around them, the mood was light and songs began to issue from throats as they celebrated the union of his youngest son. In that place, with the town of Nur having surrendered only two days before, Genghis felt more relaxed than he had for many months of war. The destruction of Otrar had not lanced the corruption from his rage. Instead it had grown. He had pushed them all hard, but with the Shah still alive, Genghis felt driven to wreak devastation on the man's lands. A line had been crossed in the attack on the women and children, and in the absence of the Shah himself, Genghis had punished his people in the only way he knew.

"I do not like the idea, Temuge," he said at last. His brother's face fell before Genghis went on. "But I do not forbid it. I do not want these Arabs to come creeping back when we have passed by. If they live, it will be as slaves." He struggled not to let anger surface in him as he went on. "Ruling a city would be a good reward for old warriors, perhaps. A man like Arslan might be renewed by the challenge."

"I will send scouts to find him," Temuge replied instantly.

Genghis frowned. He had not meant Arslan himself. Yet, he still missed the old man and he could not find a reason to object.

"Very well, brother. But send for Chen Yi in Baotou as well, if he is still alive."

"That little criminal!" Temuge said, spluttering. "I did not mean to give power to just *anyone*. He has the city of Baotou already, brother. I can name a dozen men more suited to the work I have in mind."

Genghis waved a hand impatiently. He had not wanted to begin the discussion, and now it threatened to overwhelm him and spoil the day.

"He understood the sort of thing you mean, Temuge, which makes him valuable. Offer him gold and power. He may still refuse, I do not know. Do I have to repeat myself?"

"Of course not," Temuge said. "We have spent so long at war, it is hard to think of what must come after, but…"

"*You* haven't spent much time at war," Khasar said, poking him with an elbow. "*You* have spent your time with sheaves of paper, or playing the khan with your servant girls."

Temuge colored instantly and would have replied, but Genghis held up a hand for peace.

"*Not* today," he said, and both men subsided, glowering at each other.

Near the city, Genghis saw a group of his warriors surge to their feet. He rose instantly, suddenly wary as three of them trotted through the lively crowd toward him. Whatever disturbed their meal had not yet spread to the rest, and more than one family cursed aloud as the warriors jumped over or darted around them. Many had brought dogs to the feast and those animals barked excitedly.

"What is it?" Genghis demanded. If one of the young idiots had started a fight on his son's wedding day, he would have his thumbs.

"There are people coming out of the town, lord," the warrior replied, bowing low.

Without another word, Genghis, Kachiun, and Khasar strode through the crowd to the edge facing the city. Though they were on foot, they were all well armed in the habit of men who always had a blade or a bow in easy reach.

The men and women coming out of Nur did not look dangerous. Genghis watched curiously as perhaps sixty men and women walked across the ground between the wedding ceremony and Nur. They were dressed in bright colors that were the match of Tolui's marriage robe, and they did not seem to be carrying weapons.

The wedding crowd had fallen silent and many more men had begun to drift toward their khan, ready to kill if the need arose. By the time the group drew close, they faced a line of fierce veterans, men Genghis had honored with the invitation. The sight of such warriors made them falter in their steps, but one of them called to the others in their strange language, clearly steadying their nerves.

When they were close enough to speak, Genghis recognized some of the town elders who had surrendered to him. He brought Temuge forward to interpret.

His brother listened to the leader from Nur, then nodded to himself before speaking.

"They have brought gifts to the khan's son, on his wedding day," Temuge said.

Genghis grunted, half tempted to send them back to their homes to leave him alone. Perhaps because of the conversation he had just had, he relented. Enemies were to be destroyed, of course, but these had declared for him and done nothing to make him suspicious. He was aware that having an army encamped around a town made peace talks run surprisingly smoothly, but in the end he nodded.

"Tell them they are welcome, just for today," he told Temuge. "They can give the gifts to Tolui when the feast is over." His brother spoke a guttural stream and the group relaxed visibly as they joined the Mongols on the felt mats and accepted tea and airag.

Genghis forgot about them as he saw little Tolui come out of his father-in-law's ger and grin at the crowd. He had taken tea with the family and been formally accepted by them. He led Sorhatani by the hand, and though her robe showed a bulge at the front, no one commented on it with Genghis watching. Kokchu was ready to dedicate the union to the sky father and earth mother, bringing blessings on their new family and asking for fat, strong children to fill their gers.

As the shaman began to chant, Chakahai shivered and looked away from the man. Borte seemed to understand and laid a hand on her arm.

"I cannot look at him without thinking of poor Temulun," Chakahai murmured. At the name, Genghis's mood soured on the instant. He had lived with death all his life, but the loss of his sister had been hard. His mother had not even left her self-imposed seclusion for the wedding of her grandson. For that alone, the Arab cities would rue the day they had ever scorned his men and forced him to come to their lands.

"This is a day for new beginnings," Genghis said wearily. "We will not speak of death here."

Kokchu danced and spun as he chanted, his voice carrying far on the breeze that dried their sweat. The bride and her family remained still, with their heads bowed. Only little Tolui moved as he set about his first task as a husband. Genghis watched coldly as Tolui began to erect a ger from the piles of wicker lattice and thick felt. It was hard work for one who was barely a man, but his son was quick-fingered and the dwelling began to take shape.

"I will avenge Temulun and all the rest," Genghis said suddenly in a low voice.

Chakahai looked at him and nodded. "It will not make her live again," she said.

Genghis shrugged. "It is not for her. The suffering of my enemies will be a feast to the spirits. When I am old, I will remember the tears they have shed and it will ease my bones."

The light mood of the wedding had vanished and Genghis watched impatiently as the bride's father stepped in to help little Tolui raise the central pole of the ger, white and new. When it was complete, his son opened the painted door to usher Sorhatani into her new home. In theory they would seal the marriage that evening, though it was clear that particular task was already accomplished. Genghis wondered idly how his son would procure a bloody rag to show her virginity had been taken. He hoped the boy would have the sense not to bother.

Genghis put aside a skin of airag and stood, brushing crumbs from his deel. He could have cursed Chakahai for spoiling the day, but it had been a short break in the bloody work he faced. He felt his mind begin to fill with the plans and stratagems he needed, settling into the cold rhythms that would take cities and scour the sands clean of all who resisted them.

Those with him seemed to sense the change. He was no longer the devoted father. The Great Khan stood before them once more, and not one of them met his calm gaze.

Genghis looked around the camp, at those who still lay and ate or drank, enjoying the warmth and the occasion. For some reason, their indolence annoyed him.

"Get the warriors back to the camp, Kachiun," he ordered. "Have them work off the winter fat with a long ride and archery practice."

His brother bowed briefly, striding away and scattering men and women with barked orders.

Genghis breathed deeply and stretched his shoulders. After Otrar, the Shah's city of Bukhara had fallen almost without a blow being exchanged. Its entire garrison of ten thousand had deserted and still lurked somewhere in the hills, terrified of him.

Genghis clicked his tongue to make Jochi look up.

"Take your tuman to the hills, Jochi. Find that garrison and destroy them."

When Jochi had gone, Genghis felt a slight relief. The Shah was held in the far west by Tsubodai and Jebe. Even if he evaded them and returned, his empire would be reduced to ashes and rubble.

"Temuge? Have your scouts ride to Samarkand and bring back every detail they can learn of the defenses. I will lead the attack, with Chagatai and Jochi when he returns. We will make dust of their precious cities."

Jelaudin stood with his back to the door of the rooms they had rented in the town of Khuday, shutting out the noise and stench of the souk. He hated the grubby little place on the edge of a great expanse of sand where nothing but lizards and scorpions lived. He shuddered. He had known beggars before, of course. In the great cities of Samarkand and Bukhara, they bred like rats, but he had never had to walk among them, or suffer their diseased hands tugging at his robe. He had not stopped to press coins into their palms, and he still seethed at their curses. In other days, he would have ordered the town burned for the insult, but for the first time in his life, Jelaudin was alone, stripped of power and influence that he had barely noticed before it vanished.

Jelaudin jumped when a knock sounded right by his head. He cast a desperate glance around the tiny room, but his father was lying down in the other and his brothers were out buying food for the evening meal. Jelaudin wiped sweat from his face with a sharp gesture, then opened the door wide.

The owner of the house stood there, peering suspiciously inside as if Jelaudin might have sneaked half a dozen others into the tiny hovel he had rented. Jelaudin dipped with the owner, blocking his view.

"What is it?" he snapped.

The man frowned up at the arrogant young tenant, his breath pungent with spices. "It is noon, sir. I have come for the rent."

Jelaudin nodded irritably. It seemed a mark of distrust to pay each day rather than by the month. He supposed the town did not see too many strangers, especially since the Mongols had come to the area. Still, it rankled for a prince to be treated like a man who might run from his debts in the night.

Jelaudin found no coins in his pouch and had to cross the room to a rickety wooden table. He found a small pile there, placed and counted the night before. It would not keep them for more than another week, and his father was still too ill to be moved. Jelaudin took five copper coins, but he was not quick enough to prevent the owner from coming inside.

"There," Jelaudin said, pressing the money into his hand. He would have ordered him out, but the man seemed in no hurry to leave and Jelaudin was aware that his manner was wrong for one reduced to such poor lodgings. He tried to look humble, but the owner remained where he was, passing the greasy coins from one hand to another.

"Is your father still unwell, sir?" the man said suddenly. Jelaudin took a step to stop him seeing into the other room as he went on. "I know a very good physician. He is expensive, but he was trained in Bukhara before he returned to his family here. If you can pay?"

Jelaudin looked again at the small pile of coins. In his hidden pouch, he had a ruby the size of his thumb joint. It would buy the house he stood in, but above all else, he did not want to bring attention on his family. Their safety lay in anonymity.

In the back room, he could hear his father's wheeze and he nodded, giving in.

"I can pay. I will need to find a jeweler first, one who will buy."

"There are many such men, sir. May I ask if there are other claims on the jewel you wish to sell?"

For a moment, Jelaudin did not understand what was being asked. When he did, he flushed in outrage.

"It is not stolen! I . . . inherited it from my mother. I want an honest man who will give me a good price for it."

The owner dipped his head, embarrassed at the insult he had given. "My apologies, sir. I have suffered through hard times myself. I recommend Abbud, who has the red stall in the souk. He deals in gold and valuable items of all kinds. If you say his brother-in-law sent you, he will give you a fair price."

"And then a doctor?" Jelaudin continued. "Have him come this evening."

"I will try, sir, but there are few men as educated in Khuday. He is very busy."

Jelaudin was not used to bargaining, or paying bribes. A long moment went by and the owner of the house had to glance deliberately at the pile of coins before understanding dawned. The young prince swept the pile off the table into a hand and gave it to the man, trying not to recoil as their hands touched.

"I will tell him it is a favor to me, sir," the man replied, beaming. "He will come at sunset."

"Good. Now get out," Jelaudin replied, his patience dissolving. This was not his world. He had hardly even seen coins before manhood and then only to use for gambling with his father's officers. He felt tainted by the trade, as if he had indulged in some intimacy. As the door closed again, he sighed to himself, despairing.

CHAPTER TWENTY-TWO

THE JEWELER ABBUD weighed the man before him almost as carefully as he had the ruby he had brought. Both of them made him suspicious, though his brother-in-law had a nose for profit that equaled Abbud's own.

The man who claimed to be a merchant's son had no experience of trade, that much was obvious. The way he had gawked and stared at the stallholders as he made his way to Abbud's place of business was very odd indeed. What sort of man had never before visited a souk? Then his arrogance brought the hairs on Abbud's neck standing upright, every instinct warning of danger. He had survived forty years of trading in three cities, and he trusted his senses. The man had sword-hardened hands for a start. He looked more like a soldier than a merchant and strode through the market as if he expected others to get out of his way. Abbud had watched in amusement as they failed to do so and the young man had stumbled over two market bullies selling chickens. If not for the sword on his hip, they might have followed their jeering with blows.

The sword too was very fine. Abbud itched to hold the blade and could only wonder at the stupidity of a man carrying such a thing in the souk. Judging by the worked silver of the scabbard, it was worth even more than the ruby he had laid on the stall's outer bench for all to see.

Abbud had covered the gem with his hand and beckoned him inside before the fool got them both killed, but the sword might achieve that anyway. Lives were cheap in Khuday and such a blade would be worth the risk to a few young devils with knives. It would feed their families for a year if they sold it to the right man. Abbud sighed to himself, wondering if he should warn his customer. The chances were that he would be offered the sword himself before the day was over, perhaps with blood still on it.

None of his thoughts showed as he brought Jelaudin to the rear of his little stall. He had a table there, away from the prying glances of the market. He tapped a chair for Jelaudin as he sat himself and held up the gem to a candle, looking for flaws before weighing it with great delicacy on a tiny pair of brass scales.

Was it stolen? He did not think so. A thief would not have tumbled it onto the cloth so openly. The man owned it, certainly, but still the itch of worry would not leave Abbud. He knew the reason he was successful lay in his ability to read desperation in those who came to him. He had already been told about the man's need for a doctor. He suspected he could have the gem for a fraction of its worth, but laid it down as if it scorched him. There were too many things wrong about the man and his ruby. Abbud told himself he should send him away. He would have if the gem had been less perfect.

"I cannot sell such a jewel in Khuday," he said reluctantly. "I am sorry."

Jelaudin blinked. Was the old man turning him down? "I don't understand," he said.

Abbud spread his hands. "My business is in taking a cut on fine items of gold. Khuday is a poor place and no one here is likely to give me more than I could give you. I would have to send the jewel with a caravan to Bukhara or Samarkand, or perhaps Ashgabad or Mashhad in the south." He rolled the gem with a finger as if it were just a bauble. "Perhaps Kabul would have a buyer, but the cost of taking it so far would equal the profit I could make. As I say, I am sorry, but I cannot buy it."

Jelaudin was at a loss. In his entire life, he had never bargained for anything. He was not a fool and he recognized the man was probably toying with him, but he had no idea what to offer. In a sudden flush of anger, he thought of snatching it up and leaving. Only the thought of his father's physician arriving at sunset held him in his seat. Abbud watched him closely, hiding his own delight at the young man's transparent emotions. He could not resist twisting the knife and he pushed the jewel across the table as if ending the meeting.

"May I have tea brought?" Abbud suggested. "I do not like to turn a man away without even refreshment."

"I must sell this," Jelaudin said. "Can you not recommend someone else who will take it tonight and give me a good price?"

"I will send for tea," Abbud replied as if the question had not been asked. He ignored the warning voices that had troubled him at the beginning. *I must sell this?* Let Allah bring him a queue of fools like this one, and he would retire to a palace blessed with cool breezes.

As his servant boy brought tea in a silver pot, Abbud took note of the way the customer checked the sun outside. His naïveté was intoxicating.

"You are in need, my friend," Abbud said. "I would not like it said that I took advantage of that need, do you understand? My reputation is everything."

"I understand, of course," Jelaudin replied. The tea was very good and he sipped the hot drink in confusion, wondering what to do. The old jeweler leaned forward and dared to pat him on the arm as if they were friends.

"My brother-in-law told me your father is ill. Should I turn away a good son? Never in this life. I will make you an offer for the gem, enough to pay the physician at least. If I keep the ruby, perhaps I will find a buyer in years to come, no? My business is not all about quick profit. There are times when I must think of my soul." Abbud sighed audibly. He thought he might have overdone it with the last sentiment, but the young man brightened and nodded at him.

"You are very kind, sir," Jelaudin said, his relief painfully obvious.

"Will we not all be judged?" Abbud said piously. "My stall has not been profitable of late, with all this talk of war." He paused then, observing a tightening in the young man's face.

"Have you lost someone, my friend? Allah gives and he takes away. All we can do is endure this life."

"No, it is nothing," Jelaudin said. "I have heard of great battles in the east."

"Indeed. These are hard times." The prickle of warning was back in force and once more Abbud considered sending the man away. The ruby gleamed on the table and his eyes were drawn to it again.

"For you, my friend, I will offer you four gold coins. It is not what the gem is worth, nor half of it, but it will cover your debt to the physician. I cannot offer more."

He settled back for the negotiation, but to his amazement, Jelaudin stood up.

"Very well. You are a good man," he said.

Abbud covered his startled confusion by rising as well and taking the outstretched hand. Could it be possible? The stone was worth forty times what he had offered!

Abbud hid his delight as best he could as he passed four small coins over. The sword scabbard shone brightly in the gloom and he had to drag his eyes away from it. He owed the fool something.

"My friend, I will give you a piece of cloth to wrap that blade you carry. There are thieves in the souk, though it grieves me to admit it. They may have already marked your arrival here. If you have friends, let me send for them to walk with you back to your place of lodging."

Jelaudin nodded uncertainly. "That is kind, sir. More than I could have hoped in such a place."

Abbud chuckled. "I have sons myself. I will pray for your father's quick recovery."

It took almost until sunset for Abbud's servant boy to fetch three men from his brother-in-law's house. They were as haughty and strange as the one with the gem, and Abbud wondered if he should set a watch on their house. If they had other gems to sell, he did not want them going to one of his competitors. They would pick such innocents clean to the bone. Yes, it would be good to have forewarning if there was going to be trouble. Something about the four young men told him that trouble was very close indeed.

Jelaudin was elated as he strode back through the crowds with his brothers. It was almost sunset and the doctor would be on his way. He had traded and come away with gold in his pouch. It was a giddy feeling and he did not see his brothers' nervous expressions at first. They walked quickly beside him and the sight of their stern faces was enough to warn off a pair of skinny young men who loitered near Abbud's stall, staring rudely. As they closed on the tiny house where they had taken rooms, Jelaudin noticed the tension in his brothers at last.

"What is it?" he muttered.

They exchanged glances. "The Mongols, brother. We saw them in the markets. They are here."

*   *   *

The physician pressed his long fingers into the Shah's belly, manipulating the organs beneath. Jelaudin watched in distaste as his father's skin wrinkled and sagged as if it were no longer attached to the flesh. He could not recall seeing his father so exposed and vulnerable at any time in his life. The doctor seemed coolly professional, but Jelaudin was used to dealing with physicians of the court. Each of those had established a reputation before the Shah accepted them. Jelaudin sighed silently. For all he knew, this man was a charlatan.

The doctor massaged his patient's flesh, peering closely and listening to the tortured breath. Jelaudin's father was awake, though his eyes were yellow around the iris and his face was pale. Jelaudin could only watch as the man pulled his father's lower eyelid down and tutted to himself.

The doctor murmured quick orders and his servant boy began to boil water and crumble herbs into it. It was a relief for Jelaudin to pass his father into the care of another, and for the first time in months, he did not feel completely helpless.

At last the inspection ended and the doctor rose.

"His liver is weak," he said to Jelaudin. "I can give you something for that, but his lungs are the most urgent problem."

Jelaudin did not point out that anyone could have made such a diagnosis. He was paying gold for this man's attentions and he hung on every word. The physician took him by the arm to the brazier, where dark leaves leaped and bubbled in their liquor.

"Have your companions sit him up and drape a cloth over his head. These herbs give off a powerful scent that will help him to breathe."

Jelaudin nodded to his brothers and they helped their father up. The wheezing became instantly worse.

"How quickly will it work?" Jelaudin asked.

The doctor blinked. "Not quickly at all, young man. Your father is very ill indeed. He must sit over the fumes until the liquid has gone cold, at dawn, noon, and evening. Give him beef broth for strength and make sure he drinks as much water as he can hold. In a week, I will come back to you and judge how far he has improved."

Jelaudin winced at the thought of spending a week in the cramped rooms. Would the Mongols have passed on by then? Surely they would. He blessed his decision to hide in the town. Unless the Mongols destroyed it out of sheer spite, they were as safe in Khuday as anywhere.

With rolled blankets to support him, his father drooped over his outstretched legs. Jelaudin watched as another blanket was laid in the Shah's lap to protect him from the heat. With metal tongs, the physician's boy lifted the steaming pot from the brazier and set it in front of the old man. The wheezing became slightly muffled as Jelaudin's brothers placed a cloth over his head. The Shah coughed twice at the acrid fumes, but then he settled into it and the wheezing did seem to ease.

The doctor listened closely before nodding to himself.

"I can leave you enough of the herbs for a few days. After that, you must buy your own supply in the markets." He smiled slightly. "Ask for 'bordi' or 'pala.' They will not know its Latin name. For his liver, Silymarin, the milk thistle, will suit us well. Have him drink it with a little honey."

"Thank you," Jelaudin replied. He tried not to show his relief, but the doctor seemed to sense it anyway.

"Do not worry too much for your father. He is old, but strong. A month of rest and he will be back to his old self. I see you have no brazier of your own?"

Jelaudin shook his head. His brothers had been buying food from the hot coals of sellers in the souk.

"I will lend you this one, though you will have to get your own charcoal."

Jelaudin bowed his head and watched as the physician gathered his materials and measured out portions of the bitter herbs, sealing them in waxed paper packets. It was left to the servant boy to hold out his hand for payment, and Jelaudin flushed at having to be reminded. He pressed four gold coins into the boy's hands, noticing how clean they were in comparison to the urchins of the street.

As the money changed hands, the doctor straightened subtly, relaxing.

"Excellent. Do as I have told you and all will be well, inshallah." He swept out of the tiny rooms into the bright sunshine, leaving the sons with their father.

"We have no more gold," Jelaudin's youngest brother said suddenly. "How can we buy the herbs and charcoal?"

Jelaudin winced at the thought of returning to the market, but at least he had a friend there. Half a dozen smaller rubies still remained, though at the speed he was burning through them, he doubted they would last. Still, he and his brothers were safe. In a month, the Mongols would certainly be gone, and with their father's strength returned, they could head east at last. Let him just reach a loyal garrison and he would bring hell and destruction on the head of the Mongol khan. Far to the south, there were many men of Islam who would ride to his banner against the infidel. He had only to send word to them. Jelaudin prayed silently as his father choked and labored over the fumes, the skin of his neck red with heat and steam. There had been many insults to him, but they would yet be repaid.

By sunset two different men had come to take tea in Abbud's red stall. It was unusual for him to delay rolling up the awnings and walking to the town's small mosque as his final act of the day. As the last rays of the sun lit the alleys of the souk, he could hear the call to prayer echoing across the town. Abbud dismissed the last of the men, pressing coins into his hand as a gift for the information he had brought. Lost in thought, Abbud washed his hands in a small bowl as he prepared for the evening prayer. The ritual set his mind free to consider what he had learned. The Mongols had been asking questions. Abbud was pleased he had set a boy to watch the house of his latest customer. He wondered how much the information was worth.

All around him, the market was vanishing. Some of the stalls were loaded onto donkeys and camels, while more established businesses opened wooden doors set into the ground itself, that could be barred and locked until dawn. As he finished rolling the last bolt of cloth, Abbud nodded to the armed guard he had hired to sleep on the door. He was paid well to complete his prayers on his own, and Abbud left the man laying out his mat and scrubbing his hands symbolically with dust.

The sudden rush of activity that came with sunset seemed to surprise the Mongols wandering through the town. As the stalls were packed away, the strangers were revealed one by one, standing in small groups and looking around them like fascinated children. Abbud avoided catching their eye as he strode toward the mosque. His wife would be entering the decorated building through another entrance, and he would not be able to see her until the prayers were over. She would not approve of what he was considering. Women did not understand the business of men, he knew. They saw only the risks and not the rewards that came only with risk. As if to remind him, he felt the ruby bump against his thigh as he walked, proof of Allah's blessing on his house.

Out of the corner of his eye, Abbud saw a tall young Arab standing with the Mongol warriors. The crowd heading to the mosque ignored them as if they were not there, a combination of contempt and fear. Abbud could not resist glancing at the Bedouin as he passed, noting the distinctive stitching of his robes that marked him as a desert dweller as surely as a sign on his chest.

The stranger missed nothing and he caught Abbud's quick glance, stepping quickly to block his path. The jeweler was forced to halt or lose dignity in trying to dart around him.

"What is it, my son?" Abbud said testily. He had not had time to consider how best to use the information he had bought. The best profits never came from hasty action, and he had intended to use his time in the mosque to think it through. He watched in suspicion as the Bedouin bowed deeply. None of the desert folk could be trusted.

"My apologies, master. I would not disturb you on your way to prayer if the matter was not important."

Abbud could feel the stares of the other traders as they passed by. He cocked his head to listen to the call to prayer, judging he had but moments.

"Quickly, my son, quickly."

The young man bowed again.

"We are seeking five men, four brothers and their father. Do you know of any strangers who have come here in the last few days?"

Abbud held himself very still as he considered.

"All information can be bought, my son, if you are willing to pay the price."

He watched as the young man's face changed, his excitement showing. He turned and barked strange words to the Mongols who stood watching. The jeweler knew the leader before he spoke from the way the others deferred to him. It was strange to think of these men burning a trail of fire across the world. They did not look capable of it, though each man carried a bow, sword, and dagger, as if they expected war to break out in the souk itself.

The Bedouin's chatter was met with a shrug from the leader. Abbud watched closely as the man untied a bag from his belt. He tossed it almost disdainfully to the jeweler and Abbud caught it. One glance at the gold inside was enough to cause new sweat to break out on his face. What *had* he walked into this day? He would need to hire armed guards at the mosque even to get home with such a fortune. No doubt dangerous eyes had seen the pouch and it would not be hard to guess the contents.

"I will meet you after prayers, in this place," he said, turning to go. Like a desert snake striking, the Mongol leader caught his arm, holding him even as he growled at the Bedouin.

"You do not understand," Yusuf said to Tsubodai. "He *must* leave to attend the prayers. Old as he is, he will fight us if we try to hold him here. Let him go, General. He cannot escape." Yusuf pointed deliberately back to where Abbud's guard sat on the trapdoor over his goods. The gesture was not wasted on the jeweler, though he felt a pang of anger that his foolish guard was not even facing them. The man could look for other work, he swore to himself. To have hands laid on him in an open street was bad enough, but to see the fool dreaming away his evening made the insult almost unbearable. Almost. The gold in his hand gave him that word a thousand times over.

With a sharp tug, Abbud shook his arm free, his heart hammering. He was tempted to hand back the gold and walk away with dignity, but in truth Khuday was a small town and he carried the profits of five years or more in one bag. He could even consider retiring and passing the business on to his son. Truly, God was good.

"My friend will not let you leave with the gold," Yusuf said, his face flushed. "He does not understand the insult to your honor, master. I will be here, if you have the information we need."

With great reluctance, Abbud passed back the bag, wishing he could count the coins first. He would know if they had lightened it by the time he returned, he told himself.

"Do not speak to anyone else," Abbud said firmly. "I am the man you need."

He caught the ghost of a smile on the young man's face as he bowed a third time and Abbud passed between the twitchy warriors with their hands on their sword hilts.

As the jeweler left, Yusuf chuckled.

"They are here," he said to Tsubodai. "I was right, was I not? This is the only town for forty miles and they have gone to ground."

Tsubodai nodded. He did not like having to depend on Yusuf, but the language was still a confusion of sound to him, more like the song of birds than real speech.

"We will not have to pay this man if we find them ourselves," he said. The streets had cleared around them and the market that had bustled all day had somehow disappeared. The ululating call from the mosque had ended to be replaced by a dim and muffled chant.

"You Arabs would not kill good horses, I think," Tsubodai said. "They will be somewhere close by in stables. While they pray, we will search. How many good mounts can there be in this dirty little town? Find the horses and we find the Shah."

CHAPTER TWENTY-THREE

JELAUDIN COULD NOT SLEEP as he lay in darkness, his mind torment-ing him with bright images. It was hard not to give in to melancholy as he scratched fresh flea bites and pulled a thin blanket tighter around his shoulders for warmth. At least in the dark, none of his brothers were looking to him to tell them what to do, and his father's once-piercing gaze could not find him. He retired as early as he could each night, seeking sleep as a release and willing each day away into nothingness. Yet sleep evaded him and his mind worked as if it were a separate thing, alive and twitching in his head. When he closed his eyes, he was tormented with visions of revelry in his father's palaces, lit by a thou-sand candles and lamps. He had danced until dawn many times and never once thought of the cost of tallow or oil. Now their single candle needed to be eked out as much as food or charcoal. Running a house-hold was a revelation to him, even one as poor and meager as the rooms in Khuday.

When Jelaudin opened his eyes in frustration, he could see moonlight through the cracks in the roof. The air was thick with the stench from a slop bucket. He had put it outside on his first night in Khuday, but it had been stolen in the morning and they had been forced to buy another. He had learned to pay a boy to carry it to a public pit outside the town, but of course his brothers had forgotten.

Everything cost money in Khuday. Life was more complicated than he had realized, and at times, he wondered how poor merchants could afford to live.

Jelaudin jerked upright as a noise sounded and the small door shuddered in its frame. Someone was knocking and his heart thumped painfully in his chest as he reached for his sword.

"Jelaudin?" one of his brothers called fearfully.

"Be ready," he whispered back, pulling on his clothes in the dark. The leggings stank of old sweat, but the water bucket was as empty as the other was full, without even enough to splash his face. The knocking sounded again and he took a deep breath as he drew his sword. He did not want to die in the dark, but if the Mongols had found them, he knew better than to expect mercy.

Jelaudin yanked open the door with his sword ready, his bare chest heaving. The moon was bright enough to see a small boy standing there, and relief flooded through the young prince.

"Why do you disturb our sleep?" he demanded.

"My master Abbud sent me while he went to the mosque for evening prayers, master. He said to tell you the Mongols know where you are staying. You must leave Khuday."

The boy turned to go, his message delivered. Jelaudin reached out and grabbed him, making him yelp in fear. The life of a boy in Khuday was even more precarious than their own, and the little one squirmed in his grasp.

"They are coming here?" Jelaudin snapped. "Now?"

"Yes, master," the boy replied, his fingers jerking at Jelaudin's hand. "Please, I must run back."

Jelaudin released the boy to stagger away. He faced the moonlit street for a moment, seeing enemies in every shadow. He gave a swift prayer of thanks for the old jeweler's kindness, then turned inside, pulling the door shut as if it could hold back his fears.

His three brothers were dressed and ready, once more looking to him for leadership. Jelaudin grimaced at them.

"Light the candle and get our father into his clothes. Run to the stables, Tamar, and take our horses."

"Do you have coins, brother?" Tamar replied. "The stable owner will want payment."

Jelaudin felt as if a noose were tightening around his neck. He opened a pouch and handed a small ruby to his brother, leaving only five as the total of their worldly wealth.

"Give him this and tell him we are devout followers of the prophet. Tell him there will be no honor for any man who aids our enemies."

His younger brother darted out onto the dark street, and Jelaudin began to help the others with his father. Shah Ala-ud-Din groaned as he was moved, and his wheezing became louder in the gloom. Jelaudin winced at the sick heat coming off the old man's skin, but there was no help for it. His father murmured meaningless words, but none of them stopped to listen.

Once his father was dressed and the candle lit, two of his sons supported him and Jelaudin cast a last look around the infested little place that had been home for a time. As mean as it was, it had given them sanctuary. The thought of returning to their hunted lives wrenched at them all, but Jelaudin could not ignore the warning. The jeweler had done him this one favor and he would not waste it.

He cast his eye over the small brazier, but the doctor had left it in trust and Jelaudin would not steal for the first time in his life. Though he took the papers of bitter herbs, he left that behind. He had been consumed with the need to get out and hardly dared think of his father's illness. It was wrong that an old man should be forced to run again. Jelaudin's hopes withered in him as he stood there, replaced by a desperate rage. If he was granted just one chance to revenge himself on the Mongol khan, he would take it if it meant his own life. He prayed to be given that chance.

Jelaudin closed the door as he left with his father and brothers. He did not want thieves to steal the doctor's brazier, though if anyone wanted the slop bucket, they could have it, contents and all.

The streets were not empty so early in the night. Jelaudin could see many men returning from the evening prayers to their families, looking forward to warmth and food. Only he and his brothers had tried to banish another night with sleep. The stables were some way away, a decision meant to protect them when he had made it. Their father stumbled as he walked between them, and Jelaudin did not know if the old man even understood what was going on. When he heard a slurred question from his father's lips, Jelaudin shushed him softly.

"The men you seek are in there," Abbud said. Tsubodai snapped orders and the warriors moved instantly, kicking open the door and vanishing inside.

Abbud waited, sweating, listening to strange noises. The warriors came back almost as quickly and he did not miss the looks of anger they turned on him. The young Bedouin took Abbud by the arm, his grip almost painful.

"Old man, this is not a night for games, do you understand? I have searched stables for half a night waiting for you. Now you have led me to an empty house. It will be hard for me to stop them killing you."

Abbud winced, but he did not try to pull away.

"They were here! It is my brother-in-law's house and he talked of them in the markets. Four young men and an old one who was very sick. That is all I know, I swear it."

In the moonlight, the Bedouin's eyes were covered in shadow, making him frightening. He let Abbud's arm fall, then exchanged a flurry of words with Tsubodai that Abbud could not understand.

The one Abbud had marked as leader stared at the old jeweler for a long moment of silence. Then he gave new orders. Abbud could only stand and watch as the warriors kicked in other doors and the night was broken with screams. A struggle started in a house nearby and Abbud cried out in shock as one of the warriors drew his sword and killed a young man with a thrust to his heart, stepping over him to search his home.

"There is no need for this!" Abbud shouted. "They are not here!"

The Bedouin turned to him and to Abbud's astonishment seemed to be smiling.

"I cannot stop them now, old man. They will search every house in the street, perhaps the whole town. Then they will burn Khuday down around you."

It was too much for the jeweler.

"There are stables nearby. If they have gone anywhere, it is there."

"Take me there, old man," the Bedouin said. "If you are right, perhaps Khuday will not be destroyed."

Jelaudin brought his horse to a clump of straggly bushes on the crest of a hill. The air was sweet with the scent of lemon leaves, and his heart was heavy as he looked back at the town that had sheltered them. On his right hand, the North Star shone in the heavens, the air clear and bright.

To the east, far away, he could see the fires of the Mongol camp as a dim glow. To the west, the Caspian Sea waited, a final barrier to his fleeing family. He knew he could not ride along its banks for a hundred miles with the Mongols searching for them. They would be caught as easily as running hares. He felt the east as a hunger, desperate to return and seek out the cities he had known as a boy.

The night was still and his father's tortured breath hurt him to hear. Jelaudin and his brothers had tied the old man to his saddle and led his horse out of the town, heading across scrub wasteland and avoiding the eastern road.

If the Mongols had been certain they were in Khuday, they would have surrounded the city. As it was, the sons of the Shah had walked their horses away from the town and not seen a living soul. Yet escaping such a place was a small thing. If they could not turn east, the sea would trap them as surely as any net. As his father's wheezing intensified, Jelaudin was overwhelmed for an instant. He was too tired to run again, too tired even to mount.

His brother Tamar heard the sound of his weeping and laid a hand on his shoulder.

"We must go, Jelaudin," he said. "There is always hope while we live."

Jelaudin nodded despite himself, rubbing at his eyes. He swung a leg into his saddle and took the reins of his father's horse. As they moved away into the darkness, he heard Tamar gasp and looked back at Khuday.

The town gleamed in the night. At first, Jelaudin could not understand the strange light that flickered over the huddled streets. He shook his head as the light spread and knew the Mongols were burning the town.

"They will glut themselves on that place until dawn," another of his brothers said. Jelaudin heard a note of triumph in the younger man's voice and wanted to strike him for his foolishness. He wondered if Abbud and his servant boy would survive the flames they had brought to Khuday, as if the brothers trailed pestilence and destruction in their wake.

There was nothing to do but ride on to the sea. Though he felt his own death like dark wings beating at him, Jelaudin kicked in his heels and made his horse trot down the slope beyond.

The brothers led their father's horse for four more days before they saw riders following them. They could not hide their tracks on the dusty ground, and Jelaudin had known they would be followed, though he had still clung to thin hopes that the Mongols would miss them. He had ridden to exhaustion through night and day until he could smell the salt of the sea ahead and hear the calls of gulls. For a time, the clean air had revived them all, and then he had seen dark figures in the distance, a mass of warriors on their trail, riding them down.

Jelaudin looked at his father's waxy face. There had been no time to stop and make a fire for the bitter herbs, and the old man's condition had worsened. More than once, Jelaudin had pressed his ear to his father's lips, listening to see if he still breathed. He could not leave him to be torn apart by these hunting dogs of the khan, but his father slowed them all.

For a moment, Jelaudin wanted to roar out his hatred and terror at the distant lines of those hunting him. He hardly had the strength even for that, and he shook his head wearily, looking up as he and his brothers passed over a sandy dune and saw the shimmering blue vastness of the sea ahead. Darkness was coming and they would have one more night before the Mongols found and killed them. Jelaudin looked along the shore and saw just a few huts and fishing boats. There was nowhere to hide and nowhere they could run any longer.

He ached as he dismounted and his horse shivered as his weight was removed. The animal's ribs were showing and Jelaudin patted the mount's neck for its faithfulness. He could not remember when he had last eaten, and light-headedness made him stagger.

"Are we to die here, then?" one of his brothers asked plaintively. Jelaudin barely grunted in reply. He had set out strong and young, losing men and strength at every turn for the best part of a year. He felt old as he stood on the shore, taking a piece of gray rock and casting it into the salt water. The horses dipped their heads to drink and Jelaudin did not bother to pull them away. What did it matter if they drank salt when the Mongols were coming to kill the sons of the Shah?

"I will not stand here and wait for them!" Tamar was the next in age after Jelaudin. He strode up and down the sandy ground, straining his eyes for a way out.

With a sigh, Jelaudin eased himself down to the ground and dug his fingers into its dampness. "I am tired, Tamar," he said. "Too tired to rise again. Let it end here."

"I will not!" his brother snapped. Tamar's voice was hoarse from lack of clean water, his lips cracked and lined with blood. Even then, his eyes were bright in the evening sun. "There is an island out there. Can these Mongols swim? Let us take one of the fishing boats and smash the others. We will be safe then."

"Like trapped animals are safe," Jelaudin said. "Better to sit and rest, brother."

To his amazement, Tamar stepped close and slapped him hard across the face.

"Will you see our father butchered on this beach? Get up and help me put him in a boat, or I will kill you myself."

Jelaudin laughed bitterly without replying. Nevertheless, he stood almost in a daze and helped his brothers carry the Shah to the shore. As he struggled through the damp sand, he felt some life come back to his limbs and some of the despair seep away.

"I am sorry, brother. You are right," he said.

Tamar only nodded, still furious.

The fishermen came out of their driftwood huts, shouting and gesturing as they saw the young men hammering at their boats. The sight of drawn swords reduced them to sullen silence, standing in a knot of fury as they watched the strangers break the single masts, batter holes in the hulls and then push them into deep water so that they vanished in frothing bubbles.

As the sun set, the brothers pushed the last boat into the calm water, wading in after it and clambering over the sides. Jelaudin raised the small sail and caught the breeze, the moment strangely reviving to his spirits. They left their horses behind and the fishermen took the reins in astonishment, still yelling curses after them, though the animals were worth far more than the crude boats. As the breeze freshened, Jelaudin took his seat and pushed the rudder down into the water, tying off a rope that held it in place. In the last light, they could see the white line of breaking waves on a small island out on the deep. He looked down at his father as he set their course and felt numb calm steal over him as he left the land behind. He could not last much longer and it was true the old man deserved a peaceful death.

CHAPTER TWENTY-FOUR

THE NAME *SAMARKAND* MEANT "TOWN OF STONE" and Genghis could see why as he gazed on its buttressed walls. Of all the cities he had known, only Yenking was more of a fortress, and he could see the minarets of many mosques towering behind the walls. Built on the flood plain of a river running between huge lakes, it was surrounded by the most fertile soil Genghis had seen since coming to Arab lands. He was not surprised to find Shah Ala-ud-Din had made the place his jewel. There was no dust or sand there. The city was a crossroads for merchant caravans traveling thousands of miles, secure in the protection it gave them. In times of peace, they trundled across the plains, bringing silk from the Chin and collecting grain at Samarkand to take even further to the west. There would be no more of that trade for a time. Genghis had broken the line of cities that supported each other and grew rich. Otrar had fallen, then Bukhara. To the northeast, he had sent Jelme, Khasar, and Kachiun to batter other cities into submission. He was close to obliterating the spine of the Shah's trade routes. Without trade and messages, each city was isolated from the others and could only suffer as they waited for his warriors. While the Shah still lived, it was not yet enough, nor even close to enough.

In the distance, Genghis could see white smoke rising into the air from the last of the trading caravans to have tried reaching Samarkand before he entered the area. No more would come now, not until the Mongols had moved on. Once again he considered Temuge's words on the need to establish more permanent rule. The concept intrigued him, but it remained a dream. Yet he was no longer a young man, and when his back ached in the mornings, he would think of the world running on without him. His people had never cared for permanence. When they died, the troubles of the world slipped away from them. Perhaps because he had seen empires, he could imagine one lasting beyond his life. He enjoyed the thought of men ruling in his name, long after he had gone. The idea eased something in him that he hardly realized was there.

As Genghis watched, the tumans of Jochi and Chagatai rode back from the city walls, having spent the morning riding close enough to terrorize the population. They had raised a white tent before Samarkand when the siege was in place, but the gates had remained closed. In time, they would replace it with a red one and then the black cloth that signified the death of all those within.

With the Shah gone, the Arabs had no one to organize the defense of Khwarezm, and each of his cities fought alone. Such a state of affairs suited Genghis very well. While the cities sweltered in fear, he could bring two or three tumans to bear on a single point, breaking the resistance and moving on to the next with only death and fire behind them. This was war as he preferred it, the breaking of cities and small garrisons. His Arab interpreters claimed that half a million people lived inside the walls of Samarkand, perhaps more now that the farms were empty all around. They had expected him to be impressed, but the khan had seen Yenking and he did not let the numbers trouble him.

He and his men rode with impunity and those who lived behind stone could only wait and fear. It was hard to imagine choosing that sort of life over the ability to move and strike where he pleased, but the world was changing and Genghis struggled with new concepts every day. His men had ridden as far as the frozen wastelands in the north and Koryo in the east. He considered those lands conquered. Yet they were far away. They would rebuild and forget they owed tribute and obedience to him.

He pursed his lips at the thought of city dwellers making new walls and burying their dead. That thought did not sit well with the khan of the Mongols. When he knocked a man down, he stayed down, but a city could rise again.

He thought of Otrar then, of the wasteland he had left behind him.

Not one stone had been allowed to sit on another, and he did not think there would be a city there again, even in a hundred years. Perhaps to kill a city, you had to dig the knife in deep and wrench it back and forth until the last breath escaped. That too was a prospect that pleased him.

As he rode slowly around Samarkand, Genghis's thoughts were interrupted by the thin notes of warning horns. He reined in, jerking his head back and forth to hear the sound more clearly. Jochi and Chagatai had heard, he could see. Between Genghis and the city, they too had come to a halt to listen.

In the distance, Genghis could see scouts riding in at full gallop. The horns had been theirs, he was almost certain. Could there be an enemy in sight? It was possible.

As his mount reached down to wrench a mouthful of dry grass, Genghis saw the gates of Samarkand swing open and a column ride out. He showed his teeth, welcoming the overconfidence of the enemy. He had Jebe's tuman as well as ten thousand of his own veterans. Between those and the tumans of Jochi and Chagatai, they would crush any army Samarkand could vomit at them.

The scouts reached Genghis, their horses almost dead under them from the manic ride.

"Armed men to the east, lord," the first one called before two of his companions. "As many as three tumans of Arab warriors."

Genghis swore softly. One of the other cities had responded to Samarkand after all. Jochi and Chagatai would have to meet them. He made his decisions quickly, so that his warriors saw only certainty in his responses.

"Ride to my sons," Genghis said to the scout, though the young warrior still panted like a dog in the sun. "Tell them to attack this enemy to the east. I will hold against whatever Samarkand can bring to the field."

The tumans of his sons moved quickly away, leaving Genghis with just twenty thousand men. His lines formed with the khan at the center of a shallow crescent, ready to move easily into enveloping horns.

More and more riders and men came out of the city, almost as if Samarkand had been a barracks for a wing of the Shah's army. As Genghis moved his mount into a slow trot and checked his weapons, he hoped he had not sent too many warriors away to take the victory. It was possible, but if he attacked only one city at a time, it would be the work of three lifetimes to subdue the Arab lands. The cities of the Chin had been even more numerous, but he and his generals had taken ninety in a single year before reaching Yenking. Genghis had ridden against twenty-eight of them.

If Tsubodai or Jebe had been there, or even Jelme or one of his brothers, he would not have worried. As the plain blackened with roaring Arabs, Genghis laughed aloud at his own caution, making the warriors around him chuckle. He did not need Tsubodai. He did not fear such enemies, nor a dozen armies like them. He was khan of the sea of grass and they were just city men, soft and fat for all their bluster and sharp swords. He would cut them down.

Jelaudin sat cross-legged on a narrow beach, staring over the choppy waters of the Caspian at the black shore he had left earlier that day. He could see fires of driftwood burning there and moving shadows flickering around them. The Mongols had reached the sea and there was nowhere left to run. Jelaudin wondered idly if he and his brothers should have killed the fishermen and their families. The Mongols would not have known then where he had taken the Shah, and perhaps they would have given up the chase. Jelaudin grimaced at his own desperation. He did not doubt the fishermen would have fought. Armed with knives and sticks, the dozen boatmen would probably have overwhelmed his small family.

The island was barely a mile offshore. Jelaudin and his brothers had dragged the boat into the cover of straggling trees, but they might as well have left it. No doubt the fishing families had told the Mongols where they had gone. Jelaudin sighed to himself, more tired than he could ever remember before. Even the days in Khuday seemed a dim dream. He had brought his father there to die, and after that, he half suspected his own end would come quickly. He had never known an enemy as implacable as the Mongols who stayed on his trail through snow and rain, always coming closer until he could hear their horses in his sleep. Sound carried across the water between them and occasionally Jelaudin could hear reedy yells or voices raised in song. They knew they were close to the end of the hunt, after more than a thousand miles. They knew the prey had gone to ground at last, with all the hopelessness of a fox vanishing into its den, waiting in terror to be dug out.

Once again Jelaudin wondered if the Mongols could swim. If they could, it would not be with swords at least. He heard his brothers talking amongst themselves and could not summon the energy to rise and tell them again to be quiet. The Mongols already knew where they were. The final duty of the Shah's sons was to watch him die, to allow him the dignity he deserved.

Jelaudin rose, his knees protesting as he unbent and cracked his neck. Though the island was tiny, it was covered in trees and thick foliage, so that he and his brothers had been forced to hack a path. He followed the route they had cut, using his hands to remove the slim branches that snagged his robe.

In a clearing formed by a fallen tree, his father lay on his back with his sons around him. Jelaudin was pleased to see the old man was awake to see the stars, though every catch and wheeze of breath made his chest shudder with effort. In the moonlight, he saw his father's eyes turn to him, and Jelaudin bowed his head in greeting. His father's hands gestured feebly and Jelaudin came close to hear the man he had always thought was too vital to fall. Those truths of his childhood had crashed around him. He knelt to listen and even there, so far from home, part of him yearned to hear his father's old strength, as if his frailty could be banished by will and need. His brothers shuffled closer and for a time they forgot the Mongols across the deep waters.

"I am sorry," the Shah said, gasping. "Not for me. For you, my sons." He broke off to suck at the air, his face red and sweat running freely.

"You do not have to speak," Jelaudin murmured.

His father's mouth jerked slightly. "If not now," he wheezed, "when?" His eyes were bright and Jelaudin ached at seeing the gleam of an old, dry humor.

"I am...proud of you, Jelaudin," the Shah said. "You have done well." The old man choked suddenly and Jelaudin rolled him onto his side and used his fingers to wipe a gobbet of phlegm from his lips. As he turned his father back, his eyes were wet. The Shah gave out a long breath, then filled his tortured lungs slowly.

"When I am gone..." the old man whispered. Jelaudin began to object, but his words died away. "When I am gone, you will avenge me," he said.

Jelaudin nodded, though he had left his own hopes long behind him. He felt his father's hand clutch at his robe, and he gripped it in his own.

"Only you, Jelaudin. They will follow you," the Shah said. The effort of forcing out the words was hastening the end, and every breath came harder. Jelaudin wanted the old man to find peace, but he could not look away.

"Go to the south and call holy war on ... this khan. Call the devout to jihad. All of them, Jelaudin, all." The Shah tried to struggle up, but it was too much for him. Jelaudin gestured to Tamar and together they helped their father to a sitting position. As they did so, he breathed out completely and his mouth fell slack. His thin body jerked in their hands as it struggled for air, and Jelaudin wept as he felt the bristles of his father's beard brush across his hand. The Shah threw his head back in a great spasm, but breath did not come and the shuddering became twitches and then nothing. Jelaudin heard a hiss of foul air as the old man's bowels opened and his bladder released, pungent urine drenching the sandy ground.

Gently the two brothers laid the old man back and Jelaudin opened out the clawed fingers, stroking the hand as he did so. He watched as Tamar closed their father's eyes, and they waited, hardly believing that he was truly gone. The chest remained still, and one by one, the sons stood and looked down at him. The world was quiet and the stars shone overhead. Jelaudin felt they should not, that there should be something more than the gentle lap of waves to mark the passing of a great man.

"It is over," Tamar said, his voice catching.

Jelaudin nodded, and to his surprise and shame, he felt a great weight lifted from his shoulders.

"The Mongol animals will come here in the end," he said softly, glancing back to where he knew they camped, though the dark trees hid them from sight. "They will find the ... they will find our father. Perhaps it will be enough for them."

"We cannot leave him here for them," Tamar replied. "I have a tinderbox, brother. There is enough dry wood and what does it matter now if we are seen? We should burn the body. If we live to return, we will build a temple here to honor him."

"That is a good thought, brother," Jelaudin said. "Very well, but when the fire takes hold, we will leave this island and cross the sea beyond. The Mongols are not sailors." He recalled the maps he had seen in his father's library at Bukhara. The sea had not looked too wide to cross. "Let them try to follow us across the deep waters where we leave no trail."

"I do not know the lands across the sea, brother," Tamar replied. "Where will we go?"

"Why, south, Tamar, as our father told us. We will raise a storm with the Afghans and in India. We will return with an army to crush this Genghis. On my father's soul, I swear it."

*   *   *

Jochi and Chagatai caught up with the Arab army as it began to descend into a bowl of hills to the east of Samarkand. The scout's estimate of numbers had been low if anything. As Jochi conferred quickly with his younger brother, he thought the best part of forty thousand men had come to the aid of the Shah's jeweled city. He did not let the thought worry him. In Chin lands and Arab, Genghis had shown quality of men was more important than sheer numbers. Tsubodai was credited with winning against the best odds when he had routed a city garrison of twelve thousand with only eight hundred men on a scouting raid, but all the generals had proved themselves against larger forces. They were *always* outnumbered.

The bowl of hills was a gift and neither brother delayed long as they sighted the enemy. Veterans of mounted battles, they knew the extraordinary benefit of having the high ground. Arrows flew further and horses became unstoppable in a charge as they struck the enemy. Chagatai and Jochi talked briefly, their enmity put aside for the moment. Chagatai merely grunted his assent when Jochi suggested he ride around the bowl and hit the Arab formations on the left flank. It would be Jochi's task to meet them head-on at the foot of the valley.

Jochi's men formed under his orders into the widest line the land would allow, the rest assembling in a block behind the warriors with the heaviest armor. Jochi could see spears and bows ready in the Arab ranks, though he was disappointed they had not brought elephants with them. The Arab princes seemed very attached to the idea of elephants in warfare. In return, the Mongols enjoyed sending them wild with arrows, then delightedly watching them trample their own troops.

Jochi looked down into the valley, judging the steep slope he would descend. It was crisscrossed with wild goat tracks, but scrub grass grew and the horses would fare well charging on such soil. He glanced left and right along the lines as he took his position in the very center of the front rank. His bow would sound with the first volley, and he felt the swelling confidence of men around him as they stared down at the army marching stolidly toward them. The Arabs blew horns and crashed drums as they marched, their horsemen visibly nervous on the flanks. The sloping ground was already compressing them and Jochi thought they had to be led by some young fool promoted for his blood rather than talent. The irony of his own position amused him as he gave the signal to walk the ponies down the central defile. There could be very few sons of kings or khans who led *despite* their fathers rather than because of them.

As his tuman moved to a slow trot, Jochi constantly scanned the lines, looking for flaws. His scouts were out for many miles, as Tsubodai had taught him. There would be no ambush, no sudden appearance of reserves. Whoever led the force to relieve Samarkand had treated the Mongols too lightly and would pay for it. Jochi blew a single note on the horn around his neck and saw the heavy lances brought out of saddle cups, held now only by shoulders and arms trained to iron strength. As he increased the speed to a canter, Jochi nodded to a flag bearer and watched the order to widen the line stretch across them. For this moment, he had practiced and practiced until the men's hands were bloody from shooting arrows at the gallop or punching lance points into straw targets a hundred times a day.

The army they faced loosed a volley of shafts on a barked order. Too early, Jochi thought, watching half of them fall short while the rest skipped uselessly off shields and helmets. He moved into a smooth gallop then and he could not have held back his men if he had wanted to. He put aside his nervousness and let the rhythm of his mount control his movement as he stood in the stirrups and placed a shaft on the cord.

All along the Mongol lines, men followed suit. The lancers began to dip the points, judging the moment when they would strike and kill.

Jochi released his arrow and six hundred more followed it on the instant. As they reached for another, the lancers dug in their heels and came together as an armored spike, lunging ahead of the rest. They hit at full speed and went through or over anything they touched, ripping a hole like a red mouth. Those behind could not stop and Jochi lost sight of falling men as he was carried deep into the enemy, bending his bow once more.

Ahead of him, his lancers threw down the shattered poles and drew swords as one. The archers behind them loosed another volley to the sides, widening the hole and driving men back as if burned. It was the best use of lances and bows Jochi had found and he exulted at the destruction they had wrought in just a few heartbeats. His rear lines rode out wide to overwhelm the wings, the tactic almost the reverse of his father's favored horn maneuver. In just instants, the head of the enemy column boiled, all order lost as it fell back on itself.

Jochi drew his own sword as his mount came almost to a stop, unable to press any further through the ranks facing him. He could feel the moment was perfect for the flank attack and looked up for his brother. He had time only for a single glance at the steep left flank before he was defending desperately, knocking aside a spear point that threatened to sweep him off the saddle. He looked again, not believing, but Chagatai's tuman remained where it was on the slope.

Jochi could see the figure of his younger brother quite clearly, sitting his horse with relaxed hands resting on the saddle horn. They had not arranged a signal to bring him into the flank, but Jochi blew his horn anyway, the note ringing over the heads of his men. They too saw their kinsmen standing still and those who did not understand gestured furiously for them to join the fight before it turned.

With a curse, Jochi let the horn fall loose, fury filling him so that the next two strokes seemed effortless, his strength surging in his right arm. He wanted it to be Chagatai as he caught a man in the joint between his armor and neck, gashing him terribly as he fell beneath the hooves.

Jochi stood in his stirrups once more, this time searching out a way to free his men from the crush. The odds were good that he could disengage, with the front ranks still embroiled in the horns of his finest warriors. If they had not been betrayed, they might have fought clear, but he sensed the shock running through his men and it cost them in lives. The enemy had no idea why a Mongol general would sit and do nothing, but they were quick to take advantage.

Jochi called orders in frustration, but the Arab cavalry widened its line, arcing heavy horse ranks up to the rising ground and then hammering back down against his beleaguered men. Even then, they did not dare to pass too close to the left flank, where Chagatai waited to see Jochi butchered. In breathless moments between blows, Jochi could see senior men remonstrating with his brother, but then he was swept back into the fight.

His own officers were looking to him to call for a retreat, but Jochi was filled with fury. His arm ached and his father's sword had lost part of its edge on armored men, but he felt berserk rage fill him, and everyone he killed was his brother or Genghis himself.

His men saw that he no longer looked to the hills. The son of Genghis fought with his teeth bared, and his sword arm swung lightly as he dug in his heels and sent his pony over dead men. They grinned to see his lack of fear and followed with a howl. Those who were cut ignored the wounds, or did not feel them. They too were lost for a time as their blood responded. They had pledged their lives to Jochi and they had ridden an army into the ground. There was nothing they could not do.

His Chin soldiers fought with insane intensity, cutting their way deeper and deeper into the enemy column. As the Arab cavalry impaled them with spears, they grabbed the weapons, pulling the riders from their mounts and stabbing wildly as both men died. They would not turn from the swords and arrows of the enemy with their friends in ranks around them. They could not.

Under the relentless pressure of madmen who grabbed with bloody hands at swords that killed them, the Arabs turned and broke, their fear rippling even to those who had not yet joined the fight. Jochi saw one of his Chin officers wielding a broken lance as a club, stepping over dying men to smash it into the face of an Arab on a fine stallion. The Arab fell and the Chin soldier roared in triumph, calling a challenge in his own language to men who could not understand. The Mongols laughed to hear his bragging tone and fought on as their arms became leaden and wounds sucked at their strength.

More and more of the enemy turned from the ferocious attack, and Jochi was blinded for a moment by a spray of blood across his eyes. Panic filled him at the thought of being hit when he could not see, but then he heard Chagatai's horns moaning across the valley, followed at last by the sound of thunder.

Chagatai's tuman struck an enemy already desperate to get away from those who assailed them. Jochi watched panting as a space cleared around him and fresh shafts tore into the fleeing Arabs. He saw his brother again for an instant, riding like a king before he reached the foot of the valley and vanished from sight. Jochi spat hot phlegm, his battered body aching for the blow he wanted to land on Chagatai's neck. His men knew what had happened. He would be hard pressed not to have them pick fights with those who had stood and watched in safety. Jochi swore to himself as he imagined Chagatai defending the delay, words like sweet grease in his mouth.

There were no enemies near Jochi as he ran a thumb along the edge of his sword, feeling the nicks in the steel. He was surrounded by bodies, many of them men who had ridden through the hills and destroyed the Shah's best cavalry. Others looked to him with anger still fresh in their eyes. Chagatai was busy gutting the remainder of the Arab column, his horses trampling flags and banners into the bloody ground.

If he dealt with Chagatai as his brother deserved, both tumans would fight to the death, Jochi warned himself. His brother's officers would not let him anywhere near Chagatai with a blade, not when they knew the reason for his anger. Their shame would not prevent them drawing swords, and then his own men would respond. Jochi struggled with a powerful desire to race across the battlefield and see his brother cut into pieces. He could not go to Genghis for justice. It was too easy to imagine his father pouring scorn on his complaints, dismissing them as a criticism of tactics rather than a charge of murder. His breath shuddered with frustration as the sounds of battle moved away from him, leaving him empty. *Still* he had won, even in the midst of betrayal. He felt pride for his men mingle with the hatred and impotence forced on him.

Slowly, Jochi wiped blood from the blade he had won from Chagatai. He had faced death that night against the tiger, and he had faced it again on that day. He could not simply let pass what had been done to him.

He flicked droplets of blood onto the ground and began to ride slowly to where his brother sat his horse. With grim glances at each other, his men followed, ready to fight again.

CHAPTER TWENTY-FIVE

SAMARKAND WAS AN ATTRACTIVE CITY. Genghis walked his pony along a wide street lined with houses, the unshod hooves clicking over uneven stones. Somewhere ahead, smoke hung in the sky and he could hear the sounds of fighting, but this part of the city was deserted and surprisingly peaceful.

His men were wary for him as they walked on either side with bows bent, ready to punish the slightest sign of movement. They had beaten the garrison back inside the city in an orderly retreat that would have done honor to his own tumans. Genghis was surprised to find they had prepared a second position within the city itself, but then Samarkand was a surprising place. As with Yenking, he had begun to think he would have to starve them out, but they had risked it all as soon as a relieving army was in reach. His reason for insisting on speed had borne fruit once again, facing an enemy who vastly underestimated the strength of the tumans.

If he stayed in the Shah's lands, he suspected they would eventually communicate, with the most able officers working out ways to counter his attacks. He smiled to himself at the thought. By the time they ever did, the whole of Khwarezm would be under his control.

Trees grew along the edges of the streets, full grown but somehow neat. Genghis could see the fading white discs of pruning cuts as he passed as well as dark stains on the dusty roots where they had been watered just that morning. He shook his head in wonder at the labor involved. He supposed city men enjoyed the shade the trees cast in the summer, and he had to admit they gave off a pleasant scent in the warm breeze. Perhaps even city men needed to see a touch of green leaves from the stone balconies. Standing in the stirrups, Genghis could see an open bowl of bare earth ringed in tiered wooden benches. Samarkand had many strange things within the walls. It could have been a place where the Arabs gathered to hear speakers, or race horses even. His men were bringing prisoners there and it was already dark with a huddled mass of people, bound and numb with fear.

He passed a stone well at a junction of roads and dismounted to examine it. As he peered over the edge, he saw a dark circle of water far below. On impulse he took the leather bucket on its rope and dropped it in, just to hear the splash. When he pulled it up, he drank deeply, clearing the dust from his throat before passing it to one of his archers and getting back in the saddle. Samarkand was well placed, in its position in the bow of a river and lakes. On such soil you could grow anything and Genghis had seen empty markets full of fresh fruit and vegetables by the main gate. He wondered what the inhabitants did with their days if food and water were so plentiful. It was clear they did not spend it in practice of arms after the way the garrison had retreated. His tumans had simply followed them into the city, too close for them to shut the gates.

The sheer size of Samarkand was difficult to comprehend. Genghis was surrounded by roads and houses, large buildings and small. The Shah's palace dominated the maze around it, but Genghis aimed his mount at a needle minaret to the west of the city, his curiosity aroused by such a strange structure looming over the rest. If anything, it seemed to grow taller as he approached.

The minaret stood over a large open square, surrounded by squat buildings with shuttered windows. Genghis hardly noticed as his officers kicked in doors and checked each one for enemies. Grunts and scuffles sounded, but the warriors knew their business and the noises did not last long. More prisoners were trussed and dragged back to the racetrack, some of them staring wildly at the man who stood alone at the foot of the minaret.

Genghis ran his hand along the base of the structure, enjoying the feel of the intricate tiles on the surface. Each one interlocked with the next and he was tempted to take his knife and work one loose just to look at it. The narrow tower shone in the sunlight and he had to crane his neck to see the top from where he stood. As he leaned back, the hat he wore suddenly tipped and fell at his feet. He smiled in amazement that men could build such a thing, then reached down to pick it up.

Genghis chuckled to himself as he placed the hat back on his head. One of the men heard the sound.

"My lord khan?" he asked, ready for any order.

"I was just thinking that I have never bowed to anyone since coming to these lands," Genghis replied lightly. "Until this tower." The man smiled to see his khan in so mellow a mood. Perhaps it was the open nature of the city they walked through. Chin towns were cramped in comparison and Genghis could not imagine ruling such places. Here, in the sun, it was possible. The citizens would have fresh water and food from the markets to feed their families. Farmers would bring it in each morning before dawn and take their payment in coins of bronze and silver. For an instant, Genghis saw the whole workings of a city clearly in his mind, from the merchants to the artisans, to teachers and scribes. Somehow it all worked, though he could not yet understand where all the coins came from in the first place. Were there mines nearby? And if there were, who made the metal into coins and gave them away to start the commerce of Samarkand? The Shah? It was confusing and complex, but he turned his face to the sun and felt at peace. He had won a battle that morning and sent his sons to break another army come to relieve Samarkand. It was a good day.

The smell of smoke came stronger into the square and Genghis put aside his wandering thoughts. His men roamed everywhere to collect prisoners, but the garrison fought on and he remounted to oversee the fighting. With his line of archers, he walked his horse to where gray smoke billowed over the stunned city. As he rode, he firmed his mouth. What was the point of wells and courtyards if you could not hold them? There were always hungry men willing to take what you had built. A ruler had to be a fool to let them peer into his cities and take what they wanted. Yet a city could be defended, Genghis knew. He had broken enough walls in his time to have a good idea what worked best against his catapults and wall hooks. He was tempted to test the idea with one of his generals the next winter, Tsubodai for preference. His favorite general would relish the challenge. If Tsubodai could hold a city against the tumans, perhaps Genghis would consider leaving them intact to be ruled by his own family. Otherwise, he might as well leave them staked out like the goats they used to catch wolves at home.

As he turned into a main street, Genghis saw sprawled bodies, most of them in the armor the Arabs of Samarkand favored. A doorway was splashed with drying blood, still bright in the sunlight, but with no sign of how it got there. The snap of bows was louder by then, and he passed two more streets before he reached the Shah's palace grounds and the high wall around them. The smoke was thicker there, though it seemed to be limited to a few houses nearby. No doubt someone had knocked over a lamp in a struggle, or kicked a cooking fire as they rushed through. The flames were roaring away, making the day even hotter. His men milled around the Shah's wall like furious ants, suddenly aware that the khan watched.

Genghis reined in to observe his men assault the home of Shah Ala-ud-Din. Beyond the wall, he could see a rising hill set with flower gardens, and on the crest a great palace stood. Whether by accident or design, the walls of the grounds came right down to the street itself, their length broken only by wide gates of heavy iron bars. Genghis looked up and down the long street that ran alongside. The houses were in deep shade, but looked cleaner than he had expected. Perhaps the people of Samarkand had cesspools running under the houses, or some system to carry the nightsoil away. There were problems in having so many people in one place, and Genghis was beginning to appreciate the intricate cleverness of Samarkand.

There was no room for catapults, even if his men had troubled to drag them through the streets to that place. Though the walls were barely ten feet high, the garrison had chosen a good place to defend to the death.

Genghis watched as the best archers stood back, sending shafts at any face that appeared over the high edge. Was there a platform on the other side? There must have been. Genghis could see armored men ducking back to it as arrows whirred past their heads. Not many survived at such a range, though they carried heavy shields and wielded their swords and bows from behind that protection. Genghis saw his shaman, Kokchu, exhorting the warriors to greater efforts. The man wore only a breechcloth around his waist, his body painted in lines of dark blue so that his skin seemed to writhe as he moved.

With the shaman and the khan present, the warriors worked themselves into a frenzy, using spiked poles to pull at the top edge of the wall, trying to bring it all down. They had already loosened part of it and Genghis saw a great crack appear in the brickwork. He had been about to give the order to stand down while catapults were brought. The closest houses could have been leveled to make a platform, and then the wall would have fallen easily. Seeing the crack, he relaxed. It would not be long.

Kokchu had spotted him, of course. Genghis could see the shaman watching out of the corner of his eyes. He remembered the first time they had met, when Kokchu had led the Naiman khan to the top of a hill away from a battle. Genghis had given him just a year of life, but many more had passed since then and he had grown in influence, part of the handful of loyal men who ruled under the khan. Genghis approved the shaman's naked ambition. It suited him well to have his warriors in awe of the spirits, and who could really say if the sky father had blessed their khan? The victories had come and Kokchu had played his part.

Genghis frowned suddenly, his thoughts shifting to another memory. Something nagged at his mind as he played words over in his head, but it would not come clear. With a sharp gesture, he summoned one of his scouts, always watching for orders.

"Go to the camp outside the city," Genghis told the fresh-faced young warrior. "Find my wife Chakahai, and ask her why she cannot look on Kokchu without thinking of my sister. Do you understand?"

The man bowed deeply, nodding as he memorized the question. He did not know why the khan should look so thunderous on a day when they had taken a new city, but his task was to obey and he did so without question, riding swiftly away and not even looking back when the wall tumbled outward, crushing two warriors who had not moved in time. Under the cold gaze of the khan, Kokchu capered like a painted spider and the warriors rushed in with a roar.

Chagatai watched his brother ride toward him. The bulk of his tuman were walking the battlefield, looting the dead or dispatching those who still moved. A core of warriors and officers remained with him, and he did not have to give them orders. They knew why Jochi approached, and moved subtly to surround their general. Many of the older men deliberately sheathed their swords rather than face a general with a bared blade, though Chagatai sneered at them and called out in anger as he saw it. Those closest to him were all young and confident. They kept their weapons high and visible, their faces arrogant. They did not care that Chagatai had left his brother to be killed. Their loyalty was not to the rape-born son, but the true one, who would one day inherit and be khan.

Even the young warriors became nervous at the sight of Jochi's men. Chagatai's personal guard had not fought that day, and those Jochi had with him were wet with blood, from their hair and spattered faces to the soaked cloth of their leggings. They stank of sweat and death and the sneers faded from the faces of Chagatai's young warriors as they came close. This was not a game. Jochi shook with strong emotion and he had already killed that day.

He did not rein in as he reached the warriors with Chagatai. His gaze never wavered from his brother as his mount pushed two standing men aside even as they opened their mouths to warn him off. If he had paused even for a moment, they would have firmed their nerve and stopped him, but he did not. He passed two more men before a senior officer swung his horse in hard and blocked Jochi's path to Chagatai.

The officer was one of those who had put aside his blade. He sweated as he came within reach of Jochi's sword and hoped the general would not strike him down. He saw Jochi's gaze pull away from his smiling brother and settle on the man in his path.

"Get out of my way," Jochi said to him. The officer paled, but shook his head. Jochi heard Chagatai laugh and his hand tightened on the wolf's-head hilt.

"Are you troubled, brother?" Chagatai called, his eyes bright with malice. "After such a victory as well? There are too many nervous hands around here. Perhaps you should return to your own men before there is an accident."

Jochi sighed, hiding the flare of his anger well. He did not want to die in such a place, but he had been mocked too many times in his life. He had held his temper until his muscles knotted, but on this day, he would take his grinning little brother with him.

He dug in his heels and his mount leapt forward. Jochi backhanded the officer across the face, knocking him off his saddle as Jochi's mount went past. Behind him, his men roared and attacked.

Jochi had the pleasure of seeing Chagatai's face turn to shock before more men stood in his way. Warriors around them gaped at the sudden crash of arms and came rushing in. Jochi had known they would, but his own men were close enough to force a path and their blood was already up. They killed without compunction, feeling his rage as keenly as their own.

Chagatai's young hotheads were not slow to respond. In heart-beats, they were struggling and stabbing men who hacked at them. Jochi felt his horse cut from under him and slid free, staggering as his leg buckled. His right leg was dark with blood from an earlier wound. He took another step forward, ducking under a wild swing and draw-ing his ragged blade across an armpit, cutting deeply.

Chagatai saw his wounded brother on foot and shouted, kicking his horse forward through his own men. The shoulders of the animal knocked them aside and suddenly he was there facing Jochi. He brought his sword down in a sweeping arc and Jochi almost fell under the hooves as he dodged, his leg giving way again. Chagatai gave up any pretense at style and swung wildly. He had been attacked among his own men and there had never been a better chance to remove the thorn that was his brother.

With a sickening jolt, Chagatai's horse had its leg broken by a berserk warrior standing at Jochi's side. The animal went down side-ways and Chagatai could not free his legs from the stirrups. He screamed as his shin snapped and almost passed out from the pain. He felt his sword kicked roughly away from his hand, and when he looked up, Jochi was standing there, a terrible triumph on his face.

Chagatai's tuman howled as they saw him go down. They lost all caution then, hacking at the last of Jochi's men in berserk fury.

Jochi could feel his spattering blood leeching out his strength. He struggled to bring his sword up as he stared into Chagatai's eyes. He did not speak as he chopped it down. He did not feel the arrow that took him in the chest, spinning him around before the blow could land. His awareness drained away and he did not know if he had killed the brother who wanted so desperately to kill him.

Chagatai yelled fresh orders and if anything, the fighting intensified as more and more of Jochi's tuman flooded in. The fighting continued and hundreds died to revenge their fallen general, or save him. They did not know. A knot of Jochi's men broke free with his flopping body held between them, the arrow still sticking out. As they pulled back, se-nior men blew the signal to disengage on both sides.

Snarling and in pain, the tumans wrenched apart and at last there was clear ground between them. Minghaan officers bullied and kicked their men away, using their sword hilts to knock down more than one who tried to dart around them. The chain of command reclaimed them and each jagun of a hundred, each arban of ten, had its officer growling at the men to hold.

The tumans stood panting, aghast at the dead and what they had done. The name of Genghis could be heard in whispers, and every man there feared what would happen when the khan heard. No one moved while Jochi was checked by his men, then a ragged cheer echoed across the bowl of hills. The arrow had not penetrated his armor. He lived yet, and when Chagatai heard, he spat on the ground in fury at the luck that followed the rape-born whelp. He endured his leg being splinted with a shard from a broken lance, biting his lip as the swollen flesh was bound to wood in three places between knee and ankle. His men helped him to mount and they echoed the cheer to see him alive, though it was muted and echoed in fear. The battle had been won and now they would leave the bowl of hills together, a blood feud begun that could only be bled or burned to see an end to it.

In the night, Chakahai walked her gray pony through dark streets, with darker men riding beside her. The air was warmer in the city than in the camp, as if the stones of the street kept the heat to breathe it out slowly in darkness. It was easy to be fanciful as she made her way to the palace on a hill, where Genghis waited for her. The city was full of birds, murmuring on every ledge and rooftop. She wondered if they had been disturbed by the movement of soldiers, or always came to sit on the warm tiles of Samarkand. For all she knew, it was a benign, natural thing, but she felt uncomfortable at their presence and could hear fluttering wings overhead.

Away on her right, a woman cried out, unseen. She could see the dim glow of torches as warriors without wives went to the racetrack and took young girls from the arms of their fathers and husbands, leaving the rest for Genghis's judgment the following dawn. Chakahai winced at the thought, feeling for those who could expect rough hands in the dark. She had lived among the Mongols for many years and found much to love in the people of the sea of grass. Yet they still took women from those they conquered and thought nothing of it. She sighed to herself as she reached the broken wall that gave onto perfumed gardens. It was the tragedy of women to be lusted after and stolen in the night. It happened in her father's kingdom, in Chin lands and Arab. Her husband saw nothing wrong in the practice, saying that raids for women kept his men sharp. Chakahai shuddered to herself as if a sudden chill touched her bare arms.

She could smell death over the scent of flowers in the Shah's gardens. Bodies still lay in huge piles by the wall, already beginning to corrupt in the heat. The air there seemed boiled and old and could not refresh her as she breathed through her nose and tried not to think of the staring eyes of corpses. The odor carried disease, she knew. In the morning, she would make sure Temuge had them taken away and burned before some plague ripped through her husband's army.

With the armed guards, her horse walked carefully up wide steps designed for men to the palace that loomed blackly on the crest of the hill. As she went, she mulled the question Genghis had asked and what it could mean. She did not understand it and could not shake a sick feeling in her stomach as a result. Surely Kokchu would not be there when she spoke to her husband. If he was, she would ask to see Genghis in private. The thought of the shaman's fierce eyes boring into her made her illness worse. She sighed, wondering if she was pregnant again, or whether it was just the result of so much grief and anger around her for so long.

Her friend Yao Shu was no great hand with medicine, but he knew the principles of rebalancing. Chakahai resolved to seek him out when she returned to the camp. The Mongols did not seek inner peace and she thought the concentration on violence and hot blood was dangerous to maintain for long periods. There had to be rest and calm, though they knew nothing of the teachings of the Buddha.

Chakahai dismounted as the steps opened into a walled courtyard. Her guards handed her over to others waiting there, and Chakahai followed them through dark corridors, wondering why no one had bothered to light the lamps she saw. Truly, her husband's race were a strange people. The moon rose outside, casting a gray light through the high arched windows, so that at times, she felt like a ghost walking with dead men. She could still smell the corpses on the sluggish air and struggled to remain calm.

Chakahai found Genghis on a throne in a great vault of a room. Though she wore soft slippers, her steps still echoed like whispers on all sides. The guards remained at the doors and she approached her husband, looking nervously around for sign of his shaman.

Genghis was alone in the Shah's throne room, staring out over the city revealed to him through a great arch. The moon made Samarkand looked like an intricate model, stretching away in all directions.

Chakahai followed his gaze and stood for a time in silence, drinking it in. Her father had ruled from such a palace, and the view brought a surprisingly powerful pang of nostalgia. No doubt her husband would move on soon and she would return to a life in the gers, but here, for a time, she could remember the peace and beauty of a great palace and forget the dead who littered the ground around it.

"I am here, husband," Chakahai said at last. Genghis turned to her, stirring from his reverie.

"Have you seen?" he said, gesturing to the moonlit city. "It is very beautiful."

Chakahai smiled and nodded. "It reminds me a little of the Xi Xia and my father's capital."

Genghis nodded, but she could see he was troubled, his mind barely with her.

"You sent a man to ask me a question," Chakahai prompted.

Genghis sighed, putting away his thoughts on the future. The day had begun so well, but it had ended with Jochi and Chagatai fighting in front of the men, ripping wounds in his army that even he would struggle to close. He turned weary eyes on his second wife.

"I did. We are alone here," he said. Chakahai glanced at the guards still standing on the edges of the room, but Genghis did not seem aware of them as he went on. "Tell me why you cannot look on Kokchu without thinking of my sister. What did you mean by that?"

Chakahai stepped close to Genghis and placed her cool hands on his brow as he opened his arms in an embrace. He groaned softly at the touch, letting her ease him. "He found her, husband, after the attack on the camp. When I see him, I see the moment when he came from her ger. His face was wild with grief and it haunts me still."

Genghis was like a statue as she spoke and she felt him withdraw from her. He took her hands and detached them gently, his grip almost painful.

"He did not find her, Chakahai. One of my men brought me the news when he checked the gers after the Shah had run."

His eyes were cold in the moonlight as he thought through what she had said.

"You saw him?" Genghis whispered.

Chakahai nodded, a knot of horror stopping her throat. She swallowed it to answer, forcing the words out.

"It was as the fighting ended. I was running and I saw him come from her ger. When I heard she had been killed, I thought he must have carried the news to you."

"No," Genghis replied. "He said *nothing* to me, then or after." He released her hands then and Chakahai staggered slightly, overcome with what she now understood.

"Say nothing, Chakahai," her husband said. "I will deal with the shaman in my own way." He cursed softly, tilting his head suddenly so that she could see the grief rising in him. "This has been an evil day."

Once more she stepped into his arms, touching his face and smoothing away the pain.

"I know it, husband, but it is over now and you can sleep."

"Not tonight, not after this," Genghis said in a whisper.

CHAPTER TWENTY-SIX

IT WAS ANOTHER THREE DAYS before Genghis summoned his sons to the audience chamber of the palace in Samarkand. On his orders, Kachiun, Khasar, and Jelme had returned with their tumans, leaving cities in ruins behind them.

The day had been hot and the smell of flames, sweat, and grease was strong in the confined space. Temuge too had been ordered to attend, and with him, almost seven hundred senior officers filled the echoing hall as they waited for Genghis. Yao Shu was there among them, perhaps the only man there who did not command others. The shaman Kokchu crouched at the foot of the throne facing the crowd, his empty stare fixed on the floor.

As the sun set and torches were lit on the walls, Genghis entered without fanfare or retinue, his eyes passing across the crowd and noting the faces of his brothers and his children, from Jochi, Chagatai, Ogedai, and Tolui down to the youngest girl his wife Chakahai had borne for him. The smallest ones stood with their mother and Borte, awed at the high ceiling. They had not seen a city before and they looked up nervously, wondering what prevented it from falling on their heads. One of Chakahai's boys began to bawl, but it was Borte who picked him up and crooned to him. Other wives of senior men were also in attendance, though Genghis's mother Hoelun was missing, still isolated in her grief for a lost daughter. Since Temulun had died, Hoelun had withdrawn from the affairs of the tribes, and both Chakahai and Borte felt the loss of her wisdom keenly.

The khan wore no armor that day. Instead, he had dressed in the simple clothes of one of his herdsmen. A deel robe covered tunic and leggings over soft leather boots. His skin was clean and gleaming with fresh mutton fat. His hair was tied back under a square hat, barely marked with decorative stitching. As the hall filled with yellow light, those closest to him could see gray at his temples, but he looked vital and alert, his presence enough to still the slightest movement in the crowd. Only Tsubodai and Jebe were missing with all their minghaan and jagun officers. Genghis might have waited for them, but there was no word of the hunt and matters pressed upon him, each more urgent than the next.

As he stood with the throne at his back, he met the eyes of Jochi and Chagatai, standing to the fore of the silent crowd. Both bore marks of the battle they had fought. Chagatai leaned heavily on a stick to favor his splinted leg and sweated visibly. Jochi's face was badly bruised and he too limped when he moved, his cuts barely stanched and beginning to form scabs. They could read nothing from their father. He had adopted the cold face, and even those who knew him well could not judge his mood or guess why he had called them. As Genghis watched, Jochi raised his head, his expression the match for his father's. He at least did not expect the gathering to turn out well, but he refused to show fear. He had spent three days waiting for some kind of summons. Now it had come, it was almost a relief.

Genghis let the silence grow as he faced them. He knew many of the men and women in the hall. Even those who were strangers were still his people. He knew their faults and weaknesses as well as his own, or better. He had brought them from the hills of home, taken the paths of their lives in his hands and wrenched them together. They were no longer tribes as they waited for the khan to speak. They were his, down to the last child. When he spoke at last, his voice filled the hall, his tone calmer than anyone there expected.

"Tonight I will name my heir," he said. The spell held and no one moved, though Chagatai and Jochi exchanged a silent flicker of a glance, both very aware of the other.

"I will not live forever," Genghis went on. "I am old enough to remember when each tribe was at the throat of the rest. I would not see those days return when I am gone. In this room, I have called every man and woman of power in the nation, barring the ones with Tsubodai and Jebe. I will speak to those separately when they come home. You have all pledged your lives and honor to me. You will do the same for my son."

He paused, but no one dared to move. In the stifling air, some even held their breath. Genghis nodded to himself.

"I give thanks in front of you to my brother Kachiun, who took the burden of being my heir while my sons grew to manhood." He sought his brother out and caught Kachiun's fractional nod.

"Your children will not rule the nation, Kachiun," Genghis said, knowing his brother understood the need to speak the words aloud. "They may come to rule other peoples and other lands, but the Great Khan will come from my choice and my seed alone. You will be the first to give an oath to my son, then my brothers Khasar and Temuge and every other man and woman here."

He looked up again at them all, his yellow eyes seeming to strip them bare.

"We are nothing but the oath we give. If you cannot bend a knee to my son, you may leave and take your lives before sunrise. That is the only choice I will allow." He paused again, closing his eyes for an instant when grief and anger threatened to break through.

"Step forward, Ogedai, my heir," he said. All eyes turned to the sixteen-year-old warrior. He had grown almost to his father's height in their time in Arab lands. The slim boy who had returned from a Chin city with Kachiun was barely visible in the hard planes of his face, but he looked very young, rocked by his father's words. His eyes were as pale as the khan's, wide and unblinking. He did not move and Borte had to nudge him forward so that he stepped through the packed room, older men making way. Only she and Chakahai had known it was coming. Both women had advised Genghis over the previous days, and for once, he had listened. Tears of pride brimmed in them both.

Genghis ignored the hot eyes of Chagatai and Jochi as he turned his stunned third son to face them.

"The man who leads the nation must not be weak," Genghis said. "He must not be given to rash acts or spite. He must use his mind first, but when he *does* move, it must be as the snap of a wolf, without mercy. The lives of many rest on him and one wrong decision can destroy everything my brothers and I have built."

Genghis showed a touch of his inner rage in his clenched fists as he took a deep breath.

"I am the khan of the sea of grass, the silver people. I have chosen my heir, as is my right. Let the sky father and earth mother destroy any man or woman who stands in the way."

Heads bowed nervously in the crowd and Kachiun stepped through them to stand before Genghis and Ogedai. Genghis waited with his hand on his sword hilt, but Kachiun merely smiled. Seeing Ogedai was nervous, Kachiun winked at him before going down onto one knee.

"I give my oath freely, Ogedai, to you, the son of my brother and his heir. May the day you inherit be many years from now, but until then, I vow to honor your father's command. On that day, I will swear to follow you with gers, horses, salt, and blood."

Khasar followed closely behind Kachiun and he too knelt and spoke, his eyes proud. They could not give the full oath to the khan while Genghis lived, but each man swore to honor the boy as heir. As the tension faded, Genghis took his right hand from his sword and let it rest on Ogedai's shoulder. Temuge completed his vow and Jochi and Chagatai stepped forward. Of all in that room, Genghis needed to hear the two young generals give their word publicly, so that there could be no doubt. The senior men and women of the nation were all there as witnesses to this moment above all the others.

Jochi winced as he knelt, though he forced a grin for Ogedai. In his deepest heart, Jochi had known he could not inherit. He was not certain yet that his father would leave it at that, or dole out some other punishment for the folly of his fight with Chagatai. There, at least, he was triumphant. Chagatai would not inherit either and he had been certain he would one day lead the nation. Chagatai's dashed hopes were like hot airag in Jochi's blood.

With his broken leg, Chagatai could not kneel with the others. He hesitated under his father's gaze and the officers around looked on in fascination as the problem became obvious.

"The Chin kowtow, outstretched, Chagatai," Genghis said coldly. "As you are injured, you may do that."

Chagatai's face flushed brightly as he eased himself onto the floor and touched his forehead to the cool stone. It was not difficult to guess that his father would inflict a brutal punishment on him if he tried to delay.

For his part, Ogedai seemed delighted to see Chagatai lying flat on the floor. He beamed as his brother spoke the ritual words before using the stick to clamber painfully to his feet. In the crowd, Yao Shu too could not prevent a smile from breaking out on his face. Truly, there was a place for karma in the world, that he should have lived to see the young fool humbled before the nation. The need for revenge seeped out of him, leaving him feeling empty and soiled. Yao Shu shook his head in sadness at what he had allowed himself to become in the Mongol camps. This was a second chance and he vowed to renew his studies and his teaching of the khan's sons. He brightened at the thought of working with Ogedai. The lad was quick-witted and if the family violence in his blood could be tempered, he would one day make a fine khan.

It took a long time for each man and woman in the hall to make their vows to Ogedai. By the end of it, the night was almost over and the sky was gray in the east. Genghis had not troubled to have water brought to them. As the last arban officer rose to his feet, the rest broke into cheering, understanding that they had seen the beginning of a dynasty in that night, in a city on a hill. Under the eye of the Great Khan, even Jochi's and Chagatai's officers joined in enthusiastically, relieved that no blood had been shed.

Genghis held up his hands to quiet them.

"Now go, and tell your families what you have seen here. We will throw a feast in Samarkand this day to mark the occasion." His expression tightened as the crowd began to chatter and smile, flowing toward the great doors at either end.

"Kachiun? You and Khasar will stay. You too, Temuge. I need my brothers around me for what I still have to do."

As his three brothers halted, looking surprised, Genghis turned to where Kokchu still crouched at his side.

"I have horses ready outside, shaman. You will accompany me."

Kokchu bowed his head, hiding his confusion.

"Your will, my lord khan."

As the sun rose, Genghis rode slowly out of Samarkand, his three brothers and the shaman with him, accompanied by one spare mount. Temuge had called questions at first, but when Genghis did not answer, he had fallen as silent as his brothers. None of them knew where Genghis was leading them, or why his mood seemed so dark on that day.

The families of the nation were encamped just a few miles from Samarkand, out of reach of battle lines. Genghis did not hesitate as he reached the first lines of gers, each one with its line of white smoke rising slowly into the air. The camp was already busy. The Mongols enjoyed this part of the summer days, before the heat became intense. With the river and lakes to the north, there was even enough moisture in the air to coat the grass with dew, and the sun made it sparkle for the short time before it burned away.

Those who were up and about already looked to the khan and his brothers in awe as they passed, standing with their heads bowed rather than look on the great ones of the nation. Dogs barked excitedly, but Genghis ignored them all as he walked his horse through the maze. He passed his own great ger on its cart and dismounted at last at the small home of his mother.

"*Nokhoi Khor,*" he called softly, a greeting as much as a request to have his mother's old hound held before it could rush out and attack. Genghis had never liked dogs and kept none himself. He waited for a few moments, then turned to the small group with him. Between them, they represented the ruling powers of the Mongol nation. Only Ogedai ranked with them and then only after that night.

"Wait for me," Genghis said, ducking low and opening the painted wooden door to his mother's home.

It was still dark inside. His mother had not yet thrown off the cap of felt that let light in during the day. The light from the open door let him see a huddled figure on the bed. Her old hound slept curled up by her legs and showed its teeth as he approached, a low rumbling in its throat. Genghis swallowed dryly.

"Send your dog out, Mother. I need to speak to you."

Hoelun opened her eyes blearily, still bloodshot from the airag she used to bring sleep without dreams. She closed one again almost immediately, wincing at the pain that throbbed in her head. Genghis could smell the tang of urine in the ger and the strong scent of unwashed flesh. It saddened him to see his mother's gray hair wild and unkempt, and he knew he should have roused her from grief long before this. She looked ancient and worn out as she watched him. While he had buried his sadness in the attack on the city, filling his days with plans and action, she had been left alone to grieve and the process had eaten her away.

Genghis sighed to himself. He stuck his head outside once more, blinking against the light.

"I need you to take her dog, Kachiun. And I need food and tea and firewood for the stove. Will you fetch those, Khasar?"

He stepped back to let Kachiun remove the old hound from their mother's bed. As Kachiun reached for it, the dog erupted, snapping. Kachiun simply cuffed it on the muzzle and dragged it off the bed, giving it a kick toward the door so that it ran outside, still barking.

"Leave the dog alone," Hoelun said irritably. As she sat up and realized two of her sons were in her ger, she ran a hand automatically over her hair and glared at them. Genghis could see she had lost weight alarmingly over the previous few months. Guilt swept him that he had not made sure someone was looking after her. Surely Chakahai and Borte had brought food and changed her clothes?

"What is it?" Hoelun said, wincing as her head pounded. She gave up on her hair and let her hands fall to the blankets on her lap, the yellow nails dark with dirt.

She had addressed Kachiun, but he only shrugged and looked to Genghis.

"Get some hot salt tea inside you and we will talk," Genghis said flatly. In the small ger, he heard her belly rumble with gas and was not surprised when she threw back the greasy blankets and heaved herself to her feet. She did not speak as she pushed her feet into soft boots and left the ger to visit a toilet pit nearby.

Kachiun looked at his brother in shame.

"Is it for this you called us?" he said. "I did not know she was so far gone, I'm sorry."

"Neither did I," Genghis said. "Have I not had my hands full with a thousand things since Temulun died?" He looked away then, aware that his words were weak. "We will make it right, after today," he added.

Khasar returned just before their mother, so that she followed him into the ger. He too was subdued at the skeletal figure who took her place on the bed. He embraced her formally, but winced to himself as he laid a fire in the stove and lit tinder with a flint and steel, blowing on it in his hand until a small flame puffed there.

The tea seemed to take an age to boil, and it was Genghis himself who poured the first cup for his mother. She sipped at it and her eyes lost some of their blankness as the warmth spread through her old body.

"What do you want, Temujin?" she said at last, using his boyhood name as no one else in the camp dared to do.

"Vengeance for my sister," Genghis replied, his voice almost a whisper.

Hoelun's eyes were wide and dark in the gloom, and she closed them as if he had struck her. "I do not want to hear this," she said. "Come back tomorrow and I will be stronger."

Genghis was unrelenting and he took the empty tea bowl from her hands, shaking his head.

"No, Mother. Get yourself dressed, or I will send a servant to you. You will ride with your sons today, away from this camp."

"Get out, Temujin," she said, her voice stronger than it had been before. "Take your brothers with you. I am waiting to die, do you understand? I have played my part in your life and your nation. I was there at the beginning and it has brought me only sorrow. Just get out and leave me behind you as you have always done."

When Genghis replied, his voice was gentle. "I will not, Mother. Kachiun? Tell Temuge that he will have to wait for us for a while. I will wash and dress her and make her ready."

Defeated, Hoelun slumped back on the bed. She remained limp as Genghis used a water bucket and cloth to smooth back her hair. He found a bone comb on the floor of her ger, and she sat in silence as he began to draw it through the knotted gray mass, his hands taking infinite care not to hurt her further.

The sun had risen completely by the time they finished dressing Hoelun. She had not spoken again, though she had welcomed the dog when it returned to its place at her side, darting in when it saw its chance. The will to resist seemed to have deserted their mother, and both Genghis and Kachiun were silent as they helped her into the saddle and placed her feet in stirrups. Hoelun sat badly, so Khasar passed her reins over the horse's head and looped them over his saddle horn to lead her.

As he too mounted, Genghis looked around him at the family who had hidden from their enemies in a lost and distant cleft in the ground when he was just a boy. They had walked with death then and the memories were cold on his skin. He could imagine the spirit of Bekter with them, and he knew the brother he had killed would approve of this day. He hoped Bekter could see it. Temulun too was missing from that small group of survivors, though she had been just a squalling baby when they had been forced to run. In her place, the shaman rode in sullen silence, watching the khan from under heavy-lidded eyes. As Genghis began to trot away from the camp, he heard hawks calling overhead. Their high voices reminded him of Temulun's cries, when every meal was a victory and every battle was still to come.

*   *   *

They rode south and east through the heat of the day, drinking water from the skins Genghis had supplied with each mount. He had prepared for the journey and the saddlebags were full of dried mutton and hard cheese. In the afternoon, as the ground began to rise, Genghis stopped to break the cheese on a flat stone, using the hilt of his knife to crumble the blocks before mixing them in a skin of warm water and passing the bags under each saddle. The bitter broth would sustain them when they stopped again that evening, though he did it mainly for his mother, who was not used to hard riding.

Hoelun had woken from her stupor of the morning, though she still winced at the hot sun and had stopped once to vomit weakly before going on. Her eyes sought out Genghis as he rode ahead, and she too recalled the first days of hardship, when the hand of every man was set against them. Five sons and one daughter had been with her then, where now only four sons remained. Had she not given enough for Genghis's ambition and dreams? She saw the mountains rise before her as she rode, her horse picking its way carefully when even the goat trails ended. As the sun beat down, the ground rose more and more steeply and still Hoelun did not speak to any of the men with her.

Kokchu was sweating profusely and drank more than Genghis and Khasar together. He too was not used to riding broken ground, but he did not complain while Hoelun remained silent, knowing it could only shame him in the eyes of the khan. He had no idea why he had been called to attend Genghis, though as he looked up and saw the snow line of the peaks, he knew the spirits were strong in high places. The Mongols were never truly content in hot lands, where flies and sweat and strange rashes assailed them and rotted clean flesh. In the clean air of the mountains, Kokchu knew they would feel more at home. Perhaps he had been called to intercede for Genghis there.

They climbed a ridge until the sun hung low in the west, casting long shadows before them as if they walked on darkness. The going was hard, but the horses walked with sure steps, following Genghis on the spine of the ridge. It was rarely steep enough to force them to dismount. They had led the horses only twice that day, and the grim silence seemed to have seeped into them all, so that their throats and dry lips would find it hard to speak again.

The dark mood did not survive reaching the snow line, at least for Temuge, Khasar, and Kachiun. They had not seen snow since leaving the mountains of their home, and they sucked in the cold air, enjoying the way it bit deeply into them.

Genghis did not seem to feel it, or hear the way the hoof sounds changed to the muted trudge of snow. The peak of the ridge was still ahead. He fixed his gaze on it and did not even look down to the vast lands revealed from that height.

The long, tiring day was ending as he reined in at last. The sun was half hidden on the western horizon, and the golden light struggled with shadows, so that they had to squint as they dismounted. Khasar helped his mother down and passed a skin of airag to her, which she accepted gratefully. The hard spirit brought a little life back to her exhausted face, but she shivered as she stood there, looking around in bewilderment. They could see the smudge of Samarkand across the farmland and even further, to a bright line of the lakes in the north. It seemed as if she might see all the way to home, and the thought brought tears to her eyes.

Genghis drew his sword and the sibilant sound had every eye on him. He too felt the comfort of the snow. In the high places, it was easier to feel the breath of the sky father and the whispering presence of spirits. Even in such a distant land, he felt them on his skin. Though the feeling eased him, it hardly touched the hard lump of rage in his chest that had ached for many days.

"Stand before me, Kokchu," he said, watching the shaman closely as he approached. Kokchu's expression was wary and a line of sweat shone on his high scalp, but Genghis could see the gleam of something else in his eyes. The wind grew suddenly as the brothers gathered with their mother around Genghis, scattering a dusting of snow across them.

Genghis did not take his gaze off the shaman as he spoke to his brothers and Hoelun.

"This is the man who killed Temulun, not one of the Shah's guards. He is the one."

Kokchu might have leapt back had Khasar not been standing behind him.

"That is a lie!" the shaman spat. "You know it is."

"No, I don't think so," Genghis said. He was ready for Kokchu to attack or flee, with every nerve straining as he spoke. "My sister's body wasn't found until dark and that man came straight to me. Yet you were seen coming out of her ger long before that."

"More lies! My lord khan, someone is trying to destroy me. There are those who think you show me too much trust, that you favor me too openly. I have many enemies, lord, *please...*"

Temuge spoke suddenly and Kokchu turned to him in desperate hope.

"He could be right, brother," Temuge said. "Who can say which ger they saw him at when the fires were burning in the camp?"

Kokchu fell to his knees, his clawlike hands shaking as they grabbed handfuls of snow.

"It is true what he says, lord. I have given you everything, gers, horses, salt, and blood, *everything.* This is all wrong."

"No," Genghis muttered. "It is not." The shaman turned up his face in terror as he saw the khan's sword lift into the air.

"You may not shed the blood of a shaman, lord. It is forbidden!"

He did not turn in time to see Hoelun smash her hand across his face. The blow was weak, but Kokchu cried out as he fell backwards in the snow. As he came up against Khasar's feet, the general lashed out without thought, kicking him hard in the ribs.

Genghis stood very still and his family turned to him questioningly as he let the sword fall at his side.

"You cannot let him live, Temujin," Hoelun said, her eyes brighter than he had seen them that day. Some of her old vitality had returned at the sight of the shaman struggling on that cold peak, and she did not seem to feel the wind any longer. Genghis handed her the sword and held her wrist when he thought she might lash out with it.

He flexed his empty hands for a moment and Kokchu cowered before him, trapped between the legs of the family he had served. His mind spun crazily as he looked for fresh words. Temuge's foolish face was full of doubt and weakness, and even the khan had put aside his sword. There was still hope.

"I have done nothing, lord. Whoever told you made a mistake and it must not cost me my life, or my service to you. If I die here, ill luck will follow you to the end of your days. You *know* I speak the truth."

Genghis reached down and took him by the shoulders in a terrible grip. For an instant, Kochu thought he was being raised to his feet and gasped in relief. Then he felt Genghis shift his grip to a bony leg, the hard fingers cupping his knee and digging into the flesh. The shaman struggled wildly as Genghis lifted him with a grunt.

"*Please,* my lord, I am innocent!" Kokchu yelled.

Genghis lifted the shaman higher, then dropped him, falling to one knee as he did so. Kokchu struck the khan's outstretched thigh cleanly.

They all heard the spine crack and Kokchu's mouth opened sound-lessly. His legs fell limp and his hands scrabbled in the snow and the sun's fading light. Temuge turned away then, sickened, but Kachiun and Khasar stared as if they were determined to remember every detail.

Genghis knelt at the shaman's side, speaking softly.

"There are wolves in these mountains," he said. "Some of my men have hunted them for skins. They will find you here tonight and at first they will only watch. As the cold makes you weak, they will come closer and begin to nuzzle your legs and hands. They'll scatter when you call out and move, but they won't go far and they'll come back with more courage. When they start to tear your flesh, when the smell of blood excites them, think of me then."

He stood and the shaman's wild eyes followed his movement, blurred in tears. His mouth hung open, revealing brown teeth. He saw Hoelun put an arm around Genghis and squeeze his shoulder as they turned back to the horses. Kokchu could not hear the words the family exchanged. He had never known such pain and all the tricks and rituals he knew crumbled before the flame that lanced through him.

The darkness came quickly after that and he moaned as he found his legs were useless. Once, he pushed himself almost to a sitting posi-tion, but the wave of fresh agony stole his senses away. When he awoke again, the moon was up and he could hear the soft crunch of paws on the snow.

CHAPTER TWENTY-SEVEN

AS THE SUMMER ENDED, Genghis remained in Samarkand, though his generals roared through the region in his name. The cities of Merv, Nishapur, Balkh, and Urganj fell in quick succession, the populations slaughtered or enslaved. Even the news of the Shah's death and the return of Tsubodai and Jebe did little to raise his spirits. He wanted to return home to the plains he had known as a boy, but dismissed the urge as weakness. It was his task now to train Ogedai to lead, to pass on everything he had learned as khan in decades of war. He had repaid the Shah's insults a thousand times, but in the process discovered lands as vast as any he had ever known.

He found himself as a wolf let loose in a sheepfold, and he could not simply take the nation home. Ogedai would rule his people, but there were other thrones. With new energy, Genghis walked the Shah's palace and city, learning everything he could about how such a place supported its people.

Temuge brought new maps to him as they were captured or drawn by prisoners. Each one revealed more and more of the land around Samarkand and the shape of the world itself. Genghis could hardly believe there were such vast mountains to the south that no man had ever climbed them and the air was said to be thin enough to kill. He heard

of strange beasts and Indian princes who would make the Shah of
Khwarezm look like a local governor.

The people of Samarkand had been freed to return to their homes
for the most part. In other places, Genghis allowed the young warriors
to practice sword blows on bound prisoners. There was no better way
to demonstrate the damage a sword could do, and it helped prepare
them for real battles. In Samarkand, the streets were choked with people, though they stayed out of his way as he walked with guards and
maps. His curiosity was insatiable, but when he returned to the palace
each night, he could feel it close on him like a tomb until he could
hardly breathe. He had sent a scout into the mountains to where
Kokchu had been left. The warrior had brought back a package of
splintered bones, and Genghis had burned them in a brazier. Even that
had not brought him peace. The stone walls of the palace seemed to
mock ambitions built on men and horses. When Ogedai was khan,
what would it matter if his father had once taken a city or left it intact?
Genghis practiced each day with a sword, working himself to a sweat in
the mornings against the best of his guard. It depressed him how much
speed he had lost with the years. His stamina was still the match for
younger men, but his right knee ached after a bout and his eyes were
not as sharp over distance as they had been.

On a morning that held the first breath of winter, in his fourth year
in Khwarezm, Genghis rested with his hands on his knees, having
fought a young warrior to a standstill.

"If he comes at you now, you are dead, old friend. Always leave
something, if you can."

Genghis looked up in surprise, then smiled slowly at the sight of
the wiry old man on the edge of the training ground. Arslan was darkly
tanned and as thin as a stick, but the sight of him was a pleasure
Genghis had not expected again.

The khan cast a glance at his opponent, who stood barely breathing
hard, his sword ready.

"I am hoping to surprise this young tiger when he turns his back,"
he said. "It is good to see you. I thought you might have been content
to stay with your wife and goats."

Arslan nodded. "The goats were killed by wolves. I am no herds-
man, it seems." He stepped onto the stone square and took Genghis's
arm in a familiar grip, his eyes weighing the changes in the khan.

Genghis saw that the old general was marked with thick dust from
months of riding. He pressed his grip tighter, showing his pleasure.

"Eat with me tonight. I want to hear about the plains of home."

Arslan shrugged. "They are the same. From west to east, Chin merchants do not dare cross your land without asking permission from one of the road stations. There is peace there, though there are fools who say you will not return, that the Shah's armies are too much even for you." Arslan smiled at the memory of a Xi Xia merchant and how he had laughed in his face. Genghis was a hard man to kill and always had been.

"I want to hear it all. I will invite Jelme to eat with us," Genghis said.

Arslan brightened at word of his son.

"I would like to see him," he replied. "And there are grandchildren I have not seen."

Genghis winced slightly. Tolui's wife had given birth to her second son within a few months of Chagatai's firstborn. He was a grandfather three times over, though part of him was not at all thrilled at the idea.

"My sons are fathers now," he said. "Even little Tolui has two baby boys in his ger."

Arslan smiled, understanding Genghis better than he knew.

"The line must go on, my friend. They too will be khans one day. What did Tolui call them?"

Genghis shook his head, amused at Arslan's fatherly interest.

"I named the first Mongke. Tolui called the second Kublai. They have my eyes."

It was with an odd sense of pride that Genghis showed Samarkand to the man who would rule the city. Arslan was fascinated by the water system and the markets, with the intricate web of suppliers from a thousand miles all around. By then Genghis had discovered the gold mines that fed the Shah's treasury. The original guards had all been killed and the mine looted by the time he realized its significance on the maps, but he had new men working and some of his brightest young warriors learning the process of taking gold and silver from the ground. That was one benefit of the city, he had found. It supported more men than the life he had known on the plains. Those men could be used to build other things, perhaps even greater.

"You will have to see the mine," Genghis told Arslan. "They have dug into the ground like marmots and built great forges to separate the silver and gold from the rock. More than a thousand men dig and half as many again crush the rock into powder. It is like a nest of ants, but from it comes the metal that makes this city run. Everything else works from that. At times, I feel I am very close to understanding how they came to have value. It feels like a thing built on lies and promises, but it works, somehow it does."

Arslan nodded, watching Genghis rather than listening too closely to things he could not have cared less about. He had answered the call because he knew Genghis would not have summoned him without reason. He had yet to understand why the cities had suddenly become important to the younger man. For two days, he walked with Genghis through Samarkand, talking and taking note of the khan's inner tension. Arslan's wife had been given a suite of rooms in the palace and seemed entranced with the great baths and Chin slaves Genghis had procured for her. It interested Arslan to note that neither of Genghis's wives had left the camp of gers outside the city.

On the third day at noon, Genghis stopped by a market, taking a seat on an old bench with Arslan. The stalls were busy, their owners nervous at the presence of the Mongols in their midst. Both men sat comfortably, waving away those who came to offer them fruit juices or salted bread and meat.

"Samarkand is a fine city, Genghis," Arslan said. "But you did not care about cities before. I have seen you staring out to the camp of gers every time we walk the walls, and I do not think you will stay here much longer. Tell me then why *I* should."

Genghis hid a smile. The old man had not lost his sharpness in the years apart.

"I thought for a time that I would take cities for my people, Arslan. That this would be our future." He shook his head. "It is not, at least for me. The place has beauty, yes. It is perhaps the finest rat warren I have ever seen. I thought if I could truly understand the way it works, perhaps I could rule from a city and spend my final days in peace, while my sons and grandsons conquer." Genghis shivered as if a breeze had found his skin. "I cannot. If you feel the same way, you may leave and go back to the plains with my blessing. I will destroy Samarkand and move on."

Arslan looked around him. He did not like being surrounded by so many people. They were everywhere, and for a man who had spent much of his life on open plains with just his son or a wife, their closeness made him uncomfortable. He suspected Samarkand was no place for a warrior, though it may have been a place for an old man. His wife thought so, certainly. Arslan was not sure if he could ever feel at ease there, but he sensed Genghis was reaching for something and struggled to understand.

"You cared only about razing cities once," he said at last.

"I was younger then," Genghis replied. "I thought a man could throw his best years against enemies and then die, feared and loved, both." He chuckled. "I still think that, but when I am gone, the cities will rebuild and they will not remember me."

Arslan blinked to hear such words from the great khan he had known almost from boyhood.

"What does that matter?" he asked incredulously. "You have been listening to Temuge, I think. He was always chattering about the need for history, for records."

Genghis cut the air with his hand, impatient with the way the discussion was going.

"No, this is from me. I have fought all my life and I will fight again and again until I am old and feeble. Then my sons will rule lands even greater and their sons after them. That is the path we made together, Arslan, when I had nothing but hatred to sustain me and Eeluk ruled the Wolves."

He saw Arslan's astonishment and went on, searching for the words to give voice to his hazy ideas.

"The people of this city do not hunt to eat, Arslan. They live longer than we do and it is a softer life, yes, but there is no evil in that alone."

Arslan snorted, interrupting him without caring for the blaze of anger it provoked. It had been a long time since anyone broke in while Genghis was speaking, even in his closest family.

"Until we come and kill their kings and shahs and knock their walls down," he said. "Of all men, you have shown the weakness of cities, and you would now embrace them? Perhaps you will build statues to yourself like the ones by the walls. Then every man can look on the stone face and say 'That was Genghis.' Is that it?"

The khan had gone very still as Arslan spoke, except for the fingers of his right hand drumming silently on the wooden bench. Arslan sensed danger radiating off Genghis, but he did not fear any man and he refused to be cowed.

"All men die, Genghis. All. Think what it means for a moment. None of us are remembered for more than one or two generations." He raised a hand as Genghis opened his mouth to speak again. "Oh, I know we chant the names of great khans by the fireside and the Chin have libraries running back for thousands of years. What of it? Do you think it matters to the dead that their names are read aloud? They don't *care*, Genghis. They are gone. The *only* thing that matters is what they did while they were alive."

Genghis nodded slowly as Arslan spoke. It eased him more than he could say to have the old man's advice once again. He had lost himself for a time with the dream of cities. Hearing Arslan was like a bucket of cold water on his dreams, but he relished it. To hear that voice was almost like being young again, when the world was simpler.

"When you are afraid and you do nothing, that matters," Arslan went on. "It eats at men when they think they are cowards. How you raise your sons and daughters matters. The wife who warms you at night matters. The joy you take in being alive, the pleasure of strong drink, companionship and stories. *All* that matters, but when you are dust, other men go on without you. Let it all go, Genghis, and find peace."

Genghis smiled at the stern tone. "I take it you will not be ruling Samarkand in my name then, old friend."

Arslan shook his head, "Oh, I will take what you offer, but not to be remembered. I will take it because these old bones are tired of sleeping on hard ground. My wife likes it here and I want her to be happy as well. Those are good reasons, Genghis. A man should always care about pleasing his wife."

Genghis chuckled. "I can never tell when you are playing games or not," he said.

"Never, Genghis, I am too old for games. I am almost too old for my wife as well, but that is not important today."

Genghis slapped him on the shoulder and rose. He almost used his arm to help Arslan to his feet, then withdrew it just before the old general took offense.

"I will leave you five thousand men. You may have to level part of the city to build a barracks for them. Do not let them get soft, old man." He smiled as Arslan showed his disdain for such an idea.

Genghis trotted his mount through the markets to the main gate of Samarkand. Just the thought of riding with the families and the tumans once more was enough to cast aside the feeling of constriction he had suffered within the city. Winter, such as it was, had come again to the lands of the Shah, though there were still warm days. Genghis scratched a sore on his hand idly as he guided his horse along the paved road. It would be good to have sweet grass under the hooves once more. Eight tumans waited for him to leave the city, drawn up in battle order on the farmland around Samarkand. Boys reaching fourteen had filled the gaps in the ranks, and he had found five thousand good men to leave with Arslan.

Beyond the tumans, the gers were packed onto carts and the people were once again ready to move. He did not know yet where he would take them. It did not matter and he repeated an old nomadic idea to himself as he approached the gate in winter sunlight. They did not have to stand to live, not like those around them. In the tribes, the important parts of life went on whether they were encamped on a sunny riverbank, or assaulting an enemy city, or waiting out a cruel winter. He had lost sight of that for a time in Samarkand, but Arslan had helped him to put his thoughts in order.

The crowds in the city kept well back from the man who might order the death of anyone he saw. Genghis hardly noticed their staring faces as he approached the gate and looked out through the open space to the ranks of his warriors.

His pony jerked without warning and Genghis was jolted forward. He saw a man had stepped out of the crowd to grab the leather straps attached to the bit. One hard pull had turned the mount's head and stopped the khan in his tracks. His guards were drawing their swords and opening their mouths to shout, but Genghis turned too slowly to see a second attacker rush to his side, a yelling face too young for a beard. A knife was shoved up at him, the boy trying to jam it beneath the layered armor into his flesh.

From instinct Genghis struck the youth hard across the face. In full armor, his forearm was sheathed in plates of beaten iron, and the metal ripped open the boy's cheek, knocking him down. Genghis drew his sword as the crowd seemed to erupt around him. He saw more knives held in fists and lunged at the one holding his horse, punching the blade downwards into his chest. The man he had struck was dying, but he gripped Genghis's foot and his arm flailed wildly, a blade gashing the khan's hip. Genghis grunted in pain, lashing out again and this time almost taking off the head. He could hear the attackers yelling all around him, but his guards were moving to protect the khan. They did not know or care particularly which of the crowd were the attackers. They went through them all, hacking men and women aside until bodies lay everywhere.

As Genghis sat panting on his mount, the boy with a torn cheek recovered and leapt at him. One of his guards impaled the boy from behind, then kicked him off the blade so that he sprawled with the rest. The marketplace was empty by then, though the nearby streets still echoed to screams and running feet. Genghis reached down to touch the wound he had taken. He'd known worse in his time. He nodded to the guards, knowing that they would fear his anger for letting him be cut at all. In fact, Genghis had already decided to see them all hanged for their inattention, but the moment to tell them was not when they were within sword's reach of him and still ready to kill.

Genghis waited until fresh soldiers rode in from the tumans, Tsubodai and Kachiun with them. He ran a hand across his throat as he glanced at the guards, and they sagged as they sat their mounts, all the fight going out of them as their weapons were taken.

"I should have expected it," Genghis said, furious with himself. Perhaps the city itself had made him careless. For a man who broke empires, there would always be those who hated him. He should never have relaxed inside a city, even Samarkand. He cursed under his breath at the thought that his enemies had known exactly where to find him for months. That was one benefit of a nomadic life—enemies had to work hard even to locate you.

Kachiun had dismounted to check the dead. Almost forty people had been cut down by the guards, and some of them still lived and bled. The general had no interest in finding guilt or innocence, or any pity for them. His brother had been attacked and he was about to order his men to put an end to those who still crawled when he hesitated, holding up a hand.

Two young men had fallen closely together, right by the first attack. Each wore a robe such as those that protected the desert Arabs from sandstorms. They were bare-chested under it, and in death, Kachiun could see the same mark low on their throats. He pulled the cloth further aside, then gestured to a warrior to do the same for the rest of the dead. Male and female, they had their clothes torn. Kachiun found six other men with the mark, none of them alive.

Genghis saw him turn to a young Arab standing with Tsubodai.

"You. What does this mean?"

Yusuf Alghani shook his head, his lips tight. "I have never seen it before," he replied.

Genghis stared down at the man, knowing that he hid something. "It is a word in your writing," he said. "Read it for me."

Yusuf made a show of inspecting the first man Kachiun had found. He read it right to left and Kachiun could see his hands were shaking.

"Master, it is the word for serenity. That is all I know."

Genghis nodded as if he accepted it. When Yusuf did not look at the others, he made a hard sound in his throat and dismounted, showing his teeth as weight came on his leg.

"Hold him," he said. Before Yusuf could react, Tsubodai's sword was at his throat, the metal warm against his skin.

"You knew they would all be the same, boy," Genghis said. "Tell me who might wear this word on their chests. Tell me and live."

Even with the threat, Yusuf's eyes still moved around the deserted market, looking for anyone who might be watching. He could see no one, but he knew someone would be there. His words would find their way back to the men who had ordered a kill.

"Will you leave this city, master?" he asked, his voice slightly choked by the pressure of Tsubodai's blade. Genghis raised his eyebrows, surprised at the courage he saw. Or madness, or fear, though who could inspire more fear than a sword at the throat, he did not know.

"I will leave today, boy, yes. Now speak."

Yusuf swallowed dryly. "The assassins bear such a mark, such a word, master. That is truly all I know."

Genghis nodded slowly. "Then they will be easy to find. Put your sword away, Tsubodai. We need this one."

"I have found him useful, lord," Tsubodai replied. "With your permission, I will send a runner to the general with this news. He will want to have all his staff checked for the mark, perhaps everyone in the city." As the thought formed, he turned and grabbed Yusuf, yanking his robe aside before he could react. The skin was bare and Yusuf glared at the general as he rearranged himself.

"That would be wise," Genghis said. He looked around him at the dead bodies, already attracting flies. Samarkand was no longer his concern.

"Hang my guards before you join me, Tsubodai. They failed today."

Ignoring the pain from his hip, he remounted and rode out to the tumans.

CHAPTER TWENTY-EIGHT

THE MOVEMENT OF THE KHAN'S GER rocking on its cart was a strange sensation for Yusuf Alghani. The young Bedouin had seen many astonishing things since offering his services to the Mongols. As the day wore on and the tumans moved out with the families, he had expected to be summoned once more to face the khan. Yusuf had watched in interest as every Arab man and woman was checked for the mark of serenity. There were a surprising number of dark-skinned faces in the camp once Yusuf had noticed. In the years since the Mongols had crossed to Khwarezm, they had picked up almost a thousand Arabs in their wake, both young and old. They worked as interpreters for the most part, though some practiced medicine and others joined the Chin as engineers and craftsmen working for the khan. Genghis didn't seem to care when they broke off their labors to roll out prayer mats, though Yusuf was not sure whether it was from respect or indifference. He suspected the latter, as the camp contained Buddhists and Nestorian Christians as well as Moslems, with far more of the infidel faiths than true believers.

Yusuf waited for the khan to speak as the man finished a meal. He had even allowed Moslem butchers to kill goats and sheep in the way they desired, and the Mongols did not seem to care how they ate or lived as long as they obeyed. Yusuf could not understand the man who sat across from him, idly picking something from his teeth with a splinter. When the word had come to attend the khan, Tsubodai had taken him by the arm and said to do whatever he was told.

Yusuf hardly needed the warning. This was the man who had slaughtered his people in the tens of thousands, more. Yet the dead Shah had done the same in his wars and persecutions. Yusuf accepted such things. As long as he survived, he did not care whether the khan succeeded or was left for the crows.

Genghis put aside his plate, but kept a long knife ready on his lap. The warning was not wasted on the young man watching him.

"You seemed nervous in the market," Genghis said. "Do they have such a reach then, these assassins?"

Yusuf took a deep breath. He was still uncomfortable even talking about them, but if he was not safe surrounded by tumans of warriors, then he was already dead.

"I have heard it said they can reach a man anywhere, master. When they are betrayed, they bring terrible vengeance on those who defied them, relatives, friends, whole villages even."

Genghis smiled slightly. "I have done the same," he said. "Fear can hold men in chains who would fight to the death otherwise. Tell me about them."

"I do not know where they come from," Yusuf said quickly. "No one knows that."

"Someone must," Genghis interrupted, his eyes growing cold, "or they could not accept the payments for death."

Yusuf nodded nervously. "That is true, master, but they protect their secrets and I am not among those who know. All I have heard are rumors and legends." Genghis did not speak and he hurried on, wanting to find something that would satisfy this old devil who played with a knife.

"They are said to be ruled by the Old Man of the Mountains, master. I believe it is a title more than a name, as it has been the same for many generations. They train young men to kill and send them out in exchange for vast sums of gold. They do not ever stop until the life is taken."

"They were stopped this morning," Genghis said.

Yusuf hesitated before answering. "There will be others, master, always more until the contract is complete."

"Do they all carry this mark on their skin?" Genghis asked. He thought it would not be too hard to guard his family from men who identified themselves in such a way. To his disappointment, Yusuf shook his head.

"I thought that was part of the legend, master, until I saw it in the market. It is a sin against God for them to mark their bodies in such a way. I was surprised to see it at all. I do not believe they will all carry the mark, especially now you have been seen to discover it. The ones who come now will be young men, their skin untouched."

"Like you," Genghis said softly.

Yusuf forced a laugh, though it sounded hollow. "I have been loyal, master. Ask your generals Tsubodai and Jebe." He struck his chest. "My allegiance is only to you."

Genghis snorted at the lie. What else would the young man say, even if he were an assassin? The notion that any one of the Arabs in his camp might be a killer was worrying. He had wives and young children, as had his brothers. He could guard himself against armies, but not enemies who came in the night and gave their lives to take his.

Genghis recalled the Chin assassin who had come out of Yenking to kill him in his ger. Luck had saved him that night and then only barely. The poisoned knife had caused him more pain and weakness than he had ever known. Even the thought of it brought sweat to his brow as he glared at the young Arab. He considered having Yusuf taken out away from the women and children. His men would have him telling them anything they wanted to hear in no time at all.

Yusuf squirmed under the fierce gaze, his senses screaming that he was in terrible danger. It was the effort of a lifetime not to dart from the ger and run for his horse. Only the fact that the Mongols could ride down anyone alive held him in place. The cart lurched as the wheels passed over a rut in the ground, and Yusuf almost cried out.

"I will ask, master. I promise you. If anyone who knows how to find them crosses my path, I will send them to you." Anything to make him more valuable to the khan alive, he thought to himself. He did not care if the Mongols destroyed the assassins, only that Yusuf Alghani was standing when the killing stopped. They were Ismailis, after all, a Shia sect and not even true Moslems. He had no loyalty to them.

Genghis grunted, toying with the knife in his hands.

"Very well, Yusuf. Do that and report anything you hear to me. I will search in different ways."

The young man heard the dismissal in his words and left quickly. Alone, the khan cursed under his breath. He threw the knife so that it struck the central post of the ger and stayed there, quivering. He could destroy cities that sat where he could see them. He could break armies and nations, both. The thought of insane killers lunging for him in the night made him want to lash out. How could he protect his family against such people? How could he keep Ogedai safe to inherit? There was only one way. Genghis reached for the knife and worked it free. He would have to find them and burn them out, wherever they hid. If they moved as his own people did, he would find them. If they had a home, he would destroy it. The conquest of cities would have to wait.

He sent for his generals and they came to his ger before the sunset.

"These are my orders," Genghis told them. "I will remain with one tuman to protect the families. If they come for me here, I will be ready for them. You will go out in all directions. Find me anything about these assassins and come back. Rich men can hire them, so you will have to break wealthy towns and cities to get at those men. Take no prisoners except the ones who claim to know something. I want the location."

"News of a bribe will spread as fast as we can ride," Tsubodai said. "We have cartloads of gold and jade and this could be a use for it. With your permission, lord, I will also promise some great sum to anyone who can tell us where the assassins train. We have enough to tempt even princes."

Genghis waved a hand, accepting the idea. "Offer to spare cities that bring us the information if you want. I do not care how it is *done*, just get the information I need. And take the Arabs in the camp with you. I don't want them anywhere close until we have met and destroyed this threat. *Nothing* else matters until then. The Shah is dead, Tsubodai. This is the only threat we face."

Jelaudin felt the crowd surge as if he held their hearts in his hand. He had them hanging on his words and the feeling was as intoxicating as it was new. In his father's army, he had dealt with men already sworn to obedience. He had never had to recruit them, or persuade them to his cause. To find he had that skill, that he had a genius for it, had surprised him almost as much as his brothers.

He had begun by visiting mosques in the Afghan towns, small places with just a few hundred of the devout. He had spoken to the Imams of those places and relished the horror they showed when he told them of Mongol atrocities. He had learned what worked then, and the tales grew wilder with each telling. He had come away from the very first village with forty strong men of the Pathan tribe. Until he had arrived in their midst, they had not even known the infidels had invaded Arab lands, never mind that they had killed the Shah of Khwarezm. Their righteous anger had surprised Jelaudin at first, until he saw it echoed in every village and town he visited. The numbers of loyal men had grown and more than two thousand sat outside in the dust, waiting for the charismatic leader they had vowed to follow.

"With my own eyes," he said, "I saw the Mongols destroy a mosque. The holy men raised empty hands to stop them, but they were killed and tossed aside, their bodies left to rot." The crowd murmured angrily, the largest he had addressed since coming south. Most of them were young men and there were many boys with them, their heads bare of the turbans the older men wore. Jelaudin had found the young were the ones he reached first, though they brought experienced warriors in from the hills to hear him speak. If his father had lived, Jelaudin thought the Shah might have tried the same, but his death was the perfect event to have strong men taking up their swords. He spoke with passion of the foreigners who laughed at the faith and despoiled the holy places. They drank in his words. Jelaudin raised his hands to quiet them and they fell silent, gazing on him with perfect attention. He had them.

"I saw our women and children killed and taken by their warriors, torn from the hands of their husbands. Those who wore veils were stripped and abused in public. In Bukhara, they killed an Imam on the steps of the blue mosque and their young men urinated on the body. I would tear out my eyes for what they have seen, if I did not need them for Allah's vengeance!"

Many in the crowd surged to their feet, overcome with rage and excitement. They raised their swords and jabbed them into the air, chanting holy words of war. Jelaudin turned to exchange a glance with his brothers and found them already on their feet and roaring with the rest. He blinked at that, hardly expecting them to be so affected by his words. Yet they too drew swords and their eyes were bright with anger. They had seen all that Jelaudin had seen, but still the words, the hot, lifeless air, the *need* fired their blood. Even Tamar began to chant with the warriors of Islam, intoning the words of the prophet. Jelaudin's heart swelled as the noise crashed over him. Had his father known of this? He felt as if he were balancing a sword. If it slipped, he would lose everything, but the weight of their belief brought reality to his dreams. Already men were coming to him as word spread throughout the region. He had called for a holy war on the Mongol aggressor, and his words and promises had set the land alight. Imams preached in mosques he had never seen that he was a warrior of God. His task was merely to feed that fire and then send it north.

Jelaudin smiled down at the crowd who had gathered that night, knowing they would leave with him to the next town and the next. He would arrive at Kabul as the spiritual leader of an army, and he thought that city would swell his numbers more than anything he had seen. Perhaps the hand of God truly guided him in this; he did not know. He was a poor vessel for Allah, but how else did God work if not through the hands of men? Perhaps he was the instrument of vengeance. Allah was truly good to give him a second chance.

The Mongol tumans rode hundreds of miles in all directions, an explosion of men and horses that attacked every place where there were people to make afraid. The word of their quest spread almost as fast, and rumors of great treasures for information seemed to have wings. By the tenth day, Jebe found a man who said he knew the mountains where the assassins had their base. Jelme found two more who claimed to be related to a family serving them in their fortress. In each case, the destruction of their cities stopped on the instant and that brought even more to talk to the Mongol generals, desperate to save themselves. Twice Mongol scouts returned from a fruitless ride, with no sign of a city of assassins. The men who had misled them were fools or liars, but they were killed and the tumans moved on.

Chagatai had ridden north with Tsubodai, almost in the track the general had ridden to hunt the Shah. In the foothills of steep mountains, they found a village and burned it to the ground, then moved on to another. There they were met by a group of senior men, pleading for a private audience. Tsubodai arranged it and when he heard what they had to say, one of the men did not return to his home. Instead, he traveled with the Mongol general, riding as fast as possible back to Genghis. By the time they reached the khan, three others were there to claim the gold, each with a different location for the assassins.

Genghis greeted Tsubodai as he rode in, his expression weary. "Another one, Tsubodai?"

The general's excitement dropped away. "There are more?" he said.

Genghis nodded. "Either they are thieves who believe I will give

carts of gold for lies, or the assassins have whispered different locations in a dozen places. If they are as ancient as your Yusuf claims, I
think it is the last."

"I have one man who claims to know, lord. I do not think he is a
fool or a thief like the rest."

Genghis raised his eyebrows, knowing Tsubodai's judgment was
sound.

"Bring him to my ger when he has been searched for weapons," he
replied.

Tsubodai brought Yusuf to interpret, still dusty from the long ride
back to the camp. The village elder was painfully nervous as he faced
the khan. Sweat poured off him and he smelled strongly of excrement
and garlic in that small space. Genghis breathed shallowly as he came
close.

"Well? You told my general you knew something," he snapped, already tired of the men who had come with gold in their eyes. He waited
impatiently as Yusuf turned his words into gibberish and the stranger
nodded, already terrified. Three dead men lay in a shallow pit outside.
Genghis had made sure this one saw their upturned faces as he passed
into the khan's ger. It explained the sour smell that hung around him
like a mist.

"My sister lives in a village in the mountains, master, perhaps two
days north from where I found your men." He swallowed nervously as
Yusuf interpreted, and Genghis tossed him a skin of airag to clear his
throat. The man drank and choked, having thought it was water. Red in
the face, he had to be thumped on his back before he could continue.

"I am sorry, master. Strong spirits are forbidden to me," he gasped.
Yusuf grinned as he relayed the words.

"Tell him that is not a strong spirit," Genghis growled. "And tell
him to speak before I have him thrown in the pit and covered over
while he still breathes."

By the time Yusuf finished speaking, the little man was pale and already babbling.

"My sister says that men live in the mountains and take food and
servants from the village. They answer to no man, master, but she said
they sometimes carry quarry stones on carts up into the high peaks."

As Genghis listened to Yusuf, he grew more irritable.

"Ask him if that is all he knows. It is not enough."

The Arab paled still further and shook his head. "She told me two
young men of the village followed the carts once, three, perhaps four

years ago. They did not come back, master. They were found dead when their families went to search for them, each with his throat cut."

Genghis stared as he heard the last part of the translation. It was not confirmation, but it was the most promising of all the wild tales that had come in.

"It is possible, Tsubodai. You were right to bring him to me. Give him a cart of gold with two oxen to pull it." He thought for a moment. "You and I are going north, Tsubodai. He will accompany us as far as this village of his sister. If we find what we need, he can take the gold. If not, his life is forfeit."

The little man listened to Yusuf and fell to his knees in relief.

"Thank you, master," he called as Genghis left the ger.

CHAPTER TWENTY-NINE

GENGHIS FORCED HIMSELF to be patient as he prepared to fight an enemy unlike any other he had faced. He moved the families back to the shelter around Samarkand, leaving Jelme and Kachiun with them for protection. Jelme came to thank him personally for the posting, which left Genghis blinking in surprise, quickly masked. It had not occurred to him that the general would prefer to spend time with his father in the city rather than hunting the assassins who threatened them.

For that task, he took his own tuman, as well as Tsubodai's. The best part of twenty thousand men were still a force that awed him when he remembered his first raiding bands of a few dozen. With them, he could bring mountains down if he had to. Even so many could cross sixty to eighty miles a day if they traveled light, but Genghis had no idea what lay ahead of them. The artisans of Samarkand were there to be used and he had them construct siege equipment and new carts, piling on just about anything he thought they might need and tying it down with canvas and rope. The khan was a whirlwind of energy as he planned for the attack, and none of his men were left in doubt as to how seriously he took the threat. Of all men in the tribes, Genghis understood the danger of assassins, and he looked forward to the assault to come.

The new carts had the stronger spoked wheels Tsubodai had

brought back from Russia, but they groaned and creaked as the two tumans moved off at last. Even after a month of preparation, Jochi had not returned to the camp. It was possible he still sought out information on the assassins, but events had moved on. Genghis sent two warriors riding east after him, then two more after Khasar, freeing their hands. The region was still fat with wealthy cities, and while he sought out the assassins, Genghis knew Khasar and Jochi would enjoy taking them at their leisure.

Chagatai had asked to assist his father in the search for the mountain stronghold, but Genghis had refused him. Nothing he knew of the assassins spoke of large numbers. Their strength lay in secrecy, and once that was broken, Genghis expected to dig them out like sticking a knife into a crack. Chagatai was still under a cloud with his father, and Genghis could hardly look at him without feeling anger and dashed hopes surface. He had not made the decision to raise Ogedai lightly. Thoughts of his legacy had been troubling the khan for many months, but he had planned for Chagatai to inherit for far longer. It was not that he regretted it, at all. The decision was made. Genghis knew his own temper well, however. He knew that if Chagatai showed the slightest resentment, there was a chance he would kill him.

Instead, Genghis sent him south with Jebe to raze the land in his name. All his generals were warned not to let Arabs too close to them, even those they knew and trusted as interpreters. Genghis left all but a few of his behind the walls of Samarkand, forbidding them from going anywhere near the camp. Arslan would be merciless to any who disobeyed the order, and Genghis felt he had secured his people in all ways as he rode north.

With the laden carts, they made barely thirty miles a day, starting at dawn and riding at walking pace for all the hours of daylight. They left behind the green fields around Samarkand, taking the carts across a shallow fording point of the northern river before crossing into lands of dust and scrub grass, hills and valleys.

By the fourth day, Genghis was chafing at the pace. He rode up and down the lines of carts, urging the drivers to make their best speed. What had seemed good sense and restraint in Samarkand now ate at his confidence. The assassins surely knew he was coming. He worried that they would simply abandon their position in the mountains and leave it empty for him to find.

Tsubodai shared the opinion, though he said nothing, knowing that a good general does not criticize a khan, even to those he trusts.

Yet Tsubodai was convinced Genghis had handled it badly. The only thing that might work was a massive strike, surprising the assassins where they were strongest before they even knew enemies were in the area. This slow-moving caravan of carts was almost exactly the opposite of what Tsubodai wanted. Riding with barely more than blood dust and mare's milk, he and his men had raced from the mountains to Genghis in twelve days. Now, as the moon waxed and waned for almost a full turn, Tsubodai eyed it with more and more misgiving. He was already planning what to do if the assassins had vanished as they came to the village Tsubodai had sacked. This time Genghis did not stop, though ash-marked figures ducked and scrabbled in the wreckage, searching for anything they might salvage. The Mongol tumans rode past without a thought for those who hid from them.

The mountains could be seen for days before they reached the foothills. In response to his own nervous energy, Tsubodai gained Genghis's permission to ride out with the scouts, searching for new information. He found the second village when the carts were still forty miles and more than a day's ride behind him. It was there that Tsubodai had met the village council and the man he had brought to Genghis.

No one lived there any longer. Tsubodai's heart sank as he walked his horse through the gutted shells of homes. It was not the work of his men, and in this dead place, there were not even urchins to sift the ruins for food or coins. If Tsubodai had needed any final confirmation of the assassins' presence, he found it in the bodies that lay everywhere, gashed and burned where they had fallen. Only flies, birds, and wild dogs lived in the village, and the buzz and flutter of wings sounded all around him, rising in choking clouds as his horse walked through.

Genghis came up when Tsubodai's riders told him the news. He kept the cold face as he rode through to his general, jerking sharply only once when a fly landed on his lips.

"This is a warning," Tsubodai said.

Genghis shrugged. "A warning or a punishment. Someone saw you talking to the merchant." He chuckled at the thought of the man's oblivious approach with a cart full of gold. His sudden wealth would be worth nothing in that place.

"We could find the same in this village further into hills that he spoke of, his sister's home."

Genghis nodded. He did not care particularly that villages had been destroyed. If the burned houses *were* meant as a warning, there were few men in the world that could have taken it as lightly as he did. He had seen much worse in his years as khan.

That thought reminded Genghis of something his mother used to say when he was a boy and he smiled.

"I was born with a clot of blood in my right hand, Tsubodai. I have always walked with death. If they know me at all, they know that. This destruction is not a warning for me, but for anyone else who might consider dealing with me." He frowned to himself then and drummed his fingers on his saddle. "It is the sort of thing I might do if I were leaving the area."

Tsubodai nodded, knowing the khan did not need to hear his agreement.

"Still, we must push on to see where they hid themselves," Genghis said, his mood souring, "even if they have abandoned it."

Tsubodai merely bowed his head and whistled for the scouts to ride with him into the mountains. The sister's village was a day's trek for a fast-moving warrior, perhaps three for the carts. The trails needed to be checked at all points for ambushes, and Tsubodai had to resist the urge to race ahead and see if the assassins had left anyone behind. The mountains were steep beyond that point, with only a narrow path leading the scouts through to the deep valleys and peaks. It was a hard land to assault and worryingly easy to defend. Even sound was muffled in such a place, swallowed by the steep slopes on either side, so that a horse's hooves could be heard as echoes, while the rest of the world receded. Tsubodai rode warily, his hand always near his bow and sword.

Jochi halted his tuman when he heard a warning note from his scout horns. He had ridden hard for more than a month, covering a vast distance into the east, so far that he was convinced the plains of his home lay a thousand miles north. Beyond them the world was endless, unmapped even by Tsubodai.

Jochi had known his father would send men after him eventually. Part of him had considered turning north before this point, though it would hardly have mattered. All the scouts could track a single rider, never mind the seven thousand who formed his tuman. The trail they left could have been followed by a blind man. If rains had come, their hoofprints would have been washed away, but to Jochi's frustration, the sky had stayed cold and blue all the way, with barely a wisp of clouds.

His warriors allowed their ponies to crop the dry grass at their feet as they waited for new orders. Until they came, they were content and relaxed, giving no more thought to the future than a pack of wild dogs. Jochi did not know if they guessed at his internal struggle. At times, he thought they *must* know. Their eyes seemed aware, but he knew that was probably an illusion. As the khan's scouts came closer, Jochi summoned his officers, from those who commanded a thousand down to those who led just ten. They had all stood in the palace at Samarkand and taken an oath to honor Ogedai as khan, the words still fresh in their minds. He did not know what they would do.

More than seven hundred came at his order, walking their mounts apart from those they led. Each had been promoted by Jochi himself, given honor with the trust of other lives in their hands. He felt their questioning gazes on him as he waited for his father's scouts. His hands shook slightly and he stilled them with a tight grip on his reins.

The scouts were two young men from Genghis's own tuman. They wore light deels, made dark and greasy by sweat and constant use. They rode in together and dismounted to bow to Genghis's general. Jochi sat his horse in stillness, a great calm sweeping over him. He had believed he was prepared for this, but he had not been. Now the moment was finally upon him, he felt his stomach churn.

"Deliver your message," Jochi said, looking at the closest man. The scout bowed again, still relaxed and easy after a long ride.

"The Great Khan has moved against the assassins, General. He has good information as to where they have their stronghold. You are free once more to subdue the cities and widen the lands under his control."

"You have ridden far today," Jochi said. "You are welcome in my camp and you must stay to eat and rest."

The scouts exchanged a quick glance before the first one replied.

"My lord, we are not tired. We can ride again."

"I will not hear of it," Jochi snapped. "Stay. Eat. I will speak to you again at sunset."

It was a clear order and the scouts could only obey. Both men dipped their heads before remounting and trotting to the bulk of the tuman, away from the gathering of officers. Rough cooking fires were already alight there and they were made welcome by those who cared for the freshest news.

Jochi raised his hand for his officers to follow him, angling his mount down a hill away from his warriors. A river ran along the bottom of it, shaded in old and twisted trees that overhung the water.

Jochi dismounted at the bottom and let his horse drink before reaching down and taking mouthfuls of the water in his cupped hands.

"Sit with me," he said softly. His men did not understand, but they tied their horses to the trees and gathered around him on the dusty ground until half the slope was filled with them. The rest of the tuman could be seen in the distance, too far to hear his words. Jochi swallowed nervously, his throat dry despite the water he had drunk. He knew the name of each of the senior men in that glade by the river. They had ridden with him against the Arab horses, the Shah's army, cities and garrisons all. They had come to his aid when he was lost and alone amidst his brother's warriors. They were bound to him with more than oaths, but he did not know if it would be enough. He took a deep breath.

"I am not going back," he said. To a man, the officers became still, some of them freezing in the act of chewing on meat or reaching for a skin of airag from their saddlebags.

For Jochi, saying the words was like a dam breaking. He sucked air in again as if he had been running. He could feel his heart pounding and his throat was tight.

"This is not a new decision. I have thought this day might come for years, ever since I fought the tiger and we began our journey to these lands. I have been loyal to my father, the khan, in every action. I have given him my life's blood and those of the men who followed me. I have given him enough."

He looked around at the silent faces of his officers, judging how they received his words.

"I will turn north after this. I have no desire to cross into the southern Chin lands, or go anywhere near Xi Xia in the east. I will see home again and be refreshed in streams that have given us life for ten thousand years. Then I will ride so far and fast that even my father's hunting dogs will never find me. There are hundreds of lands still unknown to us. I saw some of them with General Tsubodai. I know him well and even he will not be able to find me. I will ride until the end of the world and make a home there, a kingdom of my own. There will be no tracks where I go. By the time my father even knows I am not returning, I will be lost to him."

He could see the whites of the eyes in many of his men as they listened, stunned.

"I will not order you to stay with me," he said. "I cannot. I have no family in the gers, while many of you have wives and children you would not see again. I make no demands on you, who are bound by oath to my father and Ogedai. You will be oath-breakers if you ride at my side, and there will be no return to the nation, no truce with my father. He will send hunters and they will search for many years for us. He will not show mercy. I am his son and I know this better than anyone."

As he spoke, his fingers ruffled the stiff hair of the tiger skin at his pommel, feeling the rough edge where Genghis had hacked the head away. He saw one of his Chin minghaan officers rising slowly to his feet, and Jochi paused to hear him.

"My lord...general," the man said, his voice breaking under immense strain. "Why do you consider this thing?"

Jochi smiled, though bitterness flooded through him. "Because I *am* my father's son, Sen Tu. He made his tribe by drawing in all those around him. Shall I do less? Should I follow Ogedai too until I am old and my life is just regrets? I say to you now, it isn't in me. My little brother will be khan to the nation. He will not search for me when the time comes. Until then, I will find my wives and sons and daughters in a place where they have not heard the name of Genghis."

He swept his gaze across the gathering of men on the riverbank. They met his eyes without flinching, though some of them sat as if they had been struck.

"I will be my own man, perhaps for just a few years until I am run down and killed. Who can say how this will end? Yet for a time, I will be able to say that I am free. That is why I stand in this place."

The Chin officer sat down slowly and thoughtfully. Jochi waited. His officers had adopted the cold face to a man, hiding their thoughts from those around him. There would be no rabble-rousing by the river. Each would make the decision alone, as he had.

Sen Tu spoke up again, suddenly. "You will have to kill the scouts, General."

Jochi nodded. Those two young men had put their heads into the mouth of the wolf, though they did not know it. They could not be allowed to return to Genghis to betray his position, even if he turned north as they left. Jochi had considered sending them back with some false story for his father, but killing them was safer by far than playing games and hoping to mislead men like Tsubodai. He did not underestimate that man's fierce intelligence, nor his father's. If the scouts simply vanished, they would wait months before sending others. By then he would have gone.

Sen Tu was deep in thought and Jochi watched him closely, sensing like the men around him that the Chin officer would speak for many of them. Sen Tu had seen upheaval in his life, from the appearance of the khan in his Chin homeland, to the Arab nations and this peaceful spot by the river. He had stood in the front rank against the Shah's best horsemen, and still Jochi did not know what he would say.

"I have a wife in the gers, lord, and two boys," Sen Tu said, raising his head. "Will they be safe if I do not come back?"

Jochi wanted to lie, to say that Genghis would not touch women and children. He struggled for just an instant, then relaxed. He owed the man the truth.

"I don't know. Let us not fool ourselves. My father is a vengeful man. He may spare them, or not, as he chooses."

Sen Tu nodded. He had seen this young general tormented by his own people for years. Sen Tu respected the Great Khan, but he loved Jochi as a son. He had given his life to the young man who now stood so vulnerably before him, expecting yet another rejection. Sen Tu closed his eyes for a moment, praying to the Buddha that his children would live and one day know a man to follow, as he had done.

"I am with you, General, wherever you go," Sen Tu said. Though he spoke quietly, the words carried to those around him.

Jochi swallowed hard. "You are welcome, my friend. I did not want to ride alone."

Another minghaan officer spoke then. "You will not be alone, General. I will be there."

Jochi nodded, his eyes stinging. His father had known this joy, this vow to follow one man, even if it meant death and destruction of everything else they loved. It was worth more than gold, more than cities. A ripple spread through his officers as they shouted out to him, calling their names and joining him one by one. For each it was a personal choice, but he had them all and always had. When there were enough, they gave out a raucous cheer, a battle shout that seemed to rock the ground on which he stood.

"When the scouts are dead, I will put it to the men," he said.

"General," Sen Tu said suddenly, "if some of them choose not to come, if they decide to ride back to the khan, they will betray us."

Jochi looked into the man's dark eyes. He had considered his plans for a long time. Part of him knew he should have such men killed. It was less dangerous to let the scouts live than have his own men return to Genghis. If he let them live, his own chances of survival vanished to almost nothing. His knew his father would have made the decision in a heartbeat, but Jochi was torn. He felt the eyes of all his officers on him, waiting to see what he would order.

"I will not stop them, Sen Tu," he said. "If any man wants to return to his family, I will let him leave."

Sen Tu winced. "Let us see what happens, lord. If it is just a few, I can have men waiting with bows to make an end of them."

Jochi smiled at the Chin officer's unrelenting loyalty. His heart was full as he looked over the crowd gathered on the riverbank.

"I will kill the scouts," he said, "and then we will see."

CHAPTER THIRTY

THE VILLAGE IN THE MOUNTAINS WAS UNTOUCHED. For three days, Tsubodai had ridden with Genghis and the tumans, at times following a narrow track that was barely three horses wide. The Mongols could not see how a village could even survive in such a place, though before noon on the third day, they had reached a heavily laden cart drawn by a mule. With a sheer drop on one side, the tumans could not pass in safety, so Jebe forced the owner to cut the mule free before his men heaved the cart over the edge. Tsubodai watched it fall with interest until it shattered on the rocks below, spilling grain and bolts of cloth over a wide area.

The terrified owner did not dare protest and Tsubodai tossed him a pouch of gold for his stoicism, which then broke as the man realized he had more wealth than he had ever seen before.

The village itself had been built from the stones of the mountains, the houses and single street made of cut blocks the color of the hills, so that they blended in like natural growths. Behind the small collection of buildings, a thin trail of water fell from dizzying heights above, making the air a mist. Chickens scratched in the dust and people stared in horror at the approaching Mongols before dipping their heads and hurrying away.

Tsubodai watched all this with interest, though he could not escape a sense of unease. Warriors and carts stretched back along the mountain trail for many miles, and if there was to be a battle, only those in front would be able to fight. The land forced the general to break every rule he had devised for warfare over the years, and he could not relax as he rode along the street with Genghis.

Tsubodai sent a scout back to bring the man who had a sister in the village. With him went a dozen warriors to carry the gold and tip the cart off the cliff. If he had not, it would have blocked all the men behind and cut the army in half. As it was, Tsubodai could not see how to bring up the supplies from the rear. Without a staging area, the string of carts had to remain behind the warriors. Tsubodai struggled with the positions and terrain, hating the way the mountains held his men in a single, vulnerable line.

When the merchant arrived, he was almost in tears to see the village intact, having feared its destruction for days of travel. He found his sister's house quickly and tried to calm her terror of the Mongols strolling outside. She watched openmouthed as warriors dumped bags of gold coins on her step, but the sight did not calm her. Instead, she paled further and further as the pile grew. As the warriors stood back, she slapped her brother hard across the face and tried to bar the door to him.

"You have killed me, you fool!" she screeched as he struggled with her in the doorway. He fell back a step, astonished at her rage, and as he did so, the door slammed shut and all the men could hear her weeping inside.

"That was touching," Genghis murmured to Tsubodai.

Tsubodai did not smile. The village was surrounded by rocky heights and he was certain they were being watched. The crying woman had certainly thought so. Tsubodai had seen her eyes dart up to the surrounding peaks for an instant before she closed the door in her brother's face. Tsubodai raised his head and scanned every high point, but nothing moved.

"I don't like this place," Tsubodai said. "This village exists to serve the assassins, I'm certain of it. Why else would it be so far from anywhere else in the mountains? How do they even pay for supplies brought by cart?" At the thought, he eased his horse nearer to Genghis, feeling the narrow street close in on him. A single lucky arrow could end it all, if the villagers were foolish or desperate enough.

"I do not think we should stop here, my lord khan," he said.

"There are two paths further into the mountains and only one back. Let me send scouts along them both and find the way in."

Genghis nodded, and at that moment, a bell rang, the sound muffled but echoing. The Mongols had bows and swords drawn before the notes died away, jerking in shock as the street doors thumped open and armed men and women rushed out.

In just heartbeats, the village went from being silent and deserted to a bloody attack. Tsubodai's horse kicked out at a woman behind him, knocking her flying. They were converging on Genghis, he saw, swinging his sword in a great arc to take a screaming young man across the neck.

To Tsubodai's surprise, the villagers were determined and desperate. His men were experienced in dealing with rioting crowds, but the violence could not be quelled with the shock of sudden bloodletting. He saw one of his warriors dragged off his horse by a man with an arrow in his chest, dying as he yanked with failing strength. Some of them screamed all the time they fought, the noise almost painful as it came from a hundred different throats and echoed back from the hills all around. Yet they were not warriors. Tsubodai took a blow from a long knife on his forearm bracer, turning the block into a short punch that cracked into his attacker's jaw. The villagers had no defense against armored men and only their ferocity made them hard to stop. Tsubodai fought with manic concentration, risking his own life to protect Genghis. They were alone for just moments as more of the khan's tuman struggled to reach him and face outward with their swords and bows. Arrows hissed through the throats of anyone who moved after that, and the iron circle fought its way through them, moving with Genghis at the center.

The sun had not moved above the hills by the time the streets were covered in the dead. The merchant's sister lay among them, one of the first to be cut down. Her brother had survived and he knelt by her gashed body, weeping openly. When one of the warriors dismounted to pull her clothing aside, the man struggled briefly in tearful rage before he was cuffed onto his back. Tsubodai's men found no one with the mark of serenity at their throats.

Tsubodai leaned over his saddle, panting with exertion and relief at having survived. He truly hated the enclosure of hills, and the feeling of eyes on him was even stronger than before.

"If they are not assassins, why would they attack us so wildly?" he demanded of one of his minghaan officers. The man could not reply to such a question, so he merely bowed his head and looked away.

Genghis trotted his pony to Tsubodai as the general stared around him, still shocked by what had happened.

"I imagine they were ordered to get in our way," Genghis said lightly. He was maddeningly calm and not even breathing heavily. "Against thieves or a raiding band, they would have done very well. It would take a determined army to get through this village to the stronghold of our enemies." He grinned. "Fortunately, I have such an army. Send out your scouts, Tsubodai. Find me the way through."

Under the yellow gaze of his khan, Tsubodai gathered himself quickly and sent two arbans of ten men racing deeper into the mountains. Both routes turned sharply after only a short distance, so that the warriors quickly vanished from view. He ordered others to search every house, making certain there were no more surprises hidden in them.

"I hope this means the assassins have not abandoned their home," he said.

Genghis brightened still further at the thought.

By sunset, Tsubodai's men had piled the dead at one edge of the village, by the icy waterfall. There was a pool there, before the water found its way further down the cliffs. Tsubodai organized the watering of the horses, a task which was maddeningly slow and laborious, but vital. For those too far back to come in, he used buckets from the village and had his warriors walk miles to them. Many would be forced to sleep on the narrow trail, just a few feet from a drop to their death. There was no grumbling from them, at least that reached the ears of the general. They accepted their lot as they had always done.

Only one group of Tsubodai's scouts came back as the hills were lit with gold and the sun sank. The other had vanished and Tsubodai nodded to Genghis as the road remained empty. A single scout might have fallen or broken a leg. For ten young warriors to disappear in the mountains, another force had to exist, ruthless and patient. The Mongols had found the path to the assassins, and they slept where they stood, half frozen and with just a few mouthfuls of dried meat and water to keep them alive as they waited for dawn.

Tsubodai was up before first light, in part to be certain he could put a rank of men onto the narrow path before Genghis tried to lead them.

The general was convinced the first ones in would die, and he chose well-armored archers from his own tuman, giving them the best chance he could. He did not want Genghis to risk himself against an unseen enemy in such a place. The rock walls that lined the path were too easy to defend. As Tsubodai stared into the lightening gloom, he guessed they would face stones and arrows at the very least. He hoped the assassins did not have stocks of fire oil, but he was not confident. There was no point regretting past decisions, but the assassins had been given a long time to prepare the way. If they had chosen to fight, it would be a hard path to walk and many of his men would not return from the mountains.

The sun could not be seen for much of the morning in that place of peaks and stone, so that Tsubodai wondered at the half-lit existence of the villagers. Even in high summer, their homes would have been cold for most of the day. Only when the sun was overhead would light and warmth reach the street below. By then he did not doubt that the villagers were all servants of the ones he had come to root out from their stronghold. Nothing else explained why they would choose such a life.

Tsubodai rode in the second rank and looked back only once as the army began to move, a vast slow tail that stretched back almost to the first village he had found destroyed. Some of them still had no idea what had happened the day before, but they followed in his steps and wound their way further into the hostile terrain.

The path narrowed still further as he left the village behind, forcing his men to ride two across. It was almost a crack in the mountain, the air cold from constant gloom and shadows. Tsubodai kept his weapons ready, straining his eyes ahead for some sign of the arban he had sent. Only hoofprints remained and Tsubodai's men followed them slowly, wary of an ambush but still going on.

The sense of enclosure became stifling as the slope began to rise. To Tsubodai's discomfort, the trail narrowed again, so that only one man at a time could squeeze his horse through. Still the hoofprints led them. Tsubodai had never felt so helpless in his life, and he had to struggle with swelling panic. If they were attacked, the first ones killed would block the path of those behind, leaving them easy targets. He did not think he could even turn his mount in such a narrow pass and winced every time his legs brushed the mossy rock on either side.

Tsubodai jerked his head up as one of his men gave a low whistle and the horses came to a sudden stop. He cursed under his breath as he realized he could not even ride to the front to see what they had found.

The finest army in the world had been reduced to a single line of nervous men. No wonder the assassins had not abandoned their fortress. Tsubodai squinted upwards at the strip of bright sky above his head. All it would take was a few men with stones up there and the mountains would become a tomb for all their hopes and ambitions. He took a sharp breath when a pebble dropped from somewhere above, but nothing followed it.

One of his men came back on foot, ducking under the legs of the horses and making them shy nervously. They too felt hemmed in by the rock on all sides, and Tsubodai was worried one of them might panic. In such a small space, it would be chaos.

"There's a wall built across the path ahead, General," the warrior said. "It has a gate, but it's made of iron. If you have hammers sent up, we can knock out the hinges, but it won't be quick."

Tsubodai nodded, though the thought of sending orders back along a line of stationary horses would have been farcical if it hadn't been for the constant threat of an attack. Despite himself, he glanced up again with a wince.

"You'll have to go yourself. Have the hammers brought from man to man and have an officer break out the mantlets from the closest cart that has them." The portable wooden barricades would be useful, at least. Genghis had insisted on having dozens of the things made in Samarkand to protect his archers, a decision that was only now bearing fruit.

Tsubodai waited impatiently as the runner clambered back along the line. The carts of siege supplies were far behind, and time passed slowly as the men talked amongst themselves and waited. Only Genghis seemed cheerful, as Tsubodai looked back at him. The khan was sharpening his sword with a whetstone from his saddlebags, raising the blade at intervals to inspect the edge. He caught Tsubodai staring and chuckled, the sound echoing as he continued with the task.

In the stillness, some instinct made Tsubodai look up for a third time. He saw the strip of blue sky speckled in dark objects. His jaw dropped and he shouted to those around him to duck, raising his armored forearms above his own head just before the first stone hit him.

The stones fell in waves, causing the Mongols to grunt and snarl in pain. Those who had shields heaved them up, but they were only a few. Their horses suffered the barrage without helmets or armor, bucking and kicking in fear and pain. More than a few were stunned, slumping and scrabbling as their legs gave way. Tsubodai clenched his fists over his head as he saw some of them would not rise again, their skulls broken. He saw men with their arms hanging loose, the bones broken despite the armor, and still the stones fell into the confined space. The one thing Tsubodai could be thankful for was that the stones were small. Rocks capable of snapping a man's spine either wedged in the pass above their heads or bounced and shattered into smaller pieces. Even as he took note of that, one of the large stones survived the fall and struck the forehead of a horse only feet away from him, killing the animal instantly. A memory came back to the general of the first fort he had taken with Genghis. Men had stood above him then in a killing hole, driving shafts almost straight down. They had been saved by wooden barriers, held above their heads. Tsubodai felt his heart thump painfully as he realized he had forgotten about the carts behind him. They could not be drawn into the narrowing path, and he had a vision of the whole army being blocked, unable to reverse as the sides of rock closed on them. His men reeled under the barrage of stones, crying out in pain and frustration.

"Where are those mantlets!" Tsubodai roared. "We need mantlets here!" His voice carried far down the lines, snapping back and forth from the walls. As the trail turned, he saw men gesture urgently to those behind them, passing on his order. How far back were the carts? He waited, wincing at the crack of stones as he crouched over his saddle with his arms protecting his head.

He thought he had been listening to screams and his own breath forever when he heard a shout. Tsubodai risked looking out over his shoulder. Stones still rattled off his armor, rocking him. Even the small ones hurt. He breathed in relief to see the heavy wooden shields being passed from rider to rider overhead. They could not come fast enough.

The trail of wooden barriers halted as those under the falling stones held on to them instead of passing them down the line. Tsubodai shouted furious orders at them. More were coming, he could see. Already the stones could be heard thumping off the wood, hard enough to hurt the ears. Tsubodai grabbed the first mantlet to reach him, seeing that Genghis was already safe. He did not think the khan would be giving his up, and it took a wrench of will to pass his on to those ahead. They could move them only by tilting them up. When the mantlets were turned like shells to protect the men, they often wedged in the walls and hardly needed holding.

Bareheaded once more, Tsubodai looked to Genghis and saw the khan had lost his calm. Genghis grimaced as he saw his general unprotected and then shrugged as if it were nothing. He heaved his mantlet off where it had stuck and reached back for another. Tsubodai saw stones falling around the khan. One rocked his head back when it struck Genghis's helmet, but another mantlet was dragged forward and the general breathed in relief to see him secure once more.

The rain of stones dwindled and then stopped, leaving battered and dying men beneath the heavy boards. Without armor, they would have been destroyed. Whether the assassins had seen the wooden barriers or simply run out of missiles, Tsubodai did not know. He did know he would move sky and earth to pay them back for the agony of being helpless.

Hammers came forward under the shell of mantlets, handed from man to man until heavy blows began to ring out from somewhere ahead. Maddeningly, Tsubodai could not see the front ranks. The wall they tried to break was twelve horse lengths in front of him, and he could only wait and sweat.

Tsubodai thought he could have the dead horses butchered and sent back in pieces along the line. He dismissed the idea as quickly as it had struck him. They needed to get out of the chimney of rock, and gutting horses would take too long, even if they had room to swing the axes.

Instead, Tsubodai saw the mantlets could be used to cover dead men and horses, allowing the rest to walk over them. It would be grisly business, but without a way forward, it didn't matter if the iron gate could be battered out or not.

The echoing crash of the gate falling could be heard far back along the line, bringing a ragged cheer from the warriors. Tsubodai saw the men ahead lunge forward and then cry out as they were struck by something unseen. Tsubodai squinted, but there was little light in that place and the mantlets reduced it almost to nothing in their shadow. Just ahead of him lay the horse he had seen struck. Its rider had been pinned against the wall as the animal slumped. Blood had come from his nose and he was pale and still. Tsubodai did not know if he lived, but he gave orders without hesitation.

He passed his own mantlet forward to cover the battered pair. With Tsubodai urging him on, the closest warrior dug in his heels, forcing his mount up and onto the unstable platform.

It lurched under the weight and the terrified pony resisted, but Tsubodai and the rider yelled at it. The warrior belted its flanks with his sword scabbard until the animal lurched over, whinnying in distress. Tsubodai grimaced and followed, trying not to hear the sound of breaking bones under his weight. He told himself the man beneath was surely dead.

Tsubodai's horse almost bolted free at the sight of an empty path ahead. He reined in desperately, knowing that whatever had silenced his men was still waiting. Only one warrior rode ahead of him and that man raced forward madly, calling a war cry and brandishing his sword.

Tsubodai passed through the rubble of the gate and sunlight struck his eyes, almost blinding him. Beyond, he caught a glimpse of a wide spot in the path. His horse was running for it, desperate to get away from the fear and stench of blood in the pass. Tsubodai yanked the reins savagely, turning his mount left as arrows whirred past him. The other warrior had ridden straight in and arrows appeared in his chest. Tsubodai saw him stagger, but his armor held and he had time to kill a bowman before another shaft took him under the chin at close range.

The general gasped for breath, blinking as more warriors clattered out of the pass to join him. Those who had broken arms and collarbones were unable to use their weapons, but they ran into the arrows to clear the pass behind them.

The archers facing them were dressed in white robes, pulled open by the action of drawing their bows. Tsubodai could see they wore the mark of serenity, and fury swept over him. He kicked his mount at the massed lines of men. There was nowhere to run or maneuver. His warriors would either break the line or die in twos and threes as they came out.

It helped that the horses ran mad with terror. The Mongol warriors hardly tried to stop them as they charged. Tsubodai's horse went straight at an archer fumbling another arrow onto the string. The shot went buzzing past the general and he swung his sword as he plunged past, his horse kicking the next man down. Tsubodai showed his teeth in cruel pleasure as his warriors began to cut further into the lines. Each man's chest bristled with arrows, but the armor was good and the archers poor. The assassins were not warriors, for all the fear they created. They had not trained every day from the moment they could walk. They could not crush fear and pain to make one last cut into an enemy. The warriors of the khan could and did.

The pass ahead was wide enough for five horses to gallop abreast. Perhaps a hundred bowmen stood on tiers of rock, cut almost like steps. They could not hold the flood coming out at them. Volleys might have broken the first ranks, but Tsubodai saw every man shot alone. He swung his blade at another, cutting a great gash in the man's side as he whipped past. His horse was foundering, with two arrows deep in its chest. Only its panic kept it running, but Tsubodai was ready when the strength in the animal vanished and it fell hard. He leapt lightly down, staggering almost into the arms of an Arab. Tsubodai spun in a frenzy, so that his sword came round at neck height. The man died and the next he faced was caught helpless between shots. Tsubodai took two sharp strides and plunged his sword into the bare chest, right at the level of the serenity tattoo. A warrior who had come through still mounted kicked out as Tsubodai braced to block a third, sending his intended victim tumbling backwards. Tsubodai looked up in thanks and saw it was Genghis, bloody and jubilant.

Against unarmored men, Tsubodai thought the archers would have stolen victory even from a large number. The chimney of rock was the best defense he had ever seen, and he understood why the assassins had stayed there to fight. No doubt they thought they could hold against anyone. Tsubodai wiped his mouth, where he tasted something foul and sticky. His hand came away red and he spat on the ground.

Around him, the last of the archers were being cut down, and the Mongol riders let out a bellow of victory, releasing all the fear and anger they had not shown before. Tsubodai did not join them. His body was aching from a hundred impacts, and he sat down on the stone steps, using his foot to shove away a body and make a space. He found himself panting hard for air, as if his lungs could not fill properly. The sun was high above their heads, not yet even at noon, and Tsubodai laughed weakly at the sight. He felt like he had been trapped in that dark place for years and every breath was a struggle to find calm.

He looked further up the path, past the warriors and the dead. He had seen the fortress standing over them all the time they had fought, but only now did it enter his thoughts.

The assassins had made their stronghold from the mountain stones, building it right across the pass so that there was no way around. The cliffs on either side were too smooth to climb, and Tsubodai sighed as he studied the single great gate that blocked him still.

"Hammers here!" he shouted. "Hammers and mantlets."

CHAPTER THIRTY-ONE

THE CATAPULTS GENGHIS HAD BROUGHT FROM SAMARKAND could not be dragged through the narrow pass, even in pieces. Instead, the work fell to men wielding hammers and wall hooks. The door into the fortress was made of bronze and brass, set well back into stone columns. Progress was incredibly slow and the work was exhausting. Tsubodai organized the hammer teams, with other men to bring up the mantlets so they could work under their protection. By the end of the first day, the columns on both sides of the door were chipped and battered, with great gouges from where iron bars had been struck with hammers. It still held. Above their heads, arrows came at intervals, but the best archers in the nation were standing ready for them, sending shafts up before the assassins could even aim. Even then there were not many defenders and Tsubodai wondered if the main force of the assassins already lay dead on the bloody steps to the fortress. The assassins worked best in darkness and with stealth. They did not have the numbers to stand against a determined army, as Genghis had said. All their strength lay in their home never being discovered.

It was a tedious business arranging supplies through the crack in the mountain, but Tsubodai organized torches and food as he relieved his men and fresh warriors took up the task of smashing in the door columns. The archers on the walls had an easier task during the night.

They could see the Mongols working, though the mantlets were still held over their heads. Those warriors who passed close to the torch-light risked a sudden arrow humming down at them. As dawn came, seven of Tsubodai's men had been struck and one holding an iron bar had slipped and had his wrist broken with a hammer. Only three died. The others were dragged back beneath the steps, where they nursed and bound their wounds, waiting for daylight.

As the door held through the morning, Genghis gave orders to level the village of stone behind him. His minghaan officers went back with instructions to knock the stone houses apart and drop them down the cliffs so that more men could use the open space as a staging ground. Almost twenty thousand men waited impotently, unable to reach an enemy, while just a few sweated at the wall. Tsubodai seemed confident his men would break in, but as the second day wore on, Genghis had to force the cold face to conceal his impatience.

The Old Man of the Mountains stared down at the armored soldiers working in the sunlight. He could hardly contain the fury that swept over him. Over the course of his life, he had been honored by princes and shahs, from the Punjab in India to the Caspian Sea. He demanded respect, even deference, from the few men who knew who he was, without regard for their wealth and blood. His fortress had never been attacked since his ancestor first found the crack in the mountains and formed the clan that would become the most feared force in Arab lands.

The Old Man gripped the stone sill of an open window as he stared out at the ants working to get to him. He cursed the Shah of Khwarezm, who had tried to buy the death of this khan, as well as his own fate for taking the man's note. He had not known then that the Shah's cities would fall to the invader, the stocks of gold with them. He had sent his chosen men to bring down just one, but somehow it had stirred the khan to this desecration. The Old Man had known within days of the failure in Samarkand. His followers had become overconfi-dent, seduced by having the enemy within easy reach. They had died well enough, but in doing so, brought these mindless attackers to his sanctuary.

The Mongols did not seem to care how many lives they lost. The Old Man could almost admire them for that, if he did not consider them less than men. It seemed it was his fate to be brought down by godless wolves, after all he had achieved. The khan was a relentless, driven enemy and the old ways were falling in pieces around him. It would take a generation to rebuild the clan after this day, at least. He swore to himself that his assassins would eventually repay this blood debt, but at the same time, he was afraid, close to terrified of the man who had thrown himself so hard against the fortress stones. No Arab would have done it. They would have known that to fail was to invite destruction down to three generations of everyone they held dear. Even the great Saladin ceased to trouble the assassins after they had found him in his own command tent.

The Old Man heard footsteps behind him and turned reluctantly from the window arch. His son stood in the cool chamber, dressed for travel. At forty years of age, the younger man knew all the secrets of the clan. He would need them all to start again. With him went the last of the Old Man's hopes. They shared a gaze of grief and anger before his son touched his forehead, lips, and heart and bowed in respect.

"You will not come with me?" his son asked one last time. The Old Man shook his head.

"I will see this out to the end. I was born in this fortress. I will not be driven from it." He thought of the garden of paradise to the rear of the stronghold. The women were already dead at his order, poisoned wine allowing them to drift into sleep. With the last of his men on the wall, there was no one to remove the bodies and the garden was heavy with the smell of corrupting flesh. Still, it was a better fate for them than to fall into the hands of the invaders. The Old Man thought he might spend a little time there while he waited for the khan. The garden had always brought calm to the turbulence in his soul.

"Remember me and rebuild, my son. If I know that you will reach out and snatch this khan from the world, or his sons, I can die in peace."

His son's eyes burned into him before he bowed again.

"I will not forget," he said. The Old Man watched him stride away, his steps sure and strong. There was a hidden path behind the fortress that his son would take, leaving behind only destruction. Two men would travel with him, experienced assassins well versed in all the forms of death. Even they had needed his own order to send them away. They saw no shame in dying to defend their home. Just thirty more waited for the Mongols to break the wall. They knew they would be killed and enter paradise, and they were full of joy.

Alone once more, the Old Man of the Mountains turned from the setting sun. He made his way down marble steps to the garden for the last time, breathing in the air with pleasure as it became thick with the scent of flowers and the dead.

The right-hand column of the door shattered into two pieces at noon the following day, leaning out under the weight of stones above it. The khan stepped forward, hungry to see what lay within. The door yawned open without its support and Tsubodai's men put their hooked poles into the gap and heaved at it, the leading edge cutting a furrow in the dusty ground.

Genghis was in full armor and carried sword and shield ready in his hands as he waited for the gap to open. Tsubodai saw his intent to be first into the fortress, and the general joined his men at the gate, taking a grip on the edge with his bare hands so that he would be closer. He did not know if Genghis guessed his thoughts, but Tsubodai was the first man through to the courtyard beyond. He heard the rattle of shafts breaking on the stones and ducked to one side as he surveyed the fortress they had worked so hard to win. There were still men on the walls, but when Genghis came through, he took their shafts on his shield, seeming to pluck them out of the air so that they vibrated in the surface.

Tsubodai's archers followed, walking backwards into the courtyard and loosing shafts up at anything that moved. The assassins had no protection inside the walls. The black-garbed figures were outlined against the lighter stone and they fell quickly. Genghis watched them strike the courtyard with no expression on his face, then nodded, satisfied, as silence came again. The hammer men walked with him, still red-faced and sweating as the general and the khan made their way deeper into the fortress. Others climbed stone stairs to the walls, determined to root out every possible survivor as well as checking the dead. Tsubodai did not look back as he heard a struggle on the wall before someone fell with a cry. He knew his men would sweep the courtyard and the rooms beyond. He did not have to watch over them; *could* not while his khan walked so carelessly into the nest of the assassins.

Beyond the courtyard, a pillared cloister supported the main building. Genghis found a door there, but it was just wood and his hammer men smashed it open in just a few blows. There was no one waiting for them, though Tsubodai held his breath as Genghis walked into shadow as if he strolled among his gers. The khan seemed determined to meet his fear head-on, and Tsubodai knew better than to try and hold him back while they searched the stronghold.

The home of the assassins was a maze of rooms and corridors. Tsubodai passed halls set with weapons and iron weights, open ground with bows set in racks, even a dry fountain, with water gathered in a pool where golden fish still swam. They found single rooms set with beds of fine linen as well as dormitories where rough wooden bunks lined the walls. It was a strange place and Tsubodai had the sense that it was freshly abandoned, that at any moment, the occupants would return and fill the echoing halls with noise and life. Behind him, he could hear his men calling to each other, their voices muffled as more and more spilled into the fortress and began looking for anything worth carrying away. In one place with barred windows, Tsubodai and Genghis found an overturned cup with the wine barely dried. Genghis walked on, taking it all in, but never pausing to rest.

At the end of a hall hung with silk banners, another heavy door blocked their path. Tsubodai summoned the hammer men, but when he lifted the iron locking bar, it moved easily and the door swung open to reveal steps. Genghis hardly slowed, so Tsubodai darted in ahead and went up as quickly as he could, his sword ready. The air was thick with strange scents, but even then he was not prepared for what he found and came to a sudden stop.

The garden lay at the rear of the fortress, overlooking mountains stretching into the blue distance. Flowers were everywhere, but they did not hide the smell of death. Tsubodai found a woman of surpassing beauty lying beside a bank of blue flowers. Her lips were dark with red wine that had stained her cheek and throat as she fell. He nudged her body with his foot, forgetting for a moment that Genghis was just behind him.

The khan did not look down as he passed. He strode over the perfectly tended paths as if they did not exist, moving further in. There were other women lying in that place, all beautiful and all wearing very little to cover the perfect musculature of their bodies. It was sickening even for one used to death, and Tsubodai found himself raising his head and gulping for clean air. Genghis did not seem to notice, his gaze on the mountains in the distance, snowcapped and clean.

Tsubodai didn't see the man sitting on a wooden bench at first. The robed figure sat so still he could have been another ornament in that extraordinary setting. Genghis was almost abreast of him when Tsubodai jerked and called out a warning.

The khan stopped and raised his sword to strike with some of his old speed. He saw no threat from the man and lowered the blade as Tsubodai caught up.

"Why did you not run?" Genghis said to the man. He spoke in the Chin language and the man raised his head and smiled wearily, before answering in the same tongue.

"This is my home, Temujin."

Genghis stiffened to hear his childhood name from a stranger. The sword jerked in his hand from instinct, but the man on the bench raised empty palms slowly before letting them fall.

"I will take it down, you know," Genghis told him. "I will tip the stones off the cliffs so that no one will even remember there was once a fortress in these mountains."

The Old Man shrugged. "Of course you will. Destruction is all you know."

Tsubodai stood very close, looming over the man on the bench and ready to kill at the first sharp movement. He did not seem a threat, but his eyes were dark under heavy brows and his shoulders looked massive despite the lines of age on his face. Out of the corner of his eye, he saw Genghis sheathe his sword and Tsubodai did not dare turn away as the khan sat on the bench, blowing air from his lips in relief.

"Still, I am surprised you did not run," Genghis said.

The Old Man chuckled. "When you have given your life to building something, perhaps then you will understand; I do not know." His voice took on a bitter tinge as he went on. "No, you would not understand, even then."

Genghis smiled, then roared with laughter until he had to wipe his eyes. The Old Man watched him, his face twisting into a mask of hatred.

"Ah, I needed to laugh," Genghis said. "I needed to sit in a garden surrounded by dead women and have an assassin tell me I have built nothing in my life." He chuckled again and even Tsubodai smiled though his blade remained ready.

The Old Man of the Mountains had intended to pour scorn on the khan before going to his death with dignity intact. To have the man guffaw in his face made him flush, his sense of cool superiority torn apart.

"You think you have achieved something with your life?" the Old Man hissed. "You think you will be remembered?"

Genghis shook his head as amusement threatened to overwhelm him again. He was still chuckling as he stood up once more.

"Kill this old fool for me, would you, Tsubodai? He is nothing but a bag of wind."

The assassin spluttered in rage as he tried to reply, but Tsubodai chopped down, leaving him gurgling in his own blood. Genghis had already dismissed the man from his mind.

"They left me a warning, with the village they destroyed, Tsubodai. I can do no less for them, if any still survive. I want them to remember the cost of attacking me. Have the men start on the roof and pitch the tiles and stones off the cliffs. I want nothing left here to show they ever had a home."

Tsubodai nodded, bowing his head. "Your will, my lord khan," he said.

Jelaudin lit a cone of incense to his father, thinking of him on the anniversary of his passing. His brothers saw tears in his eyes as he straightened and spoke soft words on the morning breeze.

"Who will give life to bones when they are dust? He will give them life who made them first." He paused and lowered himself, touching his forehead to the ground as he honored the Shah who, in death, had become the light of his son's followers.

Jelaudin knew he had changed in the year since his despair on the tiny island of the Caspian. He had found his calling and many of the men who had come to defend the faith regarded him as a holy man. They had grown in numbers, traveling for hundreds of miles to join his war against the invading khan. He sighed as he failed to keep his mind clear for prayer on this day of all days. His brothers had become his staff officers, though they too seemed to regard him almost with reverence. Yet for all the faith, someone had to provide food and tents and weapons for those who had none. It was for those things that he had answered an invitation to meet a prince of Peshawar. They had met only once as boys in Bukhara, when both were spoiled and fat with sweetmeats. Jelaudin had only a hazy memory of the boy and no knowledge of the man he had become. Still, the prince ruled a region where the fields were rich with grain, and Jelaudin had come further south than he had ever known. He had walked until his sandals fell apart, then further, until the soles of his feet were as leathery as his shoes had once been. Rains had quenched his thirst and the hot sun had burned him thin, making his eyes fierce over a beard which had grown thick and black.

Smoke drifted up from the brazier as he remembered his father. The Shah would be proud of his son, Jelaudin thought, if mystified at the ragged robes he chose to wear. His father would not understand that he now disdained any show of wealth and felt the cleaner for it. When Jelaudin looked back on the soft life he had led, he could only shudder. Now he read the Koran and prayed and fasted until his thoughts were all on vengeance and the army that swelled around him. He could hardly imagine the vain young man he had been, with his fine black horse and clothes of silk and gold. All those things were gone and he had replaced them with faith that burned hot enough to destroy all the enemies of God.

When he turned from the smoke, Jelaudin saw his brothers waited patiently with their heads bowed. He rested his hand on Tamar's shoulder as he passed, striding up the steps to the prince's palace. Armored soldiers averted their eyes from him, then stared after the ragged figure who had come to see their master. No one raised a hand to stop the holy man who had brought an army to Peshawar. Jelaudin walked with firm steps until he reached the audience hall. Slaves drew open the doors and he did not bow as he saw the man who had called him to his home.

The rajah of Peshawar was a slim warrior, wearing a silk tunic cut with a sash that fell loosely by his hip, barely covering the golden hilt of a sword. His features were soft and fleshy, despite his narrow waist, and there was little to remind Jelaudin of the boy he had met so long ago. As Jelaudin approached, the Indian prince sent away two advisers and stepped down from a throne to bow.

Jelaudin raised him with one hand, though the gesture pleased him.

"Are we not equals, Nawaz? You do me great honor with your hospitality. My men have not eaten so well for months."

The young rajah flushed with pleasure. His gaze wandered over Jelaudin's dark brown feet, made hard with callus and dirt. Jelaudin grinned, wondering how he would have received such a ragged visitor when he was the son of Khwarezm.

"I have heard wonderful things, Jelaudin," the younger man replied at last. "Men from my own guard have volunteered their service against this foreign khan."

"They are welcome, my friend, but I need supplies more than men. If you have horses and carts to offer me, I will fall on your neck with gratitude. If you have food for my army, I will even kiss those golden slippers you wear."

Prince Nawaz flushed even deeper at the wry tone, overcome.

"You shall have all those things. I ask only that you let me ride with you when you go north."

Jelaudin weighed the young man, seeing in him a flicker of the same fire that sustained his army outside the palace. They burned, these young ones, whether they were rich or poor, blessed or cursed in their lives. They wanted to be led. That was the great secret he had discovered, that the right words would ignite them to a fervor that could never again be put out. Warmed by it, they would turn against their tribes, even their families, to follow him. He had witnessed fathers walking away from weeping wives and children without looking back as they came to him. If his father had ever discovered the right words, Jelaudin was sure he could have led his armies to the end of the world.

Jelaudin closed his eyes briefly. He was exhausted from the long march over mountains, and even the sight of the river Indus that fed a continent had not banished his weariness. At first he had walked because he did not have a horse. After that, he had walked because to do so impressed his men. Yet the miles and hills had sapped him, and it was tempting to ask for just one night in a cool bed before he sent his brothers scurrying around to feed the army and he had to walk those hills again. He resisted, knowing that it would lessen him in the prince's eyes. The young man did not feel his equal, no matter that he dressed in a robe that a beggar might scorn. Instead, Nawaz saw his faith and was humbled in its presence.

Jelaudin came to himself with a start, realizing he had not spoken for a long time, instead swaying as he stood in silence.

"Will your father not object, Nawaz?" he said at last. "I have heard he does not follow the great faith." He watched as the prince's face twisted in dislike.

"He does not understand, with his thousand shrines and foolish temples. He has forbidden me to go with you, but he has no power over me! These lands are mine and all the wealth of them I give to you. My men are sworn to me alone and my father cannot take them from me. Let me call you master and walk beside you on the road."

Jelaudin smiled tiredly, feeling the younger man's enthusiasm ease some of the ache in his bones.

"Very well, Nawaz. You will lead your men to a holy war and throw back the infidel. You will stand on my right hand and we will triumph."

PART
THREE

CHAPTER THIRTY-TWO

GENGHIS SMILED to see his grandson Mongke paddling at the lake edge. His scouts had found the body of water some hundreds of miles to the northeast of Samarkand, and he had brought the gers and families there, while his army administered the lands and cities of Khwarezm. The caravans moved again, from as far as Russia and Chin lands, but now they were met by Mongol officials trained by Temuge and backed by warriors. A part of every merchant's cargo was removed, but in return, they needed no guards of their own. The khan's word protected the roads for a thousand miles and more in any direction from Samarkand.

Mountains surrounded the lake and plain, far enough away so that Genghis did not feel enclosed. He knew his warriors would be watching on every peak, but he could not see them. It was somehow comforting to know that the mountains would still be there when all those who lived were dust.

Ogedai had taken well to his new position as heir. Genghis had sent him out with the tumans, learning every detail of the men he would command. That was expected, but Genghis had also placed Ogedai with Temuge, who taught him how to keep an army fed and clothed. Ogedai soaked up every skill the tribes could impart, as well as languages and even writing. The heir was never seen without a group of tutors at his back, but he seemed to thrive on it.

Genghis stretched his back, feeling at peace. The sounds of war were distant in that place, and he was enjoying the cries and laughter of the boys in the water, sunning themselves and learning to swim like fish. Some even dived below the surface, launching from rocks in great splashes. Their mothers called and peered anxiously into the depths, but they always surfaced, blowing and laughing at those who worried for them.

Genghis felt a small hand tugging at his leggings and he reached down to swing Kublai into the air. The tiny little boy was just three years old, but from the age of just a few months, he had beamed whenever he saw his grandfather. Genghis had taken a liking to him.

With a jerk, the khan put his grandson on his shoulders and walked to the water's edge, wincing a little as Kublai gripped his hair too tightly.

"I will not let you fall, little man," Genghis said. He saw Mongke catch sight of the rare treat and hold his arms out to be lifted up in turn. Genghis shook his head.

"In a while. Until then, Kublai rides."

"Another story!" Kublai called from above his head. Genghis thought for a time. Kublai's mother had said his tales were too violent for a little boy, but Kublai seemed to enjoy them regardless. Genghis could see Sorhatani watching him from a little way off down the shore. At nineteen years old, she had grown into a woman of unusual beauty. Genghis sometimes wondered how little Tolui had snared her.

"Would you like to hear about the khan of the assassins?"

"Yes, tell me!" Kublai shouted joyfully.

Genghis smiled, turning this way and that so that the boy giggled at the sudden movements.

"He was a *huge* man," Genghis said, "with arms strong enough to bend an iron bar. His beard was like black wire and it stretched almost to his waist! It was two years ago that I came across him in his fortress. He leapt on my back as I passed underneath an arch, and I could not break his grip. I felt his hands around my throat, squeezing and *squeezing* until I thought my eyes would pop out from my head!"

He mimed a terrible grip, while Mongke came out from the water and watched with his eyes wide.

"How did you get him off?" Mongke asked.

Genghis looked down and thought for a moment.

"I could not, Mongke. I tried to shake him free, as I am doing with Kublai here, but he was too strong for me. He squeezed even harder and suddenly I saw my eyes rolling on the ground in front of me."

"How could you see them if they were on the ground?" Kublai asked immediately.

Genghis laughed and lifted him down. "You are a clever boy, Kublai, but you are right. I could not see them. In fact, I could see *me*, with just holes where my eyes used to be and the assassin still clinging to my back. Yet as my eyes rolled, I saw a great ruby flashing in his forehead. I did not know it was his weakness, but I was desperate. With my hands, I reached up and ripped it out. His strength went with it, for the gem was the source of all his power. I collected my eyes and sold the ruby to buy a white horse. I survived, but even today, I have to be careful that my eyes do not come out again when I sneeze."

"That is not true," Mongke said scornfully.

"It *is*," Kublai said, determined to defend his grandfather.

The khan chuckled. "Who can say if I have remembered every detail correctly? He may not have had a beard."

Mongke snorted and struck his leg, which Genghis did not seem to notice. When Kublai and Mongke looked up, they saw their grandfather gazing into the distance, where two men were riding across the pebble beach toward him. A change came over the khan at the sight, and both boys watched quizzically, not understanding why the light mood had come to an end.

"Go to your mother now. I will tell you another story tonight, if I have time."

Genghis did not watch them as they pelted away, sending sand and pebbles skittering from their bare feet. Instead, he straightened fully to receive the scouts. He knew the men who rode to him. He had sent them away from the families more than a year before, with carefully worded orders. Their return meant they had either failed, or found his missing son. He could not tell from their faces as they reached him and dismounted, bowing deeply.

"My lord khan," the first said.

Genghis had no patience for polite greetings. "Did you find him?" he snapped.

The man nodded, swallowing nervousness. "In the far north, lord. We did not stop to check once we saw gers and ponies of the sort we know. It could not be anyone else."

"Gers? He took none with him," Genghis replied. "He has made a home then, so far away from the memory of me. Did his men see you?"

Both scouts shook their heads with utter certainty, remaining silent. The khan would not want to know the details of how they had crept close to Jochi's rough settlement, hiding themselves in snow though they almost froze to death.

"Good," Genghis replied. "You have done well. Take six fresh horses from my herd as your reward: two mares, two stallions, and two of the younger geldings. I will commend you to your general for this work."

The scouts bowed again, flushed with success as they mounted and rode to the maze of gers along the banks of the lake. Genghis was left alone for a moment, looking out over the waters. In all his life, not one of his generals had refused an order or even considered betraying him. Not until Jochi had vanished, taking seven thousand valuable warriors with him. Genghis had sent scouts in all directions, searching lands new and old for his son. It had taken almost two years, but he had found him at last. Genghis shook his head as his thoughts grew dark. It would end in blood, after all he had done in raising another man's son as his own. The entire nation spoke of the vanished army, though not in the presence of the khan. Jochi had given him no choice.

He looked along the shore to where the gers clustered, covering miles of land around the lake. It was a good place, but the grazing was very poor and the goats and sheep that fed them had to be walked back to slaughter each day. It was time to move on, he thought, enjoying the idea. His people were not made to stay in one place, with just one view, not when the world stretched around them with an infinite array of strange things to see. Genghis arched his back, feeling it click unpleasantly. He saw another rider setting out from the gers and sighed to himself. Though his eyes were not as sharp as they had once been, he knew his brother Kachiun from the way he rode.

Genghis waited for his brother, enjoying the breeze coming off the water as the sun beat down. He did not turn as Kachiun called a greeting to Sorhatani and the boys.

"You have heard then?" Genghis said.

Kachiun came to stand by him, looking out over the same pale waters. "The scouts? I sent them to find you, brother. They have found Jochi, but that is not why I am here."

Genghis did turn then, raising his eyebrows at his brother's serious expression.

"No? I thought you would be full of advice on how I should deal with my son the traitor."

Kachiun snorted. "Nothing I can say will change what you do, Genghis. You are khan and perhaps you should make an example of him to the rest, I don't know. That is for you to decide. I have other news."

Genghis studied his brother, seeing how his once smooth face had taken on lines around the mouth and eyes. The age showed most when he smiled, which was less and less often since coming to Arab lands. Genghis owned no mirrors of the sort the Chin made, but he supposed his own face was just as weathered, or even more.

"Tell me then, brother," he said.

"You have heard of this army in the south? I have had men watching it for some time."

Genghis shrugged. "Tsubodai and Chagatai have both sent men to watch them. We know more about that gathering of farmers than they do themselves."

"They are not farmers, Genghis, or if they are, they have the armor and weapons of soldiers. The latest reports are of sixty thousand men, if my scouts have learned to count so high."

"I should fear only sixty? They grow, then. We have watched them for a year or more. They shout and chant and wave their swords. Are they coming for us at last?" Genghis felt a cold hand clutch at his belly for all his lightness of tone. He had heard of the gathering army and their revered leader almost a year after he had returned from the assassins' stronghold. His generals had prepared for attack, but the seasons had crept by and no army had marched against them. At times, he thought it was only the threat of them that kept him in lands where heat and flies bothered him every day.

"My men captured three of their number," Kachiun answered, interrupting his thoughts. "They were wild, brother, almost frothing at the mouth when they realized who we were."

"You made them talk?" Genghis said.

"We could not, that was what surprised me. They merely spat threats at us and died badly. Only the last gave me anything and that was the name of the man who leads them."

"What do I care for names?" Genghis asked incredulously.

"You know this one: Jelaudin, whose father was the Shah of Khwarezm."

Genghis stood very still as he digested the information. "He has done well. His father would be proud of him, Kachiun. Sixty thousand men? At least we know for sure that he will come north, after my head. There will be no more talk of purges into India, not now we know it is Jelaudin."

"They cannot move a step without me knowing, brother."

"If we wait for them," Genghis said thoughtfully. "I am tempted to end their shouting with my tumans."

Kachiun winced, knowing that if he were to guide Genghis, it would have to be subtle. "The Shah's army was far larger, but we had no choice then. Your own tuman and mine are proven. Tsubodai's Young Wolves and Jebe's Bearskins bring twenty thousand more to the field. Chagatai, Khasar, and Jelme another thirty. Seven tumans of veterans. Ogedai is barely blooded. I would not want to throw his men against such an enemy."

"I gave him good officers, Kachiun. They will not let me down."

Genghis considered the gers along the shore. The families bore children in the thousands each year, but many of them went into the tumans to replace the dead and injured. It had been difficult to create a new tuman for Ogedai, but his heir had to learn command and the other generals had gone begging for a year. He did not mention his plans to form a ninth tuman for Tolui to lead. His youngest son's wife had approached him on the subject just a few months before. Genghis glanced over to where she now played with Kublai and Mongke, tossing one after the other into the water, to their delighted shrieks.

"Find a good second for Ogedai, Kachiun. Someone who can stop him doing something stupid until he learns."

"Even then, eight tumans against almost as many?" Kachiun replied. "We would lose many good men." He hesitated and Genghis turned to him.

"You have not worried about numbers before, brother. Spit it out, whatever it is."

Kachiun took a deep breath. "You brought us here to avenge men killed by the Shah. You have done that and repaid them a thousand times over. Why should we stay and risk destruction? You do not want these lands and cities. How long is it now since you saw the mountains of home?" He paused to gesture at the peaks around the lake. "This is not the same."

Genghis did not answer for a long time. When he spoke at last, he weighed each word carefully.

"I brought the tribes together to take the Chin foot off our necks.

Then I *took* it off and we humbled their emperor in his capital. That was my path, the one I made and chose and fought for. I wanted to send the Chin reeling still further, Kachiun, right to the sea in all directions. I would not even have come here if they had not provoked me. They have brought this on their own heads."

"We do not have to fight the entire world," Kachiun said quietly.

"You are getting old, Kachiun, do you know that? You are thinking of the future, of your wives and children. Don't splutter, brother, you know I am right. You have forgotten why we do this. I was the same for a time in Samarkand. I told Arslan these people live longer than us and have safer, softer lives. They *do,* just as camels and sheep live happily on the plains. We could choose that for a time, though wolves would still come for us in the end. We are herdsmen, Kachiun. We know how the world truly works and everything else is just an illusion." He looked over to his grandsons, seeing Sorhatani comb their hair as they writhed and struggled to get away from her. Her own hair was long and black and he toyed with the idea of getting himself another young wife like her to warm his bed. It would invigorate him, he was certain.

"Brother," he said, "we can live our lives at peace, so that our sons and grandsons can live *their* lives at peace, but what is the point? If we all live to eighty in a green field, without ever holding a bow or sword, we will have wasted the good years. You should know the truth of that. Will our grandsons thank us for a peaceful life? Only if they are too afraid to take up arms. I would not wish a quiet life on my enemies, Kachiun, never mind my own family. Even cities prosper only when there are rough men on the walls, willing to stand and die so that others can sleep in peace. With us, we *all* fight, from the first yell to the last breath. It is the only way to take pride in who we are."

"I do take pride!" Kachiun snapped. "But that does not mean—"

Genghis raised a hand. "There is no 'but,' brother. This Jelaudin will sweep north with his men, and we could run before them. We could let him take back every city we have won and call himself Shah in his father's place. He might think twice before provoking me again when I send envoys to him. But I came to these lands because when a man threatens me and I look away, he has taken something important from me. If I fight and die, all he can take is my life. My courage, my dignity remain. Shall I do less for the nation I have made? Shall I allow them less honor than I claim for myself?"

"I understand," Kachiun murmured.

"Be sure you do, brother, because you will be riding with me against this host. We will win or die, one or the other. But I will *not* look away when they come. I will not bow down and let them trample me." He paused and barked a laugh. "You know, I was going to add that no one will ever say I ran from a battle, but Arslan reminded me of something in Samarkand. It does not matter what others think of how I lived my life. It does not matter if we go down in Temuge's histories as tyrants or even cowards. All that matters is what we do now. We are our only judges, Kachiun. Remember that. Those who come after will have other trials, other battles to worry about."

He saw Kachiun had listened and at least tried to understand. Genghis clapped him on the shoulder.

"We have come such a long way, Kachiun. I still remember the first days, when it was just us and we were starving. I remember killing Bekter and I sometimes wish he could be here to see what we went on to make. Perhaps you and I have fashioned something that will last a thousand generations, or disappear with us. I do not know. I do not even care, brother. I have grown strong to defeat powerful enemies. I welcome this horde from the south to grow stronger still."

"You are a strange man," Kachiun said. "There is no one else like you, do you know that?" He expected Genghis to smile, but his brother shook his head.

"Be careful of raising me too high, brother. I have no special strength, unless it is in choosing good men to follow me. The great lie of cities is that we are all too weak to stand against those who oppress us. All I have done is see through that lie. I *always* fight, Kachiun. Kings and shahs depend on people remaining sheep, too afraid to rise up. All I ever did was realize I can be a wolf to them."

Kachiun nodded, his worries lifting away under his brother's pale eyes. He led his horse at Genghis's side as the two men walked back to the gers to eat and rest. As they drew close, Kachiun recalled the arrival of the scouts.

"And Jochi? Have you made a decision?"

Genghis tightened his mouth at the mention of the name. "He took seven thousand men from me, Kachiun. I cannot forgive him for that. If he had gone on his own, perhaps I would have left him to find his own path. As it is, he has stolen a tenth of my army and I want them back."

"You would take them? Honestly?" Kachiun said, surprised.

"I thought at first that I would have them killed, but I have had time to think while I waited for word, Kachiun. They left their wives and children and followed him, just as others followed me and gave up everything they knew and loved. Of all men, I know what a leader can do. They allowed themselves to be led, but I need them now, if Jelaudin is gathering a storm. Send scouts out to bring Tsubodai in. Jochi admired him more than any man. He will let him speak."

Tsubodai came, though his heart was heavy. The great camp was buzzing with the news that Jochi had been found, and he had hoped Genghis would not ask for him. He found Genghis with Ogedai, watching his son train his young men. The khan gestured for him to follow and they rode away from the gathering tumans, walking their horses together like old friends.

Tsubodai's heart beat hard as he listened. He had revered Genghis since he had first met the man who had forged a nation from warring tribes. He had been there when they took their first fortress in Xi Xia, then the region itself. Tsubodai had no false modesty. He knew he had played a vital part in the khan's success. Genghis treated him with respect and Tsubodai returned it as he did with no other man alive. Even so, what he was being asked caused him bitterness and pain. He took a shuddering breath as Genghis looked at him, waiting for a reply.

"My lord khan, I do not want to do this. Ask me for anything else and I will ride, anything."

Genghis reined in, turning his horse so that he faced his general. The man was brilliant, more gifted at war than anyone else Genghis knew, but he demanded obedience first and only the khan's surprise held back a sharp reply.

"If I send Khasar or Kachiun, I think Jochi will resist. His men have broken oaths to follow him. They will not balk from fighting to prevent him being taken. You are the only man he will let speak, Tsubodai. You are the only one who can get close."

Tsubodai closed his eyes for a moment, overcome. Genghis must have understood how Jochi looked to him or he would not have chosen Tsubodai for the task.

"My lord, I have never refused an order from you, ever. Remember that when you ask me for this."

"You trained him when he was just an angry boy, but I warned you then that his blood was bad, that he could turn against us at any moment. I was right then, was I not? I trusted him with warriors and authority and he took them and ran. As my general, tell me how I should deal with such a man!"

Tsubodai clenched his fists on the reins. He did not say that Genghis had brought it on himself, that the pride he showed in Chagatai had eaten at Jochi until there was nothing left but hatred. None of that would matter to the khan who sat before him. He tried a different tack, desperately.

"At least let it wait until we have ridden against the Shah's son, lord. My men are vital there. If you send me away now, I will be gone for six months or more. If they attack us before then, I will be useless to you."

Genghis lowered his brows, growing angry that his general was still struggling.

"This prince has just sixty thousand, Tsubodai. I could send two or three tumans and gut him where he stands. This concerns me more. You are the only man Jochi will allow to speak. He respects you."

"I know it," Tsubodai said softly. He felt ill, torn between obedience to the khan and his friendship with Jochi. It did not help that his tactical mind saw the truth in Genghis's words. Tsubodai knew he could get close to Jochi as no one else could. He sat in despair on the lakeshore. Genghis seemed to sense his utter misery and his face and voice softened slightly.

"Did you think all your orders would be easy, Tsubodai? That I would never ask for something hard? Tell me when a man is tested. Is it when his khan orders him into battle, with warriors of proven skill and courage? Or is it now, when he is given work he does not want? You have the finest mind of any of my generals, Tsubodai. I will grant you this. If you can see another way, tell me now and I will try it."

Tsubodai had already considered and discarded a dozen plans, but none of them were worth his spit. In desperation, he tried one more time.

"The tumans are gathering, lord. Let me stay with them and we will take the war to the prince in the south. I am more valuable to you there. If you send me north, you will lose my tuman as well, just when you need every man."

"It took me more than a year to find him the first time, Tsubodai. If my scouts were seen, he will already have left. You can follow his trail, but could you find it another year from now? This is the time to take him quietly. You are my general, but I will begin this war without you if they come. Join me when you return or *give back the marks of rank*

I gave to you!" His anger surfaced at the last and Tsubodai almost flinched from it. The khan's arguments were weak and both of them knew it. Genghis was obsessed with punishing Jochi. That was the truth that whispered behind the words. The khan could not be reached with reasoning when his heart was filled with bitterness. Tsubodai bowed his head, defeated.

"Very well," he said. "I will ride fast and far, lord. If the prince brings his army from the south, look for me in the hills."

CHAPTER THIRTY-THREE

THE MONGOL SCOUT SENSED SOMETHING. He had followed two
men into the mountains for three full days, staying well back as he
watched their progress. They had led him deep into the maze of
canyons and high mountains around the Panjshir valley and the
Afghan town of Parwan, with its ancient fortress. It was hard country,
but the scout was experienced and knew every twist of the land. In the
gathering dark, he could not follow the tracks any longer and he looked
for a safe place to spend the night. It bothered him that he had lost the
men. Something about them had aroused his curiosity from the first
sighting. From a distance, they had looked like one of the Afghan hill
tribes, swathed in cloth to protect their faces from the sun and wind.
Still, there was something odd about them and he had been drawn in.
In the canyon, he felt an itch, as if someone was watching. Could they
have prepared an ambush? It was possible. The hill tribes knew the
land even better than he did. They moved like ghosts when they
wanted to, and the scout was tempted to pull back and find the tracks
again when the sun came up. He hesitated, sitting very still and listening for any noise over the moaning wind that wound its way through
the hills.

He heard the snap of a bow, but he was not fast enough to throw
himself down. The shaft struck him hard in the chest, where there was

no armor to protect him. The scout grunted, rocking back in the saddle. His hands held the wooden saddle horn between his legs, keeping him upright as his horse whinnied in distress. He sucked air, spitting blood as he yanked at the reins. His eyes had filled with tears of pain and he was blind as he turned his mare, trusting her to find the way out.

Another arrow buzzed out of the gloom and struck him in the back, piercing his heart. He fell with the impact, sliding over the horse's head. She would have bolted, but men came running toward her, grabbing the reins and opening their arms wide so that she was forced to turn in place.

"He's down," the archer said to the man with him.

Jelaudin dropped a hand to his shoulder. "That was good work, in this light."

The archer shrugged and removed the string from his bow, folding it neatly into a pouch at his waist. He knew he was a fine shot, perhaps the best that the prince of Peshawar could offer. His master had given his service to Jelaudin, but the archer's loyalty was only to the prince, not this ragged holy man. Still, Jelaudin clearly knew the enemy. He had been able to predict the movement of the scout, tempting him just enough to bring him in for the shot.

Jelaudin seemed to sense the way the archer's thoughts were running, despite the gloom of the canyon.

"Take away their eyes and these Mongols are not half so fearsome," he said softly. "God guided your arrow, my friend."

The archer bowed his head out of respect, though he was a craftsman and took pride in his skills.

"Will we be able to relieve the fortress at Parwan, master? I have an old friend who lives in the town. I would like to think we could bring him out alive."

Jelaudin smiled in the darkness. "Never doubt it, my friend. By morning the Mongols will be blind, their scouts dead. We will come out of the hills and fall on them like a landslide."

As dawn came, the sun revealed the dusty lands around Parwan and the fortress that stood at its back. Four Mongol minghaans surrounded the high tower of its castle, left over from the days when raiding parties roamed the region from the hills. The people of the town had abandoned their possessions to rush inside its walls, safe for a time.

The Mongol warriors had surrounded the fortress completely,

knowing there could be little water inside. A deep river ran through the valley and they could water their horses freely while those in the fortress felt only dust in their throats. Some of the Mongols roamed the deserted town while they waited. Others had built a bridge across the river so they could hunt in the wooded hills beyond. They were in no hurry. The fortress would fall and another place would accept a new ruler, or be utterly destroyed. The officers were pleasantly idle as they watched the sunlight stretch shadows across the dusty ground. They did not need the town, or anything in it, but it lay across a route to the west and Genghis had ordered the way made clear.

In the two years since Genghis and Tsubodai had ridden against the assassins, this work had become commonplace. They always had maimed men or old ones to man forts in the road. Tribute came in the form of gold, slaves, or horses, and every season brought a tighter grip on the Afghan lands. There were always some who refused to bow their heads to their new rulers, but if they fought, they were killed to the last man. The ancient stone tower at Parwan suited the Mongol needs, and the townspeople had lost all hope as the days passed and the only small well ran dry. They knew nothing of the great wars going on around them, only that a grim force of merciless warriors waited just outside the wall.

Jelaudin came out of the mountains as the sun rose, the words of the dawn prayer still fresh on his lips. His best trackers knew this region better than any Mongol scout alive, and they had hunted them in the valleys and canyons, until the last scout fell with Jelaudin watching. The Mongol force had no warning of the attack. Jelaudin exulted as his men poured down into the valley of Panjshir, its river shining in the sun. The Mongols barely had time to run to their horses before his army was in formation. He had called his men in faith and they had answered, walking or riding to him from thousands of miles away. Turkoman nomads had come, some of them as good as the Mongols themselves with a bow. Berber warriors rode on his left, who shared the faith if not the Arab blood that ran in Jelaudin's veins. True Arabs, Bedouins, Persians, even Turks: he had bound them all to the men of Peshawar and their prince. Around that core, Jelaudin had trained his army.

The Mongols met them with whirring arrows, but Jelaudin knew his enemy and all his men carried long shields of layered wood and cured leather. With the prince's gold behind him, he had found a design that did well against the Mongol bows, and few of his men fell in the first vicious volleys. As the distance closed, Jelaudin rode with wild courage, shouting aloud as the Mongols changed their aim to his precious horses. They too wore the best armor Peshawar could produce, fish-scales of metal overlapping on their long muzzles and chests. It slowed them in the charge, but arrows could not easily bring them down.

They hit the Mongol lines that formed before them out of chaos, crashing with stunning force against men who did not give way. The last volley of arrows had ripped through his men and even their armor and shields could not protect them at just a few paces. Jelaudin saw them fall, but then he was among the enemy, his sword swinging. He misjudged his first blow in his hunger for vengeance, so that it cracked across the helmet of a Mongol warrior. His speed gave the blow power and the man went flying backwards, trampled instantly under hooves. Jelaudin's army had survived the first contact, and the Mongol center fell back in confusion.

Jelaudin saw horns form on the wings and the prince of Peshawar was there to send his men around the outside, trapping the horns almost before they could begin the maneuver. The Mongols had never fought men who knew their tricks and tactics as well as Jelaudin. He shouted, manic with rage and joy as the Mongols fell back, their scout horns blowing retreat.

Even then they fought and the carnage was terrible when the Arabs pressed them too closely. The warriors kept tight formation, withdrawing in groups while the closest lines covered their backs with arrows and swords. Jelaudin raised his hand and bows bent along his front rank. As the gap opened, they sent a volley into the Mongols, each man aiming at the enemy archers, who carried no shields. Dozens of them were killed and the army of Jelaudin pressed on, step by step, forcing them back from the fortress while the citizens of Parwan cheered on the walls.

The river by the town was less than a mile away when the Mongols gave up the running fight and raced for the bridge. Jelaudin galloped after them with his men, intent on their deaths. He had seen them ride in triumph too many times not to take pleasure from the sight. He rode lightly, the breeze cool on his face.

The Mongols did not stop at the bridge. The surviving warriors galloped across without slowing down, risking their lives in the crush of men. It was well done and Jelaudin's men did not hesitate to follow them.

Jelaudin saw Mongol warriors leap from their horses and take axes to the ropes and timbers of the bridge, ignoring those who rode them down. Perhaps a hundred of his mounted men had crossed, and with terrible clarity, Jelaudin saw the Mongols intended to cut the force in half, leaving those on the fortress side helpless while they turned on the rest like mad dogs. The sight of such calm thinking broke through his frenzy and he reined in. He could direct his men to kill those who hacked at the bridge supports. If it held, he would destroy the Mongol forces to the last man, but if it fell, many of his men would die. He had done enough, he thought. He had wounded and bloodied an enemy who had not known defeat before. He took a horn from his waist, where it hung on a strap. It had once belonged to a Mongol scout, but his men were ready for the blaring note.

Those who had not yet reached the bridge turned back and formed into shining ranks, already cheering the victory. Those who had already gone over pulled away from the enemy and started to retreat across the river. Jelaudin watched with pride as they followed his orders without question, raising their shields to take the arrows that sailed after them.

The bridge fell, slapping into the river in a great spray. Perhaps fifty of his men were still on the other side and Jelaudin rode to the edge, looking down into the waters. It was too deep, he thought. Perhaps the men could have swum their horses across on another day, but not with enemy archers ready to rush them as they forced their mounts down the banks. Jelaudin raised his sword in salute to those who watched him from across the river, enemy and friend alike.

His men returned the gesture and turned their horses back, riding into the Mongols in one last charge. They were cut down, though each man went without fear, killing as many as he could.

The two forces faced each other across the torrent, panting and bloodied. Jelaudin could hardly describe the ecstasy of the moment. He saw the Mongol officer trot his mount to the opposite bank, and for a moment, they stared at each other. The Mongol shrugged at the trail of dead leading to the fortress in the distance. He raised his sword then, copying the gesture of respect before wheeling his mount and riding away. Genghis would hear and the subdued officer did not have to utter threats on his behalf.

*   *   *

"The news is in the mouth of every city, Genghis," Kachiun said bitterly. "Before now, they saw us as unbeatable. This is a crack in that belief, brother. If we let it go unanswered, even for a season, they will grow in confidence and more will come to Jelaudin's banners."

"One successful raid does not make a general, Kachiun. I will wait for Tsubodai to return." Genghis gestured irritably to the open plain he had found, eighty miles south of the lake where Kublai and Mongke had learned to swim. The nation could not remain anywhere for long. Lush grass was hard to find in Arab lands, but the world was large and Genghis had two sites picked out to move them to in another month. That was simply the way of their lives, and he did not think of it beyond quick decisions when the time came. Kachiun's voice irritated him, interrupting his thoughts of Jochi and Tsubodai. It was true that Jelaudin's army had killed more than a thousand of his men, the event sending ripples of disquiet through the Arab cities. The first tribute due from the Afghan city of Herat had not come, and Genghis wondered if it was delayed or whether they had decided to wait and see what he would do.

Kachiun waited, but when Genghis said nothing, he spoke again, his voice hard.

"The men lost were from my tuman, Genghis. Let me at least ride to the area and make this bastard prince nervous. If you won't give me the army, let me raid his lines, striking and vanishing in the night as we have done before."

"You should not fear these farmers, brother. I will deal with them when I know that Tsubodai has found Jochi."

Kachiun held himself still, biting back the questions he wanted to ask. Genghis had not shared Tsubodai's orders with him and he would not beg to be told, though he wanted very much to know. He still found it difficult to believe that Jochi had taken his men away and tried to lose himself. The spirits knew Jochi had been provoked, and at times, Kachiun could only curse the blindness of the father that had led to it, but the reality of betrayal had stunned them all. No one had ever turned against the man who had made the nation. For all his faults, Genghis was revered and Kachiun could hardly imagine the strength of will that allowed Jochi to wrench apart from everything he had known. He saw Genghis set his jaw obstinately, guessing at his thoughts as Kachiun tried again to make him understand.

"You are the one who built an empire in this place, Genghis, instead of just ruins. You put Arslan into Samarkand and Chen Yi into

Merv when he came. They rule in your name, just as kings and shahs ruled before them in those places. Yet they are still invaders and there will always be those who want to see them torn out. Give these Arabs one glimpse of weakness and we will have rebellions in every place we have taken." He sighed. "I am too old to do it all again, brother."

Genghis blinked slowly and Kachiun did not know if he was truly listening or not. The khan seemed utterly obsessed with the son who had turned against him, perhaps because no one else ever had. Each day he would scour the horizon for some sign of Tsubodai. It was too soon, Kachiun knew. Even if Tsubodai had ridden as fast as light scouts, he would hardly have reached the northern land where Jochi had hidden himself. Once more Kachiun itched to know what Tsubodai had been told to do. He suspected he knew, and pitied Tsubodai for the task. Kachiun was aware that Tsubodai thought of Jochi almost as a son. It was typical of Genghis that he should test the man's loyalty to the breaking point by sending him. His brother had always been ruthless with those around him, as well as himself.

Kachiun prepared to try once more, desperate to have Genghis understand. He swallowed dryly, realizing he could have used Tsubodai then. His brother listened to Tsubodai above all others, and he would not delay here while the cracks appeared in everything they had built.

"They countered horns, Genghis, swinging out around them. They have shields as good as any we have seen and armored horses that survive our arrows. It is not the numbers I fear, brother, but the way this Jelaudin uses them. If you will not come, let me send them back on their heels. They will not surprise my tuman with the same tactics. We will counter *them* and send a message to anyone who imagines we can be defeated."

Genghis opened his mouth to suck at one of his back teeth.

"Do as you will, Kachiun," he said, then thought better of leaving his brother with complete authority to act. "Take three tumans, your own and two others. Not Ogedai or Tolui. Their men are still fresh from the teat and I do not want them with you."

Kachiun spoke quickly. "Jelme then, and Khasar."

Genghis nodded, still staring into the north where his thoughts rested with Tsubodai.

"Skirmish, Kachiun, do you understand? If they are as terrible as I have heard, I do not want you to lose your men in the mountains. Bleed them a little, as you have done before, as you did at Yenking and against the Shah. I will come with Tsubodai."

Kachiun bowed his head, relieved beyond words. "I will, brother," he said, then paused at the point of turning away. "Tsubodai will not fail. I used to think you mad for raising him, but he is the best I have ever seen."

Genghis grunted. "The problem is, Kachiun, that I do not know if I want him to fail or to succeed." He saw Kachiun open his mouth to ask what he meant, and Genghis waved him away irritably.

"Go, brother. Teach these desert dwellers not to interfere with me again."

CHAPTER THIRTY-FOUR

STANDING BETWEEN TWO PILLARS OF ROCK, Kachiun looked down into the Panjshir valley, seeing the tents and horses of Jelaudin's army. The late morning was already hot and he was sweating and scratching idly at an armpit where a boil needed lancing. With Jelme and Khasar, he had ridden as hard as any scout, half killing the horses to bring swift vengeance for the defeat at Parwan.

The army of Jelaudin knew the Mongols had come. Kachiun could see robed figures watching them from every peak, men who had climbed hand over hand up sheer rock to their positions. One of them was far above his head, out of reach of any arrow. Kachiun could not snatch them down and he was uncomfortable under that silent scrutiny. All the watchers were turned toward him and some of them signaled the army in the valley with flags, keeping Jelaudin informed.

There too Kachiun could see evidence of a controlling mind, one who had learned from the enemy at last. The Arab camp was three miles across the river from the town of Parwan, on a stretch of open plain backed by mountains that rose like blades from the flat ground. The position allowed no ambush and could not be ridden around. It did not rely on walls, though Kachiun could see stone blocks and wooden stakes had been dragged into position before the enemy camp, perfectly placed to foul a charge. Squares of tents fluttered in the morning breeze, and even as Kachiun watched, flag signals from the peaks brought men out into solid ranks. They showed their confidence in such a position, daring the Mongols to ride against them.

"We must cross that river," Jelme said at Kachiun's shoulder. "Now we know where they are, we can search for a ford."

Kachiun had overall command of the three tumans and he nodded, still staring into the valley as Jelme sent scouts riding to find the best place across the barrier. He bit his lip at the thought, knowing that Jelaudin would have marked the fording places for a hundred miles. There was no chance for a surprise attack when the Shah's son knew exactly where they would come from. Still, they had to cross. Jelaudin had chosen the spot for the battle. He knew the land; he had the numbers and every other advantage that mattered. Once again Kachiun wished Genghis had sent more men with him, this one time.

Kachiun squinted at the watcher far above him, hundreds of feet above his head. The man squatted in white robes, having climbed a face of rock that reached almost to a point. Kachiun resisted the urge to send warriors up to cut him down. The man may have taken days to reach the precarious position overlooking an entrance to the valley. If he had waterskins and supplies with him, he could defend it against climbing men for as long as he wanted.

His brother Khasar rode up to the front. Kachiun saw he too glared at the man on the heights.

"We cannot sit here all day, brother," Khasar said as he reined in. "I could ride down and destroy that little town, at least. The Arabs might lose heart when they see the smoke rise."

Kachiun looked over the valley. The minghaan officers who had been defeated had described the ground in great detail, pathetically eager to please after the shame of their loss. Kachiun could not see figures moving anywhere in the town, and he assumed the people had retreated again to the fortress that loomed above the plain. If he'd thought there was the slightest point to it, he would have sent Khasar down like an arrow. Instead, he shook his head.

"What is one more town, to us or them? When we have beaten this army, we can take that fortress as we please."

Khasar shrugged at his reply and Kachiun went on, speaking his thoughts aloud to make them clear.

"He is confident, Khasar, with the mountains at his back."

"He is a fool then," Khasar said lightly.

"He is *not* a fool, brother. This man has seen us gut his father's army. He knows our tactics and strengths, perhaps our weaknesses. See how has placed blocks of stone to interrupt our lancers and bow lines. He is confident and that worries me."

"You think too much, Kachiun. When Jelme has found a way across the river, we will pin him against those hills. We will make an example of him."

Kachiun nodded warily. Genghis had not demanded a quick victory, only that he take first blood from the enemy. Yet the first rule of war was to avoid letting the enemy choose the terrain and set the terms. Kachiun cracked the knuckles of his hands, then his neck, wishing Tsubodai were there for his insight.

It was not long before Jelme's scouts returned, reporting a shallow ford barely five miles away along the river. Kachiun gave the order for the tumans to move, and he could not help glancing up at the flicker of bright flags from one peak to the next as the movement was reported.

"They come," Jelaudin murmured, reading the flags.

"They have no choice," Nawaz replied.

Jelaudin glanced at the rajah from under lowered brows, hiding his amusement at this peacock he had made his second in command. Under his armor, the rajah was dressed in silk of purple and gold, topped by a turban of pale blue. To Jelaudin's eyes, he looked as if he had been dressed by a prostitute or an actor, but he did not doubt the man's resolve.

Once more Jelaudin reviewed the lines of his men, though he had inspected them a thousand times. There were no flaws, he was certain. The mountains protected their rear, while heavy slabs from Parwan's walls lay in clusters ahead, exactly where they would disrupt the Mongol riders. If the enemy had sent someone to the town, they would have found great sections of the walls missing, floated across the river on rafts of wood taken from homes. The people of that place had lost much for this defense, but they did not begrudge the sacrifice, not when the army had brought success against the unbelievers already. The fortress that sheltered them was too far away across the river for Jelaudin to see individual faces, but he knew they watched from the heights. They at least would have a spectacular view of the fighting to come.

"We have until this afternoon, if they use the first ford across the river," Jelaudin said. "Let us walk among the men one more time. Some will be nervous and it will help them to see us calm and cheerful."

His own eyes belied the casual tone, but Nawaz did not comment, merely ducking his head and dismounting to walk with him.

"I had expected more than thirty thousand of them," Nawaz said as they passed between tents. "Are they so arrogant?"

Jelaudin nodded. "They are justified in their arrogance, my friend. They took my father's army apart when he had three times their number. This will be a hard fight, even after all I have done."

Nawaz blew air from his lips, showing his scorn for the idea. "I have emptied my treasury to give you the shields and armor you wanted. In turn, you have fired the men's hearts." He saw Jelaudin glance at him and went on. "I am not a fool. You know them better than any man, but by tonight we will be burning piles of their dead."

Jelaudin smiled at the rajah's confidence. It was true that he knew the Mongols for the force in war that they were. He could hope for victory, but nothing in this life was guaranteed.

"I will lead the men in prayers today at noon. If Allah looks kindly on us, we will shatter the legend of this khan, so that his strength bleeds out. Win here and all those cities that watch and wait will throw in with us to root the man from our land. Lose and he will not be challenged again. Those are the stakes, Nawaz."

The rajah lowered his head, abashed. He held Jelaudin in awe, even before he had sent the Mongols running across their bridge. More than anything, he wanted to impress this man he had known as a boy, just a year older than him. His gaze swept the lines of men Jelaudin had brought under a single banner. Turkomans, Berbers, Bedouins from the far deserts, and dark-skinned warriors from Peshawar, marked from the rest by the armor of his personal guard. There were Afghans too in the ranks, serious men who had come down from the hills with heavy, curved swords. None of them were mounted for the battle to come. Jelaudin had chosen a position that would remove the advantage of the Mongol horses. His army would fight on foot. They would stand or be destroyed.

He had worked hard over the previous days to prepare the position, knowing that the Mongols would not be slow in their response. Nawaz had even labored with his men to take the stones from Parwan across the river. The rajah hoped they saw that he could put aside his dignity to work with them, though his self-conscious efforts had made

Jelaudin laugh. Nawaz flushed as he recalled Jelaudin's words on the subject of pride. He was a prince of Peshawar! It came naturally to him, though he strove to be humble.

Nawaz wrinkled his nose as he and Jelaudin walked past a latrine strip, flies swarming angrily as men shoveled earth back into it. Even in that, Jelaudin had taken a part, choosing the site of the strip so that when it was filled in, it would make a rough earth bank on their right flank. Nawaz looked away from the men who heaved earth into the trench, but Jelaudin called to them by name and reduced their shame at such unclean work. Nawaz watched him with feverish intensity, trying to learn everything he could. He had spent his father's gold like water to outfit the army. Somehow it was not enough and he hoped to show Jelaudin that he could command and fight with as much courage as anyone there.

The sun moved across the heavens, throwing shadow onto the army that waited. It would dwindle to nothing as noon approached, but until then, the men were cool. The Mongol tumans would be hot and thirsty by the time they crossed the river and rode back. Jelaudin had planned for everything and he nodded with approval at the young boys waiting to run among the men with waterskins when the fighting began. The horses were safe, tethered at the rear where they could not panic and bolt. He saw piles of arrows bound in twine as well as fresh shields and swords by the thousand.

"I have not eaten this morning, Nawaz," Jelaudin said suddenly. "Will you share a little food with me?" In fact, he had no appetite at all, but he knew his men would grin and point to see their leader eating without a care while the feared enemy approached. Nawaz led the way to his own tent, larger than the rest. It was as opulent as the clothes he wore, and Jelaudin smiled again to himself at the ostentatious prince. As he reached the entrance, Jelaudin looked over the plain he had chosen to avenge the Shah of Khwarezm, searching for anything out of place or that he might improve. There was nothing. All that was left was to wait.

"Have your servants bring the food out here, Nawaz," he murmured. "Let the men see me sitting as one of them, but keep the meal simple, as they would have themselves."

The rajah of Peshawar bowed his head, hurrying inside the tent to do Jelaudin's bidding.

The fording place had soaked the tumans as they crossed in a spray of muddy water, but the sun leached moisture away so that they were

almost dry by the time they rode five miles back to the Panjshir valley.
The sun was long past noon when they saw the enemy once more in
the distance. Kachiun walked his horse at the head of the three tumans,
conserving its strength as Jelme and Khasar rode beside him.

"This will be a hard fight, brother," Kachiun said to Khasar.
"Follow my orders and put aside all thoughts of an easy victory."

Khasar shrugged as the valley opened up in front of them. They had
found another entrance to the central plain, but it too had a man on a
peak and he stood to raise a banner that could be seen for miles. The
river ran on their left as they trotted toward Jelaudin's camp. The three
generals could see his army had formed on foot in a bow across the land.
Sixty thousand standing men made a formidable sight, and the Mongols
rode with grim concentration, looking to their generals for orders.

Kachiun felt his bladder fill as he crossed the plain. On a long ride,
he would simply have let the liquid run down the horse's flank. With
the enemy so close, he grimaced and held it rather than have the men
think he did it from fear.

When the lines of the enemy were a mile away, Khasar and Jelme
rode back across the face of the tumans to their positions. They had at-
tended Kachiun on the ride to and from the river, and both men knew
what they had to do. In that, at least, Kachiun knew he was well served.
He raised his hand and thirty thousand warriors moved into a trot.
Ahead of them, Jelaudin's front rank raised swords and shields, the
heavy blades resting on their shoulders and gleaming in the sun as it
moved west.

Kachiun stared ahead at the blocks of stone littering the open
ground. He did not know if Jelaudin had dug pits in front of his men,
and he tortured himself trying to guess where they might be placed.
Should he leave the center open and concentrate on the flanks alone? It
was maddening to think that Jelaudin knew their tactics. Surely he
would expect horns to form, in which case Kachiun should send the
tumans down the center. That would leave their own flanks vulnerable
and he felt his armpits grow cold with running sweat as he rode. His
generals knew his plan, but they were ready for anything and he could
change the orders, right to the moment they struck the enemy.

Jelaudin had seen Genghis fight, Kachiun told himself. One or
both of the flanks would have traps in their path. At half a mile, he was
suddenly certain of it. This prince thought he had made himself safe in
a position where he could not maneuver. Kachiun decided to show
him the flaw in his thinking.

"Swing wide right!" he roared, raising his arm and jerking it in a circle. The scouts near him raised red banners on their right side and the tumans flowed. They would attack the right flank alone, sending everything they had against that one part of Jelaudin's army. Let the rest fret as they stood behind their rocks and spikes.

It took years of practice to move so many men without fouling each other's lines. The Mongols managed it as if it were nothing to them, the tumans sliding into a new formation far out on the wing of the enemy. They increased their speed to a canter to match Kachiun and bent their bows. Behind them a plume of dust rose high enough to cast a shadow across the valley. With the sun behind, they rode with darkness fleeing ahead.

Kachiun saw the enemy shake their swords in anger as he thundered past the first piles of cut stones on his left. If he had led Jelaudin's men, he would have already had them coming forward like a door swinging shut on the tumans. Yet they stood, as they had been told to stand.

At four hundred paces, Kachiun counted aloud as the distance shrank at terrifying speed. He rode in the fifth rank, keeping himself alive to direct the battle. His heart pounded in his chest and his mouth was dry as he forced himself to breathe through his nose, snorting each breath. All three tumans raced toward the enemy. They had run so wide that they would strike almost along the line of hills.

The first ranks hit the trenches, concealed with river rushes and loose soil. At full gallop, the horses went down hard, sending their riders flying. Some of them had their feet trapped in the stirrups and dislocated their legs as they were brought up short. The army of Jelaudin roared, but the Mongols recovered quickly. More than a hundred had fallen, but those who still lived curled into a ball and used their mounts as shelter as the ranks behind leaped over them. A few more fell as they misjudged the barrier of broken horses, but the line hardly slowed. No other army could have loosed a volley in the strip of land between the trenches and the enemy. The Mongols sent shafts as thick as flies into the enemy, knocking them back. As they reached the lines of swords, some of the warriors threw down their bows, while most took a moment to secure the weapon on a saddle hook, drawing a blade with the other hand. They did not consider the dead men they left behind at the trenches, only that they avenged them.

The roaring line hit Jelaudin's soldiers at close to full speed, the weight and power of the horses as dangerous to a standing force as the blades themselves. The Mongols spent their mounts ruthlessly, using them as battering rams to break the lines apart.

Kachiun could see the curved blades of the Arabs swinging in flashes of sunlight as they resisted. His tumans had struck only a small part of the line, and more than half of his men could not bring their weapons to bear. Instead, they sent arrows over their own ranks, the black shafts rising high to fall anywhere in the enemy host. They tore into the Arab force, but as Kachiun had been told, the enemy shields were well made and their discipline held. He saw shields raised high overhead, so that they formed a wall against the dropping shafts while the men sheltered safely underneath.

Jelaudin's men fought with fury and discipline as they were forced back a step and then another, over their own dead. The Mongol charge lost its speed against their packed ranks, and the curved swords still rose and fell in unison. Warriors were cut from the saddle, and to Kachiun's horror, he saw his men pushed back as the Arabs surrounded any warrior in their midst, like islands in a sea.

The rest of Jelaudin's army begin to swing out against him. They had abandoned the safety of their position, but the advance was in order, rather than a mad rush. The far flank moved forward and Kachiun swore to himself. His column had cut into just one part of the enemy, and he reached for the horn at his throat to counter this latest threat. When he blew the note, Khasar answered, pulling his men back with just a single order that flowed down the chain of command. Kachiun saw his questioning glance and pointed to the closing door of men that was swinging across the plain. Jelaudin's men knew where the trenches lay and they stepped across them with barely a pause. In just moments, they would have encircled the Mongol tumans and then the killing would begin in earnest.

Khasar had ten thousand archers, each with a quiver of thirty arrows on his back. They formed up in the widest line they could make, though the leading edge was quickly sucked into the fighting on the wing. The rest bent their bows at those who marched toward them. Khasar dropped his arm and thousands of shafts bit the air, thumping into armor and men. Another volley followed on the instant and one more.

Kachiun shouted in frustration as he saw the Arab lines shudder. Hundreds of them fell, but they walked with shields high and merely grunted as they took the shots. Kachiun was exposed, and for the first time, he truly feared defeat.

He blew the horn again, a double note repeated that would send his men running. Those who were closest to him responded first, but the order spread like a ripple through the tumans. Khasar cried out in anger, but then he too turned his horse from the enemy and pulled back.

The Arab forces howled in triumph to see their enemy run. Thousands of them tried to cut down the Mongols riding away from them, racing after them with swords held ready for a vicious blow. Kachiun waited for the rest, making sure he did not ride so quickly that he left them all behind. The false withdrawal would have been easier against mounted men, where each rode alone in a wild frenzy of bloodlust.

Kachiun took a sharp breath when a new horn signal sounded across the plain. It was not one of his. To his amazement, he saw the running Arab lines stagger to a halt and turn back. Some gaudy prince among their line had blown the note, and they gave up the chase on the instant. Kachiun had already been planning the point when he would turn and cut them to pieces, far from the protection of the ground they had prepared. Instead, they re-formed where they had first stood and the tumans were left alone on the plain, panting and bloody in their frustration.

Only a few of the Arabs were too slow to respond and were cut down by Mongol warriors. The rest stood in solid ranks and bellowed insults, raising their swords and shields as if daring the Mongols to come and take them. Kachiun could see Khasar's appalled expression as the two brothers met half a mile away from the battlefield.

"Jelaudin," Khasar said, gasping for air. "That bastard knows us too well."

Kachiun nodded grimly. The son of the Shah had seen false retreats against his father and he had been ready. The Mongols had been made to look foolish as they ran from the enemy, and he struggled to find the calm he needed.

The sun had moved astonishingly far during the fighting, so that early evening shadows leapt from him as he dismounted and tipped a waterskin to his mouth. There was time for another attack, but Jelaudin had out-thought him at every step and his confidence had been shattered. Khasar sensed his confusion and spoke again, needing his brother to start thinking.

"What about taking up a position outside their lines tonight and sending arrows at them? It might draw them away from the hills at their back."

Kachiun shook his head. "With no other threat, they would just gather under shields. The shafts would be wasted."

"Then *what*, brother? Leave them to their victory?" Khasar asked. His eyes widened in shock as Kachiun did not reply. "You would let these dog-raping farmers have the day?"

"Unless you have a better idea," Kachiun snapped. Khasar gaped at him and both men looked up gratefully as Jelme rode up, covered in dust.

"They are cut off from the river, at least," Jelme said. "Whatever supplies of water they have must run out eventually. We can wait them out."

Khasar looked scornful at the idea. "I wish Tsubodai was here," he said. "He would not have us waiting for an enemy to die of thirst or old age."

Kachiun grimaced, though he shared the same thought. "It comes down to this," he said. "No tricks, or maneuvers. Bows and swords alone against twice as many."

"That's all you have?" Khasar asked incredulously. "Genghis will have your thumbs for a plan like that. We'd lose more than half our men."

"We have never faced another one like this, Khasar, and we *must* win." He thought for a moment while the other two men watched him anxiously. "If they will not leave the position, we can approach slowly, clearing the ground as we go." He looked up and they saw his confidence return.

"Archers to the front to keep them down and under their shields as we come in. Lancers behind them, ready to charge. Without the pits and stones, they are just an army of foot soldiers. We will cut them down." He glanced at the sun approaching the western hills and grimaced. "But it will not be today. We must wait for dawn. Have the men rest and eat and bind their wounds. Tomorrow will test us all, but we cannot fail in this place."

When Khasar spoke, his voice held none of his usual mockery. "Brother, you must send men to Genghis. Get him to bring reinforcements."

"He could not reach us in less than half a month, Khasar."

"So we wait! We wait and watch those farmers get thirsty while we drink their river."

Jelme cleared his throat and both brothers were relieved to have another break the tension between them.

"The losses would be fewer if we had the rest of the tumans. There is that."

Kachiun knew it was good advice, though every part of him wanted to resume the battle. He could not remember ever being forced to such a position before, and it rankled. He cursed for a time, in three languages.

"Damn them to hell! Very well, I will send riders to Genghis."

Khasar knew the decision had cost his brother in pride, and for once he chose not to mock him, merely clapping his hand on Kachiun's shoulder.

"The point of war is to win, Kachiun. It does not matter how we do it, or how long it takes. By the time Genghis arrives, they will be dry throated like chickens in the sun. I will enjoy what comes after that."

As dawn came the following day, bringing a gray light to the Panjshir valley, the Mongols rose from their camp on the other side of the river, where they could not be attacked in the night. At first Kachiun could not understand why his sharp-eyed scouts were shouting. The night had been freezing and he had slept with his arms tucked into a deel robe over his armor. He pulled the sleeves back to free his sword hand, reaching for it from instinct as the scouts came running toward him.

"Is it an attack?" he demanded, still numb from sleep and the cold. The scout looked terrified at having to deliver his news.

"No, General. The enemy have gone in the night. The plain is empty."

Kachiun sagged. The valley of Panjshir was a labyrinth of cracks and passes on all sides. Jelaudin's men would have known them all.

His mind turned to the scouts he had sent riding to Genghis the evening before. He had not done well in the Panjshir valley, and now he would have to send more men to keep Genghis informed. Even worse was the thought he did not voice, that Jelaudin's men had taken another victory with them to the hills. It was a hard land to track an enemy on the move. The prospect of searching for them among the maze of rocks and valleys that formed this part of the world made him sick with fury. It did not matter that he had most of his forces intact. The enemy had seen them retreat. Kachiun swallowed dryly as he realized he had let a spark leave the valley that could set the world alight. Word would spread that the Mongols could be defeated, and whether he liked it or not, Genghis would have to be told.

"Get the trackers out," he snapped. "We will have to run them down."

CHAPTER THIRTY-FIVE

THE SNOW SWIRLED ALL AROUND HIM, but Tsubodai welcomed the cold. He had been born in such a place, and it suited the numbness he had felt ever since he had accepted the orders of the khan. His face was set, with ice from his breath gathering on his upper lip no matter how many times he rubbed it away.

With ten thousand men at his back, he had not tried to hide his presence. Jochi was no fool and he suspected he knew exactly where the tuman was. Tsubodai thought there was a chance he would find only an abandoned camp, and then he would be forced to hunt the khan's son across the frozen landscape under the sun. He made sure his banners were held high, bright yellow streamers of silk that would be visible for miles ahead. Jochi would know a tuman had come searching for him, but he would also know Tsubodai commanded.

Tsubodai dipped his head, pulling closer the deel robe that he wore over his armor. His teeth chattered and he bit down. He did not seem to have the strength he remembered as a boy and wondered if the sudden change from heat to cold had robbed him of some of his endurance. The body needed time to grow used to such extremes, even for those born to winter.

He had wrestled with his orders for the entire trip north, climbing mountains and riding empty valleys as well as passing sleeping towns in the dark. This was not a journey of conquest and he and his men had ignored ripe settlements. They had taken sheep and goats wherever they found them, but that was only good sense and the need for fresh meat. Ten thousand men had to be fed, no matter where they rode. Their ponies had been born to snow and they seemed to adjust faster than those who rode them, using their hooves to dig through the ice to grass whenever they were allowed to rest.

The scout who had found Jochi the first time rode just ahead of Tsubodai. For thirty-eight days of hard riding, he had been a near-silent companion. Now Tsubodai saw he had become alert, his head turning constantly. They had ridden for more than a thousand miles since leaving Genghis, using the spare mounts carefully. At last they were close and none of them knew how they would be met. The first sign of Jochi could be an empty village or a song of arrows coming out of the whiteness. Still, they rode on and the general struggled with himself, making and discarding a dozen different plans each day. At times, he tormented himself with the vision of meeting the young man he had fostered and trained for three years, much of the time spent almost as far in the north. The memories were strong and he found himself looking forward to seeing Jochi again, just as a father might want to see his son. He ran entire conversations through his head, one after the other, but they did not bring him peace.

When his scouts brought a stranger back to his tuman, it was almost a relief to be nearing the end of his journey, though Tsubodai felt his stomach clench. He was not ready for what would come, even after so long waiting for it.

He did not recognize the man, though he wore Mongol armor and a deel over it, much as Tsubodai did. More, he had an air of authority as he rode between two scouts, and he did not bow his head as he reached Tsubodai. It had to be a minghaan officer, Tsubodai assumed, staring unblinking as the stranger was disarmed and allowed to come close. The tuman halted and the blinding wind seemed to intensify around them, howling across the land and dragging loose snow around the hooves of their horses.

"General Tsubodai," the man said in greeting. "We saw your banners." Tsubodai did not reply. The man would have no authority to act on his own, and he merely waited to see how Jochi would play it out.

"I am to say that you are not welcome here, General," the officer went on. The warriors around Tsubodai raised their heads at the challenge in the words, but the man did not flinch. "We have no quarrel with you, of all men, but out of respect, we ask that you turn away and leave this place."

Tsubodai pursed his lips, feeling the ice crack as it clung to him.

"Your master said more than that, Minghaan," he said. The officer blinked and Tsubodai knew he had guessed the rank correctly. "What did he tell you to do if I would not leave?"

The officer cleared his throat, reminded suddenly that he spoke to the most revered man in the nation after Genghis. Despite the strain, he smiled briefly.

"He said you would not, that you would ask me that question, almost word for word."

"Well?" Tsubodai demanded. He could feel the cold seeping into him and he was tired from riding. His mind felt dull and he wanted to get out of the wind.

"He told me to say that he will not be there when you come. If you ride against us, you will find nothing. Even you cannot track us in the snow, and we know this land. You will begin a hunt that will take you even further from the khan, but it will be wasted time." The man swallowed, nervousness growing in him as he sat under the glares of Tsubodai's warriors. He summoned his courage to continue. "He said you have taught him well and you will not survive the hunt if you begin it."

Tsubodai held up his hand to halt those who would surge forward and kill the messenger. More than a few of them drew swords with cold-numbed hands, growing angry on his behalf. The moment had come, and though it hurt worse than the cold, he knew just how to reach Jochi.

"I have not come to hunt, Minghaan. Lead me to a place where my men can make camp, eat, and rest. Then I will come with you alone. You will take me to him."

The officer did not reply at first. Those with Tsubodai began to clamor at him, demanding the right to protect him amidst their enemies. He shook his head and they fell quiet.

"He will see me, Minghaan," Tsubodai went on. "Did he say that? That he would see me if I came alone? I trained him. He should have thought that far ahead."

The officer bowed his head. His hands shook as he held the reins, though it was not from the cold.

"I will guide you in, General," he replied.

*   *   *

It was another night and dawn before Tsubodai and the minghaan officer walked their horses into Jochi's camp. From the instinct of years, the general could not help taking note of the defenses. They had chosen a spot surrounded by deep woods and forested hills. Even the path to it wound its way on fresh snow between ancient trees. Tsubodai's respect for the scout who had found them increased sharply. He would commend the man if he lived to return to his tuman.

There were gers there, the thick felt walls far better than stone or wood at keeping out the cold. A wooden palisade sheltered the settlement from the worst of the wind. As he rode through an open section, Tsubodai could see sheep and goats in wooden pens, huddled together in whitish clusters. The numbers were small and he was not surprised to see wooden huts made from the trunks of pines lashed and pinned together. Smoke rose from them and the village had a sense of being warm and snug that Tsubodai enjoyed. He had grown up in just such a place, each home separated from the rest by frozen, muddy tracks.

His arrival had not gone unnoticed. Men whose faces he vaguely recognized stood watching him. His memory was legendary amongst the tribes, but away from the tumans, he could recall only whispers of names and none strongly enough to be certain. Some of them made a point of continuing their work as the general passed, but most stood idle and stared, almost yearning as they recalled a different world. He saw piles of tanned furs, with fresh skins being trimmed and washed in wooden tubs. To his surprise, he also saw pale-skinned women, some of them even pregnant. They worked as hard as the men to make a life in that frozen village, and they did not look up as he passed. The name of Tsubodai meant nothing to them.

Jochi stood waiting at the door of a log house, the building squat and small, but solid looking compared to the gers. Jochi's shoulders were more powerful than Tsubodai remembered, perhaps from the hard work of creating the settlement. Tsubodai felt his heart quicken with pleasure to see him, despite the circumstances. He would have urged his mount to a trot, but the minghaan officer reached out and took his reins before he could do so. Under that man's silent warning, Tsubodai dismounted, watched all the time by Jochi.

The general kept his expression cold as he allowed two warriors to search him for weapons. They were very thorough, inspecting the lining of his deel and removing every sharp edge from his armor, even if they had to cut them free with knives. He endured their inspection without looking at them. One of them jerked roughly to free a piece of iron from his armor, and Tsubodai turned his gaze on the man, making him flush as he finished his work. When they were done, there was a pile of sharp-edged scales where they had been tossed into the snow, with his sword and two daggers lying on top. The heavy canvas underneath his armor was revealed in many places, and some of his dignity had been stripped away. Only then did Jochi come forward, while his men stood close with swords ready to take the general's head.

"You should not have come, Tsubodai," Jochi said. His eyes were bright and for an instant Tsubodai thought he saw affection there, quickly smothered.

"You knew I would," Tsubodai replied. "Even though you will abandon this place when I have gone."

Jochi looked around him. "I thought it was worth the price, though many of my men wanted you killed in the woods." He shrugged. "I have other sites marked out, far away. We will rebuild." His face hardened. "But you have cost me already, Tsubodai, just because you knew I would let you come to me."

Tsubodai held himself still, knowing that a single sharp movement would end his life. As well as the swordsman at his back, he did not doubt there were archers sighting on him.

"Then be sure it is not a waste, Jochi. Make me welcome in your camp and we will talk."

Jochi hesitated. The man before him was one of his oldest friends, one he respected above all others. Still, he could not shake the sense of dread that came with his presence. He could not out-think Tsubodai and it was hard to crush a swelling sense of fear.

"It is good to see you," Tsubodai said gently.

Jochi nodded. "And you, old friend. You are welcome in my camp. Join me for tea and salt. I will let you live for the moment."

Jochi waved the warriors away and Tsubodai climbed two wooden steps that kept the little home clear of the slushy ground. Jochi stood back to let him enter first, and Tsubodai went into the little room beyond.

As Jochi pulled the door shut, Tsubodai caught a glimpse of armed men gathering outside. The message was clear enough and he tried to relax as an iron kettle began to hiss on the stove and Jochi poured watery tea, adding milk and a pinch of salt from a pouch hanging by the door. There was only one low bed in that place, and Tsubodai sat on a stool, sipping at the bowl of tea and enjoying the way it eased the cold in his chest. Jochi seemed nervous and his hands shook as he held his own.

"Is my mother well?" Jochi asked.

Tsubodai nodded. "She thrives in the hot lands, more than most of us. Your brothers too are growing stronger each year. Ogedai now has a tuman of his own and Tolui as well, though his are but boys. I would not like to see them fight. Your father..."

"I do not care how my father is, Tsubodai," Jochi snapped, cutting him off. "Has he sent you to kill me?"

Tsubodai winced as if he had burned his lips. Carefully, he put aside the bowl, still half full. He had thought his way through this conversation many times, but nothing could have prepared him for the feeling of desolation on seeing Jochi again. At that moment, he would have given anything to be far away, riding different lands for the khan.

"Genghis has given hard orders, Jochi. I did not want them."

"Yet you are here, his faithful hound," Jochi said, without softening. "Tell me then what he wants from me."

Tsubodai took a deep breath. "You have barely seven thousand men, Jochi. They cannot stand against my tuman. Their fate lies with what I must ask you."

Jochi sat like stone, giving him nothing until Tsubodai went on.

"If you come back alone, they will be left in peace. If you do not, I must kill them all."

"If you *can*," Jochi said, his anger flaring.

Tsubodai nodded. "Yes, but you know I can."

"*Not* if I have you killed here, General. I know these woods. My men will fight for their homes."

"If you break truce," Tsubodai said quietly, "mine will fight to avenge me. Think as a leader, Jochi. You have brought them here, far from your father. They look to you for honor and life. Will you see them all killed?"

Jochi rose to his feet, his bowl of tea falling to the floor and shattering.

"You expect me to come back to be butchered by my father? To leave everything I have built here? You are insane."

"Your father does not want your men, Jochi. In betraying him, you wounded him publicly. He does not care about hunting them, if you come back. Yes, you will die, did you expect me to lie? You will be executed as an example to any other man who might turn against him. But your people will be left alone. When they leave this camp, no one else will come searching for them, not while I live." He too stood to face Jochi, his expression becoming stern.

"You have brought them to this, Jochi. You hold their lives in your hands alone. They will either be killed, or you will come with me and they will live. That is the choice you must make, and make now."

Tsubodai's chest was tight at seeing the agony in the younger man. He felt it himself, but like Jochi, he had no other choice. He saw the fight go out of Jochi in a slow breath and he slumped back to his seat on the bed. His eyes were dead as he looked into nothing.

"I should have known my father would never let me go," he said almost in a whisper. "I gave him everything and he still haunts my steps." The weary smile he turned on Tsubodai almost broke the general's heart.

"What is one life, after all, Tsubodai? Even my own." Jochi straightened his back and rubbed his hands roughly over his face so that Tsubodai would not see the glistening of his eyes.

"This is a good place, Tsubodai. We have even begun trading in furs, selling them to other places. My men have found wives in raids, and in just a short time, there will be children here who have never heard the name of Genghis. Can you imagine that?"

"I can. You have made a good life for them, but there is a price for it."

Jochi stared at him in silence for a long time. At last he closed his eyes.

"Very well, General. It seems my father sent the right man to bring me back."

He rose once more, recovering some of his poise as he opened the door and let the wind rush into little room.

"Collect your weapons, General," he said, pointing to the pile on the snow. Around it, many men had gathered. When they saw Jochi, their faces lit up. Tsubodai came out, ignoring the hostile men as he stooped to pick up his sword and daggers. He left the broken scales of armor where they were as he belted on the blade and shoved the daggers into his boots. He did not watch as Jochi spoke to the senior men. He did not think he could bear it. His horse was ready for him, its reins held by a stranger. Tsubodai nodded to him out of habit as he mounted, but the man was looking past him.

Tsubodai turned to see Jochi approaching. The younger man looked tired and smaller somehow, as if something had been taken from him.

"Return to your tuman, General. I will come to you in three days. There are things I must say here."

Tsubodai bowed in the saddle, shame eating at him. "I will wait for you, General," he said.

Jochi jerked slightly at the term, but then he nodded and turned away.

Snow still fell as the light faded on the third evening. Tsubodai was not sure that Jochi would come as he had promised, but he had not wasted the time. His men were ready for an attack as they froze and waited. His scouts were out in all directions and he could not be surprised. He stood on the edge of his men, watching the trail as it vanished under the falling snow. He wished his memories could disappear so completely, made fresh and clean rather than torturing him with what he might have done. He still remembered how it had felt to receive the gold paitze from Genghis's own hand, with the *world* before them. He had devoted himself to the khan, striving always to show that he was worthy of the honor. Tsubodai sighed. The khan was a man to follow, but he would not have wanted to be his son.

His scouts reached him before Jochi, reporting a lone rider making his way through the woods. For a time, Tsubodai hoped it was not Jochi, that the man would throw his men's lives away for his freedom. Genghis would have done just that, but Jochi had lived a different life and Tsubodai knew him too well.

When he saw it was Jochi, Tsubodai sat still in his saddle. Even then he hoped that Jochi would change his mind, but he came closer and closer until he stopped his horse facing the general.

"Take me home then, Tsubodai. Take me and let them go."

Tsubodai nodded and Jochi guided his mount among Tsubodai's staring warriors, who hardly understood what he had done. The tuman turned in place to go home and the two generals rode through them to take the lead.

"I am sorry," Tsubodai said.

Jochi looked at him strangely, then sighed. "You are a better man than my father," he said. He saw Tsubodai's gaze fall to the wolf's-head sword he wore at his waist. "Will you let me keep it, Tsubodai? I won it fairly."

Tsubodai shook his head. "I cannot. I will hold it for you."

Jochi hesitated, but he was surrounded by Tsubodai's men. He grimaced suddenly, sick of all the struggle he had known in his life.

"Take it then," he said, unbuckling the belt and scabbard. Tsubodai reached over as if to accept the sword. Jochi was looking down at it when Tsubodai cut his throat in one swift movement. The younger man was unconscious before he fell from the horse, his blood spattering bright on the snow.

Tsubodai sobbed as he dismounted to check the body, each breath torn from him.

"I am sorry, my friend," he said. "I am your father's man." He knelt by the sprawled body for a long time, and his men knew better than to speak. At last he had regained control of himself and he stood, breathing the frozen air deeply as if it could scour away the blood on his hands. He had followed his orders, but there was no comfort in it.

"At dawn we will ride back to their camp," he said. "They will come, now he is dead."

"What shall we do with the body?" one of his minghaan officers asked. He too had known Jochi when he was just a boy, and Tsubodai could not meet his eyes.

"We will take him with us. Treat him gently. He was the khan's son."

CHAPTER THIRTY-SIX

GENGHIS REINED IN AT THE VALLEY OF PANJSHIR. A howling wind swirled dust across the emptiness, and on one side of the river, hosts of carrion birds leapt and bickered, calling amongst themselves. Genghis grunted at the sight before digging in his heels and riding down. Jebe led those with him, including the tumans commanded by his youngest sons. Ogedai's men had seen the aftermath of battles and raids before, but most of Tolui's tuman were still young, some of them barely fourteen years old. They followed with wide eyes, until more senior men jabbed the most obvious gawkers in the ribs with a sword hilt.

Forty thousand men followed Genghis into Panjshir, dusty and thin after a hard ride. Only Chagatai's tuman had remained to guard the families and move them to new grazing. Genghis had taken every other man he had available, with two spare horses for each of them. Laden with waterskins and supplies, the vast tail of mounts trotted after the warriors, with just a few men at the rear to herd them.

As Genghis rode across the dusty ground, the heat increased until it seemed to beat directly onto their heads. The river ran on his left, the one source of life in a place of desolation. Genghis could see trampled banners as he approached the battle site, and in the distance, people ran from the town of Parwan to the safety of the fortress on the other side of the river. Genghis did not pause as he rode to the fighting birds, scattering ravens and vultures before the horses of his men so that they shrieked and wheeled angrily around them.

Two men still remained on that side of the river, sitting their horses like statues as the khan came in. Kachiun had left them to guide Genghis into the mountains, but they were pale with tension as the tumans approached. Surrounded by birds, they decided as one that it would be a good idea to dismount and prostrate themselves. Genghis saw the movement and angled his mount toward them, Ogedai and Tolui following. In comparison to their father, they stared at everything, and Tolui looked faintly ill, though he tried to hide it.

Genghis dismounted, showing his temper only when a raven came swinging in too close to him and he batted furiously at it, sending the bird tumbling in the air. Many of the carrion crows were almost too full to fly and merely hopped from body to body, opening their black wings and beaks as if in warning.

Genghis did not look at the corpses, except to estimate their numbers. What he saw did not please him. He stood over the two scouts and felt his patience fray in the heat.

"Get up and report," he snapped. They leapt to their feet, standing as if at an execution. No one knew how Genghis would react to a defeat.

"General Kachiun has followed the enemy into the mountains, lord. He said he will leave other men behind to bring you to him."

"You are still in contact?" Genghis asked. Both men nodded. It used valuable warriors, but the practice of establishing a line from one site to another was nothing new. Barely five miles lay between scouts and they could pass information for twenty times that distance in just a short time.

"There were false trails, lord, but the tumans are searching every valley," a scout said. "I have no news of a true sighting, not yet."

Genghis swore and both scouts tightened their faces in fear.

"How do you lose sixty *thousand* men?" he demanded.

Neither scout was certain if the question required an answer and they looked at each other in desperation. Their relief was obvious when Jebe rode up to join Genghis, looking around him at the battlefield with an experienced eye. As well as the slabs of stone placed to break a charge, he could see trenches, some with dead warriors and horses still in them. Wooden stakes bound together had been broken or knocked to one side, but the rusty stains of blood could still be seen on some. There were hundreds of bodies in Arab robes, lying in pitiful heaps as birds and other animals tugged at their flesh. It was not enough, not nearly enough, and Genghis could hardly control his indignation. Only the thought that he must not criticize his generals aloud held his tongue. He knew Jebe could see the truth, but with Ogedai and Tolui within earshot, Genghis remained silent. Jelaudin's army had fortified a position, just as a city or town. Kachiun had tried to break the defenses by force, instead of standing back and waiting for them to starve. Genghis glanced at the sun beating on the back of his neck. Thirst would have killed them first, no matter how well they had prepared. To attack such a position was reckless, though he supposed he might have done the same. Still, his brother's wits had deserted him. Genghis grimaced as he turned to Jebe, seeing the same thoughts reflected in that dark face.

"Discuss the weaknesses of strategy with my sons when we make camp, General," he said. "This prince should have been stopped here. Now we have to hunt him."

He turned back to the scouts who still stood, swallowing nervously.

"There is nothing else to see here, nothing that pleases me. Show me the way to my brother and the next scout in the chain."

Both men bowed and Genghis rode with them, his tumans coming after him in perfect order as they crossed the valley of Panjshir and entered a narrow crack, almost invisible in the brown rocks. It was barely wide enough for the horses to go through.

It took eight more days before Genghis reached Kachiun's tumans. In that time, he had not allowed his men to stop long enough to cook food, even if they had been able to find wood for a fire. The mountains in that region seemed bare of life, populated only by lizards and high nests of birds. When warriors came across a stunted tree, they chopped it down with axes and tied the wood to spare horses to be used later.

As he went, Genghis rolled up the line of scouts Kachiun had left behind, bringing each man with him as the tumans traveled deeper into the maze of canyons and valleys. At times, they rode their mounts over slopes of rock, almost too steep to remain in the saddle. There were no tracks left there. Genghis and Jebe began to appreciate the difficulty of the task for Kachiun. It was hard even to know which direction they faced at times, especially at night, but the line of scouts knew the way and they made quick progress. When they came upon the rear of

Kachiun's tumans, Genghis took Jebe and his sons through to the front, looking for Kachiun. He found him on the morning of the eighth day, at a brackish lake surrounded by towering peaks.

Genghis made a point of embracing Kachiun, letting the men see that he held no grudge for their defeat.

"Are you close?" he said, without preamble.

Kachiun saw the banked anger in his brother and winced. He knew better than to explain himself, having no doubt at all that Genghis would discuss his errors in great detail when they were alone.

"Three false trails headed east, brother, but the main force is going south, I am certain of it." Kachiun showed Genghis a piece of horse dung, teasing it apart in his hands.

"Still moist, even in this heat. We cannot be more than a day behind them."

"Yet we have stopped," Genghis said, raising his eyebrows.

"I am running low on water, brother. This lake is salt and useless to us. Now you are here, we can share skins and move faster."

Genghis gave the order immediately, without pausing to see the first waterskins brought up. He had thousands on his spare horses and the animals were used to sucking at them as if they had never forgotten their mother's teats. He felt every delay as a spur to his growing irritation. It was hard not to berate Kachiun with so many watching the exchange. When Khasar and Jelme came to greet him, Genghis could barely look at them.

"Tsubodai has orders to join us when he returns," he said to the three generals. "What is past is past. Ride with me now and redeem yourselves."

A flicker of movement caught his eye and Genghis squinted up against the sun. On a peak, he saw a distant man waving a banner above his head. He looked back at Kachiun, incredulous.

"What is *that*?"

"The enemy," Kachiun said grimly. "They have watchers on us all the time."

"Send six good climbers up and kill him," Genghis said, forcing himself to remain calm.

"They choose places one man can defend. We move past them too quickly to waste time getting them down."

"Has the sun softened your head, brother?" Genghis demanded. Once more he had to struggle to control his temper. "Those are Jelaudin's eyes. Have more men ride ahead and pick them off with arrows as they find them. It does not matter if some of the warriors fall trying to reach them. When our enemy is blind, we will find him more easily."

Jelaudin stared into the distance, watching the flag signal as it rose and dipped four times.

"The khan has taken the field," he said. His stomach clenched as he spoke, and suddenly all the strength of his army seemed insubstantial. This was the man who had destroyed his father's regiments, sent elephants mad with pain, and carved his way through the golden cities. Jelaudin had known he would come, the knowledge tainting their victories. The khan's pride demanded his presence and Jelaudin had known he would not be slow to follow.

"How many men?" Nawaz asked at his shoulder. He had not taken the time to learn the flag signals, but Jelaudin did not upbraid him.

"Four tumans, that is forty thousand more warriors in the hunt. They will move faster now."

For twelve days, they had led the Mongols into blind canyons and false trails, losing just a few men while they wound their way through the Afghan hills. The sudden withdrawal from Panjshir had always been a gamble, but Jelaudin knew the word would spread almost as fast as he could move his army. Cities waited for a thousand miles to hear that the khan's men had been defeated. Jelaudin thought of them as he stared at the setting sun. They would rise when they heard. Those places where Mongol garrisons kept the peace would be again at war. Every day he remained alive shook the khan's grip on Arab lands. Jelaudin swore a silent oath as he stood there. He would shake it loose.

Men rode ahead of him, leaving the hills far behind to take the news. Jelaudin knew if he could hold off the khan for just a season, his army would swell with every man and boy able to hold a sword. He would set the land on fire with the chance to strike back at the invader. If he survived. He smiled at Nawaz, standing at his side like a faithful servant. He was weary and his feet hurt. He had walked for many miles that day, but now the khan had come. It was time to ride, fast and far away from the mountains.

Genghis could find no fault with the way Kachiun moved his tumans through the labyrinth of passes. His brother had men out in all directions, linking back to the generals like the threads of a delicate web spreading over the hills. There were few mistakes once the routines had been learned, and while Genghis was there, they avoided two more dead ends and one false trail that would have taken them ten miles out of their way. Genghis developed a grudging respect for the prince he hunted. He would have liked to ask Tsubodai about the pursuit to the Caspian Sea. It occurred to Genghis that Jelaudin may well have been the mind that kept his family safe and not his father, as they had supposed.

It was strange how often Tsubodai's name came up in conversation between the generals. Genghis deflected their interest with curt replies or silence, not wanting to discuss the task he had set. Some things were not meant to go into the histories Temuge was writing. As he rode, Genghis wondered if he should keep a tighter rein on his brother's record of the tribes. Part of him still thought it was foolish to trap words in such a way, for all you could control it. Though he recalled Arslan's quiet scorn for fame, Genghis quite enjoyed the idea of shaping his own memory. In Samarkand he had mentioned the possibility of doubling enemy numbers in Temuge's account of battles and left his brother openmouthed at the idea.

The tumans moved faster through the hills, leaving the worst part of the maze behind them. Genghis pushed them on and they found new depths to their endurance under his gaze. No one wanted to be first to call the halt, and they survived on just a few hours' sleep, sometimes just dozing in the saddle as those who were still awake led them on.

Beyond the rocky slopes and valleys, they now followed a true trail, the marks of any large force of men and horses. As well as lumps of drying horse dung, the excrement of men buzzed with flies feasting on the moisture, fresher every day. The tumans knew they were drawing close to the enemy. In the khan's presence, they were hungry to revenge the defeats at Panjshir: they would not fail again, not with Genghis watching. Privately, Genghis thought Kachiun could have taken them through the hills without him, but he led the nation and he could not trust another with the task at hand.

Each day brought news from the chains of scouts he maintained for a thousand miles. The old days of an army moving alone and out of touch had gone with his subjugation of the Arab lands. It was a rare day that did not bring two or more dusty messengers from as far back as Samarkand and Merv as well as deep into the west. The Mongol nation had made deep prints in the dust of Arab lands.

Genghis both enjoyed and was disturbed by the stream of information. He had grown to manhood in a time where a raiding band might move unseen across the land, answerable to no one. Now, he had problems coming to him that he could do nothing about, and at times he wished he had brought Temuge with him to handle the details of the reports. He heard that the Afghan city of Herat had expelled its Mongol garrison, leaving them alive. Another stronghold, Balkh, had closed its gates and refused to send another year's tribute. The cracks were widening and he could do nothing about it. His task was to find and annihilate the enemy who had caused such a rush of confidence in once-beaten cities. In time, he would remind them of their obligations to him.

The seven tumans moved on at increasing speed, pushing the men and spare horses. Jebe organized fresh mounts every second day and each change brought a surge of new energy as the warriors felt an eager horse under them again. Small boys rode with the supplies behind the army, and Genghis took no note of them until Jebe brought two tiny urchins up on his saddle, riding right to the khan. They were so black with dirt that at first Genghis did not recognize them. Boys always accompanied the army, though these were very small. They ran errands for warriors and the largest were allowed to beat drums as they formed for battle.

One of the little boys grinned and Genghis pulled up, astonished. Mongke sat before Jebe and Kublai peeked from behind his back. With the boundless energy of young boys, they were both thin as rats and burned dark by the fierce sun. Genghis scowled at them and the grins disappeared instantly. His expression softened slightly, remembering a time when the whole world was an adventure. They were too young to come on such a journey, and he suspected their mother, Sorhatani, would take the skin off their buttocks when they reached the families once more. He wondered if their father, Tolui, had any idea they were there. Genghis doubted it.

"What do you want to do with them?" Jebe asked. His eyes were bright as he looked at Genghis and the two men shared a moment of humor. The boys had not been told to stay with their mother. It had not occurred to anyone to give such an order to ones so young. They had no inkling of the danger around their grandfather. Genghis lowered his brows, making his face stern.

"I have not seen them, General," he said. Kublai's eyes gleamed with sudden hope. Genghis chose to ignore the little face, complete with a crust of snot between the nose and upper lip.

Jebe nodded, a smile lifting one side of his mouth. "My lord khan," he replied, dipping his head as he went off to lose the boys once more in the herd of spare horses behind them.

Genghis smiled to himself as he rode on. He suspected he was a better grandfather than he had ever been a father, but he did not let the idea trouble him unduly.

The tumans rode on doggedly as they reached the edge of the mountainous region. Genghis thought they could not be more than a couple of hundred miles from the Panjshir valley, though they had ridden far further along the twists and turns. He did not know if Jelaudin had hoped to open up a gap between the armies. He had almost done so in the first days, but the tumans had gained on his army, pulling them in day by day. By the time the mountains came to an end, the dung of horses and men was barely cooling. Genghis rode with his generals at the head of the host, among the first to feel the rocky ground give way to packed earth and scrub grass. From his maps, he knew the grassy plain led south into India. It was not a land he knew, but he cared nothing for that. His scouts were riding in at shorter intervals and he knew where the enemy lay.

Jelaudin's men ran before those who hunted them. Genghis had driven his army hard for more than a month, and they were tired and thin, the meager rations of milk and blood toward the end hardly sustaining them. The river Indus lay ahead and Jelaudin's host flowed toward it, desperate to escape the storm they had brought down on their heads.

CHAPTER THIRTY-SEVEN

JELAUDIN STARED down a forty-foot drop to the swollen river Indus, the great artery that fed a continent for a thousand miles further south and more. The hills around the banks were green, lush with ancient acacia trees and wild olives. He could smell the scent of flowers on the breeze. Small birds flew in all directions, singing warnings as his army gathered. It was a place of life, but the water ran fast and deep, so that the Indus may as well have been a city wall. The region of Peshawar lay just a short way beyond the river, and Jelaudin turned in fury to the young rajah who stood with him, gazing stricken at the empty banks.

"Where are the boats you promised me?" Jelaudin said. Nawaz gestured weakly with his hands, at a loss. They had driven men and horses to exhaustion to reach the river, knowing that when they crossed, the Mongols could not follow for months, if at all. India was an unknown land to the Mongol khan, and if he dared to set foot there, a hundred princes would answer with armies greater than he had ever seen. Jelaudin had planned to take his victories like jewels among the princes, so that he could return with an even greater force. He could not help looking back at the dust cloud in the distance, rising into the air like an omen.

Without warning, Jelaudin took hold of the rajah's silk jacket and shook him furiously.

"Where are the *boats*?" he yelled into his face. Nawaz was pale with fear and Jelaudin let him go just as quickly, so that he almost fell.

"I don't know," the rajah stammered, "my father..."

"Would he leave you to die here?" Jelaudin demanded. "With your own lands so close?" He felt a mounting hysteria and it was hard to resist striking the foolish young prince who had promised so much.

"Perhaps they are still coming," Nawaz said.

Jelaudin almost growled at him, but he nodded. Within moments he had riders galloping south along the banks, searching for the fleet of merchant traders that would carry them to safety. He did not dare look at the dust cloud in the distance, knowing the Mongols would be there, coming like wolves with iron teeth to tear him apart.

Genghis rode at a light canter, staring ahead. His eyes had weakened further, so that he could not trust them for long distances. Instead, he had Ogedai call out a constant description of the army they faced. His son's voice was tight with excitement.

"They have gathered on the banks of the river. I see horses, perhaps ten thousand or more on the right wing facing us, their left." Ogedai paused, squinting.

"I see... ranks forming around the center. They are turning to face us. I can't see beyond the river yet."

Genghis nodded. If Jelaudin had been given a few clear days, he might have taken his men to safety. Instead, the hardship of the pace Genghis had set showed its worth. He had caught the prince on this side of the river. It would do. The khan turned in the saddle to his closest scout.

"Take this message to General Kachiun. I will hold the center with Jebe and Ogedai. Kachiun will have the right wing, with Khasar, against their cavalry. Tell him he can give them back the defeat at Panjshir and I will not accept less. Now go."

Another scout took the young man's place as the first rode away. The second was ready and Genghis went on. "Generals Jelme and Tolui will swing wide on my left. I want the enemy held tight in one place against the river. Their task is to block any line of retreat to the north." Tolui's tuman was still too young to be sent in against veteran soldiers. Holding the army in place would be honorable enough for hardly blooded men. Jelme would not enjoy the task, but Genghis knew he would obey. The tumans would sweep in against Jelaudin's army in three places, pinning them against the Indus.

Genghis slowed his approach as the lines formed, turning his head left and right to watch the tumans match his pace. Ogedai called out as new details came clear in the distance, but Genghis heard nothing to interfere with the swelling sense of anticipation in his chest. He recalled the presence of his grandsons among the spare horses and sent another scout racing back to be sure they were kept out of the fighting.

He came in slowly until he could see the enemy ranks as clearly as Ogedai and silenced his son with a wave of his hand. Jelaudin had picked the site of the last battle with Mongol tumans. He had not been able to choose the ground for this one.

Genghis drew his sword, holding it high as his men waited for the signal to charge. The army on the riverbanks would know better than to surrender, he knew. The prince had gambled everything when he had returned from the Caspian Sea, and he had nowhere else to run. Genghis saw the tumans of Jelme and Tolui moving ahead of the main lines, ready to cut off and hold the left wing. On his right, Kachiun and Khasar matched the maneuver so that the Mongols rode as an empty cup, with Genghis at the deepest part. They faced sixty thousand fanatical followers and Genghis saw them raise their swords as one, waiting for him. With the river at their back, they would fight for every foot of ground.

Genghis leaned forward in the saddle, pulling back dry lips to show his teeth. He dropped his arm and the tumans surged forward, kicking their mounts into a gallop.

Jelaudin stared at the lines of Mongol riders who dragged the dust of the mountains with them. His hands shook in rage and frustration as he looked again at the empty river. The far bank and safety were so close it hurt to think of it. He could swim the waters, despite their fierce flow, but most of his men had never learned the trick. For desperate moments, he considered shedding his armor and leading them into the river, away from the death he saw coming. They would follow, he knew, trusting in Allah to keep them safe. It was impossible. For those who had grown to manhood in the Afghan hills, in deserts and cities, deep water was a rare sight. They would drown in their thousands as they entered the swift current.

He saw many faces turned to him, looking for some words of encouragement as the hated enemy formed horns on either wing. His brothers were there among them, their faces bright with faith. Jelaudin fought with despair.

"We have shown they can be beaten!" he bellowed to them. "They are many, but not so many that we cannot gut them again. Kill this khan for me and you will know paradise. Let Allah guide your swords and let no man turn away from the fight so that he cannot face God with pride. They are just men!" he shouted. "Let them come. We will show them this land is not to be taken."

Those who heard turned back to the Mongol khan with new fire in their eyes. They raised shields and curved swords as the ground trembled under their feet.

At full gallop, Genghis raised his sword again, cutting the air sharply. Arrows came in a ripple down the lines on either side, slightly delayed as each tuman registered the command and loosed. Ahead, he saw Jelaudin's ranks drop to a crouch, holding the shields high. Genghis grunted irritably, sending another volley buzzing toward them. Many of Jelaudin's men survived the first and then rose to their feet too soon, so that the second flight of shafts caught them. Arrows that could punch through an iron scale rocked them back.

The tumans on his wings jammed their bows onto saddle hooks, drawing swords as they reached the enemy. On his right, ahead of him, Genghis saw the tumans of Kachiun and Khasar smash into the standing lines, while Tolui and Jelme drew up almost on the riverbanks on his left. From there, they loosed shaft after shaft in a constant hail. Arabs fell, struck from the side as they raised their shields blindly to the front.

Genghis smelled the river and the fear sweat of thousands of men as he raced his mount straight at the center. He hoped he would find the prince there, waiting for him. Jelaudin's men were ten deep, but the Mongol ponies had been trained for such an assault and did not hesitate as they plunged into them. Genghis swept through the first three ranks, swinging his sword as men were knocked down by the impact. With his knees, he turned the mount in place, feeling the solid connection as she kicked and sent someone reeling. A wedge of his best warriors came with him, protecting the khan with their ferocity as they cut their way into the mass.

Genghis saw a turbaned prince in bright fabric and lunged at him before Jelaudin's soldiers drove him back with sheer weight. He saw a shield loom at him, its owner cracking it into his horse's face and turning her. Genghis killed the man, but he was forced back another step as more came in, using their shields well and punching blows around them.

Very few reached the khan. A thousand warriors moved with him, each the veteran of more battles than they could recall. The pointed wedge they formed dug its way deeper into Jelaudin's ranks until they could see the river ahead of them. Jebe and Ogedai moved in the center of two other arrowheads on either side of the khan, forming three sharp tines that speared the army they faced. Whoever faced the leading edges were cut down, while those they passed were killed by men behind.

The noise was terrible in the press, a roar of sound that battered at the ears. Genghis felt his arm grow tired and missed a sword that slid along the layered scales of his thigh until it gashed him above the knee. It would be one more scar on his legs to add to the mass of ridged skin. The pain improved his speed and he whipped his sword across the face of the attacker.

Jelaudin's men did not break, perhaps because they had nowhere to go. Genghis was content at first to let the three wedges move in together, clawing strips in the enemy lines. From horseback, they loomed over men on foot, using the weight of the swords to swing down with greater force than those below and always seeing the next attack coming. Even so, Genghis felt hemmed in by the enemy and knew his men would be feeling the same. He saw a horse collapse as its front legs were cut, the warrior remaining in the saddle until a sword jabbed into his throat. Roaring warriors came through the gap in the wedge, fighting to reach Genghis himself. He turned, ready for them, but his men were fast and young. They blocked the path almost before it could form. He stood in the stirrups as they too were gashed and knocked from their mounts.

The rear of Jelaudin's army was swirling, with more and more men converging on the khan. They stared up at him as they pushed through their own in reckless fury. Genghis saw the left of his wedge pushed back, crumpling under the chopping blades of the enemy. Some even used their shields in threes or fours, heaving together so that the horsemen were turned in on themselves. More and more spilled into the wedge, coming straight at him. Genghis had time for a glimpse over at Ogedai, but the pressure there was nowhere near as great.

Genghis moved his horse back three quick steps, giving himself room as the wave of Arabs reached him. His horse answered every command from pressure of his knees, dancing round so that the first blow swung wide. Genghis took a man's head, but the next struck at his mare's foreleg. As she moved, the blade turned, but the weight of iron was enough to snap the bone. The horse screamed and Genghis fell badly, hitting the ground with his sword arm outstretched. He felt a sickening thump and struggled to get up without understanding he had torn the joint from its socket. There seemed to be yelling enemies everywhere and he was disoriented.

His wedge fell in on itself as his men struggled to protect the khan. More and more fought through from behind as a warrior dismounted and tried to shove Genghis into his own saddle. He died for his efforts, stabbed in the back as Genghis found his seat again. The khan's sword had gone and his arm hung limply, every movement an agony. Genghis drew a dagger from his boot with his left hand and wheeled the fresh horse away. His men roared into the space he left behind, using their strength in a mad rush that would see many of them cut down as they grew slow from weariness.

Genghis pulled back through his own ranks, raging at the weakness of his arm. For a fleeting moment, he wished Kokchu was there to put him right, but there were other men who knew battlefield injuries. He caught sight of one his own minghaan officers and shouted to him, calling him by name across the lines of fighting.

The officer almost lost his head as he turned to the khan, responding with a quick cut at a man's legs before he yanked his horse around and forced his way through.

"My lord?" the officer said, gasping.

"Put my arm back in," Genghis replied. The pain was excruciating. He sat the horse calmly as warriors streamed around them both, staring curiously at the khan. Genghis put his dagger back in his boot and held the saddle pommel tightly with his left hand as he heaved a leg over and slid to the ground. The officer stopped gaping, his face becoming set.

"Lie faceup on the ground, my lord," he said, sheathing his sword. Genghis did so with a grunt and kept his face cold as the officer took his loose arm and pressed his fingers into the joint.

"Quickly!" Genghis snapped. The officer put his boot into Genghis's armpit and heaved, twisting at the same time. There was another dull thump and Genghis saw white for an instant before the pain vanished. He allowed the officer to help him to his feet and tested the arm.

"You can still cut downwards, but avoid lifting the arm away from your body, understand?"

Genghis ignored him. The arm felt weaker than before, but he clenched his fist and smiled. He could grip a sword.

On his right, Kachiun and Khasar had destroyed Jelaudin's cavalry, sending a few dozen survivors running as they turned their swords and arrows on the center. Jelaudin's men were caught between pincers, but they fought on, seemingly intent on taking as many with them as they could. The pace of the battle had slowed as both sides tired, and Genghis saw he would lose many more men as the day ended. He flexed his arm, looking ahead to where Ogedai and Jebe still fought. Their wedges were intact, the enemy falling back from them. On a clear plain, he might have pushed on, knowing that they would break soon. Against the river, Genghis shook his head and reached for the scout horn that dangled on his chest.

He blew a long dropping note, then repeated it. It was echoed on other horns across the field and his men heard. They pulled back, killing as the Arabs tried to rush them. Those who were still mounted broke free first, while those on foot had to defend every step as the Arabs surged after them. It was bloody work, but as the light began to fade, there was clear ground between the tumans and the army on the banks.

Genghis looked for his messenger scouts and could not see them anywhere close. He sent warriors for them and it seemed an age until they could be found. After that, he had them raise the banner that would summon his generals. He passed on orders to make camp just half a mile from the river, and his men went with him. They had lost the cold face in the fighting, becoming flushed and vital. Some of them laughed wildly. Others rode in a dark mood, having seen their own death come too close that day.

They left a broken line of dead behind them, with many more of Jelaudin's than theirs. The prince's army had been torn apart, but they still jeered and shouted halfheartedly, the sounds coming from gasping, tired men. They saw the Mongols dismount, barely eight hundred paces away. The tumans ignored the army behind them on the river-bank, bringing up the pack animals for food and water as they prepared to make camp.

Jelaudin still lived, though his armor was gashed and bright in many places. He panted like a dog in the sun as he watched the Mongols ride away without looking back. The sunlight was becoming gray and though he was relieved at the respite, he knew they would return at dawn. He and his men would have it all to do again.

"I will die tomorrow," he whispered to himself. None of his men heard him as they passed skins of river water along the line to ease their throats. He could feel their eyes on him as he stood staring onto the plain, perhaps hoping that he would yet come up with some stroke to save them all.

The rajah of Peshawar came through the ranks to join him at the front, taking moments as he did so to clap men on the shoulder and exchange a few words of encouragement. Those who had taken terrible wounds were beginning to cry out, the noise suddenly loud after the crash of battle. Many of them would die before morning. Jelaudin had supplies of opium for pain, enough at least to dull their wits while they died. It was all he could do for them and he felt ill with hatred for the khan of the Mongols.

He turned to his friend and both men knew they were finished, unable to bear the knowledge in each other's eyes.

"I think my father had the boats burned," Nawaz said softly. "He is a fool, lost in old ways and old Hindu gods. He does not understand why I chose to follow you."

Jelaudin nodded, still staring out at the Mongol camp, seeming almost close enough to touch. The khan's men surrounded them in a great bow. There would be no stealthy flight from the banks that night.

"I am sorry I brought you to this place," Jelaudin replied. "I had such hopes, my friend! To see it come to this..." He hawked and spat on the ground and Nawaz winced at the grief in his voice.

"You could swim when you were a little boy, Jelaudin. Could you get across the river?"

"And leave my men here? I won't do it. You sank like a stone, Nawaz, if I remember. I had to drag you out myself."

His friend smiled in memory. He sighed to himself, staring at the Mongols who rested in the growing gloom.

"We showed they can be beaten, Jelaudin. You are still a talisman to the men. If you can cross the river, they will give their lives gladly. It does not have to end here. Take your brothers with you and live." He saw Jelaudin firm his mouth and spoke quickly to forestall the objection.

"Please, Jelaudin. Let me command the men tomorrow. If I thought you would escape, I could fight without regrets. I promised the boats would be here. Do not let me die with this guilt, my friend. It is too much for me."

Jelaudin smiled gently then, letting himself feel the weariness that ached in every joint.

"Your father would be proud of you, if he knew it all," he said. "I *am* proud of you." He clasped Nawaz on the back of the neck before letting his hand fall.

As dawn came, Genghis roused himself, instantly irritable as his arm felt as stiff as a piece of wood. As he rose from the cold ground, he tested it gingerly. With his elbow at his side, he had good movement up and down, but if he held the limb away from his body, it felt loose and without strength. He swore to himself, hating the weakness far more than pain. The minghaan officer had come to him again before he slept, testing the joint and warning him that it needed a month of rest, then two more to rebuild the muscle he would lose.

Genghis clambered to his feet and accepted a bowl of salt tea from a warrior who had waited for him to wake. He sipped it slowly, feeling the warmth banish the chill from his limbs. He had spoken to his generals, commending Kachiun in front of them to repair the damage to his brother's reputation. He had praised Ogedai as well and he was truly pleased with his son. Ogedai seemed to have grown in stature since becoming the heir. He had a quiet dignity to him that Chagatai had never had, and Genghis wondered at the strangeness of fate. Perhaps he had been led to choose the right son to inherit his lands.

Jelaudin's army was clearly visible as the light grew stronger. They had removed many of the dead and Genghis assumed the bodies had been dropped in the river to be tumbled away in the current. They did not look so fearsome now, Genghis thought. Almost half of them had been slaughtered the day before, and though it may have been his imagination, he thought he saw resignation in the way they stood so silently and waited. They did not expect to survive and that pleased him. He thought of the cities that had been so quick to rebel. They would hear of this day and consider what it meant for them. Herat and Balkh would be the first to see his armies, and this time he would not accept tribute or surrender. He would make a lesson of them, that he would not be scorned or mocked.

Genghis tossed the bowl down to the grass and signaled for a fresh horse to be brought. The tumans formed in squares and Genghis hardly cast an eye over them, knowing the officers would have worked through the night to bring new arrows and swords to those that needed them. He was no longer a young man, able to go two or three days without rest. While he slept, many of his warriors had worked, sharpening swords and tending to their horses.

As Genghis mounted, he saw Mongke and Kublai sitting with other boys nearby, sharing a piece of dried mutton. He scowled at the sight, looking around him for the nearest officer to take them to safety. Before he could find one, Jelaudin's army shouted a challenge, sending flights of startled birds soaring up from the trees by the river.

Genghis stood in his stirrups, straining his eyes to see if they would attack. Instead, Jelaudin's army parted and Genghis watched in astonishment as one man rode through them to the ground between the two armies.

The khan stared out at the lone rider. He did not know Jelaudin by sight, but it could be no other. As Genghis watched, Kublai and Mongke stood to see what was holding their grandfather's interest. Both boys watched in fascination as Jelaudin took a knife and cut through the lacing holding his armor, so that it fell away in pieces.

Genghis raised his eyebrows, wondering if he watched some sort of ritual. In just moments, Jelaudin sat his horse in just a tattered robe, and Genghis exchanged a glance with officers nearby, mystified. He saw the prince raise his sword as if in salute, then fling it at the ground so that it stuck point first in the earth. Was he surrendering? Three young men came from the ranks and he spoke to them, ignoring the Mongol host. The prince seemed relaxed in their presence and he laughed with them. Genghis watched curiously as all three men touched their foreheads to his stirrup, then returned to their places.

The khan opened his mouth to order the tumans forward, but the prince turned his horse and dug in his heels. His army had left a clear route back to the riverbanks and Genghis realized at last what Jelaudin was going to do. The khan had seen the drop on the previous day, and he winced in appreciation.

Jelaudin reached the muddy bank at a gallop. Without hesitation, horse and man leapt, plunging over the edge. The tumans were close enough to hear the great splash that followed, and Genghis nodded to himself.

"Did you see that, Kublai? Mongke?" he called out, startling the boys from their awe.

Kublai answered him first. "I saw. Is he dead?"

Genghis shrugged. "Perhaps. It was a long drop to the river." He thought for a moment, wanting his grandsons to appreciate the dramatic gesture of contempt. Jelaudin could have climbed down at any point in the night, but he had wanted the khan to see the reckless courage of his race. As a horseman born, Genghis had enjoyed the moment more than any other part of the campaign, but it was difficult to explain to the boys.

"Remember the name of Jelaudin, Kublai. He was a strong enemy."

"That is a good thing?" Kublai asked, perplexed.

Genghis nodded. "Even enemies can have honor. His father was fortunate to have such a son. Remember this day, and perhaps in time, you will make your own father proud."

Ahead of him, Jelaudin's army closed the gap and raised their swords. Jelaudin's three brothers strode forward with tears of joy in their eyes.

Genghis smiled, though he did not forget to send the boys to the rear before he gave the order to move.

CHAPTER THIRTY-EIGHT

THE RAINS HAD COME AT LAST to Samarkand, pounding on the tile roofs of the city in a constant downpour that had lasted for days and showed no sign of ceasing. The streets ran as rivers and the inhabitants could only endure. Illness spread as cesspools overflowed and added their stinking contents to standing water, some even corrupting the city wells. The air remained hot even so and Genghis abandoned the Shah's palace when a vicious new pestilence appeared. It began with vomiting and loose bowels, killing first children and the old as they grew weak. No one was safe and there was no pattern to it: in one area, hundreds would die, while no one suffered in streets all around. Chin physicians told Genghis that such a scourge could only be left to run its course.

The khan urged Arslan to leave Samarkand, but the old general refused, as was his right. The city was his. Arslan had not mentioned the first stirrings of sickness in his gut as he walked Genghis to the gates and saw them nailed shut. With the khan safe, Arslan had closed his eyes, feeling a hot iron in his bowels as he walked back to the palace through deserted streets. Genghis heard of his death just days later.

When Genghis looked at Samarkand after that, it was with fury and grief, as if the city itself were responsible. Those inside mourned the dead or joined them while the khan and his generals took shelter in the gers outside. No one died there. The families collected their water from the lakes to the north and sickness did not strike the camp.

Tsubodai was sighted as the number of deaths began to fall and the air grew cool for the first time in many months. As the general drew closer, tension mounted palpably in the camp. Genghis became more and more irritable until no one dared approach him. The death of Arslan had put the final touch on a bad year, and he was not sure he wanted to hear what had become of Jochi. No one had died for four days when he allowed the city to open its gates at last and burn the rotting dead. Arslan was among the corpses and Genghis sat by the funeral pyre as his oldest friend was reduced to clean ash and bones. The shamans of the nation gathered solemnly to chant the general's soul through to the sky father, though Genghis hardly heard them. The great fires seared the air, burning away the last of the sickness. In some ways, it felt like a rebirth. Genghis wanted to put bad memories behind him, but he could not prevent Tsubodai coming home.

As Tsubodai reached the walls of Samarkand at last, Genghis waited for him in the khan's ger, lost in dark thoughts. He looked up when the general entered through the small door, and even then a small part of him hoped he would have failed.

Tsubodai handed the wolf's-head sword to the khan, his eyes shadowed and showing nothing. Genghis took it almost with reverence, laying the scabbard across his lap and breathing out slowly. He looked older than Tsubodai remembered, worn thin by battle and time.

"The body?" Genghis asked.

"I would have brought it back, but the heat..." Tsubodai's gaze fell to a rough sack he had brought with him. He had carried its withered contents for hundreds of miles.

"I have Jochi's head," he said.

Genghis winced. "Take it away and bury or burn it," he replied. "I do not want to see."

Tsubodai's eyes flashed for a moment. He was tempted to remove the head from the sacking and make the khan look at the dead face of his son. He throttled the impulse quickly, knowing it was born of exhaustion.

"Did his men resist, afterwards?" Genghis asked.

Tsubodai shrugged. "Some of the Chin officers chose to take their own lives. The rest came with me, as I thought they would. They are still fearful that you will have them killed." He breathed deeply. "I made promises to them." Tsubodai sensed Genghis was about to speak and threw aside his caution.

"I will not see my word broken, my lord khan," he said.

The two men stared at each other for a long moment, each assessing the will of the other. Finally Genghis nodded.

"They will live, Tsubodai. They will fight again for me, yes?" He chuckled, though it was a forced and ugly sound. The silence became uncomfortable until Tsubodai spoke again.

"I heard of your victory."

Genghis put aside the sword, relieved at being able to speak of mundane things.

"Jelaudin escaped," he said. "I have scouts searching for him, but there is no sign. Do you want the task?"

"No, lord. I have had enough of the heat. The one good thing I found in going north was in welcoming the cold again. Everything is cleaner there."

Genghis hesitated as he considered how to reply. He sensed a great bitterness in his general, and he did not know how to ease it. He recalled the worst times of his own life and knew that time alone would heal the man, rather than anything he could say. Tsubodai had obeyed his orders and he was tempted to tell him to take comfort from that.

Genghis held his tongue. The brooding general brought a subtle sense of menace into the ger, and Genghis felt invisible hackles rise as he struggled for words.

"I will move the nation to Herat in the west. One sharp blow there will restore the nerve of other cities. After that, I think I will return home for a few years. It has been too long and I am tired."

Tsubodai tilted his head slightly and Genghis felt his temper begin to fray.

"Did you hear that Arslan died in the city?" he asked.

Tsubodai nodded. "He was a great man," he said softly.

Genghis scowled at the calm tone. "Even so, it was not a good death," he said.

Once more, Tsubodai did not add anything to the stilted conversation and the khan's temper came to the surface.

"What do you *want* from me, Tsubodai? You have my thanks. Do you think I am pleased that this had to be done?" Genghis glanced at the sack between Tsubodai's feet and almost reached for it. "There was no other way, General."

"I grieve for him, still," Tsubodai replied.

Genghis stared at him, then looked away. "As you please, Tsubodai. There will be many who grieve. Jebe was his friend, as was Kachiun. His mother is distraught, but they know it was my order."

"Still, I am the man who killed the khan's son," Tsubodai said grimly.

Genghis shook his head. "He was *not* my son," he said, his voice hard. "Put this aside and ride with me to Herat."

Tsubodai shook his head. "You do not need me for that."

Genghis crushed the swelling sense of anger at the man. He barely understood Tsubodai's pain, but there was a debt to be repaid and he realized the general could not simply return to the nation.

"Once more then, Tsubodai," he said, his voice hard. "For your service, I ask. What do you want from me?"

Tsubodai sighed. He had hoped to find peace when he gave the sword and head to the khan. It had not come.

"Let me take tumans to the north once more, into the clean cold. I will win cities for you there and wash away what I have done."

Tsubodai bowed his head at last, staring blankly at the wooden floor as Genghis considered. Jebe had been planning a raid to the north before Jelaudin's army had attacked at Panjshir. In normal times, Genghis would have sent the two generals away without a thought. The sick misery he saw in Tsubodai troubled him deeply, in part because he felt it himself, but resisted. He had revenged the insults of small kings. The Shah was dead with all but his oldest son, and Genghis had scorched cities from east to west. He searched for a victor's satisfaction, but could not find it. Somehow, Jochi's betrayal and death had poisoned the simple pleasures.

After an age, Genghis nodded. "Very well, Tsubodai. Take Jebe and Jochi's men. I would have had to send them far anyway, to have them relearn the discipline I expect of those who follow me."

Tsubodai raised his eyes from the floor, the warning not lost on him.

"I am loyal, lord. I have always been loyal to you."

"I know it," Genghis said, gentling his tone with an effort. He knew he did not have the lightness of touch that Kachiun would have brought to the meeting. Genghis rarely thought how he ruled men like Tsubodai, as able as any he had known. In the stillness of the ger, he felt an urge to ease the general's grief with the right words.

"Your word is iron, Tsubodai, take pride in that."

Tsubodai rose and made a stiff bow. His gaze lingered on the sack before he lifted it onto his shoulder.

"I have to, lord," he said. "It is all I have left."

Herat lay almost five hundred miles to the south and west of Samarkand, with two wide rivers and a dozen smaller ones in between. With the gers of the nation on carts, Genghis chose to approach the fortress city from that direction rather than go back to the mountains around Panjshir and strike west through the maze of valleys and hills. Tsubodai and Jebe had gone north from Samarkand, taking Jochi's tuman and a dark shadow with them. The story of that hunt and death was whispered in a thousand gers, but never when the khan was able to hear.

It was more than two months before the families sighted the orange stone of Herat, a city by a river. It rose from an outcrop of granite, and to Mongol eyes, it was impossibly ancient. On the first raids into the area, Herat had surrendered without bloodshed, preserving the lives of the inhabitants in exchange for tribute and occupation. Kachiun had left a garrison of just eighty men and then forgotten about Herat until the city expelled them, made rash by Jelaudin's victories.

As Genghis approached it for the first time, he began to appreciate the sheer mass of the fortress. It was built as a square on top of a rock, the walls rising more than a hundred feet from the rugged base, with great round towers set into them at each corner and along their length. He counted twelve of the towers, each as large as the single one that had sheltered the people of Parwan. It was a huge construction, able to give shelter to thousands racing in ahead of the tumans. Genghis sighed to himself at the sight, knowing from experience that there would be no quick victory. Like Yenking and Yinchuan, he would have to surround it and wait for them to starve.

The gates of the fortress were shut against him, but Genghis sent officers and interpreters to demand surrender as the tumans began to make camp. No answer came and Genghis barely listened as the officers raised a white tent just out of arrow-shot. He did not know if the people of Herat knew his rituals and did not care. The white tent would stand for a day, followed by its red twin and then the black cloth that signaled utter destruction for anyone inside the fortress.

It was another two days before the catapults were assembled in front of the walls, and the people of Herat remained silent. Genghis wondered if they trusted in their walls or simply understood that he could not accept a peaceful surrender a second time. He waited tensely until the first stones flew, skipping off the orange walls with just a blurred mark to show where they had struck.

The black tent fluttered in the breeze and Genghis relaxed, settling himself for a long siege as he had done many times before. It was his least favorite method of war, but such fortresses had been made to keep out armies like his own and there was no quick solution.

For the nation in the gers, life went on around Herat, punctuated by the crack of catapults through each night and day. The families watered their animals at the river, content to leave the destruction of the city to the warriors. The rains had brought sweet grass, though it was already withering in places as the sun beat down. Such concerns were old to them, and if the city did not fall quickly, they would send the herds out to the furthest grazing, leaving the closest hills to be cropped last.

Genghis rested, his wounds having faded to pale scars on his legs and arms. He did not think of Jochi, except with relief that the betrayal had been brought to an end. After Tsubodai had left, the khan had seemed invigorated, willing to fall on Herat with the nation and begin again. His shoulder had healed over time and he rode every day to strengthen his body, ignoring the aches and pains of age. He had sent Chagatai and Kachiun to besiege the city of Balkh in the east, but the main strength of the nation had come with him to the fortress and he took heart from the sight of the encampment. His wife Borte had not spoken to him since she heard the fate of Jochi, but he was oblivious to that. The world lay at his feet and he was strong as he waited for Herat to fall.

In the fourth month of the siege, Genghis was hunting with senior officers around the base of the city. After so long in one place, there were few living things that had escaped the pots of the families. Just a few rabbits remained and they were wary survivors, long used to running from the sound of horse or man.

Balkh had fallen two months before and his tumans had slaughtered the inhabitants, pulling down the stones of the city walls. Only Herat still held out and Genghis was tired of the siege and the hot lands. He had become hopeful of a quick ending when Kachiun and

Chagatai returned, but the fortress at Herat was one of the strongest they had ever tried to break.

As the season passed, Genghis had moved his catapults three times, concentrating their stones on flat sections of the walls. Cracks had appeared to great jubilation in the camp, but he sometimes felt he was assaulting a mountain, with as much effect. The walls stood, battered and marked in a thousand places. By then Genghis knew starvation and thirst would break the city, but he kept his siege weapons working.

"When this is done, we will go home," Genghis muttered to himself, looking up at the walls. Kachiun and Khasar had heard it a hundred times before from their brother and merely exchanged a glance. A rabbit darted out from cover far ahead of them, and all three kicked in their heels to chase it down. Over the noise of hooves, Genghis heard a sharp cry above his head and looked up. There was always someone staring down at his camp from the walls, but this time, he saw a man had leaned out too far. The luckless watcher had barely caught himself and now clung to the outer edge by his fingertips. Genghis whistled to his brothers, pointing as the man shouted for help above their heads.

Khasar and Kachiun returned, staring up with interest.

"A wager?" Khasar asked. "Two horses that he will fall?"

"Not from me, brother," Genghis replied. There were others reaching down to drag the man back to safety, but he gave a cry of despair as he felt his hands slip. Genghis and his brothers watched in fascination as he tumbled, shrieking as he went. For an instant, it seemed as if an arched stone window might save him. His hands caught on its ledge, but he could not hold on. The brothers winced as he struck the wall again, falling outward onto the rock base of the fortress. The body spun loosely and came to rest not far away from Genghis. To his astonishment, Genghis saw an arm flail.

"He's alive!" he said.

"For a few heartbeats, perhaps," Khasar replied. "That fall would kill anyone."

Genghis and his brothers trotted over to where the man lay. One of his ankles was clearly broken, the foot twisted. His body was a mass of scrapes and cuts, but he blinked in terror at the generals, unable to believe he had survived.

Khasar drew his sword to finish the man, but Genghis held up a hand.

"If the spirits won't kill him after that, we won't be the ones to do it." He looked up in awe at the distance the man had fallen, before addressing the man in halting Arabic.

"You have incredible luck," Genghis said.

The man cried out as he tried to move, and he too stared up at the walls above his head. "It does not . . . feel like luck," he replied.

Genghis grinned at him. "Get him to a healer, Khasar. When his wounds are bound, give him a good mare and whatever else he wants." More men could be seen now on the walls as they stared and leaned out, some of them almost as far as the man who now lay at Genghis's feet.

"When the city falls, you will know how lucky you truly are," the khan said in his own tongue. The man looked blankly at him as Khasar dismounted to help him into the saddle.

The walls of Herat slumped and fell in the sixth month of the siege. One of the towers collapsed with the section, crashing to the rocks below and leaving a gaping hole into the city. The tumans gathered quickly, but there was no resistance. As they entered Herat, they found the streets and buildings already choked with the dead and dying. Those who still lived were brought out onto the plain and made to kneel for binding. That task alone took many days as the fortress had been packed with men, women, and children. Temuge gave his servants the task of numbering the prisoners on wax slates, putting the total at a hundred and sixty-three thousand, with almost half as many dying of thirst or hunger in the siege. In their fear and despair, they cried and moaned as they were bound for execution, the sound traveling far across the gers. The warriors of the khan searched every room, hall, and basement of the city until it was just an empty shell filled with the dead. The smell of a city after a siege was like nothing else, and even hardened warriors gagged as they brought out rotting bodies.

It was sunset by the time Temuge was satisfied with his tally, and Genghis decreed the killing would begin at dawn. He retired to the khan's ger to eat and sleep, but his wife Chakahai sought him out as the darkness gathered. At first she said nothing and he welcomed her presence. She worked the iron stove, making tea and heating pouches of unleavened bread, mutton, and herbs that she had prepared that morning. He did not see the strain she hid from him, though as she passed him a plate of the pouches, he took her hand and felt her quiver.

"What is it?" he asked.

She bowed her head. She knew he would respond best to bluntness, but her heart beat so quickly that she could barely breathe. She knelt before him and he put aside his hunger, intrigued.

"Husband, I have a favor to ask," she said.

Genghis reached out and took her hand in his. "Ask, then," he replied.

Chakahai forced herself to take a slow breath. "The women and children," she said. "Let them go free. They will take word of the city falling. They—"

"I do not want to speak of this tonight," Genghis snapped, letting her hand fall.

"Husband," she said, begging, "I can hear them crying out." He had listened when she held the key to Kokchu's treachery. He had listened when she urged him to name Ogedai as heir. Her eyes implored him.

Genghis growled deep in his throat, suddenly furious with her. "You cannot understand, Chakahai," he said. She raised her head and he saw her eyes were bright with tears. Despite himself, he went on.

"I take no pleasure in it," he said. "But I can make this killing a shout that will spread further than I can ride. Word will go out from here, Chakahai, as fast as any bird. They will say I slaughtered every living thing in Herat, that my vengeance was terrible. My name alone will bring fear to those who would stand against me."

"Just the men..." Chakahai began.

Genghis snorted. "Men always die in war. Their kings expect it. I want them to know that if they resist me, they are putting their hand in the mouth of a wolf. They will lose *everything* and they can expect no mercy." He reached out once more and took her face in his hand, so she could feel the hard callus of his palm.

"It is good that you weep for them, Chakahai. I would expect it from a wife of mine and a mother to my children. But there *will* be blood tomorrow, so that I do not have to do it again, a hundred times and more. These Arabs do not send me tribute because they recognize my right to rule. They bow their heads because if they do not, I will visit fury on them and see all they love turned to ashes."

Tears streamed from her and Genghis stroked her cheek gently.

"I would like to give you what you want, Chakahai. Yet if I did, there would be another city next year and a dozen more after that. This is a hard land and the people are used to death. If I am to rule them, they must know that to face me is to be destroyed. They must be afraid, Chakahai. It is the only way."

She did not reply and Genghis found himself suddenly aroused by her tearstained face. He put the plate of food on the floor of the ger for the morning and lifted her onto the low bed beside him, feeling his shoulder creak. She shuddered as his mouth found hers and he did not know if it was from lust or fear.

At dawn Genghis left Chakahai in the ger and went out to watch the killing. He had given the task to the tumans of his sons Ogedai and Tolui. Twenty thousand warriors had cleaned and sharpened their swords for the work, but even so many would be exhausted by the time it was done.

The prisoners sat huddled together in the morning shadow of the broken city as the tumans surrounded them. Many of them prayed aloud and those who faced the grim warriors held out their hands and screamed until the blades fell. It was not quick. The warriors moved amongst them and had to bring the swords down many times as the prisoners writhed in their bonds and struggled to get away. Men and women clambered over each other, and the warriors were drenched in blood. Many of the blades were ruined on bone, the steel edges cracked or bent. Noon came and the killing went on, the smell of blood strong in the still air. Warriors left the mass of living and dead, gasping as they drank warm, sour water before walking in again.

The afternoon sun was powerful as they finished at last and the plain fell silent. The tumans of Genghis's sons were staggering with weariness, as if they had fought a long and bitter battle. Their officers sent them to the river to wash away the blood and clean and oil their weapons. The city stood silent above them, empty of all life.

The man who had fallen from the walls had wept for part of the day, though his tears dried quickly in the heat until he sobbed dryly and no more came. His broken ankle had been splinted and he was given a horse and supplies by a nameless Mongol officer, following the orders of the khan. The man rode away as the flies and birds gathered above Herat. Genghis watched him go, knowing he would take the news to all those who had ears to hear.

Genghis thought of Chakahai's tears as he stood in the shadow of Herat. He had not told her where he would take the nation. The families knew he intended to go home, but one other place had long ceased to send tribute and he would take his army there before he saw those hills and rivers again. Xi Xia was where he had first met the pale daughter of a king, the region a stepping stone that had led him to an emperor's capital. Like the elders of Herat and Balkh, Chakahai's father had thought the khan would not survive the Arab armies sent against him.

Genghis smiled lightly to himself as he gave orders for the nation to break camp at last. He had been too long away from the Chin lands, and Xi Xia would be the bloody example to bring them to heel.

CHAPTER THIRTY-NINE

THE NATION TRAVELED EAST TOGETHER, burning a trail of fire and blood through the Arab cities and towns. The tumans went ahead of the families, riding against cities that were still little more than ruins from their first experience of the Mongol khan. As survivors began to rebuild their lives and homes, the tumans came sweeping in again to slaughter and burn.

For those who traveled on the carts of the nation, the landscape was marked in plumes of dark smoke, growing as they came closer and finally left behind while fresh black threads appeared in the distance. They moved through desolation and Genghis was well pleased at the sight. He had no more use for Arab cities, nor those who lived in them. The destruction he brought would make the land a desert for a generation or more, and they would not rise again in challenge. Only Samarkand and Merv were left intact, for others to rule in his name. Even then Temuge had been forced to beg for a garrison to keep Samarkand safe, with its libraries and palace. Genghis was leaving Arab lands and it was not long before the least of those in the gers knew they were heading back to war with the Chin. Twelve years had passed since the fall of Yenking, and Genghis longed to see his ancestral enemies once more. The nation had grown in strength, and this time nothing in the world would stop him placing his foot on the Chin throat.

Six moons grew from crescents to full by the time they skirted a great desert to the south. The Mongol homeland lay north over mountains and Genghis hungered to see his own land, but pressed on. The nation traveled more than two thousand miles into a cold winter that only refreshed families who had grown sick of the endless heat. Xi Xia lay further into the east, but Genghis reveled in the changing landscape, taking delight in the waterlogged fields of green rice almost as if he were coming home. The hunting improved and they swept the land clean of anything that moved, taking herds of yaks and goats as easily as they fired villages on the edges of Chin land.

On a warm evening, with the sun setting in a cloudless sky, Chakahai came once again to the khan's ger. He looked up in pleasure to see her, and she felt the strength of the new vitality that infused him. He wore a tunic and trousers that left his arms bare, and she could see the web of scars on them, right to the fingers.

He smiled as he saw the platter of food she had brought and took it from her, breathing in the aroma of fresh meat with pleasure. She did not speak as he ate with his fingers, relaxing visibly after a long day. The peaceful sounds of the families could be heard around them as thousands of warriors ate and rested with their wives and children, ready for another day of riding.

Genghis finished the meal and yawned, his jaw cracking. He handed the plate back to her and she bowed her head.

"You are tired," she said.

He chuckled, patting the bed beside him. "Not too tired," he replied. Despite having borne four children for him, she had kept her slight figure, the legacy of her race. He thought briefly of Borte's thickening waist as he reached for Chakahai and fumbled the knot of her sash. Gently, she removed his hands.

"Let me, husband," she said. Her voice trembled, but he was oblivious as she let the deel robe and buttoned tunic fall open to reveal white flesh beneath. He reached inside the cloth, taking her around the bare waist with strong hands. She could feel the hardness of his fingers digging into her flesh, and she gasped slightly, pleasing him. Their breath mingled and she knelt before him to remove his boots. He did not see her take a long knife from one of them, and if she shook, he assumed it was at his touch on her breasts. He watched her nipples grow firm in the cool air, and he lowered his face to them, tasting the bitter jasmine on her skin.

*   *   *

Khasar and Kachiun were sitting their horses at the edge of the encampment, keeping an eye on the immense herd of animals that accompanied the nation. The brothers were in a light mood, enjoying the
last of the day and chatting idly before they went back to their families
and an evening meal.

It was Kachiun who saw Genghis first. He chuckled at something
Khasar had said while watching Genghis mount and take the reins of
his favorite mare. Khasar turned to see what had caught his brother's
interest, and both men fell silent as Genghis walked the horse through
the gers of their people, taking a path away from them.

At first they did nothing and Khasar finished a story involving the
wife of one his senior officers and the proposition she had made.
Kachiun barely smiled at the tale and Khasar looked again to see that
Genghis had reached the edge of the gers, his pony taking him out
onto the grassy plain alone.

"What is he doing?" Kachiun wondered aloud.

Khasar shrugged. "Let's find out," he said. "You are a poor audience for my troubles, brother. Genghis will see the humor in them."

Kachiun and Khasar moved at a trot across the vast encampment,
picking their way to intercept Genghis as he left the nation behind. The
light was dimming and the plain was lit in gold, the air warm. They
were relaxed as they drew close to him and called a greeting.

Genghis did not respond and Kachiun frowned for the first time.
He moved his horse closer, but Genghis did not look at him. His face
was bright with sweat and Kachiun exchanged a glance with Khasar as
they fell in on either side of the khan and matched their pace to his.

"Genghis?" Khasar said. Still there was no response and Khasar
subsided, willing to let his brother explain in his own time. The three of
them walked their mounts far onto the empty grass, until the gers were
just a whitish hump behind them and the bleating of animals faded to a
distant murmur.

Kachiun noted the sweat pouring off the khan. His brother was
unnaturally pale and Kachiun's stomach clenched as he feared some
terrible news.

"What is it?" he asked. "Genghis? What's wrong?" His brother rode
on as if he had not heard, and Kachiun felt worry bloom in him. He
wondered if he should turn the khan's horse with his own, ending this
plodding trek away from the families. The khan held the reins loosely,
barely exerting a control on the mare. Kachiun shook his head at Khasar
in confusion.

The last light of day was on them when Genghis slumped to one side and slid from the saddle. Khasar and Kachiun gaped in dawning shock and Kachiun cried out as he leapt down and reached for his brother.

In the dim light, they had not seen the spreading stain at his waist, a dark slick of blood that marked the saddle and the mare's side. As he fell, his deel came open, so that they could see a terrible wound.

Kachiun heaved Genghis into his arms, pressing his hand over the swelling blood in a vain attempt to stem the flow of life. Wordlessly, he looked up at Khasar, who still sat his horse, rooted in shock.

Genghis closed his eyes, the pain of the fall rousing him from his stupor. His breathing was ragged and Kachiun held him tighter.

"Who did this, brother?" Kachiun said, sobbing. "Who did this to you?" He did not send Khasar for a physician. The brothers had seen too many wounds.

Khasar dismounted woodenly, his legs suddenly weak. He knelt with Kachiun and reached out to take Genghis's hand in his own. The blood on the skin was already growing cold. A warm wind blew across the empty plain, bringing dust and the smell of rice fields.

Genghis stirred in Kachiun's embrace, his head lolling back so that it rested on his shoulder. His face was almost white as his eyes opened. There was a spark of recognition there and Kachiun gripped him tighter, desperately willing the blood to stop. When Genghis spoke, it was barely a whisper.

"I am pleased you are here, with me," he said. "Did I fall?"

"Who did this, brother?" Kachiun said, his eyes filling with tears.

Genghis did not seem to hear him. "There is a price for all things," he said. His eyes closed again and Kachiun coughed out a sound without words, consumed with grief. Once more, the khan roused and when he spoke, Kachiun pressed his ear to his brother's lips to hear.

"Destroy Xi Xia," Genghis said. "For me, brother, destroy them all." The breath continued in a rush and the yellow eyes lost their fire as the khan died.

Khasar stood without knowing he did so, his gaze fastened on the two men who sprawled together, suddenly so small on the vast plain. With anger, he rubbed at the tears in his eyes, breathing in sharply to hold back a wave of sorrow that threatened to crush him. It had come with such brutal quickness that he could not take it in. He swayed as he looked down, seeing how his hands were covered in the khan's blood.

Slowly, Khasar drew his sword. The sound made Kachiun look up and he saw his brother's boyish face set in rage that threatened to spill over at any moment.

"Wait, Khasar!" Kachiun said, but his brother was deaf to anything he might say. He turned to his horse, gently cropping at the grass. With a leap, he startled the animal into a flat run back to the gers of the people, leaving Kachiun alone, still rocking the body in his arms.

Chakahai sat on the bed, running a hand over the spots of blood on the blanket and staring at the red mark. She moved as if in a trance, unable to believe she still lived. Tears spilled down her cheeks at the memory of Genghis's expression. As she had cut him, he had gasped, pulling away with the knife deep in him. He had looked at her in simple astonishment. Chakahai had watched as he yanked out the blade and tossed it to one corner of the ger, where it still lay.

"Why?" he had said. The tears fell freely from her as she crossed to the knife and took it in her hands.

"Xi Xia is my *home*," she had replied, already weeping. He could have killed her then. She did not know why he had not. Instead, he had risen to his feet, still looking at her. He knew he was dying, she was certain. The knowledge had been clear in his yellow eyes and the sudden paleness of his face. She had watched as he fastened the deel around the wound, pulling it tight over a growing spot of blood. He had left her alone with the knife, and she lay on the bed and wept for the man she had known.

Khasar came back to the gers, his horse belting into the paths through the gers with no care for those who scattered from his way. Those who saw him froze as they understood something was wrong. No more than a few had seen the khan leave the families to ride out, but more saw Khasar return, his face terrible in its fury.

He reached the khan's ger. It seemed just moments since he had seen Genghis leave it, but everything had changed. Khasar jumped down before the horse halted, staggering slightly as he bounded up the steps and kicked open the door to the gloom within.

He breathed hard at what he saw there. Chakahai lay on the low bed, her eyes glassy. Khasar took two steps to stand over her, seeing the cut at her throat and the bloody knife that had fallen from her hands. It was a peaceful scene and it offended him.

He made an inarticulate bellow, reaching for her flesh so that she was jerked from the bed and fell limply to the floor. Mindless, Khasar plunged his sword into her chest, hacking at her until he was spattered and panting and her head was severed.

When he appeared at the broken door once again, the khan's guards had gathered, alerted by his shout. They took one look at the blood on his face and his wild eyes, and for an instant, Khasar thought they would charge him.

"Where is the khan?" one of them demanded, raising a bow so that the arrow centered on Khasar's chest. Khasar could not ignore the threat, though he could hardly bring himself to speak. He gestured vaguely to the darkening plain outside the ring of campfires and torches that had sprung up all around.

"He is dead," he said. "He lies on the grass and the Chin whore who did it lies behind me. Now get out of my way."

He strode down through the guards, and in confusion and horror, they fell back before him. He did not see one of the men race into the ger to check, his shout of anguish following Khasar as he mounted and raced across the camp. His rage had not been sated in cutting at dead flesh. Chakahai's ger was nearby and he sought her children, determined to take a price for what she had done.

The ger was empty when he found it, stalking in and out again in just moments. He saw a Chin servant cowering from the blood-spattered general and grabbed her by the throat as she tried to kneel in terror.

"Chakahai's children," he said, squeezing ruthlessly. "Where are they?"

The woman choked, growing red until he released her. She coughed as she lay on the ground and he raised his sword to kill her.

"With Borte, lord. Please, I know nothing."

Khasar was already moving. His horse was skittish at the smell of blood on him and had wandered away. He broke into a run, his sword held low as he loped between the gers, looking for the right one. Tears filled his eyes as he thought of his brother cooling on the plain. There would be a price.

There were many people around Borte's ger. Word was already spreading through the camp and warriors and families had abandoned their meals and beds to come out. Khasar hardly saw them, his gaze searching and finally alighting on the home he wanted. He could hear the sounds of life within it, voices and laughter. He did not hesitate and threw himself at the door so that it fell flat, the leather hinges tearing free.

He ducked inside and stood to face the shocked family of his brother. Borte was there, with Ogedai. He was on his feet before Khasar had straightened, his hand on a sword hilt. Khasar barely registered him as his gaze fell on the four young children Chakahai had borne, two girls and two boys. In the lamplight, they stared at the bloody apparition, frozen.

Khasar lunged for them, his sword rising to kill. Borte screamed and Ogedai threw himself at his uncle, with no time to draw his own sword. The two men went down, but Khasar was too full of rage to be stopped easily. He threw Ogedai off as if he weighed nothing, and came lightly to his feet. In his madness, the sound of a drawn blade reached him, and his eyes turned slowly to see Ogedai standing ready.

"Get out of my way!" Khasar snapped.

Ogedai quivered as his heart raced, but he did not move. It was Borte who broke the tableau between the two men. Death was in the air and though she was terrified, she made her tone as gentle as she could.

"Are you here to kill me, Khasar?" she said. "In front of the children?"

Khasar blinked as if returning from far away. "Not you," he said. "Genghis is dead. These are the children of his whore."

With infinite slowness, Borte too rose to stand before him, moving as she might with a snake about to strike. She spread her arms to shelter those children behind her.

"You will have to kill me, Khasar," she said. "You will not hurt them."

Khasar hesitated. The searing rage that had carried him back to the camp and from ger to ger began to fade, and he clutched at it, longing for the simplicity of revenge. His eyes met those of Ogedai and he saw a dawning realization there amidst the grief. The younger man stood taller in front of his uncle and the quiver in his hands vanished.

"If my father is dead, Khasar," Ogedai said, "then I am khan of the nation."

Khasar grimaced, feeling sick and old as the rage left him. "Not until you have gathered the tribes and taken their oath, Ogedai. Until then, stand aside." He could hardly bear to look into the yellow eyes of Genghis's heir as he stood before him. There was too much an echo of the father, and Khasar heard it too in Ogedai's voice as he spoke again.

"You will not kill my brothers and sisters, General," he said. "Walk away and wash the blood from your face. I will come with you to my father, to see. There is nothing more for you here tonight."

Khasar's head dipped, grief coming at him in a great dark wave. The sword slipped from his hand and Ogedai moved quickly to hold him up before he could fall. Ogedai turned him toward the open doorway and glanced back only once at his mother as she watched, shaking with release.

EPILOGUE

ALL THINGS WERE NEW. The brothers and sons of Genghis did not take the khan to the hills of a foreign land to be torn by crows and eagles. They wrapped his body in sheets of bleached linen and sealed it under oil while they reduced the region of Xi Xia to a smoking, desolate ruin. It was his last order and they did not rush the work. A full year passed while every town, every village, every living thing was hunted down and left to rot.

Only then did the nation move north to the frozen plains, taking the first khan to the Khenti mountains where he had come into the world. The tale of his life was sung and chanted a thousand times and once read, when Temuge told the full tale from his history. He had trapped the words on calfskin sheets and they were the same no matter how many times he said them.

Ogedai was khan. He did not gather the tribes and take their oaths while his father lay in oil and cloth. Yet it was his voice that ruled the rest, and if his brother Chagatai was sullen at Ogedai's rise to power, he did not dare let it show. The nation mourned and there was not a living soul who would have challenged Genghis's right to choose his heir after he had gone from them. With his life complete, they knew again what he had done and meant. His people had risen and his enemies were dust. Nothing else mattered at the last accounting of a life.

On a bitter dawn, with a chill wind blowing in from the east, the sons and brothers of Genghis rode to the head of his funeral column, leaving the nation behind. Temuge had planned every detail, borrowing from the death rites of more than one people. He rode with Khasar and Kachiun behind a cart drawn by fine horses. A minghaan officer sat high over the animals, urging them on with a long stick. Behind him on the cart lay a simple box of elm and iron, at times seeming too small to contain the man within. In the days before, every man, woman, and child of the nation had come to lay a hand on the warm wood.

The honor guard was just a hundred men, well formed and young. Forty young women rode with them and they cried out and wailed to the sky father with every pace, marking the passing of a great man and forcing the spirits to attend and listen. The Great Khan would not go alone into the hills.

They reached the place Temuge had prepared and the brothers and sons of the khan gathered in grim silence as the box was lifted inside a great chamber cut from the rock. They did not speak as the women gashed their throats and lay down, ready to serve the khan in the next world. Only the warriors who oversaw the ritual came out, and many of them were red-eyed with grief.

Temuge nodded to Ogedai and the heir raised his hand gently, standing for a long time as he gazed into the last resting place of his father. He swayed slightly as he stood, his eyes glassy from drink that did nothing to dull his grief. The son of Genghis spoke slurred words in a whisper, but no one heard them as he let his arm fall.

The warriors heaved on ropes that arced up into the hills. Their muscles grew taut and they strained together until they heard thunder above. Wooden barriers gave way and for a moment it seemed as if half the mountain fell to block the chamber, raising a cloud of dust so thick that they could not breathe or see.

When it cleared, Genghis had gone from them and his brothers were satisfied. He had been born in the shadow of the mountain known as Deli'un-Boldakh, and they had buried him in that place. His spirit would watch over his people from those green slopes.

Kachiun nodded to himself, breathing out a great release of tension that he had not realized he felt. He turned his pony with his brothers and looked back only once as they wound their way through the thick trees that covered the slopes. The forest would grow over the scars they had made. In time, Genghis would be part of the hills themselves. Kachiun was grim as he looked over the heads of the young warriors riding with him. The khan would not be disturbed in his rest.

Just a few miles from the nation's camp, Khasar rode to the senior officer, telling him to halt his men. All those who had met in the khan's ger the night before rode forward in a single group: Temuge, Khasar, Tsubodai, Jebe, Kachiun, Jelme, Ogedai, Tolui, and Chagatai. They were the seeds of a new nation and they rode well.

From the camp came Ogedai's tuman to meet them. The heir reined in as his officers bowed, then sent them past him to kill the honor guard. Genghis would need good men on his path. The generals did not look back as the arrows sang again. The honor guard died in silence.

On the edge of the encampment, Ogedai turned to those he would lead in the years to come. They had been hardened in war and suffering and they returned his yellow gaze with simple confidence, knowing their worth. He wore the wolf's-head sword that his father and grandfather had carried. His gaze lingered longest on Tsubodai. He needed the general, but Jochi had died at his hand and Ogedai promised himself there would be a reckoning one day, a price for what he had done. He hid his thoughts, adopting the cold face Genghis had taught him.

"It is done," Ogedai said. "My father has gone and I will accept the oaths of my people."

HISTORICAL NOTE

We sleep safe in our beds because rough men stand ready in the night to visit violence on those who would do us harm.

—GEORGE ORWELL

Describing lands as "conquered" by Genghis Khan always requires some qualification of the word. When the Romans conquered Spain and Gaul, they brought roads, trade, cities, bridges, aquaducts—all the trappings of civilization as they knew it. Genghis was never a builder. To be conquered by the Mongol army meant losing your kings, their armies, and most precious cities, but the Mongols never had the numbers to leave a large force behind when they moved on. Mongol warriors would have appeared in markets of Chinese cities, or retired in places as far apart as Korea and Afghanistan, but in general, once the fighting had stopped, there was little active government. In essence, being conquered by the Mongols meant that all local armed forces had to stand down. If word got out that *anyone* was moving soldiers, they could expect a tuman to turn up on the horizon. The Mongols accepted tribute and controlled the land, but never gave up their nomadic lifestyle while Genghis lived.

It is a difficult concept to understand eight hundred years later, but the fear induced by Genghis's mobile forces was perhaps as effective in controlling a beaten province as the stolid presence of Romans. In the seventeenth century, the Muslim chronicler Abu'l Ghazi wrote:

"Under the reign of Genghis Khan, all the country between Iran and the land of the Turks enjoyed such a peace that a man might have journeyed from sunrise to sunset with a golden platter on his head without suffering the least violence from anyone."

Sheer speed and destruction were crucial to the Mongol success. After all, in the campaign against the Chin emperor, the armies of Genghis Khan attacked more than *ninety* cities in a single year. Genghis himself was involved in storming twenty-eight, while being repulsed from only four. Historically, he benefited from the fact that China had not yet begun to use gunpowder efficiently in war. Only six years after the fall of Yenking, in 1221, a Chin army used exploding iron pots against the southern Sung city of Qizhou, with a shrapnel effect very like modern grenades. Those who came after him would have to face the weapons of a new era.

The scene against Russian knights in the first chapter takes place around the same time as the fifth crusade to the Holy Land. To put Russia in historical perspective, the huge cathedral to Saint Sophia in Novgorod was built as early as 1045 and replaced a wooden church with thirteen domes that was built a century before that. Medieval Russia and indeed Europe were on the brink of the great period of cathedral building and Christian expansion that would clash with Islam for the next four centuries. I have described the period armor and weapons of the knights as accurately as possible.

The Mongols did reach Korea—though I used an older pronunciation of "Koryo" throughout. The name means the "high and beautiful land." Mongol forces destroyed the Khara-Kitai, a branch of the Chin who had left their homeland and dug themselves into the mountains of Korea beyond the ability of that dynasty to root them out.

In men like his brother Khasar, Jebe, and Tsubodai, the khan had found a band of generals who justified the name of "the hunting dogs of Genghis." They were practically unstoppable—and yet Genghis turned toward Islamic central Asia before the conquest of China, even northern China, was complete. In the history, Jebe, the Arrow, was established in his role earlier than I have it, but the pressures of plotting make changes sometimes inevitable. Tsubodai and Jebe became the two most famous generals of their day—twins in ability, ruthlessness, and absolute loyalty to the khan.

Genghis did not fight to rule cities, for which he had no use whatsoever. His purpose was almost always personal, to break or kill individual enemies, no matter how many armies and cities stood in the way. He was prepared to treat once with the Chin emperor over Yenking, but when the emperor ran for Kaifeng, Genghis burned the city and sent an army after him. As wide-ranging as the destruction was, it was still a battle between Genghis and one family.

Other events made Genghis look away from his single-minded and personal approach to warfare. It is true that one of the Mongol diplomatic—read spy—caravans was slaughtered by the Shah of Khwarezm. Genghis sent between 100 and 450 men (depending on the source), only to see them held by the governor of Otrar, a relative of the Shah. Even then, Genghis assumed the man was a rogue and sent three more men to accept the governor as prisoner and negotiate for the release of the first group. They too were killed and it was that act that brought Genghis into the Islamic nations. At that point in time, he almost certainly intended to complete the conquest of China. He had no desire to open up an entire new front against a teeming enemy. Yet he was not a man to ignore a naked challenge to his authority. The Mongol army moved and *millions* would die. Genghis went alone to the top of a mountain and prayed to the sky father, saying, "I am not the author of this trouble, but grant me the strength to exact vengeance."

In infuriating Genghis, the governor of Otrar made what is perhaps one of the worst military decisions in history. Perhaps he thought he could scorn the khan of the Mongols with impunity. As a cousin to the Shah and with vast armies available, he may have thought little of the Mongol threat.

The original city of Otrar remains rubble today and has never been rebuilt. Inalchuk was executed by having molten silver poured into his eyes and ears. Though I have altered the order of falling cities, the Shah was routed and sent running with Tsubodai and Jebe on his trail, as I have described it. He stayed ahead of them for a thousand miles, crossing modern-day Uzbekistan and Iran to the shores of the Caspian Sea, where he took a boat with his sons to a small island. Exhausted, he died of pneumonia there and his son Jelaudin (or Jalal Ud Din) was left to take his father's place at the head of the Arab armies. He faced Genghis at last against the Indus River and escaped almost alone, while his army was crushed. The boy who would become Kublai Khan was indeed there, and Genghis is said to have made a point of noting Jelaudin's bravery to him, as an example of how a man should live and die.

The Arab assassins are perhaps most famous for giving us the word in English, from *hashishin*, by way of Marco Polo's *ashishin*, following their practice of creating a mad frenzy with the drug. However, it may have the simpler route of coming from *assasseen*, Arabic for "guardian." As Shia Moslems, they differed from the main Sunni branch of Islam. The practice of showing drug-dazed recruits a version of heaven and hell is true. One can only imagine the result of such experiences on impressionable young minds. Certainly their reputation was for ferocious loyalty to the "Old Man of the Mountains." At their height, their influence was vast and the story is true about leaving a poisoned cake on Saladin's chest as he slept, a clear message to leave them alone in his conquests. Though their strongholds were destroyed by Genghis and the khans after him, the sect remained active for many years.

Elephants were used against Mongols at Otrar, Samarkand, and other battles—a hopeless tactic against warriors whose first weapon was the bow. The Mongols were not at all intimidated by the enormous assault animals and hammered them with arrows. Each time, the elephants stampeded and crushed their own ranks. At one point, Genghis found himself in control of captured elephants, but turned them loose rather than use such unreliable creatures.

For reasons of plot, I moved the minaret to which Genghis "bowed" to Samarkand. It is in fact in Bukhara and stands to this day at around one hundred and fifty feet tall. Genghis is said to have addressed the wealthy merchants of that city, telling them through translators that they had clearly committed great sins and if they needed proof, they should look no further than his presence among them. Whether he actually saw himself as the punishment of God or was simply being whimsical can never now be known.

Note: In the Islamic faith, Abraham is considered the first Muslim, who submitted to one god. As with Moses and Jesus, the description of his life in the Koran differs at significant points from that of the Bible.

Genghis's eldest son Jochi was the only general ever to turn against him. He took his men and refused to return home. Though it is well recorded, a writer of historical fiction sometimes has to explain how something like that could happen. His men would have left wives and children behind, and that seems extraordinary to modern sensibilities. Could he have truly been so charismatic? It may seem like an odd example, but I recalled the cult leader David Koresh, whose followers were killed in a siege in Waco, Texas, in 1993. Before the end, he had taken the wives of married followers to his own bed. Not only did the husbands not object, they even accepted his ruling that they would no longer lie with their wives themselves. That is the power of a charismatic leader. For those of us who do not command that sort of loyalty, men like Nelson, Caesar, and Genghis must always be something of a mystery. The exact manner of Jochi's death remains unknown, though if it was at the order of his father, it would not have been recorded. The timing is, however, suspiciously convenient. It suited Genghis very well that the only man to betray him died shortly after taking his men north. We can be certain Genghis would not have employed assassins, but that is all.

The name of Tolui's wife, Sorhatani, is one of those with many spelling variations. The most accurate is probably "Sorkhakhtani," but I rejected that as too hard on the eye—and the "k" sounds would have been pronounced as "h" anyway. In a similar spirit, I have used the old-fashioned spelling of "Moslem" throughout, though "Muslim" is now the accepted form. Sorhatani plays only a small part in this book, but as mother to Mongke and Kublai, she had a huge influence over the future of the Mongol nation. As a Christian, she was one of those to influence Genghis's grandsons, and yet she allowed Yao Shu, a Buddhist, to become Kublai's mentor. Between them, they would create a man who embraced Chinese culture as Genghis never could.

Jelaudin gathered approximately sixty thousand men to his banners after his father's death. Cut off from his own lands, he must also have been an extraordinary leader. At the valley of Panjshir in Afghanistan, he forced a Mongol army into retreat across a river. Underestimating him, Genghis sent only three tumans to crush the rebellion. For the only time in Genghis's life, his army was routed by them. In just one year, the aura of invincibility he had worked so hard to create had been shattered. Genghis himself took the field with everything he had. He moved his men so quickly that they could not cook food, catching up with Jelaudin at last on the banks of the river Indus in what is now Pakistan. Genghis trapped the prince's army against the banks. I have not continued Jelaudin's story here, but after surviving the battle on the Indus, he made his way across Iran to Georgia, Armenia, and Kurdistan, gathering followers until he was murdered in 1231. It was his army that overran Jerusalem without him, so that it remained under Muslim control until 1917.

The man who fell from the walls at Herat is a peculiar part of the histories. The abandoned fortress city still stands today, much as I have described it. Genghis did indeed spare the man, astonished that he could have survived such a fall. As with so many other times, Genghis the man was quite different from Genghis the ruthless khan. As a man, he enjoyed displays of courage, as when Jelaudin took his horse over a sheer drop. As khan, Genghis ordered the slaughter of every living thing in Herat, knowing that it would send a message to all those who thought his control had been shaken by Jelaudin's rebellion. The killing at Herat was his last major action in Afghanistan. Like that city, the Chinese region of Xi Xia thought the Mongols were too stretched to defend distant outposts, so stopped sending tribute. Their refusal would bring the khan out of Arab lands at last, intent on resuming the utter subjugation of the Chin empire, begun more than a decade before.

In 1227, only twelve years after taking Yenking in 1215, Genghis Khan was dead. He spent about eight of those twelve years at war. Even when there was no obvious enemy, his generals were always on the move, reaching as far as Kiev in Russia, where Tsubodai made the only successful winter attack in history. Of all Genghis's generals, Tsubodai is rightly known as the most gifted. I have barely done him justice here.

Genghis died after falling from his horse in the process of attacking the Xi Xia for a second time. His last command was to wipe out Xi Xia. There is a persistent legend that the Great Khan was stabbed by a woman before that last ride. As he was on his way to destroy Xi Xia, it made sense to give that role to the princess he had taken as his wife. Given that his birthdate can only be estimated, he was between fifty and sixty years old. For such a short life, and from such humble beginnings, he left an incredible mark on the world. His immediate legacy was that his sons did not tear the nation to pieces in deciding who should lead. They accepted Ogedai as khan. Perhaps there would have been civil war if Jochi had still been alive, but he was gone.

The army of Genghis Khan was organized in tens upwards, with a rigid chain of command.

> arban: ten men—with two or three gers between them if traveling fully equipped
> jagun: one hundred men
> minghaan: one thousand men
> tuman: ten thousand men

Commanders of one thousand and ten thousand were given the rank of *noyan,* though I used "minghaan" and "general" for simplicity. Above those, men like Jebe and Tsubodai were *orloks,* or eagles, the equivalent of field marshals.

It is interesting to note that although Genghis had little use for gold, plaques of the substance known as paitze became the symbol of rank for his armies and administration. Jagun officers carried one of silver, but noyans carried one weighing approximately twenty ounces of gold. An orlok would have carried one weighing fifty ounces.

At the same time, the growth of army organization, field weapons, and messenger routes required a quartermaster type of rank to come into existence. These were known as *yurtchis.* They chose campsites and organized the messengers across thousands of miles between armies. The most senior yurtchi was responsible for reconnaissance, intelligence, and the day-to-day running of the camp of Genghis.

Finally, for those who might want to learn more about Genghis and those who followed him, I recommend the wonderful John Man book *Genghis Khan: Life, Death, and Resurrection; The Mongol Warlords* by David Nicolle; *The Devil's Horsemen: The Mongol Invasion of Europe* by James Chambers; *Jenghiz Khan* by C. C. Walker; and of course *The Secret History of the Mongols* (original author unknown, though I used an edition translated by Arthur Waley).

ABOUT THE AUTHOR

CONN IGGULDEN is the author of two previous Genghis Khan novels: *Genghis: Birth of an Empire* and *Genghis: Lords of the Bow,* as well as the Emperor novels, which chronicle the life of Julius Caesar: *Emperor: The Gates of Rome, Emperor: The Death of Kings, Emperor: The Field of Swords,* and *Emperor: The Gods of War,* all of which are available in paperback from Dell. He is also the coauthor of the #1 *New York Times* bestseller *The Dangerous Book for Boys.* He lives with his wife and children in Hertfordshire, England.